NO! I DON'T NEED
READING GLASSES!

NO! I DON'T NEED READING GLASSES!

Virginia Ironside

WINDSOR
PARAGON

First published 2013
by Quercus
This Large Print edition published 2013
by AudioGO Ltd
by arrangement with
Quercus

Hardcover   ISBN: 978 1 4713 4340 7
Softcover   ISBN: 978 1 4713 4341 4

British Library Cataloguing in Publication Data available

Printed and bound in Great Britain by
MPG Books Group Limited

For Denis Whyte

WORCESTERSHIRE COUNTY COUNCIL	
898	
AudioGO	21.06.13
	£19.99
AL	

JANUARY

1 January

Oh gawd. Woke up with the most terrible hangover, panting for water, heart beating, sweating . . . very unlike me. Haven't had one like this since the sixties. (And now I remember it, I didn't feel too hot after my retirement party, either, at the school, but that was because the booze was provided by the science master who had prided himself on Making His Own Beer.)

Managed to crawl out of bed and have a cup of coffee and a piece of toast, and overcome with great desire to have five fried eggs, but even though I've had two, nothing makes a lot of difference. It being New Year's Day, a strange silence has descended over London, which makes me feel as if I am the heroine in a very bad film in which I'm the only person alive in a world which has been struck by a strange kind of sleeping sickness. Looked out of my window to the street below and there is absolutely no one about. Hardly any cars, either. Everyone's away I suppose. And when I looked out of the bedroom window— nothing there either. Well, there isn't usually anyone around at the back, of course, and I would be most surprised to see anybody mooching around my lawn on New Year's Day, or any day come to that, but there isn't even the sound of a distant chainsaw or screaming baby or the pounding thump of a far-off radio.

Must say the garden looks particularly squalid. I

suppose the viburnum will be out soon, but it can't be soon enough. The garden's one of those long thin affairs, with grass in the middle and overgrown with bushes and trees at the sides. Last summer it looked as lush as a tropical rain forest, but nothing looks good on New Year's Day. It's just a grey swamp of mud and desolation, with the odd fat pigeon standing around wondering if he should make the huge effort of taking off to escape the claws and jaws of Pouncer, my cat, and Pouncer sitting there equally weary and bloated, wondering if he can be bothered to get himself into his wiggling position to make a move on the pigeon.

I shall go back to bed. With any luck I'll wake up fizzing with life and full of beans. With even more luck I'll sleep until next week, when life will be back to normal.

3 January

The world is slowly waking up, and so am I. I've decided to do something I haven't done since I was about ten. Make a list of New Year's resolutions. So here goes.

1. Never drink again, and certainly never mix champagne, red wine and rum punches. (I've only just begun to recover. The old brain cells are starting to return to life, like the bubbles at the bottom of a pan of boiling water.)
2. Have a facelift.
3. Try acupuncture to see if makes any difference to my increasing stiffness. I'm starting to walk around like one of those

2

little wooden Dutch dolls that were so popular in Victorian times.

4. Sort out the entire house room by room, chucking things out. I have far too much *stuff*.
5. Write a diary. (Which I've already started doing.)
6. Start painting again.

Penny, my great friend who lives round the corner, suggested I should make 'travelling more' one of my resolutions, but I'm old enough to know now that travelling doesn't get you anywhere, if that doesn't sound ridiculous. I've often thought that going away would do me good and 'get me out of myself', so I've packed my suitcase and rushed off to Timbuktu, say, and when I've got there I've opened my suitcase and out has popped the same old self I wanted to get away from.

So, frankly, I'd rather stay at home.

It may seem odd to put 'Have a facelift' so high on my list, but at the New Year's Eve party a creepy old man (I say 'old'—he was probably my age) came up to me and said in what he thought was a seductive and flattering voice, 'You remind me of a Burmese princess' and I realised exactly why I'd reminded him of a Burmese princess, and it wasn't because I looked gorgeous, Eastern and sultry. No, the seductive slit-eyed look had been achieved only because my eyelids droop over my eyes so much.

And why am I starting a diary again? I did write one when I was sixty, but it fizzled out after a year for the simple reason I was ludicrously happy. And if one's tiptop happy, why write a diary? It would

3

be so boring. Imagine: 'Monday: great day. Tuesday: Sun was out, felt marvellous. Wednesday: Saw Penny, she is really nice. Thursday: gave a great dollop of cash to charity and felt a warm glow. Friday: 'How lucky I am to be alive!' and so on.

Anyway, when you're full of beans, there's no time for writing a diary because you're so busy doing jolly things like arranging suppers with friends, putting bulbs in pots for Christmas and tucking them away under the stairs, chortling at reruns of Laurel and Hardy on YouTube, repainting the spare room, thinking about sorting out all your photographs from ages ago into neat albums (notice I just say 'thinking about') or simply sitting with a loved one doing . . . well, not very much. When you're with someone, it's not having them around to do things with that's nice. It's having them around to do *nothing* with.

And nothing was what I did a lot of with my darling Archie for quite a while after I'd rediscovered the old love of my life at the grand old age of sixty. He was a man I'd been crazy about ever since I was a teenager, but who I'd lost touch with when we'd both married different people. Once our marriages were over—I was divorced from David and Archie's wife had died—we found each other again. And though the cuddly nights together were gorgeous, we also spent a lot of time just mooching about. We'd often go for walks near his vast Victorian pile in a remote corner of Devon, tramping through the parkland, into the fields and round the farms nearby, in complete silence. Not that awful kind of seething-with-resentment silence, the sort of silence after which

4

one person says, nervously, 'What's the matter?' and the other person answers, 'Nothing!' in a loud and furious voice—thank God those days are over!—but an easy, companionable silence.

Sometimes we'd chat a bit and joke, and make plans for the future or ruminate over the past—I'd tell him about the ghastly times I'd had with David (now one of my bestest friends) and the ghastly times David had had with me, and he'd tell me about life with his late wife Philippa with a mixture of such pain and affection in his voice that I couldn't be jealous. (How could I, when she'd made Archie's life so happy?)

Sometimes we'd talk about my son Jack, his wife Chrissie and my adored and adorable grandson Gene—and we'd shared the joy of the marriage of his daughter Sylvie to Harry, her childhood sweetheart.

Now, right from the start Archie and I had decided we would never live together. Both of us were savvy enough to realise that it would have been a dreadful idea, particularly as, since I'd got divorced, I'd learned to be happy on my own. (Oddly, this is something it's very difficult to unlearn. Once you've got used to being in command of the remote control, and sitting in the driving seat of the car and deciding what to have for supper and how far apart to space the plates when stacking the dishwasher and at what point you think the dishwasher is full enough for a wash, and how thinly to chop up the carrots and where to buy the fish and when to turn out the light in bed and making all those decisions that are so important in life, it's hard to relinquish control and share.)

Sometimes I think we actually turn into a different shape when we're single. From our edges being all bumps and dips while we were searching for a partner, and constantly looking for another piece of a jigsaw puzzle to fit into, we become smooth and round and self-contained. And much less capable of slotting neatly into someone else's personality. Unless, of course, they have a personality like a great round vacuum which is, of course, not a very attractive personality in any case. But Archie and I often spend weekends together. He comes up to my Edwardian terraced house in Shepherd's Bush in London, or I go down to Devon—always packing my electric blanket, and wearing my special Heat-Tech underwear from UniGlo on top of a silk vest and pair of underleggings, *and* woolly knickers.

Unlike me, Archie has lots of money, but like a lot of grand country people really hates spending it on anything as decadent as heating. So you go into his vast and gloomy stone kitchen and it's awash with all the latest gadgets, and spotless slate worktops, and the bedrooms all have swagged chintz curtains (albeit hanging by a thread), but the actual house is perishing. Indeed, if I ever find myself doing the cooking down there, I wear a hat and a scarf and my overcoat, and I once cut down a pair of woollen gloves to make mittens to wear indoors. Sometimes I even put the oven on and leave it open, just to get a bit more heat. And I'm such a naturally cold-blooded person that the temperature only has to be one degree under freezing that, if I shield a sneeze from others by covering my face, I need a kettle of boiling water to provide enough steam to prise my frosty fingers from my icy nose. I have about as much circulation as an inland lake.

I should take up knitting, but after the huge effort of making Gene, my grandson, a pair of tiny socks on four needles, when he was born, I don't think I could ever wind a piece of wool round another pair of needles again. So *complicated!*

So, there's been no diary-writing for a time, anyway. After all, one keeps a diary not only for comfort but also in the weird hope that someone might come across it hundreds of years later and one might be heralded as the new Mr Pepys, though whether old computer files will last till another century is another matter. Perhaps I should get a quill pen and start writing this by hand rather than banging away on my laptop. Jack gave me this thing for Christmas, in an effort to drag his poor old mum into what I still call the twentieth century—though of course it is now the twenty-first. And I am determined to get the hang of it, even though the keyboard appears to be made for people with very tiny fingers, like goblins. Secretly I rather prefer the cranky old computer I have in my workroom.

Anyway, back to the diary. It's a place you can write all the stuff you can't tell your friends, where you can go over the top or be really mean about your nearest and dearest without hurting them. It's a good pal, or a chum as we used to say when I was a girl, which now seems like millions of years ago though actually I was ten in 1957. And a pal or chum is what I'm starting to need now that things aren't quite as—well, how can I put it?—quite as superlatively brilliant as they were when I was sixty. And because, while I'm still delighted not to be young and believe I'm happier now than I've ever been, things haven't worked out in quite the ecstatic way I was hoping for at the end of my sixtieth year.

What do they say now instead of 'chums' or 'pals'? Mates? Guys? I've got a friend who, when she sees me with someone else, even with another woman, always shouts 'Hi, you guys!' It always makes me feel a bit peculiar, as if I might have suddenly sprouted a moustache or gone bald in the last five minutes.

Now, why am I not as all-singing and all-dancing as I was? For one thing, I'm now nearly sixty-five—in only a couple of weeks in fact—which is rather nearer seventy than it was before. I've certainly ratcheted down a couple of notches. (When you're older, and you suffer some great blow like a major operation or even a very severe dose of flu, you never quite get back to where you started. It's a kind of ten steps back and only nine steps forward situation.) The other day I caught myself talking to myself. Actually, I never realised quite what an interesting person I was until this started. But still . . . In a way it's quite a good thing, this encroaching loopiness. I never used to exercise, but now my heart is constantly getting a work-out just by racing round the house looking for my glasses or panicking that I've left my bath running.

The main problem has been Archie. About two years ago, I realised that Archie was actually starting to behave rather oddly. It began with him forgetting my name. We laughed it off as a senior moment, but then I noticed a bit of paper on his desk one day on which he'd made a list of the names of all the characters he knew: Hardy (his

8

dog), James (our mutual friend), Philippa (his late wife), Harry (his son-in-law), Mrs Evans (his cleaner), Marie (that's me), Sylvie (his daughter), Gene (my grandson), Jack (my son), David (my ex). It looked suspiciously like a reminder list. I was also slightly miffed, to be honest, to see that I was so far down. And the other thing was that his writing looked peculiar. Not quite as strong as it used to be. A bit wiggly. Or, to be *really* honest, shaky. Jolly important as you age to keep your handwriting strong and certain. Before I write anything these days I always take a deep breath to make sure my elegant italic looks full of purpose and intent. You don't want it looking all quavery. Dead giveaway.

The next thing Archie did that struck a note of deep anxiety was to buy a very rare and expensive new rosebush for his garden and become furious when it died. First he'd been convinced that Hardy had peed on it, but just before he fired off an enraged letter to the company which had supplied it, I passed it in the garden and noticed a bit of polythene poking up through the earth around the base of the dead bush. I could see at once what the problem was. He'd planted it with the polythene packaging still on! Was that the act of a man in full possession of all his marbles? I don't think so. This was a man who used to win prizes for his roses; a man who was so scrupulous about his gardening that he actually used to double-dig, and anyone who's done that knows this is serious stuff.

And since the rose bush episode I've been noticing other heartbreaking things about him. For instance, after a day out shopping recently, he came back to my house wearing a brand-new loden coat. Now many people wouldn't think anything of anyone buying a loden coat. I mean why not? Very warm and green and full. But I understand Archie well enough to know that he's not a loden coat-man. Only certain men like loden coats. And Archie isn't one of them. He's a hairy-old-fishing-coat-from-Savile-Row sort of person. He doesn't possess a jacket that hasn't got leather patches sewn onto the elbows. Indeed, it's quite unlike him to buy anything new *at all*, being of a generation, like myself, which finds forking out for a new anything rather extravagant, particularly if we have some old rag hanging in the cupboard that can be repaired instead. I've been known to dig out the sticky remains of my lipstick from its little tube with a pin, and then smear it on my lips with my fingers, rather than go out and get a new one. And I'll never *ever* throw a chicken carcass away. I devil the legs, boil up the bones for stock, and once managed to eke out a bird for ten days. It's the spirit of austerity that still clings on from childhood. Make do and mend.

When Jack stayed the other night, just before Christmas—he was on his way back from a trip to New York and his car conked out in Shepherd's Bush before he could get home so he spent his jet-lagged night with his ma—he said in the morning that he'd slept fine except that there had been a rather uncomfortable ridge down the middle of the bottom sheet. I told him that it was because in some ghastly recession in the seventies, I decided to resort to an old wartime habit of my mother's when the centre of the sheet was worn, and I'd cut it in two, swapped the sides around and resewn it. My son gave a snort, partly of laughter

10

and partly of disgust.

'Mum!' he said. 'You may be broke, but for heaven's sake, you can surely afford new sheets! Go down the market, it'll only be a tenner! I've now got a red line down the middle of my back that will take days to disappear! What will Chrissie think I've been up to?'

But I digress. Back to Archie's loden coat.

'That's very nice!' I said, lying my head off, when he showed it to me—it was one of his weekends in London with me and he'd been to a sale in Regent Street. The coat was billiard-table green, with narrow leathery binding round the collar, a thin chain instead of a top button, and it had a split in the back with a bit more material in the pleat so that it swung out when he walked. It featured small buttons in the shapes of tiny barrels and, worst of all, there were two Sherlock Holmes-type flaps across the shoulders. Funny, those flaps. However tall a man is, those flaps always take about a foot off his height. The problem was that there was far too much material involved. The coat was slightly too long for Archie—even the sleeves—and he looked like a mixture of a small Hollywood millionaire and an insect, the big sort you find in rainforests. Not a good look.

'Do you like it?' asked Archie, attempting an unsuccessful twirl. 'I thought it had a kind of Alpine chic.'

'It certainly does,' I replied, though what Alpine chic is I have no idea, except that it obviously must involve a lot of layers and thick material not only to keep you warm but also to cushion you when you fall on your bottom in the snow. And why would Archie want Alpine chic when he appears to

11

be impervious to cold? Perhaps even he was starting to realise how freezing it was inside his house. Perhaps he was planning to wear the coat for cooking in.

Anyway, he wore this wretched coat all the time, even in the house, while he stayed with me. And just before he left for Devon, he said to me, 'I love this coat! I thought I'd grow a beard to go with it!' As he said this, he gave the strangest laugh I've ever heard. And then I knew that something was deeply wrong and a cold shiver went down my spine. I mean, I've heard Archie on the subject of beards. 'The only gentlemen who ever looked good in a beard were George V and Edward VII,' he said once. 'A beard is the sign of a weak man or a *scoundrel.'*

So I'm very worried.

4 January

I've been looking at the Christmas tree in my sitting room, and roll on Twelfth Night, I say. It just looks a bit sad standing there, its job over, and with all the presents gone from beneath it. Also the room, which is quite small and cosy, needs good lighting, and the tree, despite its fairy lights, doesn't give off quite enough. Maybe I'll just take it down anyway. Can't bear to tell anyone, but last year was the first time I bought a false tree. I just couldn't face sweeping up the needles for months on end. *And no one noticed!* Of course it didn't smell the same, but Christmas trees have stopped smelling like Christmas trees years ago. Or is it just my failing nose? False trees are brilliant. After

12

you've used them, you just fold them up like an umbrella and bung them in the back of a cupboard till next year.

This morning I rang my dear old friend Penny, round the corner. While we were gossiping, I brought up the subject of Archie's coat.

'I'm really worried,' I said. 'Archie's forgotten my name, planted a rosebush in its bag, bought a loden coat and now he says he wants to grow a beard. I think he's getting Alzheimer's.'

Penny was very scathing. 'You always look on the black side,' she said. 'For heaven's sake, we all forget names! And why shouldn't the man buy a new coat? And as for a beard, he's probably fed up with shaving! That's the reason most men grow beards. Can't be fagged to get out the old lather and strop.'

'But he's got an electric shaver!' I protested.

'Oh, don't be so stupid, Marie,' said Penny dismissively. 'Archie's one of the brightest oldies I know. Alzheimer's! Tosh! Honestly, you're so picky, and sensitive. *You're* the one who's getting Alzheimer's. You know paranoia is one of the first symptoms. Anyway,' she added, just to make everything worse, 'you've never been able to bear people wearing things you don't like. You're such a control freak.'

Now, if there's one thing that makes me hopping mad, it's people telling me I'm a control freak. Particularly shambolic, utterly hopeless, untidy and so-called 'spontaneous' people like Penny. Just because her life's a mess and mine is a meticulously filed set of folders in alphabetical order, she accuses me of being a control freak. Naturally I do not see myself as a control freak. I

13

see myself as someone who has got their act together and remembers people's birthdays and gets the trees in the garden lopped every five years, has all her skirts and dresses arranged in different sections in her wardrobe, has working smoke alarms in every room and who always at Christmas gives the dustmen, the newspaper boy and the milkman cards with ten-pound notes inside them. *And* who remembers their names, I might add. Unlike some, i.e. Penny, who is always surprised when the dustmen chuck all her rubbish over her front garden 'by mistake' because she's forgotten to tip them again.

9 January

Now Twelfth Night's well and truly over, the sitting room's all back to normal again and not a Christmas tree, paper chain or card in sight. Took me about an hour to erase all evidence of Christmas from the place, and I nearly fell off the ladder as I was dismantling some holly lights, but what a relief it's all over. Looking through my cards as I swept them from the mantelpiece, I found a very odd one from someone which read, 'With loads of love from Angie, Jim, Bella, Perry and Squeaks. Don't know if dad told you about our latest addition! He's so cuddly! Do come down and meet him, soon! Ring us! Loads of love . . .'
    ???
    Another signed herself 'Anne', but which particular Anne she was, I have no idea. And there were a couple of people who just put a squiggle at the bottom, whose names I couldn't even decipher.

14

Now, Jack rang this morning and invited me to lunch this Sunday. *Very* sinister, this. Most normal mothers would be thrilled to hear from their sons, and usually I'd jump at the chance and be round there like a shot with presents for all the family, but there was something in his voice that made me feel extremely wary. I think that the older we get the more sensitive we are to the nuances in people's voices, a sort of radar. I certainly have invisible antennae like snails' horns, when it comes to voices. Even on the telephone, I can tell at once whether people are happy or cross, ill or well, envious, resentful or bored. Sometimes I wish I weren't quite so sensitive. Because I often get it wrong and am convinced someone is absolutely furious with me and planning never to speak to me again and it turns out that they've merely mislaid their front-door keys.

Anyway, this invitation to lunch was particularly suspicious, not just because of Jack's voice but because I usually only have supper with the family when I drop Gene back after he's been to stay. Not lunch.

But I was made even more wary when he said there was something they wanted to tell me. I had the same feeling as when, at the school where I taught, the headmaster would say he wanted to 'have a word' with me. Wonder if it's connected with Jack's recent mysterious visit to New York? Or Chrissie's? She said it was to do with her job.

To distract myself from this vague anxiety, I went into the kitchen and started cooking like mad—Penny had given me the recipe for a lemon drizzle cake and I thought I'd make it and take it round when I went to see the family. Oh, the

15

longing, when you're on your own, to be able to cook for people, to do things, to nurture! I suppose that's why people love gardening so much when they get older. Instead of looking after the kids, they're out talking to the wallflowers and asking them if they'd like some more water and whether they had a good night's sleep, and saying: 'No, I don't think it's wise that you lean that way, and what about using this stick for a while to ensure you grow straight? And did you say you were being bullied by a whole colony of ragged Robin? Don't worry . . . I'll deal with it . . . yank! All gone! Better now?'

Just as I was getting the cake out of the oven, there was the sound of a key in the door and it was Michelle, my French lodger, back from her Christmas break. A few years back, she fell in love with my Polish cleaner Maciej, and they returned to France to live together, but now he's in Poland studying something and Michelle has returned here to brush up her English, which, frankly, could do with a bit of brushing up. Rather brilliantly, she suggested taking over Maciej's job so she could get her old room at a reduced rent, which suits me fine. (My cleaning days are well and truly over. I think there's a moment when you've hoovered your sitting-room floor for the hundred-thousandth time and you say, 'That's *enough!* Someone else's turn!')

She gave me a big kiss and a hug—she's almost like a daughter to me, or at least a niece—and I helped her upstairs with her huge suitcases. Then I asked if she'd like to share some soup as a welcome-back gesture.

'Oh, ze garden is looking so *triste*,' she said, as

16

she wandered to the window, and stared into the darkness.

'It is,' I said. So I'm going to order some plants for spring.

13 January

I went over to Jack's and Chrissie's for lunch. We had it in the kitchen, and Chrissie cooked an enormous sea bass which was very nice, and I brought the cake and we were all having a jolly time and, when it was over, Gene, who's now five, showed me a picture he'd done of the whole family—one of Chrissie looking completely gorgeous, like some beautiful fairy, another of Jack looking slightly mad but very big and butch, and one of me looking completely crackers, hair on end, huge pair of glasses falling off my nose, wild staring eyes and no neck.

He put his small hand on my arm as he showed me the pictures. 'I've done bags under your eyes, Granny,' he explained kindly, pointing to three lines he'd drawn under each eye, 'because you're very old.'

'Thanks, darling!' I said, giving him an affectionate kiss. 'I can see when you grow up you'll be sweeping the girls off their feet! But I haven't got bags!' I said, pointing to the lines.

'They're to show you're a granny,' said Gene. 'I've seen it in comics.'

'It's not very flattering,' said Chrissie, laughing. 'Granny *doesn't* have bags under her eyes!'

'All right,' said Gene, staring at me hard. Then he said crossly. 'But now I've got to do *another*

17

picture of you,' he said, padding over to the special drawer where he keeps his art things.

Over pudding—my delicious lemon drizzle cake and cream—I asked them how Chrissie's trip had been to New York and this is when the conversation suddenly went a bit silent and Chrissie left the table to do some washing up, and if it had all been a film, some sinister music would have started playing, with low droning violins and a throbbing drumbeat.

Jack looked down at the table and then he pushed his chair back and said, 'Well, that's what we wanted to tell you about, Mum.'

Of course at that moment I knew exactly what was coming and my heart sank into my boots. He didn't have to say another word. Everything suddenly fell into place as if I'd known all along but had just hidden it from myself. Chrissie had been offered a job in New York and they were going over.

'How long for?' I asked, as lightly as I could, trying to hide the catch in my voice.

'Don't jump to wild conclusions, Mum,' said Jack, rather snappily. 'We haven't even told you what it is!'

'Chrissie's been offered a job in New York,' I said.

'How did you know?' said Chrissie, turning from the sink.

'Sometimes you just know these things,' I said. Though actually I didn't really know how I knew at all. I just knew I knew.

'Well, anyway, yes, that's true. But there's nothing to worry about.'

'Nothing to worry about?' I said. 'But I'll never

see you again!'

In my racing mind I'd already got them living in New York forever, then moving even further away to California, and Gene growing up with an American accent, wearing a permanent baseball cap either backwards or sideways on his crew-cut head and chewing gum, and us all being completely unable to recognise each other when we did finally meet. Every ten years if we were lucky.

'Honestly, you've got us living there forever and never seeing you again before we've even thought about it properly!'

The immensity of what they were about to do suddenly hit me with huge force. I burst into floods of tears.

'But you'll all be saying "Gee whizz!"' I heard myself wailing.

'What, Mum?' said Jack, pushing his chair forward and leaning over the table to hold my hand in his. 'We'll all be saying what?'

'G-g-gee whi-whi-wh-whizz,' I hiccupped, choking, between sobs. For some reason this seemed the saddest thing I could think of. 'Gee whizz, darling,' I added, in a more composed voice, in case he hadn't understood.

Jack started laughing and so did Chrissie. 'We'll never say "Gee whizz"', said Jack, and at that point I realised how silly I must have sounded and started to laugh myself. Everyone was very sweet and pulled out their handkerchiefs and Gene came over and said he knew his alphabet now, and Jack said 'What is gee for, then? Or "g?"' he said, making the sound.

'God,' said Gene solemnly.

'And "a"?' said Jack.

19

'Apple,' said Gene.

'And "w"?' said Jack (and under his breath, to me, 'Listen to this').

' "W" is for wabbit,' said Gene.

'Mum, don't worry . . . we're not going till May . . . and anyway, we'll only be gone a year at most . . .'

'But you might stay on,' I said, miserably, trying to pull myself together. I felt that I'd known this was coming all along, and suddenly all my grief had just burst out at once. 'You might stay there for ever and ever and I'll never see you again . . .' the tears started welling up again.

'Well, I can't lie—there *is* a remote chance we might stay on, but it all depends whether we like it or not. And I'm sure we won't. Now you've introduced the appalling idea that we might all say "Gee whizz" it's sounding more unattractive by the minute.'

At this point Gene, realising I was upset, came up and put his little hand on my arm.

'Why is Granny crying?' he asked his father.

'She's upset we're going away,' said Jack, 'but it'll be fine, Mum. We'll be in touch all the time.'

'Don't worry, Granny,' said Gene to me, repeating the words of his father. 'We'll be in touch all the time.'

'I'm fine,' I said, trying to pull myself together. 'And you'll have a lovely time, darling.'

'It's all assuming I can do the job!' added Chrissie. 'They may sack me after a couple of months!'

'And I'm going to an American school!' said Gene, tugging at my sleeve. 'Look, Granny, look at the dinosaur I've just drawn! Look, can you see his

20

teeth? And that's you—you're on his back, having a ride! And you haven't got those lines under your eyes any more!'

'Oh, lovely, darling,' I said, trying to recover and, inside, to take all this in, and not burst into tears again and lie on the floor wailing and gnashing my teeth and begging them not to go. 'Well, it'll be a great opportunity!' With a superhuman effort I tried to look on the bright side.

'Oh, Mum, I know you'll miss us and we'll miss you, but you can come over and visit and we'll be coming back, it's not that far away. And there's always Skype!'

Apparently Chrissie's been offered a brilliant job, marketing her company's beauty products. As a lifelong soap-and-water girl, if I can even call myself 'girl' any more, I simply don't understand the obsession with the kind of 'products' that Chrissie markets, but she always looks gorgeous so perhaps they do some good. Personally I put a good skin down to genetics, but I keep my mouth shut when she's around. So sweet—on my birthday she always gives me amazingly expensive creams, but to be honest I just pass them straight on to Michelle, who can't believe her luck.

Anyway, I was trying desperately to convince myself it was a great opportunity for the family, and Jack can find work out there, too, and of course there was a bit of me that's really thrilled for them and it'll be exciting and good for Gene. And yet, on the other hand, I felt so frightful, and so immensely sad, I just couldn't stay for very long afterwards.

'At least it's not Australia,' I kept telling myself,

as I drove home. I had to pull over repeatedly to wipe away the tears that were misting up my glasses. 'New York is just a hop and skip away. You could almost go over for the day.'

Then, 'And there's always Skype.'

But what the hell is Skype, anyway? I mean I know it's some sort of photo thing where you can see each other, but that's all. I'll have to ask James.

When I got home at five o'clock I broke one of my resolutions and poured myself an extremely large glass of white wine—I had to get a new bottle out of the elephant cupboard where all the drink is kept. I felt so bleak I had to sing a song loudly as I passed it. The elephant cupboard? It's where Gene and I even now play 'elephants'. Children always see their parents as parents—mum and dad. But I'm convinced that until they reach a certain age, grandchildren regard their grandparents not as grandparents but, rather, as very big children, people to play games with.

Anyway—the elephant game. It involves Gene going into the cupboard under the stairs, as I walk about in the sitting room and the corridors saying, in a loud voice, 'I think there's an elephant here! Oh look, there's some elephant poo on the floor, how disgusting . . . there *must* be an elephant here . . . but a very pongy elephant . . .' and there'd be a burst of giggling from the cupboard—'but I can't *hear* an elephant, so perhaps it isn't here . . .'

At this point Gene makes a trumpeting noise from the cupboard and I say 'Good heavens, could that be an elephant!' and I look everywhere, and I look behind the sofa and say 'No elephants here!' and then behind the chair and say 'No elephants here!' and Gene still trumpets from the cupboard and finally, exasperated, he whispers loudly, 'Granny! Look in the cupboard!' and I say, 'Funny, I've never heard an elephant call me granny before, I'll go and look . . .' and open the door and he bursts out and we laugh and then he says, 'Let's do it again. You be the elephant this time . . .' and I'm stuck in the cupboard making elephant noises.

Oh dear, oh dear. I'm crying again. All over my keyboard.

Later

Ohdearthetearsseemtohavedonensomethingtomy keyboardandthespacebarwon'twork.Iwilltrytodryit outwithmyhairdryer.

15 January

MY BIRTHDAY!
Even though I'm now sixty-five, I still feel the same kind of childish excitement about my birthday that I used to have when I was three. I can almost hear my voice going back into those flirtatiously lisping tones of a little girl. It would be more appropriate, perhaps, to say: 'It'th my birfday!'

Penny shudders whenever her birthday comes round, and says she can't bear getting older, but I still adore my birthday. I remember my great friend Hughie saying, before he died, when he was discussing how he wasn't frightened of death: 'So many of my good friends have gone down the plughole I really don't mind following them down

23

the same plughole.' And nor do I. Young people wring their hands at the thought of death, and rightly, because they just can't imagine it and therefore dread it. What they don't realise is that as you get older it gets less and less frightening until finally, if the really old people I know are to be trusted, they often say things quite cheerfully like, 'Well, I've had a good life! If I don't wake up tomorrow it won't be the end of the world!'

The science master at the school where I used to teach has just emailed me, which was very decent of him (makes up for the disgusting brew he rustled up at the retirement party), an old school friend remembered as well, and I got another card from Angie, Bella, Perry, Jim and Squeaks, saying, 'Have a good one! Come soon! Xxxxx'

Hunted in the bin for the envelope and found the postmark too blurred to read. So again: ????

After the postman had been, I counted and I'd got twelve cards. Penny sent me one with a picture of a birthday cake on it covered with candles which read: 'The more candles on my cake, the hotter I am!' But my favourite was of a rabbit lying on its back, surrounded by little bunnies scampering all over her. 'Too old to carry on, too young to stop', it read. I got a card from Gene, too. He'd done a picture of a rocket going into space, with a small circle with an arrow at the bottom and writing which read 'WERLD'. And I got a telephone call from him saying 'Happy birthday, Granny, I love you! Have you got my card? We made you some peppermint creams and I've saved one for you.'

Jack took the phone from him and asked if I was okay and I lied through my teeth and said I was absolutely fine. (I realise now that though

24

mothering appears to stop when children leave home, what one's actually required to do, for the rest of one's life, is to reassure one's grown-up children that one is 'absolutely fine! . . . incredibly busy!' and end every phone conversation with the words, 'Must dash!' This is what makes them feel okay. Frightfully tiring of course, to keep up this ridiculous front, but essential.)

Penny had asked James and me round for a birthday supper and James dropped round first to have a cup of tea so we could catch up. James—oh, it's so complicated. He's my ex-brother-in-law and he's gay, and years ago he got together with a very old friend of mine, Hughie, who was a great mate of Archie's—and Hughie died six years ago, as I just said, and James hasn't found anyone else and it's all very sad. But it's always lovely to see him. He's tall, dark, and not bad looking for his age and only fifty-four. You wouldn't know he was gay until he opens his mouth, when he's quite the shrieking queen, all 'darling' and 'angel' and very emotional. Quite lovely. I wish straight men were more like that, screams and all.

'You're looking just lovely, queen of my heart!' he said, with a broad smile on his face as he came in, bearing a large bunch of flowers. 'How do you do it? Have you had any work done? I bet you have, you naughty thing, and you haven't told me about it.' He brushed a piece of hair from behind my ear and peered behind it. 'Looking for tell-tale scars, sweetie,' he said.

'How dare you!' I said, glowing with pleasure. Isn't it funny how it doesn't matter how insincere someone is, and even if you know they're born liars, it's just lovely to be told you're looking great?

I'm a sucker for compliments. The woman in the corner bakery just has to call me 'love' and I think, 'Oh, you're so kind and wonderful, let me come and live as your friend in your warm, accepting home.' I feel that way even when she calls the next customer 'love'. Strange.

'Now, let me take my shoes off,' he said. 'They're all muddy.' But as he bent down to take them off I stopped him. 'Don't take them off!' I snapped, not very kindly, I'm afraid. 'I keep telling you, my house is designed for shoes. Mud will brush off. I don't mind.'

The truth behind my not-wanting-people-to-take-their-shoes-off-in-my-house is two-fold. Firstly, it's because *I* hate being asked to take my shoes off when I go to other people's houses. I mean, what's the point of dressing up to the nines, and adding, as a final touch, a pair of achingly painful but beautiful high-heeled shoes, only to have someone order me to remove them at the door, meaning I have to pad around on my flat feet everywhere? I feel like those prisoners in the States who are forced to take off their belts by guards, in order to humiliate them. Not being allowed to wear shoes is somehow demeaning. That's why it's so horrible when you have to take them off in airports. Suddenly, you're reduced to feeling like a child.

The other reason I'm not too keen on people taking their shoes off in *my* house is that I don't want their smelly, sweaty feet imprinting themselves in my carpet and leaving damp and pongy footprints everywhere. But of course I don't *say* that.

James came into the kitchen with his shoes on,

26

and I made him a cup of tea.

'Funny you should mention "work", as you so politely put it,' I said, as he leaned over me to choose a green-tea bag from my assortment rather than the Indian I was going to give him ('More antioxidants, darling,' he said), 'I was thinking about having a facelift as a special birthday present to myself. What do you think? I know you're very sweet about my looks, but have you noticed my eyelids? I look like a basset hound. And as for this lizardy bit of neck under my chin . . . it doesn't serve a purpose, does it? I mean it's not as if I can carry my Waitrose shopping in it, like a pelican.'

James stood back, narrowed his eyes, and appraised my face. 'The problem is, my angel,' he said, at last, 'that although you look utterly gorgeous, no one wouldn't look even better with a nip and a tuck, even you. If you've got the money and could stand the pain, I'd go for it. But get someone good, won't you? You don't want to end up looking like those California freaks. When I was last in LA, I met some old movie star whose skin was actually splitting down the middle of her nose, it had been stretched so much.'

He pulled back his skin to look like a cosmonaut taking off, and gave a ghoulish laugh.

'I wouldn't dream of having it done in California!' I said, rather shocked. 'I don't want to look like Joan Rivers. No, I want an English facelift, all understated and resulting in people just saying how well I look.'

'But don't you want people to tell you how young you're looking, as well?' said James. 'Don't you want to get the young men slavering?'

'The last thing I want is a young man slavering,'

27

I said, shuddering. Then I thought again. 'Well, I wouldn't mind one slavering as long as that's all he was doing. No, I just want it done so when I look in the mirror I don't see something that looks like a suicidal maniac. I want to see someone bright and perky.'

'Someone who says "yes" to life!'

'I wouldn't go that far, James,' I replied, pursing my lips as I added the milk. 'Don't let's go mad. But someone who at least says, in the mornings, "Don't you think it's worth giving today a chance?" before throwing in the towel. Anyway, if I do have one, will you come and pick me up and put a bag over my head while you drive me home?'

James says I want to chase a lost youth. I said that's rubbish. He said he wouldn't mind chasing a lost youth himself, the more lost and youthful the better.

'But hurrah to the facelift,' he added. 'I think you'd look more cheerful, too. And that would make other people feel more cheerful when they looked at you, and then you'd feel more cheerful back . . . it would be like perpetual motion. Or do I mean a vicious circle?'

'Perhaps not vicious,' I said. 'But you've got the drift.'

Despite my moaning and groaning and all the sadness about the family flight to the States, I'm actually quite chirpy inside, but whenever I look in the mirror these days, everything's sagged. The skin has just lost its elasticity. I discovered this the other day when I was putting on my eye make-up and was making that kind of grimace that you always do to make it easier to put on the liner at the bottom. However many weird faces I pulled, nothing made the slightest bit of difference to the skin around my eyes.

Before we left to go round to Penny's, James handed me an envelope. 'This is from Marion,' he said. 'I saw her yesterday at this charitable do for the latest disaster—you know, some earthquake. She's the patron of it or something. Honestly, that woman, she's so noble! Anyway, this is your birthday present. But don't open it,' he added suddenly. 'I want Penny to see your face when you find out what it is.'

And with that he snatched it back with a mysterious smile.

Penny had cooked us a delicious supper and I'd brought some champagne, but when Penny asked how Jack was I burst into tears again as I told them the news. They were both absolutely sweet and said I mustn't be upset, and James said, 'Don't worry, I'll come over every weekend with some plasticine and we can make little people out of it and you can pretend I'm Gene,' and Penny said, 'And you can take me to the park . . . and read me bedtime stories,' and James added, 'And we'll all go over to New York and Penny and I can go and find some gorgeous men, while you make gingerbread men and play the elephant game with Gene and we'll all have a brilliant time.'

'I might meet a tall dark stranger,' said Penny, giggling slightly.

'The only tall dark stranger any of us is going to meet is the Grim Reaper,' I said, mopping my eyes and putting my glasses back on. I felt a bit better.

Then Penny turned out the lights and produced a scrumptious cake decorated with enough candles to heat Archie's kitchen. And then James said,

'Marie's going to get herself a facelift for her birthday!' and Penny said, 'You're not! But how could you possibly afford it?' and I said I thought I could sell the two Vivien Pitchforths I had, and James said who the hell was he, and I said he was a painter who'd taught me at art school and he'd given them to me, and actually I could probably get about £2,000 each for them, and then that I was thinking of selling the brooch Archie had given me—

'You can't sell Archie's brooch!' said Penny, choking, shocked, on a piece of cake she was cramming into her mouth.

'Oh yes I can,' I said. 'It's worth about £3,000. And it's hideous. And I don't dare wear it in the streets of Shepherd's Bush, anyway.'

'But what will Archie think?' asked James.

'I don't think he'll mind,' I said. 'Partly because he can't remember anything these days.'

'Marie's convinced he's got Alzheimer's,' said Penny, explaining my apparent heartlessness.

'Well, he's got *something*,' I said. 'You know he rang me up this morning to wish me happy birthday, and called me Philippa! His dead wife! But that's not why I'm selling the brooch. It's because I lost it a couple of years ago, and when I told him he said it didn't matter, and it was silly of him to have given it to me because it was far too valuable to wear, and if I ever found it again, I'd be better off selling it and getting something I really wanted. And I did find it again.'

'Where did you find it?' asked Penny.

'In my jewellery box,' I said, rather shamefacedly. 'You know, you look and look, and can't find it and then a year later you look again

30

and there it is. It's weird.'

'Oooh . . . I forgot . . . do open Marion's present,' said James, pulling it out of his pocket.

I took the envelope and checked it. 'James wants you to see my face when I open it,' I said to Penny. I turned to James. 'It isn't some kind of boxing glove on a spring, is it?'

'No, no, go on open it,' he said, leaning forward expectantly and pouring us all some more champagne.

I opened it. It was a card. And inside there was a piece of paper. Which I read out. 'This is to certify that a goat has been bought by Marion Parker on behalf of Maire Charp for the African community of Ngawa, Swaziland. Thank you Maire and happy birthday!'

'A goat!' I said. My face fell.

'Well, isn't that *sweet!*' said Penny, looking all dear-little-goatishly at me. 'What a lovely present!'

James looked at me slyly.

'It's not a lovely present, it's vile!' I said sharply. 'Not only do I not want to give a goat to Africa, I actually *disapprove* of giving goats to Africa! It's Marion who wants to give a goat to Africa! I've read all about it. They end up either eating all the villagers' vegetables or the villagers just eat the wretched animal themselves. And anyway, the person who gets the bloody goat is hated by all the other villagers because they haven't got one . . . it's loathsome! Why couldn't she give *me* the goat and then at least I could decide who to give it to?'

'But it's for charity,' said Penny. 'How can you be so ungrateful? And to be honest, Marie, you don't *need* a goat.' She got up to look for something.

31

'I can just imagine the whole of Africa swarming with goats given to them by soft-hearted liberals like Marion,' I said. 'They don't want bloody goats! They want fast cars and computers and iPods or pads or whatever they are, and football strips and plasma screens! Goats! It's as if Africans were to give us crystal sets, or tape-recorders or old manual typewriters. No thanks! Anyway,' I added, warming to my theme, 'I've got my own charities I give to—like Romanian orphans. And the whole thing's so patronising, too. It's like offering a child a fiver and then snatching it from his hand and saying he must give it to the poor.

'God, Marion! She hasn't changed has she? I do love her to pieces, but I remember at school when we were moaning about our teachers, she'd always remind us that we were very lucky to be getting an education at all, compared to all the poor children in the world. What am I expected to say? "Dear Marion, Thank you for including me as an involuntary middleman in your kind gift to Africa. I am glad you could kill two birds with one stone. When it's your birthday, I will make a contribution on your behalf to . . . to . . . to—" what's some outfit that would drive her insane with rage?'

'The Conservative Party?' suggested James.

'The Conservative Party, and see how *she* likes it! Then when it's her birthday you can both watch her face fall and report back to me. Bloody goat!'

It quite brought me down. At least she could have given me a glimpse of the poor animal before it was shipped off to cause mayhem in some tiny African community. I might have been able to rescue it and keep it in my garden. Though Pouncer would probably have objected.

Then I suddenly felt guilty. 'For God's sake don't tell her I hated her present, will you?' I said, suddenly remorseful at my outburst. 'I do know she meant well.'

'No, don't worry. It's our little secret,' said James.

'That's the great thing about being older,' said Penny, who was returning to the table with a bottle of Rioja. 'You can tell people all your secrets and know they'll never repeat them because they can't remember them.'

'Har, har, har,' said James, ironically.

We ended the evening by singing a few old Beatles songs and then reeling happily back into the night and home.

Oh dear. Champagne and red wine. Fingers crossed for tomorrow.

FEBRUARY

3 February

Every morning I clamber out of bed and brush my teeth and creak down the stairs to make myself a cup of tea and a bit of toast and Marmite. I then lie on the sofa, Pouncer purring on my lap, and work my way, page by page, through one of the most vile and scandalous right-wing newspapers known to man, the *Daily Rant* as I call it. I get it delivered. When Penny asked me why on earth I took it when I was much more of a *Guardian*-reading sort of person, I found myself giving rather an odd reply.

'It wakes me up,' I said. 'And it gets me going and puts me in touch with the world. When I read the hair-raising headlines, it gets my adrenalin flowing, like a freezing cold shower. And when it has some stupid article about how wicked abortion is, I react so strongly against it that I almost feel engaged in an argument with someone else, "back on the barricades" sort of thing.'

'Hmm,' said Penny, doubtfully. As another woman who lives on her own, she says she has the same problem with overcoming mental inertia in the mornings. 'I usually ring someone up to get myself going,' she said. 'But I never thought reading a ghastly newspaper might do the trick.'

That morning's *Daily Rant* headline read 'GLOBAL WARMING: IT'S OFFICIAL! *Half the world will be starving by 2050, warn scientists.*'

Well, I can tell you, *THAT* jolted me awake,

34

even though I was muzzy with last night's temazepam. I'm starting to reach out rather too readily for the sleeping pills, I'm afraid, since the news about my entire family leaving the country. Oh well, who cares—not about the family of course. I mean the pills. If I were twenty I could see the risk—one wouldn't want to be addicted for the rest of one's life. But at sixty-five? No problem.

Where was I? Oh yes. The *Daily Rant*. Talk about gloom and doom! It appears we are all going to boil to death (last year it was freeze to death— they never seem to be able to make up their minds, but it's always one or the other) and it seems there are only about a dozen rhinoceroses left, and the pandas won't mate and wildlife is all packing up in general. There was a particularly creepy page showing all the species that only had a few months to go before they became extinct, but I can't say, to be quite honest, I'd miss any of them. There was an exceptionally unpleasant black beetle that I'd be glad to see the back of. (Now I come to think of it, it looked just like a miniature version of poor dear Archie in his loden coat.) The weird thing is that a hundred years ago no one knew these species existed and everyone was as happy as bees (which are also DOOMED, apparently), and now everybody's wringing their hands because they're all disappearing.

The other day Penny said to me, when I'd said I couldn't care less, 'But Marie! How can you bear to think that there might be no more rhinoceroses! Think about it! They're such noble beasts!'

I did think, for three seconds, but to be perfectly frank if there weren't any more rhinoceroses it wouldn't make a hell of a lot of difference to my

35

life. After all, there used to be all these dinosaurs milling about and yet these days we seem to be able to cope without pterodactyls, not to mention dodos, perfectly well. Of course if dinosaurs—or 'dinos' as I gather they're affectionately known these days—hadn't been there in the first place, Gene would have been deprived of a lot of enjoyment since, for some reason, young children seem to learn about nothing these days at school except the lives of Tyrannosaurus rexes and diplodocuses. But if a Tyrannosaurus rex were suddenly to arrive in Shepherd's Bush I bet old Penny wouldn't be terribly delighted when it started ripping up all the trees in her back garden. Not to mention sizing her up for breakfast. We wouldn't hear much banging on about 'beautiful beasts' in that scenario, I fancy.

Of course, in the past few years, I haven't needed the *Rant* to jolt me awake because three mornings a week I've woken up beside Archie—he's either been here or I've been down there. I've always preferred going down to him, really, because despite the freezing cold, Mrs Evans, his housekeeper, has always cooked and frozen delicious meals for at least one night. Then there are the roaring fires, the open countryside outside, the lovely library with the musty smell of books, the reassuring presence of Hardy and, best of all, dear Archie himself.

Until recently he'd always spent the days striding about looking at dead trees or broken gates or reading or checking things out on the computer, and then every evening we'd settle down after supper and snuggle up together on the sofa, and either watch an old movie I'd brought down,

36

or just chatter about nothing in particular.

'Do you think it would have been as nice as this if we'd got together before I met David or you'd met Philippa?' I'd said rather sentimentally one evening. I looked at his dear old weathered face, and smiled as he gave me a regretful shake of the head.

'*You'd* have been angelic,' he said. 'Of course. But I . . . I was so immature! I remember having so many rows with Philippa during the first years of our marriage, and it wasn't till much later that everything settled down. I don't think you and I would have lasted for a second. It seems strange to say that, doesn't it,' he added, reaching out his hand to stroke my hair, 'when now we fit together like a couple of old bedroom slippers?'

'Excuse me!' I said. 'Bedroom slippers! I can think of a nicer simile than that!'

'Like what?' he said.

But I couldn't think of anything. 'I think the reverse is the case,' I said. 'I was so neurotic when I was young, so emotional, always taking offence. I'm bad enough now, but *then!* And you've always seemed so level-headed. I think I'd have driven you nuts. I agree, it's best now. But it's a shame not to have a history together.'

'Depends what sort of history,' Archie had replied, pulling me gently over to his side of the sofa. 'As far as I'm concerned, I like it just as it is now, darling.'

'So do I,' I said. And with that, we had a brief affectionate cuddle, then gathered up our bits and pieces, put a guard in front of the dying fire, turned off the lights, shut Hardy into the kitchen, and wandered up to bed, me snuggling up to

37

Archie to keep warm and him tucking me in at the sides, with his free arm, as if I were a child.

'I love you,' he said.

'And I love you,' I said. 'And now is all that matters.'

Now *was* all that mattered *then*. But now, oh so sadly, it doesn't seem to be like that any more.

4 February

Since my great friend Hughie died, James and I have become very close. 'I'm your walker, darling,' he says. 'Don't say that,' I reply. 'It makes me sound like a dog.' But it's true. Whenever I need a spare man, he's always around, and whenever I need to go up a ladder, he's always there to steady it. ('One thing you must promise me, Mum,' Jack said, after he'd found that I'd not only put up but also taken down all the Christmas decorations on my own. On a ladder. 'Yes?' I'd said, imagining he was going to ask me some enormous favour, like a guarantee that I'd never get married again, or insist I make a will leaving everything to him. 'Now you're sixty-five, will you please never go up a ladder without someone holding it at the bottom?')

I was rather touched by this request, and of course since making the promise I never have—gone up a ladder, that is. And golly, am I glad! Half my contemporaries either are, or have been, in hospital having fallen off a ladder. It's weird. The moment they hit their sixty-fifth birthday they get a craving to scramble up a ladder, and then they invariably drop off at the top. In the past month alone two of my friends have clambered up ladders and, literally, the moment they've got to the top rung they've swayed slightly and then fallen to the bottom. Just like that. No reason. Perhaps it was the thin air up there.

Anyway, James said he'd come for coffee to get cracking on putting Skype in for me, and I settled down to read the *Rant* before he arrived. I'd barely read the headline ('DUNCE NATION! *Eighty per cent of adults can't find Britain on a map*'), when the bell rang and it was James. Early.

'Now before we start on the Skype, I want to ask a favour of you,' he said, as I put the kettle on. 'You know I've been doing these art classes recently . . .'

He started to tell me about them as we went into the sitting room, and I sat down and put my feet back up again.

He has to do *something* now Hughie's died, he said, and has no one to look after—so he's taken up art. I made polite noises because it's always a bit tricky, having taught art at a school until I retired, when some complete amateur says they've started to paint. I mean it's very touching and all that, but they seem to think they can just pick up a brush or a pencil and draw and hey presto! They think they're Leonardo da Vinci. The truth is that you really have to spend years practising day after day before you can even begin to get the hang of drawing or watercolours, a notoriously difficult medium, so I always wince when retired contemporaries say that they've 'become an artist' in their old age. I mean it's just not possible. It's tricky when they show me their pictures. I'm just so bad at lying. Funny, I would never say, at my age, that I'd decided to 'become a pianist.' Particularly

39

not to someone who'd been a piano teacher all her life. I mean I might be able to thump my way through a Chopin prelude rather badly, but it's highly unlikely I'd get much further.

But back to James. 'I've decided to do some portraits, darling,' he said.

I'd had an awful premonition that was coming and I tried not to look as if I'd just opened an envelope with a gifted goat inside. I tried to change the subject.

'Funny you should say that,' I said. 'I've decided to get back to painting myself, this year. I was thinking of trying landscapes. You know I've always been keen on them . . .'

But my efforts failed.

'And I wondered if I could use you as a model?' said James, as if he hadn't heard. 'I'd love to, well, interpret your spirit.'

'What exactly do you mean, "interpret my spirit"?' I asked, suspiciously. 'I hope I'd still look like me.'

I'm clearly an old fuddy-duddy. I do prefer representations of things to look like what they're meant to represent, and I was nervous of what the 'spirit' of me might conjure up in James's mind. But I could hardly say no to a useful Skype-installer and ladder-holder.

'I'll tell you when I've thought it through,' he said guardedly.

Unfortunately, when he looked at my computer he found the broadband wasn't working for some reason, so he couldn't download it. We had to call it a day for the moment.

'By the way,' he added, before he left, 'we must see *Bitter Quinces, Poisoned Souls*. It's that new

40

Swedish film and everyone says it's brilliant. It's got five stars everywhere!'

6 February

Spent a couple of very jolly hours pulling out old canvases and sorting out paints and brushes, and even managed to dust off a portable easel I sometimes used to take with me when I went down to Archie's. I must say some of the pictures I did in the past weren't half bad, though I say it myself. Feel I've probably got a bit rusty, but it all made me very enthusiastic, and I can't wait to get started again.

I was just about to load the dishwasher this morning—my special way, with the knives all facing downwards—when blow me, as I stomped into the kitchen there was one of those beetles that the *Rant* had warned were on the brink of extinction! At least I was almost sure it was. It was quite big and black and shiny, in two parts, with long waggling antennae. It was pretty swift too. On seeing me it raced to the other side of the room and tried to hide in the crack between the floor and the skirting board.

Of course the thrill of finding one in my kitchen made me reconsider my feelings about this particular endangered species. So I immediately turned into an eco-warrior. I placed a tumbler over the beetle, slipped a postcard under it, picked it up, walked with it reverently to the garden, opened the door, bent down and sent it off with a soothing benediction: 'God speed, little fellow. May you prosper, and may your children prosper and your

41

children's children . . .' It was horribly cold out there, though, so I hope he doesn't die.

I even left a note for Michelle. 'If you see a beetle in the kitchen please don't kill it. It is an ENDANGERED SPECIES', I wrote on a little pink Post-it note. *'Espèce en danger'*, I added, hoping that made sense, *'mais pas dangereuse.'*

'Are you sure, actually, zat eet ees special beetle?' said Michelle, when I found her in the kitchen this afternoon, mixing a revolting muesli dish with yogurt and drinking some kind of bio thing called Yakult. Funny name. 'I 'ave see one like zees last week, and I try to keel heem but he runs by *frigidaire*. 'E is like bad beetle we 'ave in France, actually, 'ow you say, a *concrelat.'*

'Oh, I'm sure you have them in France,' I said, knowledgeably. 'Lots of them. But France is much richer in wildlife than England. Here we must preserve them. No, here we are lucky to have black beetles in our kitchens. Particularly endangered species.'

She looked doubtful. 'Perhaps you're thinking of a cockroach?' I said, the penny dropping. 'Because it's *not* a cockroach,' I added with certainty. I'd seen plenty of them in every lavatory I entered in Morocco when I went on a wild trip with Marion just after we'd both left school. 'Cockroaches are *brown.'*

I remember once going to a loo in Tangiers and counting twenty-nine of the beastly things inside, all grinning at me and waving their antennae about.

I might put a saucer of milk out for it if comes back tonight, and perhaps some crisps, but I am not sure what endangered species like to eat so

42

have decided against the crisps.

Shut the kitchen door in case Pouncer takes a fancy to the scuttling beast. Even though he's old in years, he can't resist anything scampering about on the floor.

8 February

I know it's only a few weeks since I made the List of Things to Do, but I don't feel I've got to grips with it yet. Time is speeding by. Honestly, within what will seem like only a few weeks, it'll be Christmas yet again. How on earth does one fill one's days? I'm at a loss to know. Before I've blinked, another week has raced by.

I suppose everything takes a bit longer these days, but not *that* long, surely? My days seem to be spent doing maintenance. Maintenance, maintenance, maintenance. Sometimes it's me who needs maintaining—a round of doctors to see about this and that, a strange patch of eczema at the back of my knee, blood tests, visiting the optician for new glasses . . . then there are the exercises we all have to do these days to stop our limbs seizing up like one of those clockwork drummers. You know the sort. They work perfectly well and then suddenly one day they just stick, frozen, as they beat—or rather don't beat—their drum. And however much you wind them to the ultimate point or tap them firmly on the side of the table, they just refuse to move and sit there, mid-beat. I'm starting to feel like that in the mornings. I wish I could have a change of oil, like a car, to get everything lubricated again.

The other day Gene said to me, 'Granny, do you go up the stairs slowly because you *like* it?'

Apparently it's all down to the little pads between one's joints wearing out, or shrivelling up—I imagine them like those old India rubbers you find at the back of drawers. All firm and bouncy when you originally put them away, but, when discovered years later, dry and cracked and unmalleable.

Not only that but there's also all the checking up on one's friends. Whenever anyone says they've got to have a scan or an X-ray or an appointment to see an oncologist, I rush to the diary and put in the date, to remind me to ring them up within hours to find out exactly how they got on.

And apart from all *that* there's the maintenance of wherever one lives. In my case, it's a hundred-year-old house. If it's not a slate off the roof, it's a drip on the upstairs tap, or the front door suddenly sticks because it's swollen by the rain. If it's not the draughts, it's the blistering paintwork, and if it's not the little holes in the shower-head getting bunged up with limescale, it's the lino that starts buckling in the kitchen—signifying that there might well be a leak from the dishwasher.

How people with jobs manage to cope I just don't know. Indeed, how I used to cope when I worked full-time as a teacher, I don't know either. Sometimes entire days are simply taken up with fixing, collecting, repairing, buying replacements—well, just *maintaining*. And when you go to bed at night, you feel you've achieved nothing because all you've done is rush around like a mad thing, just to stay in exactly the same place as you were before.

12 February

I was over at Jack and Chrissie's yesterday, picking up Gene from school and looking after him until Chrissie got back from some essential shopping before they fly off—and when she got back she made me a cup of tea. She was pink with the cold. Golly February's a cruel month. I took the chance to reapply my make-up—I always like to look my best, but particularly when immaculate old Chrissie's about—and as I was doing so, my lipstick rolled off my lap onto the floor. Chrissie said to Gene, 'Pick that up for Granny! Don't make her bend down!' and I had a completely different vision of myself as I must appear to Chrissie— rather less agile than I actually feel.

And then Jack came back from work and they started discussing a trip they'd made to the Monument. Jack said, 'You must go, Mum, it's really interesting! It's where the Great Fire of London started,' and Gene said, 'Yes and you go up all these steps to the top!' and Chrissie said, 'You can see all over London!' and then Jack turned to Chrissie and said, 'Might be a bit much for Mum, don't you think?' and then added, 'all those steps,' which I thought was pretty odd and then I heard Chrissie saying, 'Oh no, I'm sure she could manage them!'

Manage them! I'm sure no one said that about me when I was fifty!

Of course it's these little incidents I'll miss when they're in New York. Just the small encounters and closeness and estrangements and instincts and understandings that make relationships. How on earth am I going to cope without them?

It's not as if I even have Archie to keep me company, now, really. He's just a little bit too peculiar. Tomorrow I'm off to see him, and I have to admit I'm rather dreading it.

16 February

Just back from seeing Archie. Oh dear, oh dear, oh dear. I don't know what to do. I'm so worried about him. The first thing that made me nervous, as I turned the car into the drive, was to find him sitting on one of the stone lions that guards his front door, *in his pyjamas*. He hadn't shaved and his hair was sticking up on end. As it was midday and raining it was particularly odd. And then he greeted me as if I'd been there all the time—there was no surprise or pleasure in his seeing me.

I parked the car, got out quickly and went up to him. 'Darling,' I said, putting my arms round him and kissing him. 'How are you?'

'I've lost my key,' he said. 'I went out this morning to find Philippa in the garden and now I can't get back inside. I've been looking everywhere.'

'But Philippa's dead, sweetie!' I said.

'I know she's dead, Marie,' said Archie, looking at me as if I were mad. 'For God's sake, what are you talking about?'

'But you said you'd gone out to look for her.'

'I didn't. I said I'd come out to look for Hardy, my dog, in case you'd forgotten ...'

'But you said Philippa.'

46

'I didn't!' he said. 'Honestly, Marie, are you going deaf?'

I said nothing. Then, 'But what about the key?' I asked. 'Have you lost the key? Have you locked yourself out?'

'Yes,' he said. 'And I know there's a place where it's hidden somewhere but I can't remember where it is.'

'It's under the fourth flower pot outside the back door,' I said, leading him round the house. We found the key, then went back to the front of the house and opened the door. It was still drizzling. 'Now come on, go and have a hot shower and get yourself dressed. You must be freezing. It's nearly lunchtime.'

I fed Hardy who'd been inside all morning and was so desperate to get out he'd done a poo on the kitchen floor. So I cleared it up. I made lunch and got out the cutlery and plates to lay the table, but when I opened the cupboards, I found that dirty plates had simply been stacked up as if they were clean, and there was congealed food on every one of them. I knew Mrs Evans wouldn't have left things in such a state, but she usually comes on Tuesdays and Saturdays, and today was Friday, so obviously Archie had just piled the plates away without washing them up. There were clean knives and forks in the drawers—but also ones with butter smeared on them, and bits of cabbage attached.

Just as I was staring at these revolting specimens, Archie came into the kitchen, having got dressed and, peculiarly, as we were in the house, wearing his loden coat. 'You look as if you've seen a ghost,' he said. 'What's the matter?'

'These,' I said, pointing to the dirty plates. 'How

47

did they get put away like this?'

Archie appeared amazed. 'Well, that's disgusting,' he said. 'Who can have done that? Mrs Evans . . . oh, dear. She's not up to her usual standards. I'm thinking of sacking her, you know.'

After lunch, Archie made the coffee—I only just prevented him from putting salt into his—and we decided to go into the library and do *The Times* crossword, which Archie is very good at. We got to the word 'amphora', and Archie said he'd look it up in the dictionary. He got up and pulled it down from the bookshelf and sat down.

'It's a Roman vessel,' he said, as he opened the book.

'I know it is,' I said. 'And so do you. It's a well-worn crossword answer, like "retsina". Why are you looking it up?'

But he'd started poring over words.

'It's Greek,' he said. 'A two-handled vessel for holding wine, oil, etc. . . . amphitheatre . . . amphibian . . . yes, amphi means double . . . can live on sea and land . . . but ampho . . . that's different . . . amphitryon . . . the host, giver of dinners . . . that's interesting . . . you see "amphi" meaning double, where is the meaning in that . . . "ampho" on the other hand . . . ah, the two handles . . .'

'Yes, but what's 6 across, now beginning with "p"?' I asked, tetchily. But Archie wasn't to be deflected from his task. It was as if he'd forgotten about the crossword puzzle altogether. He started looking up 'Double . . . ah, yes, from the Latin here, Duo meaning "two" . . .'

I couldn't tear him away, and even though I got up and suggested we went for a walk while it was still light, he seemed transfixed. He pushed me away rather crossly when I tried to take the dictionary from him, and just carried on reading out the words like an automaton.

Eventually I gave up and went out on my own, feeling very lonely. It was nice that Hardy came with me, and licked my hand as if he knew something was wrong. We didn't go far—just to the end of the field outside the house and back, and I felt sad that Gene would miss all the wonderful English countryside when he was in New York, the damp aroma of the fields and leaves, the snowdrops, the faint smell of wood smoke, the sound of pigeons chuckling to themselves as they settled down for the night . . .

When I got back, half an hour later, Archie was still studying the dictionary, now on to 'mitriform . . . shaped like a mitre . . . from the Greek *"mitra"* a type of headdress worn by a woman . . .'

Eventually he stopped, but he'd been preoccupied for far longer than usual.

'Let's go for a walk!' he said, brightly. I didn't think it was worth explaining that I'd just come back from one, so out we went again, even though it was now getting quite dark. 'Doesn't seem as if Hardy wants to go out,' he said as he tried to persuade him through the door. 'That's odd. He usually loves a walk about this time.'

I didn't say I'd just taken him out, but after moving around a bit in the open air, Archie seemed a bit more like his old self. Although we'd been silent as we wandered down an avenue of beeches, he started singing 'Oh My Darling Clementine'.

'Our song, Philippa,' he said, affectionately

49

squeezing my hand. But of course it wasn't *our* song. I just smiled at him. We walked on, over the stile and into the darkening wood. We sat on a bench.

'Our tree, darling,' he said.

And there he was right. That old beech was indeed 'our tree'. It was here, several years ago, that we'd sat one glorious summer's day, and he'd put his arm round me and we'd just sat, staring out, happy to be together, when he'd said, 'Would you like to get married, Marie? To me, I mean!'

I hadn't known what to say. I was so touched at his suggestion and yet at the same time I felt a wave of anxiety. Marriage hadn't been very happy for me, and I didn't want to do anything that would rock the boat with Archie. I must have blushed and stammered because he looked at me, affectionately and then said, 'Don't worry. If you wanted to, of course we could. I just wanted you to know that of course it's in my mind. If you want.'

'Well, it's not that I don't want to be married to you,' I said. 'But marriage is really for people when they're going to have children, isn't it? And then we'd have to remake all our wills . . . making sure that our children would still get what they should get . . . and to be honest, I don't know how Sylvie or Jack would react . . .'

'Sylvie would hate it,' laughed Archie. 'She's a daddy's girl. And she's never got over her mother's death. So it's probably best not. But I just wanted you to know, darling, that I feel married to you, even if we're not.'

'And I feel married to you, even though we're not,' I said.

'At least until one of us goes bonkers,' added

50

Archie realistically. 'Any moment I start going funny, I do not want you devoting your life to me, and you've got to make me a promise that if it happens, you won't. I don't want any sacrifices, okay?'

'I'd find it hard not to,' I remembered saying. 'But I'll promise, if you promise me the same if I start losing my marbles.'

'Our special marriage tree!' Archie had said, looking up at the branches, pulling me close and turning, reaching down, and pulling a stalk from the ground. 'With this weed,' he'd said, winding it round the third finger of my left hand, 'I thee wed.'

But the good years had passed and now I wondered if he remembered our conversation. He just squeezed my hand, and finally we got up and walked quietly back home.

On the way back, he seemed so nearly normal that I told him that I'd found the brooch and wanted to sell it: even though he'd said in the past that it would be fine, I just wanted to make sure.

'Very good idea,' he said. 'You don't need a facelift, though, darling. But if it'll make you happy, then I'd love to think I was contributing in some way. I'd forgotten about that brooch. I had no idea I'd given it to you. I thought you'd lost it. It's a pity you can't find it.'

I didn't want to go over it all again, but I was extremely worried. And when, the next morning, Mrs Evans came in, I waited till Archie had gone out of the kitchen and then asked her directly how she thought he was. I added that I was very worried about him, and this news seemed to come to her as a great relief.

'Oh Mrs Marie!' she said, sitting down and

putting her duster on the table. 'I can't tell you how anxious I am! He's forgotten to pay me these last months, and then when he does, he forgets and gives me twice as much, and yet the other day he accused me of stealing. Mr Archie! Me, who's known him since he was a young man! Stealing! He's not right, no, he isn't. He's got demania or Alzenstein, or whatever it is. And the other day for some reason he took all the light bulbs out of their sockets and put them in a drawer. I don't know why. I had go to behind his back and put them back, or there'd have been no light for him to read in the night. I've told his daughter, Mrs Sylvie, I'm worried, but she won't hear a word about it. I think she's living in denial or whatever it is people live in these days when they don't want to hear the truth, and I can't blame her. Her father! Her lovely father!'

'I'll have a word,' I promised.

But, oh dear, I don't fancy broaching the subject.

18 February

I talked to Penny about my weekend after we'd been to see the most ghastly film. It was on up the road at one of those lovely old cinemas that everyone's so keen on tearing down these days, and we went early to take advantage of the cut-price tickets for pensioners. The woman at the box office didn't query my age at all, which made me even more determined to have a facelift.

Anyway, it was the movie James and all our friends had been raving about, *Bitter Quinces,*

Poisoned Souls, the one that all the critics have declared a masterpiece, but after about half an hour Penny whispered to me, 'I don't understand any of this, do you?' and I whispered back, 'It's total rubbish. Shall we go?' and we got up and left and crossed the road to have a jolly good supper at one of those Japanese places where you pick your food off a moving conveyor belt.

'Sometimes I think that as I've only got ten years left, or something like that,' said Penny, as she took off her coat and sat down, 'I don't want to waste two and a half hours of it staring at a film that's total crap. Time is precious these days.'

'What on earth was that woman doing, staring into space in that blighted underground car park?' I asked.

'Oh, I thought she was a character in someone else's computer game,' said Penny. 'And was it really necessary to show us that poor man's fingers being cut off one by one?'

We both shuddered and started choosing little bowls of raw fish to tuck into.

Then I told her about Archie, and even she thought it sounded as if there might be a problem.

'He can't be left on his own if he's getting locked out, and the poor dog . . . what if he forgets to feed him?' she said, helping herself to a tiny dish full of raw salmon. 'Maybe someone could stay with him.'

'Don't look at me,' I said, wrestling with some noodles. 'I'm not married to him, thank goodness. I love him dearly, but that was always the deal. No marriage and no commitment if one or other went off their heads. He always said if he ever got peculiar I was just to push him off a cliff. He made me promise I'd never waste my life looking after

53

him.'

'Would it be a waste of life? Looking after him, I mean?' asked Penny.

'While I will do all I can to make everything as happy and comfortable for him as I possibly can, I'm not going to incarcerate myself down in Devon with a man who's starting to think I'm his dead wife,' I said firmly. 'Anyway, I couldn't manage it. He might go wandering off in the fields in the middle of the night and then what would I do?'

We chatted some more and then we paid the bill and started to leave, but at the door the manager came over to us and asked us to pay extra for two dishes he claimed we'd had after we'd settled the bill.

'One of my staff saw you taking them, I'm afraid,' he said.

We were outraged.

'For heaven's sake do we look like two women who need to steal sushi dishes for kicks? How dare you!' we said.

He reluctantly let us go, but we were left with a nasty feeling. 'He probably thinks we're two barmy old ladies who pinch marinated tuna for the hell of it,' said Penny. 'Oh dear, we should never have left that film early.'

When we were young we couldn't be trusted because we were young and irresponsible and now we can't be trusted because we're old and mad. Well, I'll never go *there* again. Though their chicken teriyaki is, of course, totally scrummy.

As we walked back, Penny and I congratulated each other on living in Shepherd's Bush. Not only is it an extremely 'diverse' area—i.e. every nationality under the sun lives here in apparently

54

perfect harmony—but it's one of the few boroughs that is, in the summer, incredibly green. Each street is lined with enormous trees and at the top of our road there's even a small patch of grass on which flourish not only a huge old plane tree but a really beautiful false acacia. If you're very clever, on a particularly balmy day, and if you stand in a particular spot outside my house, and half-close your eyes and gaze up towards this bit of greenery, you can almost imagine you're looking at a picture by Claude. Or Poussin.

'Not,' as Penny pointed out when I mentioned this to her, 'that anyone has ever heard of Claude or Poussin these days.'

I wondered whether it might not be worth having a crack at trying to reproduce this oddly romantic piece of urban landscape as a picture.

Spent a happy hour rereading *Diary of a Provincial Lady* by E.M. Delafield. Now there's a diarist and a half.

19 February

Today I took my courage in both hands and gave Sylvie a ring. That's Archie's daughter. Much as I love Sylvie and we have a lot of laughs together, I'm never certain *quite* how much she loves me because I can't imagine any daughter, even a grown-up one, particularly likes a new woman in her father's life. Luckily Archie and I had reassured her early on that we had no intention of getting married, and that eased things a lot—I think she'd been nervous that the family millions (not that there are many millions but presumably the estate is worth a fortune) would be left, on his death, not to her but to me.

Still, we are very civilised with each other. But civilised enough to have a conversation about her father's deteriorating mental condition? I wasn't so sure. And anyway the last thing she wants to be burdened with is someone like me telling her that she thinks her father's losing his mind.

We went through the usual hellos and how are yous on the phone and then I said, 'Look, I wanted to ring because I'm a bit worried about your father.' I don't think I've ever uttered quite such a grown-up phrase in my life. I usually feel about eight, forty-five or fifty-three or any age except the one I am now. But after hearing myself intone this grave sentence I felt every inch of sixty-five. I'm not sure I didn't actually feel ninety. I was sure that even my voice had lowered itself in order to convey how important I thought it was.

'Well, what about him?' she said, and I thought I detected a snap in her voice.

'He does seem to be getting a bit forgetful,' I replied.

'Well of course he is!' she retorted, tetchily. 'He's seventy-five. Everyone gets forgetful when they're old. I should think *you're* getting a bit forgetful, aren't you?'

'This is slightly different, Sylvie,' I said. Using her first name added a bit more gravitas to it all. 'Even Mrs Evans has noticed.'

'Well, you shouldn't listen to what *Mrs Evans* says. She's as mad as a hatter! Not only that but my father rang yesterday to say she'd stolen a brooch of yours. She's obviously gone barmy. She'd never do a thing like that unless she was off her head.'

56

'No, she hasn't stolen a brooch,' I said, gently. 'I think your father got a little confused. I really think you ought to take him to see a doctor and see what he thinks,' I added, finally, but realising I was unlikely to get anywhere.

'Our doctor's a woman!' she snapped.

Oh dear. When I was young doctors were always 'him' so I often forget, even though my own GP is a woman, to add 'or her' when I'm talking about professionals who used in the sixties, always to be men. Or rather, whenever I hear myself saying the word 'him' I involuntarily add the phrase 'or her'— so often it makes no sense at all. (The last time I mentioned a hitman, I heard myself adding 'or her', which was of course ludicrous. It's because I'm so paranoid that someone like Penny—or, now, Sylvie—will jump on me and accuse me of being sexist.)

Quite apart from being outraged by my assumption that the doctor was a man, Sylvie was clearly furious about my suggesting there was anything wrong with her father. But she did concede that Harry, her husband, had expressed the same misgivings, at the same time claiming that she 'knew daddy better than anyone' and that he was perfectly fine, but if I insisted she'd take him to the doctor, not that there would be anything she—and she emphasised the 'she'—would be able to do if there were.

'Quite the contrary,' I said, decisively. 'There are, in some cases, things that can be done at least, before . . . er . . . whatever it is—' I didn't like to say 'dementia' or 'Alzheimer's' though we both knew what I was talking about, '—gets a grip. Things that can prolong . . .'—I was getting

57

flustered—'er, stupidity and memory . . . I mean,' I added, even more anxious and confused, 'lucidity and memory . . . senior moment.'

'Senior Moment. Exactly,' snapped Sylvie. 'Just like daddy. Nothing to worry about.'

No wonder Sylvie ended our phone call with the sarcastic words, 'Well, thank you very much—*Doctor* Sharp.'

MARCH

4 March

Had a ghastly dream last night that I was in group therapy and the therapist said she didn't trust me an inch and that I was two-faced and devious, and after she finished the entire group burst into applause, shouting 'Hear hear!' I thought it was pretty mean of whoever it is who creates my dreams, just after I'd just taken a very brave and honest and up-front step in bearding Sylvie. Sometimes I'd like to meet my dream-weavers and give them a good talking-to. I'd like to ask them for something light and amusing, full of jokes and songs, threaded through with a general feel-good atmosphere. Something on the lines of *Mamma Mia!*, perhaps. Or if they'd simply give me the name of the Derby winner, that would be fine. That would save them the trouble of constructing all these blackly complicated scenarios. But I doubt if they'd listen. I suspect the director of *Bitter Quinces, Poisoned Souls* has a say in most of my dreams. They're almost always X-rated horror stories or psychological thrillers steeped in what is known as 'the dark side'.

Oh, crikey! We're at the beginning of March and I still haven't done any of the things on my list except write a diary! Will make an appointment with the acupuncturist today—I gather they're very good with joints—and scout around for a cosmetic surgeon. I need a jolly good brush-up.

It's not that I'm 'letting myself go', don't get me wrong. The older I get, the more scrupulous I am about looking as good as I can. But what with Archie's ghastly condition and Jack and Chrissie and Gene going to the US, I have to admit I'm not quite the cheerful bunny I used to be, and, as I read today, to my horror, one in seven of us will live to a hundred years old. I realised at once that, as one of these people who's quite happy to leave the party early and bow out at a civilised time, like eighty, fate will probably decide as a nasty trick, to engineer my living till 120, so I've come to the conclusion that I've got to get my act together and see that the last years of my life aren't spent wringing my hands and bemoaning 'the state of things today'. (I did catch myself doing that once, egged on by Marion, who remembers the old 'peace and love' days, but then I reminded myself how, when I was young, I hated old people who whinged. So I shut up.)

5 March

Today I rang an acupuncturist who has her practice in Oxford Street, above a shop. I asked which end of Oxford Street she was and she said the Tottenham Court Road end. Then I asked if her place was on the north side of Oxford Street or the south side. And, amazingly, she had no idea what I was talking about. It doesn't bode well. Surely an acupuncturist ought at the very least to know the points of the compass? You would think so, wouldn't you? Made an appointment to see her some time in the distant future. Had no idea acupuncturists were so popular. Anyway, I thought it might be a nice treat to give me a lift after the family's gone away. Aaargh!

Then Penny came round with the minutes of the last Residents' Association meeting.

'So, what did Sylvie say?' she asked. She was wearing a very wet old windcheater, and carrying an even wetter umbrella which she folded up as she came in.

I told her she'd promised to take him to the doctor.

'Bet she doesn't.' she said. 'Did you hear the joke about the perks of having Alzheimer's? I can only remember one of them.'

I laughed.

'That wasn't the joke,' she said crossly. 'No— one of the things that's good about having Alzheimer's is that you can hide your own Easter eggs. That's funny don't you think?'

I thought it was, rather.

7 March

I've just been out in the garden with Pouncer. It was surprisingly warm, and I was thrilled to see that at the end of the garden there is the odd primrose, and a whole bunch of early daffodils. God knows when I planted them. Probably that funny collection that Penny gave me last year that she'd got free with some gardening order. What with a few crocuses, the whole thing down the end looked like a spring glade.

61

And I suddenly thought of an idea. I'd do a painting of part of my garden every month, for a year. The David Hockney of Shepherd's Bush.

Pouncer was looking contemplative, too, but he was probably thinking about birds. Then I heard someone yelling. Looking round rather irritatedly, I saw my Polish neighbour, Mrs Vladek, who'd come out into her garden and was shouting over the wall. She's a widow who must be at least ninety, and she always has to walk very carefully in her garden as there's not much room on her path because she still collects and hoards driftwood there, an old wartime habit.

'I want you to know, I am selling house.'

'What!' I said. For some reason I thought she'd be living there forever. 'But why?' For a brief moment I imagined that she'd somehow eavesdropped on my ghastly dream and had decided she couldn't carry on living next to such a foul and devious neighbour.

'I go to live with my sister in Poland,' she said. 'And I have offer on house. From very nice people. He is American. Lawyer, very big.' I immediately imagined a grossly fat legal eagle, having to be winched up to his room through the window, along with the grand piano. 'They have plan for house. I leave next month. I will be sad.'

Thinking about this, *I* felt rather sad as well. And *particularly* sad that I'd never made proper friends with this old lady. She'd clearly had a bad war, since she still spent her days scavenging for bits of wood for emergency heating. Once, during the biggest storm in recent history, a storm that felled a quarter of London's trees, I looked out of my bedroom window at three in the morning and saw her wrestling with a piece of tarpaulin on her roof, a tiny, game, wizened creature struggling to keep her balance in the gale, clutching on to the chimney pot while desperately trying to fix the billowing fabric in place.

With great difficulty I had managed to get the window open, waved liked a maniac, yelled at the top of my voice, and finally caught her attention.

'Get inside!' I shouted. 'It's dangerous!'

But she couldn't hear a word I said and, blow me, when I next looked out, she was still there with a hammer, banging nails into the tarpaulin as the wind howled around her, leaves and branches and birds tumbling past her. I shut the window, crept back into bed, pulled the duvet over my head and prayed.

I sometimes wonder if our generation isn't rather weedy. True, we survived the sixties, which was a dreadful stress as it was a time of such social change. But these old birds who lived through the war! What they must have suffered! Presumably all the men were away fighting, so no doubt everything at home was left to the women—sweeping away the rubble from the streets after bombing raids, boiling up weeds for soup and, without a crumb of coal for heating, just pulling on another jersey made out of the front-room carpet and getting on with it.

We're a pampered generation.

But to be honest, after the news she'd just given me, I felt rather like my neighbour herself, struggling on the roof in the middle of the night. I felt I was trying to hammer down some kind of psychic tarpaulin on my feelings. It's the strain of the family going away, I know. I suppose change is much easier to bear when you're young. But now, I only have to find my local butcher has gone away for a holiday and his daughter is serving behind the counter for two weeks instead, and I start to feel as if my whole world is falling apart. It's absolutely pathetic. I try not to show it, of course.

10 March

Have had the most horrifying morning of my life. I'd had a bath, done my hair, put on my make-up, and gone out to make some preliminary sketches at the end of the garden. I came back in—it had turned freezing again—and had sat down and written hundreds of words of my diary when I hit a key on the keyboard, quite innocently, and suddenly the whole screen went blank. It wouldn't start, or anything. It was just a silent square of black nothingness. I thought I'd lost everything I'd ever put on this wretched computer. Not only had I lost my entire diary, but I'd even lost my New Year Resolution list that said I'd got to write a diary!

Rang James and he said it was most peculiar and he'd come and take a look. But just as I was about to take to my bed in despair, he rang again.

'Just one thing,' he said, 'I suppose you haven't turned the screen off, have you?'

'I didn't know you *could* turn the screen off,' I said.

'Try this,' he said. And when I did what he said, the whole thing sprang back to life. I'm *sure* I hadn't touched the button he was talking about, but he said I must have. Crikey. I was about to start on a great rant about computers, but I suppose in

64

the pre-computer age there were other hazards— and far worse. Carlyle must have felt pretty choked when his maid used the entire manuscript of the first volume of his great *oeuvre*, *The French Revolution*, for kindling. He couldn't just press a button and retrieve it. Or get in a computer whizz who would, after hours of humming and despairing at the state of his files, eventually magic the manuscript back to life. He just had to start again from scratch.

That's not a book I'll ever get around to, actually. But I've got a huge pile by my bed. Just discovered a brilliant author called Patrick Hamilton who lived in the forties and wrote like a dream. Penny's always trying to get me to read modern books, but there's so much great old stuff I haven't read. And anyway, there's so much I want to read again before I get on to the new stuff: Chekhov. Turgenev. Wouldn't mind rereading all the old Jane Austens actually.

16 March

It's so funny, being retired. Sometimes life stretches out before you like an empty desert and you wonder how you're ever going to fill your days, and then at other times you feel you've got so many things to do you can hardly cope. Just as I was imagining my life was pretty much over—no family, no neighbours and Michelle will soon be off to get married at last—the phone rang and it was Penny in a frightful state. 'Have you seen the local paper?' she asked, referring to a free-sheet that's bunged through our doors every so often.

'No,' I said.

'Well, they're planning to build a huge hotel on the little park at the end of our road!'

'The one we were admiring just the other day?'

'Yes,' she said. 'And you know, it's not really a park. It's actually a common. I've looked it up. It was called Rosedale Park in Victorian times, but in the seventeenth century it was part of Wormly Common. They're going to build a hotel! It would mean masses more cars. Think of the parking problems! It would be hideous. There's a picture of it on the council website. It looks like an arms factory! And it would mean cutting down that huge plane tree—and the false acacia.'

'But that's the only bit of green space in the area,' I said. 'They can't do that!'

Admittedly, although I'd said it was Poussin-like the other day, that was after a very good supper at the Japanese restaurant, and a whole carafe of sake. Although it could be charming, through half-closed eyes on a foggy day, in reality it was a small triangle of green scrub used by local drug-dealers as an open-air social club and fighting-dogs' lavatory.

'Well that's their scheme,' she said. 'We've got to object.'

We made a plan to galvanise the residents for a meeting, and for Penny and me to meet there later this afternoon.

Later

Just come back from viewing the piece of green or the 'common', as we have now decided to call it. It

66

makes it sound as if it belongs to the entire community. I have to say it was terrifying. There were gangs of yobs with slavering dogs, most of them wearing nothing but vests and shorts and covered with tattoos (the yobs, that is). It is absolutely freezing still, despite the time of year, and they don't seem to need anything to keep them warm. Probably it's their rage that heats them up. Anyway, they all looked furious when, picking our way through the dog turds, we came on the scene. Penny had brought a camera, which didn't help matters, and while she was photographing the false acacia and the plane tree, one of the more aggressive-looking blokes came up to her.

'Wot you tekkin picture of? Wot you fink ya doin'?' he said, threateningly. Luckily Penny was at her most bubbly, and she stuck out her hand to introduce herself and said, 'Penny Anderson. So pleased to meet you! Did you know the council's thinking of building a hotel here? Don't you think it's ghastly? And they're going to cut down these two beautiful trees!'

Before we knew where we were, there were about five of these guys around us all nodding and muttering. 'Fuckin' disgustin'.' 'Somefink oughta be dunnabaht it.'

'I hope you'll come along to our Residents' Meeting soon,' she said. 'It's at my friend's house—Marie Sharp.'

My mind reeled as I had a vision of these hardened criminals bursting into what I like to think of as my beautiful home and eyeing my gorgeous pictures and all the things I've collected over the years. I could just imagine them storming in, tearing my Pitchforths from the walls, and

67

filling burlap sacks with cherished antiques, not to mention the special duck Gene made for me at playschool and the tape-recording of Jack speaking, when he was two, but when I confided my fears to Penny later, over a cup of tea at home, she said I was being stupid.

She looked around my immaculate sitting room with her lip curling. 'They don't want old Victorian mirrors, or embroidered cushions, or sculptured heads or old gas fittings sticking out the walls,' she said. 'Nor do they want drawings by minor English artists like Vivien Pitchfork, or whatever his name is,' she said, referring to the two delightful little landscapes I'm planning to sell to fund the facelift. 'They want tellies and iPads and things, and you don't have any of those.'

'I've got a Patrick Caulfield,' I said, defensively. I hated the idea that there was absolutely nothing worth stealing in my house. 'We were at art school together and he gave it to one of my fellow students and she didn't like it so she gave it to me.' Even though I must have been staring at it every day as I came down the stairs, I'd only just remembered who it was by, and of course he's now worth a fortune. With the brooch, the Pitchforths and the Caulfield I could afford a facelift, a breast reduction, a tummy tuck and a pair of brand-new feet—I wish!

'Who's he?' said Penny.

'He sells for quite a lot these days. And it's signed,' I said. 'And I *have* got a telly,' I added. 'And a video recorder!'

'Call that a telly?' she said, pointing to my small, wonky, scratched grey box, stuck in the corner. 'You couldn't give it away! And no one has videos any more!'

18 March

I'm really worried about these beetles. There seem
to be rather a lot, suddenly. And however many
times I catch them, by putting a glass over them,
sliding a postcard underneath and placing them in
the garden, they keep coming back. I've stopped
putting saucers of milk out for them, but still they
come. Wish I'd kept that picture of them from the
paper so I could see if they really are an
endangered species or not.

When James rang to discuss doing some
sketches of me, he was very sceptical.

'Darling, you can't have beetles in your kitchen!'
he said. 'It's disgusting, even if they are
endangered. They might eat your food and lay eggs
in your pasta, and then one day when you're
pouring out the rice or something you'll find it's
not white grains, but loads of little larvae ...'

I thought a bit. 'I wonder if the council could do
something,' I said, thoughtfully.

'No, don't be silly! The council has a waiting list
a mile long and they only put down the cheap
repellents. Get it done properly,' said James.

So I looked on the computer to find my nearest
pest control and told them about my beetles.

'But I think they're an endangered species,' I
said. 'They're black, by the way, not brown.'

There was a silence at the other end.

'It is of course possible that they *are* an
endangered species, madam,' said a man in a
cautious voice, 'but unlikely if they're in your

kitchen and only appear at night. It sounds to me as if they might be oriental—' here I gasped and interrupted, 'Oriental beetles! How rare can you get?'

'No, madam, not oriental *beetles*. Oriental *cockroaches*. The black ones. I'll send a man round tomorrow.'

Oh Lord! I felt as if my world were falling apart. My house had suddenly turned into a David Attenborough documentary. I imagined cockroaches everywhere, in my sitting room, crawling round the loo seat, in my bed . . . down my bra . . . I called on my Polish neighbour and asked if she had them, and she reluctantly said that yes, she had thought they were earwigs at first, but now she had discovered they were cockroaches.

'But are yours big and black and shiny?' I asked.

'No, they are small and brown,' she said. 'They are German cockroaches.'

Good God! Checking with my neighbours on the other side I discovered that they had German ones, too. Small and brown! Mine, for God's sake, are not only black but they're the size of Shetland ponies. Hardly dare tell Michelle.

19 March

A man with a mask and a spray came round today and asked me to leave the house for two hours after he'd finished treating the place.

He told me that cockroaches are distantly related to lobsters. They lay hundreds of eggs at a time, and scream when you tread on them. Apparently they are the only creatures to survive a

70

nuclear explosion. In the States, he told me, they used to get rid of them by laying down 'Roach motels'—little cardboard traps which feature a drawing of a cheeky cockroach in a top hat and holding a cigar with a speech bubble saying 'Roaches check in—but they don't check out!'

He charged me so much money that I realised I'd *definitely* have to sell the Caulfield if I wanted a facelift. But at least my house is now clear of vermin. Feel so ashamed of actually trying to preserve the beasts.

20 March

I've been ringing Archie every other day just to see if he's okay—I daren't ring Sylvie again—and during one conversation he admitted that Sylvie had suggested he see a doctor, but he'd refused.

'There's nothing wrong with me at all, after all. Don't want to waste his time.'

Oh dear. Well, at least she tried.

And notice the way he said 'his'. Not just me, then.

When I suggested coming down he said that Philippa had asked several friends over so there might not be room. I didn't want to point out yet again that Philippa had been dead for years, so I said nothing. I think I'll just have to ring *every* day from now on, to make sure he hasn't fallen over or anything.

I worry so much about him. The worrying space in my mind, from having been rather small, has now expanded to fill my entire brain. The moment I stop worrying about Archie, I'm worrying about the family going. The moment I stop worrying about them, there are the plans for the hotel . . . the cockroaches . . . my neighbour leaving . . . whether to have a facelift or not . . .

Talking of which, I phoned Marion because I know that even though she disapproves of plastic surgery, she's got a friend who's had it, and it was done brilliantly. I wanted the name of whoever had operated on her.

She was appalled when I told her of my plans. 'But you'll look all horrible and I won't recognise you!' she said. 'You'll be completely expressionless and you won't look like my friend any more! I won't know if you're laughing or if your face is contorted into a rictus of hate.' (The way I looked on opening your beastly goaty present, I thought sourly to myself.) 'There's nothing wrong with the way you look! You look lovely! *Don't do it!*'

She even quoted a Joyce Grenfell poem at me: 'At dancing I am no star/Others are better by far/My face I don't mind it/For I am behind it/It's the ones in the front get the jar.'

I said that unlike *some*, I didn't want the ones in front to get the jar. Funny how it's all my girlfriends who are against the facelift, and the heterosexual men feel they have to say they think it's a terrible idea just to show they're only interested in the inner rather than the outer you. Most heterosexual men are fantastically squeamish about visiting the doctor, anyway, even for some cough lozenges, let alone going in for an operation voluntarily. The only ones who agree that it's a good idea are the gay friends, like James.

I finally got Marion off the phone after she'd finished berating me for leaving *Bitter Quinces,*

72

Poisoned Souls too early, saying that we'd missed the very best bit, and that after the fingers being chopped off bit and the car park bit it was absolutely brilliant and incredibly moving, and why was I so impatient, and I'd said because my time was running out, and she said what was wrong with me, taking such a gloomy view, and me saying that she was in denial, and that knowing you weren't going to live for ever made life actually so much more interesting and vital. Anyway, after all this, she finally gave me the phone numbers of a couple of friends who'd had cosmetic surgery, and I rang them.

Each one recommended a different surgeon so I decided to make an appointment to consult both of them and see what happens.

I must say I am getting extremely nervous about the idea all of a sudden. And it does seem like so much money to squander on what's basically a vanity project. I mean, I could be giving all the money to starving orphans or donating goats to friends I don't like. I feel such a selfish creep.

But then I think it would do me good. I mean, I've always minded about how I look. I never go out without full make-up, I get my hair coloured and cut regularly, never wear laddered tights, and if someone points to a stain on my skirt I feel like committing hara-kiri.

Later

Have just got the two Pitchforths down from the walls, and the Patrick Caulfield. The Caulfield is a small oil, with no glass on, but the Pitchforths were

73

all sealed up with mounts, so I thought that before I took them to Christie's to get them valued and then, hopefully, put into an auction, I'd unpick the backs just to check there were no secret maps behind them. Even at my age I still harbour the touching hope that behind every picture I will find some amazing piece of parchment, with a note written in blood which reads, 'For the treasure, go to the church. Turn left outside the iron door, go North five paces, then East two paces, dig deep and you will find jewels beyond compare!' I must have these fantasies from reading all those *Famous Five* adventure stories when I was small. Of course I've never found anything like that, but I live in hope.

Putting the framed pictures on the kitchen table, I removed the tape behind, pulled out the panel pins with pliers and then removed the pictures themselves. Luckily I'd hung them in a shady bit of the room so they weren't faded by the sun, but I could see the glass needed cleaning, even on the inside. And what I found at the back! It was like a wild-life park. Dead flies, discarded chrysalises, endangered species, tiny squashed beetles and even a leaf. It's amazing what collects behind pictures. No treasure map, sadly. But I still had great satisfaction putting them back together, having cleaned everything up, and it was a relief to find that both pictures were actually signed, though the signatures were hidden under the mounts. So there won't be any argument about provenance, thank goodness.

26 March

Daily Rant: 'MORE RATS THAN PEOPLE IN LONDON! *Scientists predict plague!*'

27 March

Very sad phone message from Archie, who said, 'Come and see me soon! I so long to see you, darling. I sat under "our tree" the other day, and thought of you. Loads of love.'

The fact is that I ring every day now, and constantly offer to come down, but he always makes some excuse. 'Our tree' . . . oh dear . . .

29 March

Well, I've done it! I've been to see the first cosmetic surgeon. He was called Mr Mantovani and he hangs out in Wimpole Street, next door to Harley Street, home of super-expensive doctors. (The very grandest surgeons are always called Mr rather than Dr apparently.) His reception room was one of those places with giant furniture of the kind you see in *Jack and the Beanstalk* pantomimes. You sit on a chair and your legs don't reach the ground. That sort of thing. Opposite me in the ballroom of a waiting room was a battered-looking woman in a fur coat, dark glasses and swathes of expensive scarves up to her chin. There appeared to be tiny little bottles of what looked

75

like blood suspended on tubes hanging from her ears.

Not a good look.

I wondered what on earth I thought I was doing. Did I really want a facelift?

From the moment he welcomed me into his office, I realised that Mr Mantovani was a slimy old thing. His face was such an orange colour it looked as if it had been smoked, and his skin was tightly pulled back to his ears, giving him a sinister, ageless look. I immediately thought: I don't want to go to the guy who gave *him* a facelift. Or had he done it himself? Surely not. He had silver wings of hair at his temples, a very well-cut suit and a bright-yellow silk bow tie. (Why is it that all private doctors, particularly surgeons, are not only uniformly tall but also sport ridiculous bow ties? Some I've consulted even have red silk linings in their carefully tailored suits. Is it that they want to show how much money they're making, by these displays of ostentation? Or is it because they all harbour ambitions to play a clown in a circus? Actually, now I come to think of it, it's probably because if they were performing surgery, their conventional neckties would be dangling down into the blood and liver and kidneys and what-not. Not very reassuring. But then the idea of being operated on by a man in a hilarious bow-tie who looks like Coco the Clown isn't exactly comforting either.)

Mr Mantovani showed me to a huge chair and then sat down behind an enormous desk. Perhaps this ludicrous furniture is installed to make the patients feel even smaller than they do already. His desk was crowded with executive toys and lumps of crystal—presents, presumably, from grateful patients.

'What can I do for you, Marie?' he asked, cautiously. I think the first thing he'd noticed was the fact that I didn't look rich. (I certainly didn't have a red silk lining in my rather threadbare jacket.) Unfortunately there was no operation that would fix that.

'I was thinking of having something done to my eyes, Mr Mantovani,' I said, hoping my formality would stop him referring to me as Marie. I mentioned my eyes, because suddenly I thought that might be a bit cheaper than a facelift. Within seconds Mantovani was out of his chair and sitting on a stool opposite me, measuring bits and pieces with strange metal instruments, rather like the ones we used at art school when we were doing intricate designs.

After a few minutes of poking and measuring, he said: 'I can understand why the eyes need attention. But I think we should consider a full facelift. Then we could have the neck lifted, too . . . we don't want to look beautiful and young—or rather even *more* beautiful and young—with this . . .' and here he pinched at the loose skin on my neck. 'And it would be possible, at the same time, to do breast reduction. It's worth a thought . . .'

'There's nothing wrong with my breasts,' I said defensively.

'Not at all!' he said hastily. 'I just thought that if they were a bit uncomfortable . . . No—you have a very good figure for a woman of your age, if I may say so.'

And, at the mention of figures, I remembered to ask about the price. 'How much would this cost?' I asked.

Turned out he was thinking of charging me £8,000 for the full works. I said I'd think about it and hurried away. Then I realised that just to consult him cost £200. Golly. Not too sure about this after all. I'll see what the other one says.

30 March

Gene came to stay. We had a great time, and did some leaf prints and made a flick-book, and baked some bread with currants in. Then I remembered I'd got an old lead soldier kit of Jack's and we had a very fun and dangerous time out in the garden with a pan full of boiling lead on top of a camping-gas stove, and produced twenty toxic little guardsmen.

He went to bed at eight. He sleeps on a camp bed in the room where I work. It's all a bit cramped, but he likes it, and he doesn't mind being surrounded by canvases and piles of books about Donatello and jars full of old paintbrushes—and there's still the reassuring smell of turps about it, which Gene describes as the 'Granny smell'. Just as he was getting into bed, he knocked one of the jars onto the floor and it broke.

He looked appalled. 'I'm sorry, Granny,' he said, very quietly. 'I didn't mean it!'

'I know you didn't, darling,' I said, picking up the pieces. 'I put the jar in a stupid place. Silly old Granny. It doesn't matter a bit. Let's put the rug over all the bits now so you don't step on them, and I'll hoover them up in the morning.'

He looked very serious as he got into bed.

'I know why you don't get cross, Granny,' he said, solemnly.

'Why?' I asked.

'It's because you're very, very old,' he said.

I read him a story, and then he turned over and closed his eyes.

I sleep next door—or try to—but when he's staying I always find it difficult to drop off. I suppose I'm nervous he'll have some frightful accident in the night and I won't hear him.

Anyway, I was still wide awake at 2 a.m. I kept worrying about those blasted cockroaches. Cautiously putting on my slippers in case I stepped on one, I tiptoed downstairs, turned on the light in the kitchen and scanned the floor. Nothing there. I poured some milk into a mug, added some Horlicks and put it in the microwave. That would help me sleep. Just as I was about to leave the kitchen, I started. There was a sinister black shape on the floor. I was sure it was a cockroach. My heart pounding, I approached it as if it were an unexploded landmine.

On closer inspection it turned out to be two enormous currants stuck together, remnants from this morning's bread-making.

Just as I was getting back off to sleep, at about six in the morning, there was a pad pad pad on the landing between our rooms, and in came Gene in his aeroplane pyjamas, clutching a very disgruntled and uncooperative Pouncer, full of beans and raring to go.

'Can we make toffee now, Granny?' he said. 'You did promise!'

Oh dear. How I shall miss him!

APRIL

1 April

Leafing through the *Daily Rant* this morning, I came across a story which read, 'Money really does grow on trees!' about how a man had buried a ten-pound note in his garden which had sprouted into a bush with tenners as leaves.

I thought this was going a bit far, even for the *Rant*, but looking up at the date I saw that it was April Fool's Day. So I was quite prepared, when I went over to Jack and Chrissie's today for Saturday lunch, to be thoroughly fooled.

There is nothing a little boy likes to do more, particularly on April 1st, than make his granny look like a complete idiot. Indeed, there is nothing anyone likes to do more than to make some powerful figure in their lives fall flat on a banana skin. Never have I seen Jack, aged about ten, laugh quite so much as when I tripped backwards into our tiny garden pond in my dressing gown. I can't remind him of it now without reducing him to helpless giggles.

When I arrived, Gene opened the door. He was wearing an enormous piece of plastic body armour with a Star Wars logo on it. I went through to the kitchen and there was barely time for me to put my bag down before he said, almost unable to contain his laughter, 'Sit on *this* chair, Granny.' He pointed to a chair with a pad on it, underneath which was a very obvious pink rubber whoopee cushion. I duly sat and pronounced myself astonished and

80

embarrassed at the resulting fart. Then he got hold of the whoopee cushion and stuck it on another chair, and I was invited to sit down again. Interestingly, although he knew I knew all along what was going on, he still found my reaction hilarious. I spent twenty minutes sitting on farting cushions and pretending to be amazed and then mortified by my noisy flatulence, and the response was always the same. Helpless laughter. Endless cries of 'April Foo–ool!'

'Shake, Granny?' asked Gene, extending his hand when the farting orgy had petered out. On his finger was an enormous ring, far too big for him, the metal buzzer quite obvious in his palm. We shook hands and there was a faint buzzing sensation. And then: 'April Fooo–ool!' Moments later: 'I did fool you, didn't I, Granny? Did you think that was a real ring I was wearing? Did you? Did you?'

And after I'd been duly shocked by that slapstick masterpiece, he wandered off to the sink and then returned, saying: 'Smell this!' displaying a very wet plastic flower through a hole in his body armour, that I'd just seen him fiddling with under the tap. 'April Fooo–ool!' he cried joyously as my face was squirted with water from the bulb he was pressing inside his armour. I spluttered and waved my arms about and gasped for a towel, as if I'd been completely drenched by the faint trickle that had emerged from the petals.

Finally: 'Are you hungry? Would you like a peanut?' he said, almost wetting himself at the prospect of my unscrewing the lid of a tin marked Peanuts and being sent into complete disarray by a caterpillar on a spring that jumped out at me.

81

'APRIL FOO–OOOL! HAHAHAHA!!!'

Whether you play along with such jokes or not is, I think, a sign of being a mature adult. When Gene insisted on playing his tricks on Tim, Marion's stuffy old husband, he, on being offered the tin of peanuts last year, had declared pompously that as it was April 1st he knew it was a joke, and no, he wouldn't like a peanut, thank you. At that point he sank down so many points in my estimation that I could barely bring myself to talk to him for weeks.

Of course when I was small, I too found all the April Fool pranks hilarious. Marion and I used to glue half-crowns to the pavement outside my house, and then fall about when we saw innocent passers-by ruin their fingernails as they scrabbled to pick them up. We constructed false parcels and left them on the pavement, beside ourselves if anyone came along and took one away. (I suppose today, if an unattended parcel were found on the street, the whole area would be cordoned off by machine-gun toting police, and helicopters brought in to monitor the situation.)

And of course it was *always* hilarious, at school, to pass another girl a half-empty water jug, pretending it was extremely heavy, with the result that when she took it, the water splattered all over her clothes.

Anyway, I spent a nice day with them. One of Gene's front teeth is wobbly. How strange it is to think that only the other day I was so excited to see it poking through his gums! Came back feeling very cosy and contented.

5 April

Oh, I do dread the idea of them going next month. I wish I could just up sticks and buy a flat in the same block as them in New York without them knowing, and then Gene could pop downstairs without anyone looking and we could make origami paper boats together or muck about on the piano. I shall miss them *so* much. Putting a brave face on it all is such an enormous effort. Every time I see them I can feel myself dragging on this cheery persona, slapping my hands together, roaring with laughter, and saying things like 'Well, of course I'll miss you, but I've got so much to do, I don't know if I'll ever have time to come and visit you all!' just so they don't worry about me.

To cheer myself up I ordered some plants from a catalogue that for some reason had been sent to me through the post. The picture showed huge foaming banks of flowers in vibrant colours, blues, pinks, yellows, all screaming to be seen and singing with scent and sunshine. So I hope they'll deliver. Caliban . . . Calibrach . . . something.

Archie was meant to be coming this weekend, but never turned up. I rang him to ask where he was, but it was clear he had no idea he was meant to be coming, so I didn't press it. He said he was in the middle of lunch.

'I'm worried about Mrs Evans,' he said. 'She's stolen Philippa's brooch.'

'It's not Philippa's, it's mine,' I said. 'I've got it.' This was starting to sound like a stuck record.

'*You've* got it?' he said. 'But I didn't give it to

83

you. You didn't steal it, did you?'

'I've got it, darling. You *did* give it to me. Philippa never had it. Don't worry. I told you, I said I was going to sell it to get the money for the facelift, and you said fine.'

'Oh,' he said, as if the light were dawning, but I could tell by his voice that he didn't understand anything I was saying. He was trying to pretend he hadn't made a terrible mistake. 'You've got it. Oh yes, I remember now. That's fine.'

We chattered on, but then he said he'd got to go. 'When are you coming, darling?' he asked. 'I haven't seen you for months. Everything's looking wonderful here. The bluebells will be out soon. And I'd like to talk to you before I sack Mrs Evans. We can't have a thief around can we? Who knows what she might steal next.'

On a complete whim, I thought, 'Why don't I pop down now?' He clearly wasn't doing anything, and I know if I'd suggested it in advance he would have become anxious and made an excuse, so I just said, in a no-nonsense way, 'I'm coming down right away. I'll be there in a couple of hours!' And I didn't give him time to change his mind.

Leaving a note for Michelle to feed Pouncer, I hurled a few things into a case and drove like a mad thing to Devon, all the time feeling choked with sadness and emotion about Archie. I realised that I'd never be going down to see him again without feeling concern. That my dear old Archie was starting to disappear slowly, and that one of the happiest periods in my life was starting to come to an end.

It was beginning to get dark when I arrived, and, much to my pleasure, it seemed as if he were expecting me! The moment my car crunched up the drive, he opened the door, and I could see a welcoming expression on his face.

'Philippa!' he said, as I got out of the car. 'How lovely! I haven't seen you for so long! Darling!' And he enfolded me in a big hug.

Was it that he thought I was Philippa? Or was it just a matter of his muddling our names? I didn't know, and I didn't really care. He took my holdall out of the car, and led me inside the house. But just before his bedroom, he stopped. 'Here you are!' he said, opening the door of one of the spare rooms next to his. 'I hope this room will suit you!'

'But darling, we usually . . . I mean . . . I usually sleep in your room . . .' I said, nervously.

'I know you do, darling,' he said, suddenly like the old Archie. 'But, sweetheart, I'm afraid I find myself wandering in the night. I don't know why. But I've woken up in some funny places recently! I don't want to disturb you,' he added, rather plaintively, 'but sometimes I feel I'm in such a muddle, darling.'

I took both his hands in mine and looked into his eyes. Then I drew near to him, kissing him.

'If it makes you feel happier,' I said. 'That's fine.'

It wasn't fine, of course, but what could I do? I could hardly badger my way into his bed. And there was something so serious and 'old Archie' about the way he spoke, that I felt he was aware that something was deeply wrong, and he knew that I knew, too.

7 April

Just got back! Oh, it's all so agonising! I *do* so hope Sylvie gets him to the doctor. If it were just me in charge I'd have had him down the surgery the first moment that he lost his glasses. But I can't steam in when I know that he's really Sylvie's responsibility, and if I did anything like that she'd be terribly upset.

9 April

Popped into my local shop to buy some frozen peas. Because I didn't have the right money, they undercharged me, letting me off 1p. Very decent of them, but I know this debt will drive me mad. What's 1p, you may say? But to me one pence still has the same sort of value as it did in the days when it bought a bag of sweets, so I *must* remember to pay it.

10 April

'NATIONAL DEATH SERVICE!' yells the *Daily Rant*. '*More people killed in hospitals than in the Blitz! The message is: if you're ill, don't see a doctor!*'

As she was making her speedy kitchen visit for her breakfast of Yakult, Michelle looked at the headline in horror. 'I 'ave to ze doctaire zis afternoon! I 'ope I will not die!' she said.

'Of course not!' I said reassuringly, stuffing the

paper out of sight. 'It's all a load of rubbish.'

Honestly, I must stop getting this ghastly newspaper. I'm certain it's not true. And all it does is scare the living daylights out of people.

11 April

Penny came round to lunch to plan the Residents' Meeting. She'd brought with her huge maps of the area, plus the council's plans, and laid them out on the table. I couldn't make head nor tail of them, but she seemed to understand everything.

'This is a big project,' she said, 'and we can't afford to lose. I'm worried that there aren't enough of us to make a credible case against the plans. We need more people on the committee.'

'There's you, me, James, Marion and Tim,' I said, doubtfully . . . 'No, you're right.' Then I was hit by a thought. 'Why don't we ask Father Emmanuel if he'd like to be on the committee?' I asked. He's the preacher at the evangelical church on the corner. 'He'd be good.'

'You mean Praise the Lord! Inc? Where the Kwit-Fit garage used to be?' said Penny. 'Do you know him? It'd be great if you could get him along. Will you ask him?'

'And what about Sheila the Dealer? I don't know her last name, but she's lived here for thirty years,' I said. She's a nightmare of a woman, a complete racist, and mad as a bucket of frogs, but she packs a good punch and when it comes to yelling she can be heard all the way down the street. She's a good person to have on your side because she's probably the longest-serving drug dealer in the borough. No doubt highly respected by all the other drug dealers around.

'Sheila what's-her-name?'

'Sheila the Dealer,' I said. 'No idea what she's really called. Presumably she has a name. You know her, always got a fag on the go.'

'And what about the man at the mosque . . . the imam? He'd be good, too. These religious leaders go down very well. They can get away with murder at the council because no one wants to offend them.'

'I'll try,' I said. 'But I think he's a bit shy. Not sure how much English he speaks.'

'Oh, do get him along. It would be so cool.'

Funny, those expressions like 'cool'. They seem to be coming back into fashion. And it must be very peculiar for young people to hear what they think of as today's slang being used by people of their grandmother's age. I gave the right change to some slip of a thing recently over the counter and she said, as she took it, 'Fab'. Now that's not a word I've heard used since the sixties. Though no doubt if you look into it, the people who originally coined the word were the ancient Greeks, or Druids or somebody.

12 April

As I was leaving to go to the acupuncturist, I looked up the road at the patch of green the council's planning to ruin. And then it occurred to me: instead of painting the garden every month, why not paint the trees every month? Like David Hockney. The trees in every season. And there'd be more *point* to it, too. We could have an exhibition of the Seasons of the Doomed Trees and get some publicity for our campaign.

Saw the acupuncturist and as I went in I told her that she was actually on the north side of Oxford Street, west of Oxford Circus. She looked completely baffled. She really should know this stuff. She wasn't much younger than me.

But she was full of enthusiasm. She was called Vishna, but she didn't look like a Vishna, being a plump, white, middle-aged woman. However, she'd done her best to look the part, having swathed herself in Indian shawls and smelling of patchouli. There were dim red lights placed all over the floor, acupuncture charts on the walls, an enormous golden Buddha squatting on a low, highly varnished table and floating candles in bowls of water placed around the room. Mingled with the patchouli was the sickly smell of joss sticks.

She looked a bit astounded when I told her that first I wanted her to do something for my rusting joints and second I wanted to relax so I could make a decision about having a facelift. But fair play to her, she just said how brave I was and that not only was I looking wonderful, but that after the operation, if I had it, I would look even more wonderful. Naturally I liked her immediately after that, despite her total ignorance about the points of the compass.

She sat me down, took notes, and told me it was the Year of the Tiger and that the Chinese spring started the following day and it was a very auspicious time to have a facelift and that June was the wellspring of energy, vitality and rebirth. Or something.

'I know you don't believe me,' she said, 'but this is going to be a great year for you! Now, let's get going with those needles!'

She was quite right, I didn't believe her, but it was still nice to be told something jolly and optimistic, and by such a very charming person.

Vishna led me into a small room with a massage table. I heard the whining, groaning sound of whale music which I instantly asked her to turn off. There is nothing more unrelaxing, in my experience, than the moaning sound of whales in the background. And what are they saying to each other, anyway? 'Get some more plankton while you're out, dear.' 'Watch out for harpoons!' Suddenly remembered the 1p I owe the local shop. *Must* pay it.

She switched off the whales, turned down the lights, and got going.

'Now, this is the one to rid you of those indecisive demons!' she declared, sticking a needle into my calf. 'And this will get your joints moving so smoothly . . . now, one just here . . .' (I winced as she put one in my lip) 'That's the one to jump-start you, it's a very good sign that you gave a little jerk there, shows you're springing to life . . .'

Once she'd finished pushing pins into me—I felt like a hedgehog—she put her hands on my head and started droning, 'Now we are into *gathering*, *enjoying* and *loving* . . . and there's a golden liquid coming all the way from your feet to your head, and back down again, in a circle, the circle of life . . . and down to your toes . . .' She moved to my feet . . . . 'Rooted in the ground, your feet are growing roots, to suck in the energy from Mother Earth, which resonates with all the planets . . .'

90

(here she rang a bell) '. . . and the vibrations will resonate with the you, the inner you, the real Marie, inside, even inside the deep inside of you, expanding like a flower petal, opening its leaves for a rebirth, and the bursting forth of all those talents you have of . . . of . . . er . . . of . . . um . . . art . . . creation . . . gyrating . . . and pushing forth green shoots in the very camaraderie of all the spirits . . .' I could hardly keep a straight face. Then she started rubbing various brass bowls that made the most frightful whining noises and before I knew where I was it was all over and she charged me sixty quid.

Admittedly, I felt pretty relaxed after it all, but thought, to be quite frank, that I could have done it all myself just by slipping into bed and lying there and staring at the ceiling.

Still, I did feel more positive about having a facelift.

13 April

James is finally coming over this afternoon to install Skype, now the Broadband is sorted. I've now discovered *exactly* what this modern wonder is. It's amazing that you can stick a mini-camera you on your computer and then you can speak to another person for free on the other side of the world, and you can see them and they can see you. All sounds rather exciting to me. Though I think I'll need a stiff drink before it's installed. Whenever anyone comes and fiddles with my computer I get so anxious I've been known to burst into tears, even when they're putting in some simple anti-virus program. I'm always so scared the whole thing will blow up, or that all my computer stuff will just dissolve, leaving me with a blank screen and the words 'Ha! Ha! V-worm strikes again'—or whatever viruses are called.

Anyway, it's sweet of James to come round to do the Skype stuff because I am hopeless with computers. But I do also realise there is something to be said for Getting a Man In, when it comes to these kinds of jobs, and Paying Him. When a friend does a practical favour for you, particularly a bloke, you have to dance around admiringly all the time, gasping about how brilliant they are, and saying 'Wow! Aren't you a total genius! I wish I were half as clever as you!' That's the deal. And you also have to listen to them moaning about the state of whatever it is they're looking at before they start. It's like going to a new dentist.

I remember the last time I went to a new dentist, ten years ago, and he took one look inside my mouth and shook his head. 'Where on earth did you last get your teeth done?' he said. 'Uzbekistan? Was he qualified?'

'Uuuuugggh,' I explained. There was nothing else I could say. But it was very annoying. Particularly as every new dentist always says it about the work done by the previous one.

Later

Yes, I was right about the dentist analogy. When we'd gone upstairs to my little office, negotiating our way around Gene's camp bed, which I hadn't yet folded away, I first had to listen to James

92

tut-tutting about my computer's desktop.

'Why have you got this here?' he said, staring at some mysterious icon in the shape of a small red cross that I'd never properly examined.

'Oh, I don't know,' I said. 'It just arrived.'

'Well, I don't like it. Let's get rid of it.'

This took about ten minutes with me just standing and goggling, while James fiddled about with my keyboard like a surgeon peering into a brain on which he was about to perform an intricate operation, and making that rather irritating noise that people make these days when they're pretending to think, which goes 'Te te te te . . .'

Then, 'That shouldn't be a short cut,' he muttered, fiddling about with more things. 'And you know it would be much easier if you . . .'

'I'm sure it would,' I said hastily. 'But I like it the way I've got it. Please don't do too much tinkering! I'll never be able to work it again!'

Shaking his head he put in the Skype disk and started umming and aaahing and te-te-te-ing and typing and tapping and waiting while the computer hummed away thinking about things.

'Is this Windows XP?' he said. Anyone who looks at my computer always asks that. I've got no idea what Windows XP is.

'I've no idea,' I said, feebly.

'Whatever it is, it's very slow,' said James. 'How many gigabytes have you got left?'

'I don't know, James,' I said, my heart thumping with anxiety. 'Don't ask me questions like that. They terrify me.' Then I added, slimily, 'I'm just not as clever as you when it comes to computers,' and he gave a gratified and superior smile.

'You know it would make life a lot easier if you got an app for your photographs,' he added.

I said nothing, just stood there white with fear, my hands gripping the arms of my chair like someone who's been told their pilot is about to attempt a crash-landing. I had a vague idea what he was talking about, but on hearing the very word 'app' I find myself starting to quake with anxiety.

Finally, the whole thing was sorted and he said that when he got home he'd ring me up and we could talk on Skype.

Before he went, he kissed me and hugged me, saying: 'Now don't forget about the portrait! I really do want you to sit for me, my darling!'

17 April

Oh God, the Residents' Meeting is only just over. What a relief. I'd managed to dragoon Father Emmanuel into coming, and Marion and Tim were there, she wearing a Laura Ashley dress that she must have bought in the sixties, and he having thoroughly let himself go, roly-poly paunch and all. They live in the past, those two, and are a very good advertisement for staying single when you're older. Then there were me and Penny, and, amazingly, Sheila the Dealer. She arrived wearing green carpet slippers, with, as per, a fag on the go.

'You don't mind me 'avin' a fag?' she said, as she shuffled in. I'm afraid to say she smelt, a mixture of old chip-fat and general filth. 'All this rubbish abar it. My nan lived to 103 and she smoked 60 a day all her life. And she drank like a fuckin' fish. Load of fuckin' rubbish, you ask me.'

Once the meeting got going over the kitchen table, she expanded on the idea that a hotel might be built at the end of the road.

' 'Oo in their right mind would pay to stay 'ere, anyway?' she said. 'Full of nig-nogs and all them men wiv dishcloths on their 'eads. Filthy streets, all this noise . . .'

Penny and I didn't know where to put ourselves. I blushed deep red and felt my heart beating, but oddly Father Emmanuel—who comes from Antigua—didn't seem to have heard a word. He was just smiling gently to himself at the end of the table.

But when it came to having his say, it appeared he didn't really know why we were all gathered there anyway.

'Surely a hotel is splendid news?' he said. 'And, our good Lord knows, we all need good news! There will be no denying that in these parts!' He hitched himself up into preaching mode, wagging a finger at each and every one of us as he scanned the table with glittering eyes. 'First and foremost,' he intoned, 'it will raise the tone of the neighbourhood. That is my first submission. And my second submission is to say . . . what is a tree? *Many* will say, and they will have a point, that there are too many trees in these parts. Who amongst us can say that a tree is good? A tree, like a man, may be good or bad. Here, I say to you, there are too many trees. Who can say why the Council will not cut them down? I have been trying to get them to cut down a bad tree outside my church and they refuse. It spills leaves into my drains every autumn, I am thinking of cutting it down myself. Let us look at these plans with the advantages in mind, not

95

only the disadvantages.'

Sheila the Dealer soon put him right about all that. She leant over the table and stuck her face into his. 'Why d'ya fink we're here you big . . . you big . . .' she seemed lost for words. 'We're here because none of us, not one of us rahnd this table, *want* the fuckin' hotel and because *we* want to keep the fuckin' trees. And pardon my French, Vicar.'

I don't think anyone had ever spoken to the good Father like that before. From what I can hear floating over the garden wall from the consecrated former garage, he spends every Sunday railing at his congregation and telling them that they're all Miserable Sinners destined for Hell, and I suspect they all happily believe every word he says, and bow and scrape when he's around, so he must have been very taken aback at being shouted at. But within a few minutes he realised what the party line was and had come round to our point of view.

Marion tried to smooth things over. 'Everyone's allowed their own perspective,' she said. She's such a sweet old hippie.

I felt like saying 'No, they're not,' but kept my mouth shut.

'What we need,' said Penny, 'is a tree expert. Someone who can tell us why those trees are essential to the environment and, hopefully, that they house a rare species of bat. Anyone here know a good tree man?'

David (my ex) used to work in local planning, so as he's coming up next week I said I thought I could ask him for advice, but, then, most surprisingly, Sheila the Dealer piped up again. 'My nephew,' she said. ' 'E worked for Wandsworth Council in the parks department. 'E knows all abar ashes, oaks, leaves, branches, ask 'im. 'E'll come round for nuffink. 'E owes me one.' Here she gave an enormous dirty wink, and all our minds boggled at what exact favour Sheila could have done her nephew that he was so malleable.

Marion said she'd contact him, and even though I was meant to be chairing the meeting, Sheila rounded if off herself.

'Any uvver business?' she yelled. 'Fought not. Well, I'll be orf, then. If they fink they can build an 'otel 'ere wiv old Sheila to deal wiv they've got another fink comin'. Cheers for the cuppa, love.' And off she went, fag on the go, drizzling ash all over the carpet. At that moment I felt a wave of affection and admiration for her. Like my Polish neighbour, she's tough as old boots. A survivor.

Father Emmanuel hung about a bit and asked if I'd be coming to his church this Sunday and I said that unfortunately I was going away this weekend and every weekend until I died, as far as I could see, which meant Sundays were completely out. I have no desire to be told I'm going to Hell. And then he shuffled out, disappointed. He can screech at his congregation all he likes from his wretched pulpit, he's never going to convince me I'm going anywhere after I'm dead—not heaven, hell, or anywhere in between.

18 April

Getting the washing out of the machine this morning I discovered I'd thrown my dry-cleaning pile in with it. A Vivienne Westwood jersey I'd bought for four pounds in a charity shop was

97

completely ruined, and a blue linen dress has come out looking like an old dishrag.

Then I remembered I hadn't paid back that 1p. Nipped out to the shop with it, but it was closed. Damn and blast.

Later

This evening I felt really sick and everything seemed to be whirling around. I couldn't even see properly. When Penny rang I told her I was certain I was about to have a stroke. Or perhaps I'd had one and was actually making no sense at all.

She asked about my balance, and what I'd eaten, and said she'd come over right away and drive me to A and E. Despite being reluctant to go anywhere near a hospital (*thanks, Rant*) I staggered to the car, everything a grey blur, and when I got into the passenger seat, Penny got out the map to find how to get to the hospital but couldn't read it, however far she held it out. So she handed it to me.

'I'll get my reading glasses,' I said, fumbling in my bag. But I couldn't find them. Only my ordinary ones.

'Are you sure you're not wearing them?' said Penny, as she started up the engine. She was right. And the moment I took them off and put on my ordinary ones, all my symptoms promptly vanished. I felt such an idiot that I had to wait till we got to the first traffic light to pluck up courage to tell her.

'I'm afraid it's my glasses,' I said, in rather a small voice. 'I've been wearing my reading glasses all day. That's why I feel sick. I'm not ill after all.'

'Well, that's a relief!' said Penny, sounding extremely pissed off, as she looked behind to see when it was safe to make a U-turn. 'For heaven's sake! You had me worried sick!'

To make it up to her, I asked her in for a drink. We cracked open a bottle of sparkling wine, and I rustled up a nice herb omelette. I was going to use ham, but Pouncer had got it first because I'd left it on the counter. And I said how jolly lucky I was to have Penny round the corner, and what would I do without her; she said no it was she who was lucky to have me round the corner, and what would she do without me, and we went to our respective beds tired but happy.

21 April

I got some smoked salmon for lunch with David and it was lovely to see him again. He lives in the country now, but we've still got lots to talk about because we were married for ten years and, being Jack's dad, he always wants news of the family as he doesn't see them quite as often as I do.

'Jack won't last out in New York, sweetie,' he said. 'Mark my words. He's just not a New York type. You forget, I've lived there. Nine months.'

'That was about a hundred years ago, David, if you don't mind my saying. Times change. And even if Jack isn't a New York man—you know, a thrusting executive—I do think Chrissie could turn out to be a New York woman.' I ladled him out some onion soup to start with and having got drinks and napkins, sat down opposite him to tuck in.

99

'No, she only pretends to be. In England she seems like a dynamic manager because everyone else is so hopeless. But she won't be able to compete with all those high-powered Manhattan broads. It's incredibly competitive. She's too nice.'

'I'm so worried that they'll stay there and they'll start to say "Gee whizz",' I said, and as I said it I felt tears coming to my eyes. It's turned into a kind of Pavlovian reaction. Somebody only has to say 'Gee whizz' and I burst into tears.

'Come on, don't be silly. No one says "Gee whizz" any more anyway,' said David, reaching over the table and giving my hand a reassuring squeeze. 'That's if they ever did. You notice they're not selling the house. That means they're going to come back. It's inevitable they want to go, and it's inevitable they'll be back before you can say . . . well, "Gee whizz",' he said.

'Oh, don't start that again, please,' I said, crossly, suddenly remembering why David and I had got divorced in the first place. 'It's not funny.'

What an old silly I am.

After lunch we went up the street to the scrubby patch of grass at the top of the road—sorry I mean 'Common'—and David said the trees were in perfect health as far as he could see, and had we thought of applying to the Open Spaces Society to see what they thought about it? He also referred me to all kinds of green charities.

'The last thing you need round here is a hotel,' he said. 'There are enough itinerant residents anyway. I bet you within a couple of years anyway it'll turn into a hostel and then you'll be in trouble.'

A hostel! I hadn't thought of that! Oh Gawd.

I'd taken a camera to take some pictures to

work from—though I've already done a few sketches. I don't fancy sitting up there at my easel day after day, surrounded by drug dealers commenting on the fact that I'm doing the grass the wrong colour. Also, even though it's April, it's still hideously cold, and you can't paint in the rain.

24 April

Today I had an appointment with the second facelift man. To be honest, Mr Mantovani was such a creep, and anyway, who needs a facelift and wasn't it just a ghastly extravagance, and who'd look at me anyway, whether I had a facelift or not?—that I was quite tempted just to ring up this new guy, a Mr Parson, and call it a day. But yesterday I read in the *Rant* that this kind of thinking is a Critical Voice, which should be Ignored. Sometimes I think what I'd really like is a major operation to remove the Critical Voice, rather than the wrinkles.

Anyway, James persuaded me not to give up and cancel, so I dragged myself along to see Mr Parson. And he was much nicer than the creepy Mantovani. All his furniture seemed a normal size, he didn't have a pair of tongs to pick up my sagging flesh, and he said absolutely nothing about my breasts. And although he did, unfortunately, have a bow tie, it was a quite discreet pale beige.

'Are you sure you can actually see out of your eyes properly?' he asked. 'Because your eyelids have dropped so much that it might be possible to get them done on the National Health. On the grounds of vision.'

He explained that it would be better if I had a facelift rather than just the eyes, 'because if you have just the eyes done, then the rest of you tends to look really—well, different, in comparison,' he said. Not only did he not say anything about breasts, but he didn't say a word about tummies or knees, either—and I felt he wasn't trying to sell me anything. He took a photograph of me (for his 'before and after' folder) and I had no idea I looked so dreadful from the side. My chin blurs into my neck like one of Gene's drawings. He says all that can be fixed. For £7,000. A thousand quid cheaper than Mr M.

So, much to my surprise, I found myself making a date for three months ahead and just hoping I have the nerve to go through with it.

What the hell am I letting myself in for?

25 April

Just back from Christie's. Like all auction houses in smart districts of London, the place was awash with sleek, fat little men with slicked-down hair wearing very well-cut pin-stripe suits with fabulous colourful hankies sticking out of their breast pockets. The premises reeked of money and opulence. Even though I'd only come from nearby Shepherd's Bush, I still felt like some country bumpkin up for the day. And I felt particularly drab as I joined a queue of elderly gentlemen clutching bundles of silver cutlery, and dear little old ladies with cherished antiques that they wanted valued.

All the staff were very kind to me—I wasn't sure

if they were kind to everyone they thought might have something good to sell, whether it was simply good manners, or whether they thought I was just another dear little old lady. Don't really care, actually. Kindness is kindness. Grab it when you can, say I.

Luckily the girl who came down from the Modern British section took one look at my hoard and was very excited about it. She said they could put an asking price of £1,000 each for the Pitchforths and £3,000 for the Caulfield. This, by the way, was a lovely picture in bold colours, of a chair against a window—and I'm very fond of the little Pitchforths, but it's time to shed things, not hang on to them. Another smoothie was sent down to look at the brooch and he said the reserve price should be £2,000.

So I put them all into the auction and hoped to raise enough money to pay for the facelift.

What am I doing? Help!

Oh, I said that last time.

26 April

The *Daily Rant*'s latest headline is 'ASYLUM SEEKERS CLOG BENEFITS SYSTEM! *Whites will be a minority by the end of the year!*'

Don't think that will go down a storm around here.

Acupuncture has made absolutely no difference to my joints. It still takes me an hour or so to get everything fully articulated.

The tree man came over at the same time as Penny and James, who was chatting to me about his plans for the portrait, while I sat only half-listening, thinking about the huge wodge of cash I'm about to squander on a Pointless Act of Vanity.

Well! Both Penny and I practically swooned when he arrived because he is, as Penny put it, a tree man to die for. He had a fantastically slim figure, great bone structure (very cool, as Penny would say), grey hair and lots of it, and his skin was all brown and tree-y. He also seemed completely on our side and was up-in-arms at the idea of anyone cutting down any bit of nature when it wasn't necessary.

His name is Ned, and though he used to work for the council he's now retired, but gives advice to residents' groups for nothing except expenses, which is very nice of him. I can't imagine how he came to be the nephew of ghastly old Sheila, but genes are funny things.

We accompanied him up to the Common and he took photographs of the trees and said they were Grade A, whatever that means, and he said the *Robinia pseudoacacia* and the *Platanus acerifolia* were habitat to a lot of birds, especially some who came over from Africa, and that the bark of one of them housed some kind of fungus that was very important to the environment . . . I didn't understand a word, but Penny was taking notes.

'He's brilliant!' she said afterwards. 'He knows all the Latin names!'

'He's dishy!' said James. 'And he's single. Do you think he's gay?'

'I thought you could tell at once by the winks they give you,' said Penny.

'No, that's all old-fashioned,' said James. 'No one winks these days. But I know what you mean.

He did mention the name of some pub he goes to, and I thought, you know, it might be an invitation.'

'Invitation!' I said, rather put out. 'Why didn't he invite us?'

'He looks like a silver birch, doesn't he?' said Penny, dreamily.

'Do you remember those children's stories where the trees actually have hair for branches and their faces were their trunks . . . ?'

'Yes—but he looks better than that,' interrupted Penny.

'Which makes it all the more irritating he's given James some kind of secret invitation.'

'Drat!' said Penny.

'Well, we wouldn't want to go out with a silver birch anyway, would we Penny?' I said.

But, significantly, she didn't reply.

27 April

Went down to see Archie again this weekend, though I was pretty nervous about what I might find. This time he seemed more eager to have me, so I've got to go. But to be frank I was particularly reluctant because it was also the last weekend to see the whole family before they left. But Jack and Chrissie were incredibly busy sorting things out, and as it would be easier without Gene, I took him down with me. Archie's always great with Gene, and loves having him, and I hoped he wouldn't be too peculiar.

On Saturday, everything went absolutely fine. We all went for a walk, and though the daffodils were over, there were carpets of bluebells in the little copses around the house. It really felt like spring. For the first time I felt like leaving my coat indoors. Though Archie insisted on wearing his loden coat. It's starting to give me the creeps. There were cracks of blue in the grey sky, and everything was full of hope and promise. Hardy seemed to sense things were looking up and charged about like mad. Could have been, of course, that he hadn't been for a proper walk for weeks.

In the evening, Archie and Gene played Snap. Mrs Evans had prepared a delicious supper and Archie had almost been his old self. The problem is that he can cope quite well as long as he doesn't have to initiate anything. He can even make polite conversation. But anything unusual and he goes to pieces. Gene and I slept in twin beds in the room next door, and though I found it hard to sleep because I was anxious about Archie's night wanderings, I managed to grab a few hours. The next day, after breakfast, when we were sitting in the library reading the Sunday papers, Gene suddenly bounced in and suggested we play the elephant game.

Archie had always been an enthusiastic player in the past, and was particularly good at making very loud trumpeting noises and even elephant pooing noises, which always had Gene in hysterics. But this time, at the mention of elephants, Archie got panicky.

'Elephant?' he said. 'Where?'

'There,' said Gene, pointing to a large oak cupboard that substituted for the cupboard under the stairs at my house. 'You know, where we always play.'

Archie suddenly became agitated. He rose from his chair and started wringing his hands.

'Why is there an elephant in the cupboard?' he shouted. 'I don't want elephants in the cupboard! How dare you put an elephant in the cupboard!' He lunged towards Gene who was laughing, thinking this was all part of the game. But I could see it wasn't. Luckily I reached Gene in time because I'm quite sure Archie would have hit him.

'Darling, there isn't an elephant,' I said to Archie, shielding Gene behind my back. 'It's only a joke!'

But by this time Archie had gone to the door of the cupboard and pulled it open. 'There's no elephant here,' he said. 'It must have got away! Close the doors and windows. Don't let it get back in! It'll smash the place up!' He went out to the hall, grabbed a walking stick and then went round the ground floor banging doors and crashing down windows.

Hardy, thinking the whole thing was a great game, started barking furiously and racing from room to room.

The worst thing was that Gene was still laughing himself silly. He had no idea what was going on.

'Get behind the sofa!' Archie shouted, as he returned to the room where we were. 'What are we going to do, Philippa?' We walked over to the back of the sofa and then he joined us, pulling us down with surprising strength. I started to panic. I pulled out my mobile and dialled Sylvie. I couldn't think of anything else to do.

'What are you doing?' Archie said to me, accusingly.

'I'm ringing the RSPCA,' I lied, 'To ask them to

107

come and take the elephant away.' The phone started to ring and I prayed Sylvie would answer. Luckily she did.

Gene, oblivious to the situation, was still killing himself laughing.

'RSPCA?' I said into it, very loudly, hoping she wouldn't ring off. 'It's Marie Sharp here and I'm with Archie Lloyd, and we're very frightened there's an elephant in the library and would you come quickly . . .'

'Let me talk to them!' shouted Archie, seizing the phone from me. 'RSPCA? Come quickly. It's about to attack us!'

Thank heavens Sylvie caught on to what was happening and she was down with her husband, Harry, in a flash, and Harry managed to persuade Archie the elephant had gone back to the zoo where it had escaped from—and I was nearly in tears of relief. Gene still had no idea what had happened and thought it was one of the best elephant games we'd ever had together. But I was really shocked, particularly by the way that Archie had been about to attack Gene.

We all had lunch at Sylvie's, which was a relief, and Archie calmed down considerably, but then Harry asked if I'd seen *Bitter Quinces, Poisoned Souls*, and I said I'd left after the first half hour and he and Sylvie had pounced on this and said I should have stayed to the end because then 'when the person whose fingers have been cut off learns to play the piano, it's so moving, and there's a shot of a torture cell in a Bulgarian prison which goes on for ten minutes and you're just, well, you're transported, really. You *have* to see it, it's as if you're really *there*.'

108

'And the camerawork,' added Sylvie. 'It was worth seeing for the camerawork alone . . .'

'And the little *boy*!' added Harry.

'The little *boy*!' echoed Sylvie, holding up her hands, and then hiding her face in compassion and misery. But they refused to tell me the end however much I begged them, because they said that I *must* go and see it again all the way through because it was *marvellous*.

Apart from that we all got on like a house on fire.

Harry accompanied Archie back to his house, with the intention of staying the night there, and, after dropping Gene back home, I drove back to Shepherds Bush.

When I arrived, I finally remembered to pop into the corner shop and give back the Debt of Honour I owed them. The Indian man behind the counter had no memory of it, refused at first to take it and when I insisted, looked at me as if I were completely mad.

29 April

Got a very apologetic email from Sylvie. Apparently the next day, she'd gone to have a cup of tea with her dad, and when she'd arrived he'd asked her who the hell she thought she was, a complete stranger, barging into his house. He was going to call the police and would she get out, the bitch. *Totally* uncharacteristic phrase for Archie. So she's finally made an urgent doctor's appointment. Thanks heavens! At last! I'm so relieved.

109

30 April

The postman left a parcel today and I opened it
eagerly. It was from the plant nursery. Golly, what
a disappointment! Thirty-six plants were all
crammed into a tiny plastic box, and when I took
them out, they were each about the size of my little
finger. They were called 'plugs'. They didn't look
anything like Calibans or whatever they were
called, I can never remember these Latin names,
nor did they look as if they would ever develop into
banks of foaming colour, at least not for another
five years. I spent a couple of hours bunging
dozens of these things into the ground feeling most
pessimistic. All I could see were specks of green.

Later Penny popped round to show me a letter
she'd drafted for the planning people. But before
she'd even taken her coat off, she said she'd got
bad news.

'What?' I asked, rather nervously.

'James is in love!'

'What do you mean, "James is in love"?' I said,
in a rather peeved way. I thought I was James's
special friend and he would have told me first had
he been in love. 'Who is it . . . ?' Then it dawned.
'It's not the Silver Birch, is it?'

' 'Fraid so. He went to the pub and they hit it off
at once, and now he's in love.'

'But he said he'd never have another
relationship after Hughie!' I said, crossly. Realising
that was uncharitable, I added, 'Oh, well, I'm very
happy for him.'

'Oh, yes, so am I,' said Penny, as she hung her

110

coat up. 'It's wonderful that he's met someone.'

And then, in the kitchen over the slowly boiling kettle, we looked at each other more knowingly. 'Bloody maddening as well, if you ask me,' I said.

'Absolutely,' said Penny. 'How dare he? He's got us, hasn't he? What's he doing falling in love. It's ridiculous.'

'Won't last,' I said.

'Hope not,' said Penny, darkly.

To cheer ourselves up, we each had two chocolate digestives with our coffee.

MAY

2 May

At first I thought the headline read: 'IT DOESN'T ADD UP! *21 in every 10 children leaves school innumerate!*' but then I realised that even the *Rant* couldn't go that far. Adjusting my glasses I saw it said that *one* child in every 10 was clueless about arithmetic. However, my blood pressure had already shot up, just as it was supposed to, which gave me the energy to ring Sylvie to find out how the doctor's appointment with Archie had gone.

'Oh, Marie,' she said, sounding much more affectionate than when I last spoke to her. 'I was just about to ring you. We went to the doctor's yesterday, and I feel awful about this, but you were quite right of course. I'm afraid he's got some kind of dementia, and the doctor's sending him to have an assessment at the clinic, but it's all changed suddenly very rapidly. It's so awful because he sort of understands what's going on and sort of doesn't. I'm trying to spend as much time there as possible and Mrs Evans says she'll stay over on the nights I can't be there, but it's all horrible. The thing is that sometimes he's just like his old self and then suddenly he seems completely different.'

'Oh Sylvie,' I said, almost crying with relief. 'I'm so glad you went. And I'm so, so sorry. It must be dreadful for you.'

'I just feel so bad I didn't notice it sooner,' she said. 'I think I did actually, but I was just trying to pretend to myself that it was just ordinary old age, losing his memory and so on, but after that terrible afternoon the other day with the elephants . . . I'm so sorry, I wasn't very sympathetic and you were doing your best . . .'

'What are you going to do? Can I help you with anything?' I asked. 'Does he need a carer? Or are you looking for somewhere for him to stay? Is there anything that can be done?'

'No, there's nothing, unfortunately. If I'd listened to you earlier we might have been able to have made it a bit better for a few months or so, but it's too late now. I'm going to start looking for nursing homes. The awful thing is that he's in perfect health, strong as a horse. It's just his brain that's going.'

'Well, if there's anything I can do, let me know,' I said. 'I can go down at the drop of a hat, so if you want some time off, it's fine.'

'Oh that would be brilliant,' said Sylvie. 'Thank you.'

The news made me feel curiously light-headed, as if someone had died. This really is the end. I suppose that, like Sylvie, although I've thought I've faced up to what's going on, I still felt that a trip to the doctor would mean his being given some magic pills that would make him better, at least temporarily. But no. It's just downhill. Poor, poor Archie. I don't think I can quite believe what's happening.

3 May

James rang today. He told me he wasn't feeling very well because he'd been buying something at

113

the corner shop and some wretched girl with a huge rucksack had turned round and literally knocked him to the ground. He was only just recovering.

I was very sympathetic and then I said, rather accusingly I'm afraid, 'What's all this about your falling in love with the tree man?'

There was a silence at the other end of the phone. Then, 'I don't know about in *love*, Marie,' said James, 'But he's really nice. He does part-time work for the Organic Soil and Hedges Society, and he knows all about plants, and I've been out with him twice, but honestly, the amazing thing is . . .' There was a long pause. 'He does seem to be interested in me, too.'

'How lovely,' I said, hoping I sounded more genuine than I felt. 'I'm so glad for you.' I injected such a great dollop of warmth that I almost found myself believing it. 'When can we welcome him into the family?'

'Oh, I'm very frightened of your meeting him— well, meeting him more than you have, Marie,' said James. 'I know how critical you can be.'

'Me? Critical? Never! Well, not with you. Anyway, even if I think he stinks, I shall absolutely force myself to like him because I love you.' That at least was true. 'Come to supper soon. Come on. I'll ask Penny, so it won't just be me staring at him through an enormous microscope and making notes.'

'No,' said James, darkly. 'It'll be the two of you. I promise you, he hasn't got leaf mould or root rot.'

'It's gone that far, has it?' I said, laughing.

114

4 May

Went out into the garden to see if my plants had turned into banks of foaming colour, but no. Believe it or not, I couldn't see any trace of them at all, not even the tiny green shoots there were last week when I planted them.

Cockroaches. Bet it's cockroaches.

11 p.m.

Tonight I had an early supper with the family—a kind of last supper—and declined their invitation to come to the airport to say goodbye to them the following day. Gene said he wanted to wave to me from the plane. Sweet. But I just couldn't face it. I knew I'd crack up.

I just said goodbye early, assuring them I'd be over, they'd be over, we'd all be over, I was frightfully busy, it was quite a relief they were going so I could catch up on *all* the things I had to do. I tiptoed upstairs to give Gene one last kiss (he was asleep) and looked around his room, so tragic with all the suitcases packed and his little satchel filled with pencils and things to do on the aeroplane and his favourite cuddly peeping out of the top, and Jack gave me a special hug and said, 'Love you, Mum. Take care of yourself'—my least favourite expression because I always think people are muttering under their breath, 'Because no one else will, that's for sure'—and I just had to rush home before I disgraced myself by falling down on the floor and tugging everyone's clothes and hugging their knees and begging, *begging* them not to go.

Just taken two temazepam and would be very happy never to wake up again. Not really, but you know what I mean.

5 May

Well, I *did* wake up. By now they'll be in the air. I thought of getting up properly, but it transpires I've only got enough energy to write my diary and now I'm going back to bed. Going to bed isn't a bad activity, actually, when you're feeling low. It's true you don't often feel a lot better when you wake up, but you usually feel a *tiny* bit better, and anyway it passes the time. Penny believes in running round the block when she feels gloomy, but the thought of pounding the streets with tears pouring down my cheeks is quite beyond me and I'm going to draw the curtains back again and go straight back to bed. Seems like a very sensible idea. Tomorrow I will start getting my life together.

Later

Just as I was trying to drag myself up at 3 p.m. the phone rang and it was Marion.

'I'm told this is a horrible day for you,' she said, very sympathetically. 'So I wondered if you'd like to come and have supper with us? So you know that even if some of your family have gone away,

116

you've got a family of friends still here—us! I know it's not the same, but it's better than nothing.'

I accepted like a shot, and immediately felt hugely cheered up. I'm so mean about Marion, what with her being part of a kind of seventies rock pool, but she's the kindest and sweetest person in the world. I know. There's always the totally unforgivable goat. But her heart's in exactly the right place, and she's a darling.

She'd cooked an enormous bean stew, the type of thing no one else has eaten since 1969, and she even supplied the sort of acid wine we used to take to parties when we were young. But it didn't matter at all. It was just so nice to be there, with old friends, that everything tasted totally delicious. The conversation turned to the subject of getting old, with everyone complaining about it.

'I was at a party the other day,' said Marion, 'and I met this charming young thing who was all of eighteen years old, and do you know she asked me if I'd ever met Oscar Wilde! Aren't young people extraordinary? No idea of history!'

'Extraordinary,' I said. 'But very nice.' We all agreed we adored them. Marion says she likes them so much that she's been known, after giving a stray young person supper, to write a letter and thank them for coming over to see them, rather than the other way round.

'Well, *someone*'s got to write a thank-you letter,' I said, rather tartly. 'And you know it's not going to be them.'

Tim was particularly affectionate, giving me a friendly wink now and again, and the odd pat—not creepily, but as if to say, 'We know what you're going through and we're here for you.'

117

Marion's organising a school reunion, and has asked if I'll go. How can I refuse?

A very jolly evening, and I came back feeling completely different. The love of friends isn't the same as the love of family, but it's pretty damn near, and Marion is a total brick.

'Any time you feel low,' she said, 'just give us a ring. We're always here. And we always love seeing you.'

Lucky old me, really. Not much to complain about. Though as I carefully lifted Pouncer off the centre of my bed in order to make room for myself, I couldn't help wondering what Gene was doing at this precise moment. Possibly sampling his first real American hamburger? And his first 'fries'? My mind is completely conflicted between hoping they all loathe every minute of being in that beastly city and at the same time hoping so much that they're terribly happy there.

6 May

Daily Rant greeted me this morning with the news, 'TV'S ANNIE NOONA BACK IN REHAB!' As I have never heard of Annie Noona and have no idea who she is, the news didn't have the desired effect on me. I was obliged to dig out yesterday's newspaper: 'NO MORE FISH IN THE OCEAN!' That perked me up.

Looked up the mysterious Annie Noona on Google. Turns out she is a superstar who is regularly being found unconscious in her glamorous New York apartment, so she must have cracked up once again.

Funny how these days people are falling from their dizzy heights before one even noticed their ascent to celebrity to start with. Let alone spotted them waving briefly from the summit.

Later

This evening Jack rang me from the States on Skype. Of course for him it was the afternoon. It wasn't particularly satisfactory. Nothing remotely like him actually being here. First he was too close to the camera, so all I could see was this huge mouth on the screen like something out of a nightmare, saying, 'Hello Mum!' At the 'u' bit of 'mum' I thought he was going to swallow me up.

We sorted that out and then it turned out that all *he* could see of *me* was the arm of the chair I was sitting on, which wasn't ideal.

Anyway, eventually we managed to work it out. But it was so strange! I mean it's not like talking face-to-face at all. It's like watching telly. It's not even as intimate, I think, as talking on the telephone when you feel all secretly close to the other person with them whispering in your ear. And they don't look at you. They're so busy looking at the picture of you on the screen, that you feel all the time as if you're at a cocktail party where the person you're talking to is constantly checking over your shoulder to see if there isn't someone more interesting in the room.

Then occasionally the whole thing jammed and Jack's image would stay flickering on the screen, mid-sentence, a mass of Jack-like pixels, until the computer had obviously coughed, got rid of the frog in its throat, twiddled itself and jumped back to life.

Skype's not all it's cracked up to be. I can't feel the family, smell them, touch them, hug Chrissie when I say hello, or give Jack's hair a motherly tousle (though of course he'd flinch if I did that; one has to be careful with sons). And however good it is, I'll never be able to feel Gene on my knee as we watch *Tom and Jerry* and laugh when Jerry gets totally squashed by an iron and ends up on a washing line. It's better than nothing. But it's not the same.

Anyway, when we got the hang of it all, I found that the family seem to be getting on maddeningly fine—which I found very discouraging because obviously I wanted them to arrive, find everything was just vile, and come steaming home. But I heard myself telling dreadful lies like, 'I'm so glad it seems to be going well,' while all the time I wanted them to say the rooms were full of bedbugs (as I gather all apartments are in New York these days), that it was so cold they were freezing—or so hot they were boiling—and that the Americans were brash and unwelcoming, but unfortunately nothing of the kind.

As Chrissie has this mega-job with a cosmetics and general beautifying company, Gene has not only been paid for to attend some weird little private preparatory school, but they've also been installed in a very glorious 'apartment', as Jack calls it, on the Upper West Side, with views across the Hudson, and a kitchen with a breakfast bar in it (can you imagine a bar in your house? At breakfast? I can barely have my tea and toast lying on the sofa with the *Rant* and my feet up in the morning, let alone balance high on a tiny stool like some nightclub chanteuse, with my legs entwined round the stem of the seat). They have the biggest and lowest white leather sofa in the world, it all looked quite hideous, just the sort of place you'd imagine Annie Noona having her latest breakdown in (Jack showed me the layout by pointing the camera at various corners), which is not the sort of place in which any right-minded granny would choose to live, but still. I had a quick chat with Chrissie, who said it was all mind-blowingly wonderful except that the air-conditioning in their apartment block had stuck, and they were freezing cold, and then Gene was put on.

My heart missed a beat when I saw him. I noticed his front tooth had finally fallen out. That and being on Skype meant he didn't really look like Gene at all—all brightly lit and rather puffy, through the fish-eye lens. I suppose I must have looked the same to him. No change there, then.

'Hello Granny!' he said, settling down and looking rather astonished and pleased to see someone just over my shoulder. 'How are you?'

'How are *you*?' I replied. 'What's it like?'

'I lost my tooth, look!' he said, trying to show me by pulling his upper lip towards his nose making him look even more grotesque.

'Well, I never!' I said. 'I hope the tooth fairy came!'

'Yes, I got a . . . a dollar,' he said.

'But how is it in New York?' I persisted.

'It's brilliant, Granny!' he said. 'I love it here!'

His little-boy enthusiasm really touched me. One of the delights of getting older, but also one of the problems, is the cynicism. 'Oh yeah, another

121

riverside apartment in New York, big deal, so what,' you think, partly because you've seen so many in movies (and I've even stayed in one on a couple of trips to the States), but also because you know they don't bring happiness. They just appear to for a couple of months. But for Gene the place was bliss. While I would just hate to live in a film set, he obviously thought it was the height of chic.

'What's the weather like?' I said. Quite unbelievable that I was asking this little boy such a pedestrian question. But it's the sort of question you ask on Skype.

'It's nice out, but here it's *freezing*!' he said. 'You'll have to knit me a jersey, Granny.'

Knit him a jersey? After those complicated socks I'd knitted him as a baby? As I've said, my knitting days had well and truly stopped. I could never take on a major project like a jersey. Particularly now he was so big. By the time I'd finished it he'd be a grown man. I'd never catch up.

'We'll see,' I said, cautiously, reminding myself of my mother's irritating way of saying 'no' to me, when I was small. A horrible phrase, 'We'll see.'

And then I was suddenly overtaken by an overwhelming urge to knit. Knitting him a jersey would be a wonderful way to feel close to him. And I could show it to him when we talked on Skype, and he could see how it was progressing.

Sadly, you can't really make conversation with a five-year-old child in the same way as you can with an adult. Children aren't very skilled at it. There was a lot of 'And what have *you* done today?' and getting not a lot back. Children haven't been trained to ask questions of other people. Had he been here, in the house, we could have made faces

122

at each other, or simply done something together like build a robot out of cardboard boxes, or read a book, or play the elephant game. Making conversation is something you do at cocktail parties, not something you do with your grandson. And then I fear that when we meet again, Gene won't even recognise me.

Oh, come off it, Marie. Stop wallowing in self-pity, you wally! Of course he'll recognise you.

(Well, not if the facelift's successful.)

Oh shut up, you big banana!

8 May

Mr Parson's secretary has just rung up to say they can move my appointment to next month. I suppose some other poor woman has finally become overcome with terror and hasn't been able to go through with it and he's got a sudden vacancy. I said I was worried that the auction to sell my money-raising pictures might not have taken place so I was a bit concerned about the bill, but they seemed quite cool about it all, saying that they were sure they could trust me. Rather sweet really. Who wouldn't trust a retired art teacher, after all? We're not renowned for our careers as swindlers.

But, suddenly terrified now the operation seemed so much closer, I rang James who shrieked, 'Go for it, girl,' which didn't help much.

'I think you'll have to wait before you start your portrait,' I said, relieved to put off the evil hour. 'I don't know how far you've got, but if you've started you'll have to paint out all those wrinkles. Sorry

123

about that.'

Penny was no help at all. She just said that I shouldn't get it done, it was all vanity and I looked perfectly okay anyway. And she said it was putting her in an awful position because she'd have to deal with the Residents' Association and the protests about the trees while I was recovering, and thanks a lot. And if I had any spare money, shouldn't I be spending it on my Romanian orphans, anyway? I was always banging on about them, she said.

'Why should you spend money on the orphans?' said James, when he phoned later and I told him what she'd said. 'Do something for *yourself* for once, my darling.'

But I'm not really of a 'do something for myself' generation. We weren't brought up to pamper ourselves. We were brought up with the strict injunction to deny ourselves everything nice and give to the poor. My grandmother even used to look disapprovingly when I left a bit of bacon fat on my plate and say, 'Think of all those starving children in India.' I remember trying to think of them, and wishing there were some way I could post them my bits of fat, but quite honestly eating them myself wasn't going to help them. So I just felt awful.

14 May

Today I had to go to Jack and Chrissie's house and check that it is all spick and span for potential tenants. I promised I would, but it makes my heart ache to go down there and know there's nobody home. Brixton, where they live, used to seem to be

124

a vibrant jolly place, a happy, laughing mix of races and cultures. Now it seems sinister and dark, with hidden threats waiting to pounce from beneath every burnt-out car rusting in the gutter. As I opened the door I felt a pang when it dawned on me properly that Gene wouldn't be at the top of the stairs, running down to greet me.

They'd left it pretty immaculate, I must say. I did find a piece of Lego under the sofa, which made my heart turn over, but otherwise Chrissie had done a spectacular job. I almost wish I could move into it myself, though it would hold too many memories.

Can it really be true they've left? I looked to see if they'd taken the last disc off the CD player and found they'd left in *The House at Pooh Corner*. I watered the plants and wondered whether to look in Gene's room but just couldn't bear to, so I came away and dropped the keys off at the estate agents and told them that, as far as I could see, everything was in perfect order and they could start showing people round whenever they liked.

16 May

The estate agents have just rung to tell me that three 'prospects' are visiting today. It seems so odd to think of other people living in that flat. I used to sit in that kitchen when Gene was tiny, feeding him bits of mush that Chrissie had prepared for him, pretending, when he didn't want to eat, that the spoon was an aeroplane going into his mouth, making him laugh and then popping in some squished-up carrot when he wasn't thinking about it.

That very spot would be in future where some ghastly young banker would be microwaving a 'dinner for two' for his leggy secretary, and then afterwards they'd go into Gene's bedroom and bonk the night away, under a newly installed plasma TV screen.

Yuk!

18 May

The *Rant* tells me today: 'COMPLETE COLLAPSE OF SOCIETY! *Social workers predict "total disintegration" of family life. Only one person in five knows how to eat with a knife and fork, and only one in 20 can boil a kettle. Ninety per cent of teens "don't know who their father is."*'

Golly. Can this really be true? Makes me want to slash my throat. No wonder the *Bitter Quinces* director is alive and well in my dreams. He's got all this grim material to work with.

When I went out today to make some sketches of the trees this month—the April picture I've done is great, though I say it myself—I thought I'd try to sprinkle a bit of joy in people's lives. Why not? So when I came across some wretched hoodie who was skulking along staring miserably at the ground—probably one of those hopeless, homeless people who have no idea who their father is—I smiled at him broadly and said, 'Lovely day, isn't it?'

Instead of getting out a knife, plunging it into my heart and seizing my handbag, he looked up, flashed a dazzlingly friendly smile and replied,

126

'Lovely, isn't it! And by the way, when's that meeting going to be?' Turned out he was one of the dealers Penny and I had spoken to about the hotel plans. I took his address—he certainly wasn't homeless—and said I'd let him know if we had a big meeting and could I rely on him to tell his mates?

'Sure! Cheers!' he said, as we parted.

Amazing.

20 May

Rang Jack on Skype. I scanned his face and tone of voice for clues about when they might be thinking of returning, but there was absolutely nothing. As far as I could tell, Chrissie was loving her job and it was still going to be a year's trial. Jack had met a web designer and he seemed to be getting some work, but still had time to look after Gene, and Gene, he said, was 'settling down' at school.

'He'll have a few problems, but he'll get used to it,' he said. 'It's difficult being a new boy in a new country.'

Gene wouldn't be drawn on the matter, but I could see by his face when I asked about school that he felt uncomfortable there.

'You should have seen Dad at his first day at school!' I said, to cheer him up. 'I picked him up after the first day and he said he didn't like it at all and was very pleased to get home. But when I said "Tomorrow it will be better" he burst into tears. "But I've *been* to school, Mum!" he said. "I don't have to go again, do I?"'

At this Gene roared with laughter.

127

'And I didn't like school the first day, either,' I said truthfully, not adding that I hated every day afterwards until the day I left. Probably best to keep that to myself.

'But tomorrow we're going to paint the American flag. It's got stars on it. Did you know it had stars on it, Granny?'

'No!' I said, as if it was the first time I'd heard it. 'How extraordinary!'

'It's for the States,' he said, ambiguously.

'Really?' I said. Honestly, sometimes talking to a small boy is rather like making conversation with some dumb man at a dinner party. You have to do nothing but feign surprise and fascination at all his fatuous remarks. Not that Gene was remotely fatuous of course.

'Now, darling,' I said, changing the subject. 'I thought I might knit you a jersey—you remember we were talking last time?—and I could do elephants on it to remind us of the elephant game!'

'Yes, Granny!' he said, smiling broadly. 'Do you remember that time with Archie? That was *so* funny!'

'Yes, wasn't it,' I said. I couldn't say anything else. 'And as I knit it I can try it on you on Skype and see if it fits.'

'You'd like it here,' said Gene suddenly.

'I'm certainly going to try to come over,' I said. 'I've just got to sort out some dates with Dad.'

'Great,' he said, staring enthusiastically at the spot above my head. 'Oh, I just farted. Did you hear my fart, Granny?'

'No, I didn't, darling,' I said smiling.

'Oh dear. I can't do another one because I haven't got any farts left at the moment,' he said, rather apologetically, as if I might have been disappointed at missing the last one and living in hopes of another. 'I'll see if I can do one next time.' He paused. 'You can't smell them on Skype can you?'

'No, darling, you can't,' I said.

And for the first time in my life, I rather wished I could.

Funny, isn't it, boys' preoccupation with farts? There was a time when Gene did nothing, I remember, but pull down his trousers and moon at me, shouting: 'Fatty bum bum!' It didn't upset me because Jack had done exactly the same at that age. Life seemed to consist only of burps and farts, and phrases like 'I done a plop' after a visit to the loo were deemed as inexplicably amusing. Sometimes Gene could hardly stand, he was so bowled over by his own smells and noises. I tried to go along with it, but just couldn't find it at all funny. It's not because I disapprove, it's just because it leaves me cold. Perhaps it's because I'm a woman. All men seem to find them far more amusing than we ladies do.

29 May

I nipped up to the John Lewis store in the West End, and went straight to the haberdashery department. It's amazing they still have these things, all lovely old wool and needles and tapestry kits and a myriad different coloured cottons. Found a pattern for a jersey which actually had a border of elephants going all the way round the bottom. I couldn't believe it! I snapped it up, bought my needles and wool and thought, oh well, if I can't work it all out I'll ask Marion, who's very good at knitting, and she can show me the ropes.

It's just so lovely to have something to do which connects me to the little chap.

Sylvie rang. The doctor's given Archie some sedatives which stop him being so anxious, so that would explain why he hasn't answered the phone recently, though I've kept trying. Apparently he's doing little else except sleep.

Oh, I do hope he has good dreams and feels at peace. That's all that matters. Dear Archie.

JUNE

5 June

Slaved away all morning to make the most
delicious game stew for this evening, because
Penny and James and Ned—the tree man—are
coming round. I'd bought some potted shrimps to
start with and had made a delicious pudding—
when James rang me.

'Just to say,' he said, 'that Ned's a vegan.'

'Oh, well that's okay,' I said, through clenched
teeth. 'He can have the baked potato and I can
make him a cheese omelette and he can have extra
helpings of potted shrimps and there's a lovely
fruit fool for pud . . .'

There was a silence. 'Oh dear,' said James. 'I
suppose I should have rung earlier. No, he's not
vegetarian. He's *vegan*. He won't eat fish, or any
dairy products either. And, er, I'm trying to go
along with it as well, actually. He said I should give
it a go. I've lasted a week so far, though I did sneak
in a steak one lunchtime, but I didn't tell him. But
we're very happy with vegetables. I'm sure we'll
be able to cope. Whatever you cook it's always
absolutely delicious. We don't want you to go to
any trouble.'

'Well, frankly, I don't think there's a single thing
I've prepared that you can eat, James,' I said,
rather tartly. 'Even the pudding's full of cream. I
suppose that's out?'

'I'm afraid so,' said James. 'Would it be easier if
we brought something?'

131

The idea that the guests had to bring their own food just didn't sit right with me. 'No, don't worry,' I said, 'It'll be fine.'

The moment I put the phone down I shouted 'BLOODY VEGANS' at the wall, crammed the game stew into the freezer, shoved the potted shrimps back in the fridge (I could always have them for lunch for the next six days) and stared bleakly at the whipped cream and blackcurrant fool that I'd made in four individual little ramekins. I didn't think they'd last for more than a couple of days and I couldn't eat them *all* by myself.

I felt like Job who was, as I remember, plagued by locusts, boils, frogs and rats—or was that someone else? No, Job was plagued by Satan, who took away his children, his wealth and his health . . . well, frankly, I'm worse off than Job because although I still have my health, up to a point, I am now not only about to be plagued with the absence of my wonderful, quiet, charming Polish neighbour (she moved out last week) but with the arrival in my life of a wretched vegan. Or, rather, vegans.

Rushed off to the corner shop and managed to buy some tomatoes and basil for a salad starter, then I bought some nice bread, vegetables to roast, followed by oranges in caramelised sugar.

Just about to have a snooze to recover before they come round.

Later

Thought I'd try to reread *Anna Karenina* before I put my head down, but discovered, after four

132

pages, that it was unreadable. So odd, that. When I read it the first time I thought it was brilliant. Second time, adored it. But this time, it's just dust. Weird.

Later had a ghastly dream that I'd had my facelift, and afterwards when I looked in the mirror there was my mother looking out at me. She (or was it I?) had mad eyes, badly put-on lipstick, far too much blusher and bottle-blonde hair. Crikey. What a shock.

Afternoon snoozes. Not all they're cracked up to be.

Midnight

Well, they came and now they've gone. By them, I don't mean the dreams, unfortunately, I mean James and Ned.

There's no question, old Ned is a dish. And he's not that old. His complexion is surprisingly good for a vegan, he smells very strongly of soap (though I'm sure soap isn't allowed for vegans so it must be something else) and he's got a really nice natural smile.

'I'm so pleased to meet you in a more personal setting,' he said, starting to take off his shoes.

'Don't take off your shoes!' I found myself screaming. 'This is a shoes-on house!'

He looked a bit put out, and then I noticed he was wearing plastic sandals. No wonder he wanted to get them off. Well, tough, I say.

We all sat down with a drink. I gave up my usual spot on the sofa so Ned and James could sit next to each other, and Penny and I perched on the slightly uncomfortable uprights. Pouncer, deprived of his habitual seat, lay curled up on the floor in the middle, his ears flat back, his tail swaying with simmering rage even as he slept, furious at being ousted from his spot.

Ned insisted on a glass of simple tap water, and refused the stuff that I keep in the fridge because he said that fridges give off too many carbon emissions or something—but luckily the conversation quickly turned to planning law and trees. He's found out more about what's going on with the Common—he has spies at the council apparently—and it seems they're sending out letters asking for comments on the plans tomorrow, so we've all got to get busy objecting.

I was delighted to see his face darken at the mention of all the shenanigans, and he definitely wasn't pleased about the prospect of the trees having to come down.

'I'll certainly write a letter on your behalf saying what I think,' he said finally. 'But now,' he said, changing the subject, 'I hear James is doing a portrait of you.'

My heart rather sank, but I tried to look as bright as I could. 'Isn't it wonderful!' I said.

'I've been trying to persuade him to do an installation that represents you, instead,' he said.

'Isn't that a super idea!' said James, moving up close to Ned and running his hand through his hair. 'All *objets trouvés*. Don't you think that would be fun, darling?'

Then James turned affectionately to Ned and planted a kiss on his cheek, before putting a hand on his knee and kneading it significantly as he worked his way up his thigh. Ned, to his credit,

134

looked mildly uncomfortable and shifted away.

'Now, now,' said Ned.

'About the installation,' I interrupted, in a rather schoolmistressy way. But they remained entwined.

'It would be much more ecologically viable than using up canvas and oil paints which are made, of course, from precious oil,' said Ned, removing James's hand from his neck and then rather prudishly, shaking his head when I offered him a top-up of his glass as if I were trying to get him drunk on tap water.

Eventually we filed into the kitchen, and James was terribly pleased that I'd bothered to make this ghastly meal of vegetables, and Penny and I managed to choke down our baked beetroots and roasted courgettes—which I persuaded her to slather with butter. Ned, of course, ate them entirely butter-free. No idea how he could actually get it all down his gullet.

'Have you got solar panels, here, by the way?' he said. 'It might be worth thinking about. And did you know you can get an insulating grant from the council?

At some point I suddenly remembered that in order to encourage the very few—about three—of the seedlings I'd planted that had survived, I'd left the sprinkler on, so sneaked out into the garden to turn it off and hide it away, realising that watering the garden would not be on Ned's list of approved activities.

When I got back, hoping I didn't look as if I'd been drenched by Gene's joke button-hole, I carefully switched the conversation round to acupuncturists, which meant I got a lot of Brownie points from Ned who believes that all doctors are in the pay of the Devil, and that inoculations actually make you ill and, even worse, that most of them actually contain timed drugs to turn us all into mindless slaves in the future. Although come to think of it who knows? No doubt the *Rant* will enlighten me on the subject.

And eventually they went home.

'Stay a moment,' I said to Penny, going to the fridge and rummaging around for some real food. 'Bacon sandwich before bedtime?'

'Oh God, yes!' she said, peering into the fridge. 'And what are those delicious little puds I see in there?'

'Ooh, wow, yes!' I'd forgotten all about them. 'Surely we could manage a couple each?'

'He's a bit of an eco-fascist isn't he?' said Penny, as she got out the spoons.

'He certainly is,' I said, grim-faced as I threw several bits of bacon into the pan. 'And I do wish they weren't all over each other all the time, don't you? Though actually, Ned didn't seem to be that enthusiastic, did you notice?'

'Yes, I did,' said Penny. 'But even so, it's disgusting! It's not a prejudice thing, either. I hate all that public slobbering, even in heterosexual couples.'

'It just rubs it in that they've got each other while we've got no one,' I said.

The bacon sizzled and crackled.

'Well, you've got Archie,' said Penny.

'I'm afraid the Archie I knew and loved has long gone,' I said, sadly. I felt so upset about Archie, that I couldn't actually talk about the situation at the moment, not even to Penny. I knew I'd just go to pieces. 'But it's clear that James is in love, so

136

we'll have to put up with all this lovey-doveyness for the moment. And Ned's a nice enough bloke. And he'll certainly be useful in the planning battle.'

'Or not,' said Penny. 'He might be a mole working for the other side. I bet there's a pay-off for the council in this scheme. There usually is. We ought to organise a petition. That would help.'

Then: 'Mmmm!' we both said as we savoured the smell of frying bacon. 'Now that's more like it!'

7 June

Was waiting hours this morning to get into the bathroom to have a long soak, organise myself for the day, dress and put my make-up on, but because it was Michelle's day off from her studies she had decided to have what seemed like a day-long spa experience. When she finally emerged, smothered in bath towels, with a great swaddling turban on her head, she looked at me and said, 'Ooh là là! Your 'air look vair' naice, Marie!'

It was only then that I realised that even though I was still in my dressing gown, I'd got up unusually early and already had a bath and washed my hair.

I think I probably ought to ring Sylvie and ask her to book an extra place in Archie's nursing home.

10 June

I must say the garden's looking sensational. All the roses are out, and the climbers have climbed everywhere. Funny, that plant. I bought it ten years ago at a car boot sale and it was out in the front doing absolutely nothing. I was just about to dig it up and throw it away when I thought I'd give it another chance at the back. Since then, it's almost overtaken the entire garden. Gorgeous.

Even the sweet peas are out, and the delphiniums. No sign of the wretched Calibans, however. Grrr.

On top of that, it's absolutely boiling and I have finally discarded my vest. Bit late, I know, but I'm pretty funny on the cold front.

Sylvie had asked if I'd go down this weekend to see Archie because she wanted a break, but I've got such mixed feelings. One bit of me is longing to see him, of course, but there is also a fear that he might suddenly get angry about something for no reason. Poor lamb, not his fault, but that thought doesn't make a lot of difference when the person you're with thinks you're a dangerous intruder and attacks you with a poker. Decided to take my knitting so at least I'll be armed with a sharp needle in case of emergency.

It's going rather well, actually, the knitting. I have done half the back—elephants included—but don't get much time, what with all this council stuff and the painting.

The other reason I rather dreaded going down to see Archie was because I felt it was so treacherous, knowing that Sylvie is looking for a home for him to go into behind his back—but it turned out Sylvie had already broached the subject.

We had a very nice supper—I'd brought down the uneaten game stew in a box and we heated it up in the Aga—and I managed to steer the conversation away from the subject of the brooch which he becomes obsessed by whenever I appear, and we were sitting having our coffee in front of the fire in the library, Hardy panting at our feet, when he said, perfectly lucidly, 'The doctor thinks I've got some kind of dementia. Rather ghastly, isn't it? I'll probably have to live somewhere else. They say I can't cope.'

Now written like that it might appear he was completely normal. But what was so odd was that he didn't appear to be upset by it at all. It was if an automaton was talking. He seemed to be in a kind of daze.

'Well, I think it's for the best,' I said, staring intently at my knitting, and trying to make out it was a perfectly ordinary sort of conversation to be pursuing after supper. 'Because you have been behaving rather strangely, recently.'

'Have I?' he said, smiling vacantly. 'Oh dear. I'm sorry.'

There was a silence. Then: 'Poor Mrs Evans. She's in prison, you know.'

'Really?' I said. I'd talked to her only hours before, arranging when she was going to take over from me the following day.

'Yes. She's in prison for stealing that brooch.'

'Oh, dear,' I said. 'Well I expect she'll be out soon.'

'I hope so,' he said. 'She's coming to make my breakfast tomorrow. I don't know how she gets out of the prison, but they must have some arrangement.'

'I'm sure they have, darling,' I said, getting up and putting my arms round him. 'Oh, dear Archie,

I do love you, you know.' I felt as if I were saying goodbye to him.

'And I love you, Philippa,' he said.

He looks the same as he always did—handsome, wonderful blue eyes still crinkling when he smiles; he smells the same—a sort of mixture of outdoorsy weather, earth, old tweeds and woodsmoke; and he feels the same . . . strong, reliable, gorgeous.

But he *isn't* the same. Oh dear. Oh dear.

16 June

My facelift operation is due all too soon, and I'm getting terribly cold feet about it. It's as if there are two parts of me at war—one part's saying, 'Don't have it. It'll hurt. You may well die under the anaesthetic. And if you don't die you may look permanently changed and wish you had your old face back. Or perhaps he'll make a mistake and instead of giving you a facelift, chop a great big chunk off your nose.'

The other part says: 'Relax! Do something for yourself for once! You'll *look* better, and as a result you'll *feel* better. Nothing ventured, nothing gained. You haven't bought anything new for about ten years, while everyone else has been splashing out on clothes, shoes, etc. With the money you've saved, surely it's only fair to do something that will have such a beneficial effect on you?'

These two sides rage against each other till sometimes I feel quite dizzy. I so wish Jack and Chrissie were around because I know they'd have some good advice, but I don't want to confide in them when they're in the States because they're

140

too far away and they've got too much on their plate. I know what Jack would say, anyway. He'd say 'Wait till you get over here and we'll talk about it,' when I really want to get it all over with as soon as possible.

17 June

I was in the kitchen making a shopping list when Michelle wandered in looking rather gloomy. At first I thought it was the prospect of having to gulp down another of those Yakults, but she sat down and sighed heavily. She looked as if she hadn't slept.

'What's the matter?' I said, putting my arm round her shoulder and kissing the top of her head.

'I seenk Maciej 'e does not love me. I reeng and 'e nevair reply. I send 'im text—nosseenk. Maybe 'e die. Maybe 'e find annuzair woman . . .'

'Oh, I'm sure it's fine,' I said cheerfully, not believing it was fine at all. 'He's probably just busy. You know—men! I was always worrying when I was your age but . . .' Just as I was running out of platitudes she added, 'And *respirateur* is 'ow you say, *ca ne marche pas . . .*'

I was starting to wonder whether she actually *was* taking English lessons on the days she was meant to, she's still so French, when she started making sucking noises. Did she have asthma, I wondered? Finally, I gathered what she was talking about. The vacuum cleaner was bust.

'I'll get a new one,' I said. 'It's gone wrong every three months ever since I bought it and I just can't

141

face getting it repaired again.'

I left her staring into her Yakult, and I felt dreadfully sorry for her. How incredibly lucky I am not to have to go through any of that 'Will he ring me? Has he got another girlfriend?' rubbish ever again! Sheer torture!

20 June

Daily Rant's headline today: 'TEACHERS UNDER ATTACK! *Twenty-five Assaults by Under-fives Every Day! "We're breeding a generation of thugs!" says Minister.*'

11 p.m.

Spent the entire evening panicking over the operation tomorrow. I have packed my little bag— nightie, spare pair of glasses, slippers, prettiest dressing gown, a whole pile of painkillers that I am NOT going to declare to the nurses. With my Nurofen Plus in my case I feel like someone trying to smuggle icons through the customs in Russia. I always remember going to the former USSR with David ages ago and we were taking some Polyfilla for a friend who lived in Moscow because he needed it to fill up the mouse holes in his flat. The customs officer immediately pounced on it thinking it was cocaine and refused to let us take it through. I've always liked the idea of him snorting it up his nose and being unable to breathe as it solidified permanently in his sinuses.

I decided on a P.G. Wodehouse because I don't

think any other author will do when you're in hospital. But then I thought it mightn't be a very good idea to take a funny book because what would happen if I were to laugh so much that I burst my stitches? And anyway, would I ever be able to laugh again? It seemed unlikely. I rang Penny in a panic and she was no use. She just hooted with laughter.

'Can't wait to see you afterwards!' she snorted. 'You'll look like someone who's been five rounds with Muhammad Ali. When I come over, I'll bring a notepad and pencil, just in case you can't move your mouth.' And she went into more peals of laughter. 'God, you're brave! I wouldn't have it done for a million pounds. Good luck!'

Not very reassuring.

Last-minute Skype with the family, because I won't be appearing on camera for a few weeks. I'll have to pretend it's temporarily broken. Or smother it with Vaseline so that they can only see a kind of smear instead of a face.

All seem tip-top though Gene has developed a maddening habit of raising his voice at the end of every sentence. So he says: 'School's okay now, Granny?' And 'Mom and Dad are giving me a goldfish for my birthday?'

'Mom.' Oh dear. Well, at least Jack isn't yet 'Pop'.

21 June

Crack of dawn. Oh Lord. Why am I doing this? I'm waiting for the minicab to take me to the hospital. What if I go to the States and Gene doesn't recognise me? What if the whole family gathers to greet me at the airport and completely ignores me as I pass? Last night I was up till three worrying myself sick. Actually worrying at three in the morning is nothing new. These days I spend half my day dozing and half my night worrying. Dozing comes particularly after I've eaten something. I can barely swallow a poppadum and have a glass of orange juice in the day without needing a lie-down afterwards. I think it's because when you're older all your blood has to rush to your tummy to digest whatever you've eaten, and can't cope with keeping you awake at the same time. And then, in the middle of the night, you wake up—at least I do—at about 3.15 a.m.—a totally God-awful hour—as if some dreadful Worrying Monster has tapped you on the shoulder and as you open your eyes staring wildly into the dark, it shouts, like a guard yelling at a prisoner: 'Okay, Marie! It's worrying time!' and then you spend the next hour panicking about the most ridiculous things.

In the end I got up and went downstairs and had a large glass of wine and washed it down with a pill (or is it the other way round), which was a very bad idea because this morning I woke up with a raging thirst which was no good because I'd been told I couldn't have anything to drink at all the morning before the op.

Fell asleep over *Anna K*. Think I'll chuck it. Still haven't got into it, and I'm halfway through. And all the mowing with the men nonsense. What a ghastly man Tolstoy was.

Midday

Now I'm in the hospital. I brought my laptop in case I found I had nothing to occupy my mind. Har har. I'm lying on my bed, gasping like one of those cartoon characters you see crawling across the desert hoping for water. It's a horrible little room, like a prison cell, boiling hot, painted magnolia, with a lockable bedside table, windows you can't open, a view over a car park, and a single stool for visitors. Screwed into the wall is a television set on a long stalk. Opposite is what I thought was a cupboard but turns out to be a tiny shower and a loo. Talk about spartan.

And for some reason I've been forced into a hospital nightdress, a humiliating blue affair which does up at the back, so that if you walk down a corridor without your dressing gown on, everyone can see your bottom.

I'm afraid I behaved rather badly just now. I got extremely anxious and then Mr P. came in, still wearing his bow tie under his green overalls, and started drawing blue lines on my face. It was as if he were a portrait painter, but instead of using a canvas to paint on, he was painting my portrait *actually on my face.* As he was about to leave—to go and do more drawing on other ladies' faces I suppose—I suddenly found myself getting furious, saying I wanted to go home and have a drink of water. Just like some tantrummy child at school! I must have seemed absolutely barmy! I suppose I was terrified. Still am really. He looked at me with alarm as he saw his blue lines smearing all over the place, rushed off and came back with the anaesthetist. I was getting out of bed to start packing my bag.

'Now, now, now, Mrs Sharp,' he said kindly, putting his arm gently round my shoulders and guiding me back to bed. 'Just let's talk about this.' I started to rant and sob again. 'I think you're just very frightened, and lots of people feel like this before an operation, but why don't you have a glass of water' (now he tells me) 'and let me give you a little injection, and then if you still feel upset, we'll get you a cab to take you home.'

God knows what he put in the injection, but I'm now lying here feeling incredibly sleepy and so relaxed and happy I think I'd like a facelift every day of the year. Wonder if this is what it feels like to be on heroin.

22 June

Crikey! I'm just waiting for James to come round and take me home. There's a limit to the number of old reruns of *Antiques Roadshow* a woman can watch without screaming, and my face doesn't contort very comfortably into screaming mode at the moment. I know it sounds cowardly, but I just can't bear to look in the mirror. Like the woman in the waiting room, I've got strange tubes hanging down from the side of my face attached to tiny little bucket things which are filled with blood.

Mr P. came in this morning and said I was doing fine, but would have to sleep sitting up for the next couple of weeks. Thanks a lot! They never tell you these really important things before they put you

146

under the knife, do they? And he also added that I might find my cheeks rather numb for a few months but that feeling wouldn't last, the feeling of not feeling, that is . . . another surprising fact that they'd kept from me. But, he added, 'I took an incredible amount of flesh from the tops of your eyes . . . I'm really pleased with the job I've done. I think you'll be very pleased, too.'

'It won't show too much, will it?' I said. Unbelievable. You pay thousands of pounds for a facelift and go through agony, and then you plead with the surgeon to reassure you that no one will notice.

'No, no one will know,' he said. 'They'll just think you've had a good holiday.'

Now I come to think of it, it would have been a damn sight cheaper and more relaxing to have had a good holiday instead.

23 June

I still feel pretty woozy. James brought me back after one night in hospital—it seemed pointless to spend two nights because it was just another sackful of money down the drain—and he didn't say very much, just looked at me worriedly and asked if I needed anything. We had a cup of tea but then he left and, overcoming my fear and trepidation, I looked in the mirror. Actually I looked dreadful—as if I'd been beaten up by a gorilla. I'm just covered with bruises. I look rather like a Francis Bacon painting—all purple and red with smears of yellow. True, there are some familiar eyes staring back at me under the swollen

147

lumps of aubergine that appear to have replaced my eyelids, and my teeth appear unchanged, but otherwise even *I* wouldn't recognise myself in the street if I bumped into myself. I'd probably run screaming to the nearest police station.

Even Pouncer gave me an odd look, and only agreed to come near me after I'd put down a bowl of his favourite food. I probably even *smell* of hospital!

24 June

Last night I tried to sleep sitting up—but it's very difficult. Apparently the bruises are drawn by gravity down your face as they lessen. So that if you walk about a lot, you find your bruises end up round your ankles before disappearing into the ground beneath your feet. Isn't that a weird idea? Anyway, I've had no desire to go out at all, though did stagger to the corner shop to get some more milk, with a pair of dark glasses on and a big polo-necked jersey and a hood to hide the little bottles. The Indian who runs the shop (and who already thinks I'm mad after the incident with the paid-back penny) looked at me with desperate pity in his eyes, as if he thought I'd been beaten to a pulp by a jealous boyfriend the night before. Still, it did me good to realise that I can get out and about if I want to. Came back and was absolutely shattered of course and had to spend the whole afternoon lying down. Or, rather, sitting up, if you see what I mean.

Thought I'd read some old classics to comfort me, but, as with *Anna K*, I couldn't get through either *Vile Bodies* or *Mansfield Park*, both favourites when I was young. I wonder what it is that happens when you're older? Does your perspective change? I think it's because when I read them as a young girl they seemed so new and fresh, but now they just seem dated and dull. Wonder if books I like now, if I could read them again in fifty years, would turn to dust as well? Probably. Actually, just after I'd thought this, I read a magazine and there was a quote in it from Muhammad Ali of all people, who once said: 'The man who views the world at fifty the same as he did at twenty has wasted thirty years of his life.'

Good old Cassius Clay, say I.

25 June

I was complaining so much about books that Penny lent me an enormous fat thriller which she said was 'rubbish'. But I don't think these books are rubbish, not if they keep you gripped. And gripped it certainly kept me. I was still reading it at two in the morning, could hardly keep my eyes open, but every time I said to myself I'd got far enough, something so frightful happened I had to pick it up again.

At one point the heroine was chained to a wall, about to be raped by a particularly insalubrious baddie, and our hero was chained to the wall opposite and couldn't do a thing about it except look on helplessly, and then at the last minute he made a huge effort, yanked the chain from the wall and knocked the baddie unconscious. I was just thinking what a good place that was to stop, now

149

everything was okay, and the heroine was saved, when I made the mistake of turning the page.

'"Not so fast, my friend," said a sinister voice from the darkness.'

Or some such. Well, of course I couldn't go to sleep after that, and had to read another chapter, and so on. As every chapter ended with a cliffhanger I was still racing through the pages at four in the morning when all the goodies were tied together in a house stacked with dynamite and the baddie was outside with a match—when I realised I just *had* to sleep. After throwing the book across the room so it wasn't too easy to retrieve, I managed to nod off at last.

26 June

'Eet weel be *magnifique!*' said Michelle when she saw me the following morning at the top of the stairs. She was just leaving to go to her English class. 'You weel look *ravissante!* My muzair she 'av done ze leefteeng and she ees vair' much badder zan you. In few weeks you weel be *superbe!*'

'I think you mean worse,' I said, ever the teacher, as I tottered downstairs in my dressing gown, clutching my thriller. The *Rant* would have to wait this morning. I just had to find out what happened in the end.

28 June

Mowed the lawn for what seems the fifty-fourth time this year, and then went back to Mr P. who took off the plastic buckets, which was a relief, and handed me over to a nurse who gave me a good wipe-down and said I should return in a fortnight to have the staples taken out of my head.

'Staples!' I said. 'I'm not being held together with metal staples, am I?'

'Don't worry. Everything will stay in place once it's all healed.'

When I spoke to Jack that night on Skype I pretended the camera had packed up, but it was good to hear him. I didn't say anything about the facelift because I'm sure he would have been worried or thought I was mad.

29 June

Rather worried that I'm missing June out of my Seasons of the Trees series, so snuck up in the evening, covered with scarves and dark glasses, and did a few sketches in the gloaming. Actually, it might be rather a good picture because it would be a contrast to the others.

One thing I *can* do in the day, even if I can't go out, is knit. But, unfortunately, as I was thundering up the back I got stuck on an armhole and couldn't make head nor tail of the pattern, so I had to ask Marion over.

Of course I had to go through all the 'I *still* can't understand why you had a facelift. You didn't need it! You looked wonderful! Waste of money!' stuff, but eventually we got down to knitting. 'It's all on the internet,' she said, and I thought how silly of me. I always forget to look. But it was nice to see her, even though she did beg me to see *Bitter*

151

Quinces, Poisoned Souls again and stay till the end this time.

'Quite simply,' she said, 'it's a masterpiece.'

'And there's a little boy in it, I hear?' I said. 'We left before that bit.'

'The little boy!' she said. She raised her eyes to heaven and sighed, her face a picture of compassion and agony. 'The little boy!'

Later

Was just about to get off to sleep at about midnight when Michelle knocked on my door and, looking very tear-stained, sat at the end of my bed. Pouncer was looking at her in a very irritated way as if to say 'For God's sake! I was just in the middle of an excellent dream about mice, and now you've woken me up!'

'What's up?' I asked, pulling myself up to a sitting position. I'm now at the lying-down stage. There's only so long you can spend sleeping sitting up, as anyone who's flown to Australia knows.

'Eet ees Maciej,' she said, sobbing. ' 'E *'as* got new girlfriend, *c'est certain, absolument!* 'E say 'e 'as not, but when I call eem last night 'e ees out. 'Ees cellphone ees off and ees flat mate say 'e 'as not been back for some days. 'E ees aizair die or wiz girlfriend.'

'I'm sure there's a good explanation,' I said reassuringly, knowing perfectly well there wouldn't be. 'Perhaps his mobile's broken. Perhaps ... er ... he's had an accident . . . perhaps he had to go off somewhere suddenly. Don't panic. He's probably, um, visiting his parents and forgot to tell you . . .

152

here,' I said, because I couldn't think of anything else to say that wouldn't sound as if I were lying through my teeth. 'Have a pill.'

I handed her a temazepam and saw to it that she swallowed it in front of me. 'Everything will look different in the morning, I promise you.'

30 June

After spending a couple of hours downstairs this morning, I started to feel worried. There was no sign of Michelle. Oh Lord—perhaps she's committed suicide, I thought, my heart racing. I noticed she hadn't had her breakfast—usually evident by the vast array of crumbs around the toaster—and her coat was still hanging up in the hall. But this was surely her early classes day, so God knows what had happened.

I called to her up the stairs, but no reply. Finally I went up to her room and knocked at the door. As there still wasn't a reply, I turned the handle and went in. Piles of clothes, open suitcases, open drawers overflowing with tights and undies, books, a television still on . . . How can people live in such squalor? And in the corner, there was her bed. And she was in it, lying completely still, her face deathly pale under her yellow duvet cover.

Oh Christ! I thought, as I picked a path through the heaps of old clothes to examine her. She's a goner. The pill was far too much for her and she's died in her sleep. I almost prayed to the God that I don't believe in for her to be alive. What had I done? I'd be accused of murder and I'd go to prison and never see Gene, or Jack or Chrissie

153

again. I should *never* have given her that pill. It always says on the bottle 'Not to be taken by anyone except the person for whom it is prescribed' or something. Why had I been such a fool?

My heart was racing and, feeling quite sick with panic, I sat on the edge of her bed and called her name softly. Nothing. Next, I shook her shoulder. Nothing. But at least I noticed she was still breathing. Thank goodness. That meant I'd only be had up for attempted manslaughter, if there is such a thing. I went on shaking her and then, amazingly, she slowly started coming to life.

I was so overcome with emotion that I took her in my arms, held her tight, and burst into tears, surprising myself with my relief.

'Marie, ees okay!' she said, alarmed at my reaction. 'I am sleeping in. No classes today. No worries! Don't cry. Ze tears . . . eez not right for your leefteeng . . .'

Crikey. I'm certainly fragile at the moment. Probably still the result of the anaesthetic. Went downstairs and made myself a strong cup of tea and took one up to Michelle, who was astonished at this outburst of attentiveness.

Later

Oh dear. The new neighbours have moved in. They appear to own a Range Rover and if I go down to the end of the garden and look back I can see they are busy installing some enormous cinema in their kitchen, presumably so they can watch DVDs or baseball all through what Americans laughingly

154

call their meals—i.e. cheeseburgers and waffles and corn cobs and hot dogs and doughnuts and more doughnuts. Washed down with Coke. Or am I just prejudiced?

As I was walking back to the house—the garden is looking brilliant even without the banks of foaming Calibans I was promised—a head popped over the wall and said, 'Hi there!'

'How lovely to meet you!' I said, turning on the charm. 'I was just spying on you—but much nicer to say hello directly! I'm Marie Sharp, oldest resident of the street. In more ways than one.'

'Hi, Marie! We're Sharmie and my husband is Brad! So glad to make your acquaintance. And don't spy! You must come see what we're doing to the house.' This charming woman had a strong East Coast accent and was about forty-five, with red hair and a lively, confident face. 'We can't get over how quaint it all is. There's even a chimney with what you call a fireplace. It's got no central heating! Can you imagine, Marie? It's like a time-warp!'

'You must first come over to see me,' I said, not to be out-polited. 'I was going to put a card through your door to ask you to drinks to welcome you to the street.'

It turns out they have a little girl, Alice, a little younger than Gene, and are only here for a year, but they've bought the house as an investment, determined to do it up and sell it for more than they paid. I immediately told them about Jack and Chrissie and Gene in New York.

'And do you leave a grieving granny behind?' I asked.

'And how!' said Sharmie. At least that's what her

name sounded like. I have no idea what it was short for. 'My mom's in Florida, crying her eyes out. She's in bits over there. Still, she'll be over, Marie. You two will get on, I know it . . . And, hey, there's always Skype.'

We were just making a date for them to come over when she hesitated, and then said, 'You okay, Marie? You look as if maybe you've been in an auto accident?'

'No, I've just had a facelift,' I said, boldly. I mean there was no point in pretending, it must have been obvious.

'Holy Moses, Marie, are you brave!' said Sharmie, pushing away a branch and getting closer to the wall so she could see me better. 'I'm having a lift when I start to sag. Does it hurt? I can't wait to see what you look like when it's all healed up! Good for you, Marie! You've sure got some balls!'

I was very touched by her enthusiasm and when Brad popped out into the garden, overhearing our friendly conversation, he seemed a jolly enough chap, too. I immediately asked if he knew anything about planning law and apparently he does. I expect he's over here advising some dreadful American billionaire about how to ruin the English countryside with strings of casinos or wind farms or something. And she designs kitchens, apparently.

They're coming over next week, with Alice.

Later

Penny came over for a drink in the garden with a couple of petunias she didn't want and didn't think were too late to plant, which she couldn't fit into

156

her garden. I didn't like to tell her about my failure with the Calibans. She also brought some shopping, and a bowl of soup with some cling-film over the top, which was very sweet of her.

We were sitting there chatting away when suddenly Penny said: 'What a lovely tinkling sound! So peaceful.'

I hadn't, frankly, noticed it until she'd pointed it out. But once she'd drawn my attention to them, I could hear them at once—deafening things, the sound of permanent jangling. I'd wondered why Pouncer had been looking so unnerved . . . probably freaked out by the sound. I got up, peered over the wall and saw the source of my anxiety. Sharmie and Brad had installed chimes in their garden.

Odd, isn't it, about chimes? The owners never put the wretched things near their own house, where they can hear them. They go down to the end of the garden and hang them as far away as possible from their own bedroom in order to insulate themselves from the sound, at the same time maddening everyone in the entire neighbourhood with their beastly tinkling.

'Peaceful!' I said, as I returned to sit down. 'It's like having tinnitus.'

'No, they're those special chimes of peace,' said Penny. 'You can hear . . . with little bells . . . they must be from Glastonbury or somewhere. They're meant to soothe and make you feel at one with nature.'

'I feel perfectly at one with nature without having the sound of bells buggering up the whole experience,' I snapped back. 'It's a vile racket, just as bad as having someone playing their blasted

157

radio all the time.'

'You'll get used to them,' said Penny. 'Don't worry. It's just the effects of the anaesthetic that's making you so edgy. You won't notice them after a while.'

Curious how some people think that if you give someone cause for irritation for long enough they'll be able to blank it out eventually. Anyway, how dare she say it was the anaesthetic. It was as irritating as those men who used to tell you you were cross because it was 'that time of the month'.

I shall have to think of a way to get rid of those chimes. Or move.

'I could always superglue them together,' I said, brightly.

'It would be politer just to ask them to take them down.'

'I don't think so,' I said. 'Because if they say "no" and then they find something's happened to them, they'll know it was me. No, I'll have to be more devious than that.'

And suddenly I thought of Archie. He'd have found a way to get them down. He was such a charmer, he'd have got Sharmie and Brad eating out of his hand. I shook my head sadly.

Now I'll have to do it myself.

JULY

2 July

It's funny the strange bits of conversation you pick up while wandering about London. Because you don't hear all of it, they come across as completely surreal. On my way back from having my staples removed—it didn't hurt a bit and afterwards I felt far less a Creature from the Black Lagoon than I had—I passed a girl by my gate who was saying to her friend, with a chatty smile on her face, 'So at least now I know what it's *like* to be raped . . .'

5 July

Finally got my act together to organise signatures for the petition against the hotel. Marion said she'd come with me and she arrived in a long denim skirt with a weird kind of crocheted top, and clutching a stick and a clipboard. It turned out she'd fallen off a ladder yesterday. It was pouring with rain.

'I don't expect you feel like walking very far, and as I'm still recovering from my op, I don't imagine we'll get a lot of signatures,' I said.

'Oh, I don't know,' said Marion, gamely. 'People will feel so sorry for us. We can play the "We're very old" card.'

Having just paid a small fortune for the facelift (or rather about to pay a small fortune when the money comes through from the auction) I wasn't

159

very much in the mood for playing that particular card, but I didn't say anything and we set out.

Amazingly, within an hour and a half, we'd each got about fifty signatures—people were very keen to sign, particularly when they found out we weren't selling anything—and I was rather struck by the number of people far younger than me who were hanging around at home on a Monday afternoon; I thought they'd all be out at work. Maybe the *Rant* knows what it's talking about. We were both exhausted and finally returned for a cup of tea. Then Marion started. (She's such a kindly and warm-hearted woman, but my goodness, she could take a PhD in moaning.)

'So many unemployed,' she sighed, as she sat down. 'What is the world coming to? I despair. And did you know that there are over half a million out of work and on benefits and so many single parents? They get pregnant just to get a council house and the money, you know, no other reason. And they spend all their child benefit on drugs.'

I waited for the kettle to boil. She went on. 'Honestly, they have such short attention spans these days, it's hopeless. I don't think anyone's going to read a book after we're dead. It's all this Facebook and Twitter—God knows what they are—no wonder they riot in the streets, they've got nothing to do and all they're interested in is material things . . .'

'Let's count the signatures,' I said firmly. 'And let's thank our lucky stars that three of them promised to collect signatures from their tower blocks . . .'

'It's so sad no one wants to get involved these

days, isn't it?' said Marian. 'In the old days we were always marching and petitioning and trying to save the world, and now no one can be bothered even to put their signature to something right under their noses. Fear I suppose. When I think of how *we* were in the seventies, so full of optimism, hoping to change the world with peace and love, and now look . . .' She shook her head dolefully.

'Oh, well, we'll all be dead soon,' I said reassuringly. I'm never comfortable with anyone, even sweet old Marion, droning on about the good old days. 'Or we'll all be wiped out in a plague. Or a nuclear bomb will blow us all up. Or the internet will collapse and it'll be the end of civilisation as we know it . . . that would fix everything wouldn't it? We could start again from scratch. Look at the Ancient Egyptians. Not a trace of them now.'

'Oh, don't say that!' said Marion.

She was so distressed at the idea of Armageddon that she shut up, clutching on to the table. Felt a bit mean, so I thanked her profusely, let her out of the door and watched her as she pottered down the street with her stick and clipboard, and then I crawled upstairs to have a rest.

6 July

Though I still look pretty peculiar, I decided to go with Sylvie to look at a nursing home she thinks might be suitable for Archie. Mrs Evans said she'd spend the day with him, so Sylvie is free, and Harry, her husband, is away on business. So I was really touched that she wanted me to go and help

161

her.

Even though I'd warned her I'd be covered in scarves and dark glasses to cover up my bruises, Sylvie still looked a bit shocked when she opened the door to me. But she politely said she was sure I would look wonderful in a few weeks. Then she showed me some brochures and said all the homes she'd visited so far were hopeless. There were only two more to see, one of which we were going to visit now. It was called Eventide—part of an American chain—and set in the kind of Devon countryside that's always described as 'rolling'.

It turned out that Eventide was frightfully posh and impressive. There was a lake and a wood, and a very large car park for all the visitors' cars (mostly urban jeeps), and even a cafe and playroom in the reception area for families who visited with children. It looked like one of those country house spas that were so popular in the seventies—I once won a week in one in a raffle and Penny had jokingly said, 'First prize, one week in luxury spa. Second prize, two weeks.' Anyway, Eventide consisted of three buildings. One was called Afternoon where there were lots of people pottering about in proper clothes. You felt you could even strike up a worthwhile conversation with them. At least I think you could. I have to say that neither Sylvie nor I tried, feeling too ashamed, nervous and generally appalled by the whole set-up to dare to speak to anyone.

Next was Evening, a long two-storey building overlooking the lake. And finally, Sunset—which was more like palliative care. This was a gloomy building with very few windows and surrounded by pines, all on one floor just in case any of the inhabitants had the sudden urge to leap from their windows. Not that many were, of course, capable of leaping.

Once inside, what struck us was how suffocatingly hot it was in all the rooms.

'Why do you keep it at tropical temperatures?' we asked a nurse.

'Our guests often lose their temperature thermostat,' said the nurse. 'Hypothermia.'

Sylvie and I looked at each other. There was nowhere colder, as I've said, than Archie's house.

We looked at the sort of room that Archie might be in, and I suppose it could have been worse. It was light. There was a very high bed with lots of levers on it, presumably for the day when he becomes bedridden and needs to be able to tip it up and down himself to make it more comfortable. There was a very nice-looking armchair for him to sit in and an upright chair for visitors. A television. And even double doors leading out onto a small walled garden full of alternately red and cream plants that looked as if a gardener had only just stuck them in that morning. Obviously not Calibans from the banks-of-foaming-colours nursery.

'What do you think, Marie?' said Sylvie, as we left. 'I know it's grim, but at least it's in the country. And it's very luxurious. And the staff seem nice.'

'It *is* grim,' I said, 'but it's a whole lot better than most old people's homes I've been in.' I remembered when I'd been to visit my aunt. The whole place had smelt of pee and it was full of tragic old gentlemen strapped to their chairs and screaming for their mothers. 'If you can afford it, I

163

don't think you could do much better. At least there are lovely views.'

'I don't think we need look at the other one. It's far nicer than anything I've seen. And I've seen some grisly places, I can tell you!' she said.

I agreed. The truth was that I suddenly felt so absolutely knackered—as one does after an operation—that the idea of going to visit anywhere else was quite beyond me. I thought I was going to faint.

'I'll book him in. Oh Marie, isn't it sad!'

It is sad, but I'm afraid that, since Archie won't really *know* where he is, it won't *matter* so much to him where he is.

8 July

Spent most of the day in bed, having driven back last night after an emotional day.

I was hoping James had forgotten about the installation, but unfortunately when he rang asking if he could bring me an early supper—always nice, even though by now I can make supper perfectly well myself—he asked if he could also bring over a collection of 'found objects'. He wanted me to sit in the garden, while he assembled these bits and decided how to put them together to make an 'impression' of me. It was one of those rather depressingly grey, humid summer days and I didn't really feel like going out, particularly as yesterday I'd done so much weeding I thought my back would break.

But he is such a sweetie. The first thing he did as he came in was to take a long look at me and say,

'Well, my darling! Shaping up nicely! The swelling is really going down isn't it? You're still a bit puffy round the eyes, but that'll soon go. Hasn't it all been a huge success? Aren't you thrilled?'

Now James has put the seal of approval on the facelift I think I can turn the camera back on Skype without Jack or Chrissie knowing anything's been done. Particularly if I sit a bit further away from the camera than usual. On Skype everyone looks as if they've just had a facelift anyway, all distorted, so I doubt anyone will notice I've actually had one.

'And how's Ned?' I asked.

'He's fine!' said James enthusiastically. 'And do you know what? I actually managed to persuade him to eat some butter yesterday! Isn't that brilliant! I think I might be turning him into a vegetarian rather than a vegan. And after that, who knows . . . lamb chops, steaks . . .'

'Boiled babies . . . lightly grilled!' I said.

James unloaded all his stuff into the garden, and looked a bit nervous when I showed such shock and horror when he unrolled a lumpy old bedspread and laid out a few clothes pegs, some rusty razor blades, half a bicycle, the skull of a fox and a rusty old walking frame.

'I hope you don't think any of that looks like me!' I said.

'No, no, it'll be quite different,' said James hastily. 'I just brought these round for inspiration.'

'Well, I was expecting you'd bring round a jug of sparkling water, a bunch of flowers, a piece of moss and a bird's nest, or something romantic, not this old crap,' I said tartly.

'Oh, no, there'll be plenty of moss and charm,'

said James anxiously, as he fiddled around. 'It's all just to give me ideas about the basic structure. This walking frame isn't there to "say" anything. I just thought it would help prop the whole thing up.'

I sat—staring suspiciously at the pile of old junk—in a rickety garden chair, with Pouncer jumping on flies around me, listening to the tinkle tinkle tinkle of the neighbour's chimes.

'Aren't they frightful?' I said.

'What?' said James.

'The chimes!' I said, and felt like adding, 'Are you deaf?'

He cocked his head, coyly. Then he said, 'Funny—I didn't hear them till you drew my attention to them. Now you point them out, aren't they lovely—so soothing!'

'*Soothing!* I can't get them out of my head,' I said. 'Honestly, these new neighbours! They're so nice, but that racket's not very neighbourly of them, is it? Sometimes I swear I can even hear them tinkling away in the middle of the night when there's not a breath of wind. I may have to move house.'

James said nothing as he fiddled with bits of wire, then broke a few small twigs from a nearby bush, and stuck them at odd angles around the fox's skull.

'You wouldn't pop over the wall and take them down, would you, angel?' I said. 'And that's not meant to be my hair, is it?'

James looked shocked. 'I'll do no such thing!' he said. 'Not even for you, my heart of hearts. I'd be had up for trespassing. You take them down yourself if you don't like them!'

Which gave me an idea.

166

Later

At about midnight, having fortified myself with three large glasses of Pinot Grigio and played *The Best of Aretha Franklin* at full volume on my CD player to give me Dutch courage, and done a bit of dancing round the room to get up my courage even more, rather like those Maori rugby players, I went out into the garden with a pair of scissors and the rickety garden chair. I took the chair to the end of the garden, stood on it, clambered up on to the wall, dragged the chair up after me, placed it in my neighbour's garden, tiptoed down on to it, and then crept, my heart in my mouth, to the tree where the chimes were hanging, and cut them down. Of course I should have brought wads of cotton wool to muffle the sound, but as the whole escapade had been a spur-of-the-moment thing and I'd had one glass too many, I'd forgotten, so I had to place the chimes carefully in my skirt to prevent any sound, put my foot on the chair and promptly stepped on Pouncer who had followed me, keen to be in on the act. I screamed, Pouncer let out an almighty 'Miaaow! and my foot went through the seat of the chair with a great crash.

I can tell you, I'd never make a burglar. It's only because Shepherd's Bush is full of such shrieks and yells at night that no one came rushing out to discover what was going on.

Somehow I managed to pick up all the incriminating pieces of the smashed chair, throw them over my wall, scramble up myself, make it back inside, and found myself, slightly drunk and sweating with horror, wondering what on earth to do with the chimes. Eventually, convinced that I'd be found out if I kept them in the house or put them in my bin, I sellotaped the chimes together to prevent them making any noise, wrapped them in newspaper, crept out of the house and over the road, and put them in the wheelie bin of Father Emmanuel's garage-cum-church.

I went to bed shaking with guilt, imagining a knock on the door and the police standing there with handcuffs. I could visualise the headline in the *Rant*, with a dreadful blurred CCTV picture of me in my nightdress, furtively dropping the wind-chimes into a bin. I could just imagine the story: 'SHAME OF PENSIONER CHIME-STEALER! *65-year-old Marie Sharp, described by her neighbours as a pillar of the community, leads a Jekyll-and-Hyde life. By day, a peace-loving retired art teacher, by night she turns, hell-bent on devastating her local area by stealing garden features. "She has just had a facelift," revealed a neighbour who did not wish to be named. "Perhaps this drove her to this crazy behaviour." Police are also questioning her about a garden gnome missing from a local hospice . . .'*

Now I'm up and it's two in the morning (the Worrying Hour) and I SO wish I hadn't done it. I'm sure they'll know it was me. But of course it's too late. I can't go over the road, collect the chimes from the wheelie bin, unsellotape them, hop over the wall again and put them back. Besides, my trusty chair is now well and truly out of action.

Isn't it awful when you do wrong like that and there's no putting it right? The guilt! At this moment, feeling as I do, I'd be quite happy to die in my sleep.

4 a.m.

While I was writing, I heard the distant sound of soul music. Surely not! No one could be playing music at this time of the morning! This was beyond a joke. I tried to block it out, but couldn't. I took a pill, but that didn't work, and at 3 a.m. I crept downstairs to go out into the garden to see who was making such a frightful racket at this hour.

The sound got louder and louder as I neared the kitchen—and then I realised that I'd left the CD player on and it was just playing and replaying Aretha Franklin. I burst out laughing, turned it off and stumbled back to bed.

9 July

Nothing from the neighbours about the chimes, but as I was going out of my front door, Sharmie came out of hers and it was too late to duck down. I gave her a sickly smile, going bright red as I did so. She returned my smile with a twinkling, knowing look. I've been rumbled, I thought. She was only smiling because she'd tipped off the police and knew they were due any minute. Her lawyer husband was at this very minute constructing a watertight case against me. I could see the pitying way she looked at me as she contemplated my last days of freedom. For a moment perhaps she was regretting what she had done . . . But no.

'Some party you had last night, huh?' she

169

boomed, in a 'gee whizz' sort of voice.

'Oh, I'm so sorry,' I burbled. 'It was the lodger. I've ticked her off. I do hope it didn't disturb you!'

'Hell no, we all sleep like logs,' she said. 'You're looking great after your op! I must get the name of your medic. By the way, what's all this about the trees at the top of the road? They're not going to build a hotel, are they?'

And thankfully I was able to turn the conversation round to a diatribe about how frightful the council was and dragoon her and Brad onto the Residents' Association Committee. Saved by the bell. Or, in this case, bells.

12 July

New vacuum cleaner arrived today, in one of those vast cardboard boxes big enough to fit a body in. At last. I tore it open—it was like wrestling with one of those endangered rhinos—and was infuriated to find one of the parts was missing. The engine bit was there, where all the fluff and dust is collected, the brushy bit at the end which picks up the dirt, and different attachments and the flexible hose, but where there should have been two straight tubes of plastic to slot into each other to give the length, there was only one.

After going mad looking up the number of the manufacturer on the internet, and waiting for hours to get on to the right person, I finally got through to someone called Nairit who asked how he could help.

'I'll tell you how!' I shouted furiously, after having crawled on the floor to get the new cleaner's model number, and rifled through the torn packaging to find my order number which had been concealed in a plastic envelope on the box, and spelled my name a hundred times and given him my postcode. 'I've waited weeks for your wretched machine to arrive, and now it's come without one of its parts!'

He asked me patiently which bit was missing and I explained. 'It's utterly hopeless! In the old days, you'd go into a shop and a nice man would give you what you wanted and explain it all to you . . .' I exploded. I was into full *Rant* mode now. 'And now it's all online there's no personal service, I don't even know what you look like, you might as well be speaking from Mars . . . You pay your money, you expect excellent service from a firm like yours, you wait in for days to take delivery of the thing you ordered and when it arrives it's missing a crucial bit! I'm furious!'

There was a pause.

'Have you looked at the instructions, madam?' asked Nairit calmly.

'That's another thing!' I shouted. 'There are no instructions! There are just meaningless pictures with crosses and ticks on them which are completely baffling to any normal person!'

'You have one of the plastic tubes?' said Nairit.

'I have. But what's the use of one without two? If I were nine inches high, the size of a goblin, yours would be the ideal vacuum cleaner for me, but curiously I am a normal-sized human being and I don't wish to have to crouch down to clean my house . . .'

'I think you'll find,' said Nairit, politely, 'that there is a little button on the outside of the plastic tube you already have. If you press it, you will find that an inner tube is released which extends the tube to the correct length.'

Well, of course, I was dumbfounded. I spluttered, and faffed around, tried to get out of it by grumbling that the instructions weren't clear, and ended up feeling like *such* a loony.

Poor old Nairit.

14 July

Oh dear, there's a bit of me that misses the family so much I sometimes think I might just drive to Land's End, jump into my bathing costume, smear myself in goose fat and simply start swimming until I get to New York. Highly unlikely, of course. I can barely do a width in our local pool, but you get the drift. I miss them so much it's almost unbearable.

'It's different, here, Granny,' said Gene firmly, when we next talked on Skype. I had managed to smother my face with make-up and sit rather far away so I knew he wouldn't be able to see me properly. He paused. 'They call poo "shit" here, Granny. That's a very rude word, isn't it, Granny?'

'What about the teacher?' I asked changing the subject. Perhaps they didn't call them teachers in American schools. Perhaps they called them 'tutors' or 'instructors' or 'mentors' or 'educators'.

'He's so dumb,' said Gene, firmly. 'He don't know nothing. And we have to sing some silly song, well Dad says it's silly, about America every morning. It ends up saying "my home sweet home", but America isn't home, Dad says, England is home.'

'Well, I'm sure Dad's right,' I said cautiously, 'but it might be best just to go along with it because people can be very touchy and if you say you don't like their country they can get very silly. I mean you wouldn't like it if people said England was stupid, would you?'

'And they call chips "fries" here. That's dumb, isn't it? They're chips, aren't they? Not fries.'

'It must be very puzzling for you,' I said, my mind aching with sympathy for the little chap. 'I wish I could be with you and pick you up from school and things sometimes.'

'It's very cold here, Granny,' he added. 'We have arcon and we can't turn it down. Do you have arcon, Granny?'

'I think you mean air-con,' I said. 'It's short for air conditioning.' That's the sort of stupid thing one says to children to try to educate them as one speaks. Who cares if it's short for air conditioning or not?

'Well, ours is called arcon,' said Gene defiantly. Then, 'How is my jersey going?' he asked. 'Can I see it?'

I went and got it. With Marion's help, I've finally managed to finish the back.

'Now that's cool!' he said, sounding far too American for my taste. 'When will you finish it?'

'Probably when you're twelve,' I said, 'When you're far too old to want to wear something with elephants on it.'

'Well, hurry up,' he said sensibly. Then he said: 'I've got to go . . . Dad's calling . . . love you, Granny.'

'Love you too, darling,' I said, blowing him a kiss.

173

3.30 a.m.

Tonight I can't sleep for worry. All I can think of is poor Gene being so cold and low, and for a brief moment I actually wished I hadn't had Jack, because then he wouldn't have had Gene and Gene wouldn't be suffering like this. And then I wouldn't be suffering. Of course I remember thinking exactly the same thing about Jack when he was at school and came back agonising about some unfair punishment. I just felt it was all my fault. To my horror I then imagined Gene grown up and having children and *them* feeling low and at that point I got a grip of myself, poured myself a glass of water, and read the horoscope that was in the copy of the *Rant* that I'd kept by my bed.

I was relieved to find it said, 'You can worry all you like. But however much you berate yourself, you cannot stop the inexorable rise of Uranus, which means that your wildest dreams are about to come true.' (I hoped he wasn't thinking of my *actual* dreams.) 'You are about to enter one of the happiest and most peaceful times of your life. For more information about the great week that lies ahead, call the number below and listen to my prediction for you as a Capricorn. Calls will cost just 75p a minute. Mobiles may vary.'

There was a curious drawing of the astrologer himself at the top of the column, an intense, balding man, with piercing eyes, staring into an astrological chart.

Batty as it was, it made me feel a lot better. I took half a temazepam, stared at my pile of books, wondered if I could possibly continue with Philip Larkin's *Letters to Monica*, that I'd started this month, decided against it, and finally went to sleep.

20 July

Well, I'm glad to see that even *I* think I'm looking a lot more normal now. Some of the bruises have dropped down to my neck, so I look rather as though someone's tried to strangle me, but if I wear a scarf or a polo-necked jersey I don't look too bad at all. I just look a tiny bit swollen. I've decided to be completely open about it—and I will tell Jack when I go over. I just didn't want him to worry beforehand. The reason I tell people is not because I'm such a frank and fearless sort of person, but because I can't bear the thought of them whispering behind my back that I've had a facelift as if I were some foolish vain woman who wanted to put the clock back in secret. I want everyone to know exactly how old I am, that I've had a facelift, and if they want to make something of it then they can jolly well step outside.

23 July

Sharmie and Brad and Alice have just been over for a drink and they are absolutely delightful. With typical American generosity they brought a bottle of champagne *and* chocolates *and* a huge bunch of roses, and I felt awful having only provided warm white wine, olives and crisps. Particularly having destroyed their wind-chimes as well.

Alice, who is a sweet little girl, immediately got stuck into the box of Gene's toys I keep in the sitting room, and right away developed an epic scenario between a stuffed kangaroo, an orange frog and a blue rabbit. I saw that a plastic Batman had also made an appearance and longed to get down on my hands and knees to enter her imaginary world, but adulthood called, and I busied myself by briefing her parents about the entire street. I told them about the dispute over the 'common' at the top of the road and told them about my project, the Seasons of the Doomed Trees, and Brad was mad keen to appear as an expert witness if there's some inquiry. They were both very enthusiastic about the idea of joining the Residents' Association. I told them about Father Emmanuel and his evangelical church. And I told them about the mosque, which adjoins their garden as well as mine.

'We're not best pleased with that mosque, Marie,' said Brad.

'You know what they did? They actually *cut down* the chimes at the end of the garden,' said Sharmie, leaning forward to pick up a crisp.

'Beats me why anyone would do such a thing,' said Brad. 'I mean who the hell would object to chimes?'

'It's because of their beliefs, we guess,' said Sharmie. 'They don't approve of musical instruments. And I think it maybe interfered with their prayers.'

'But we're letting it go,' said Brad. 'We don't want to start up a holy war. So we're backing down.'

176

'It's Alice who's really upset,' said Sharmie, selecting an olive with her immaculately painted nails. 'Those beautiful chimes were given her by her grandma back in Florida, who said, "Now every time, my little darling, you hear these chimes, you can think of me, and you'll know I'm thinking of you." Wasn't that just lovely?'

At this point I decided to kill myself with shame, Japanese-style. Her granny's lovely present! If only I'd known I wouldn't have *minded* the noise! I felt myself going redder and redder and was just about to confess when Alice piped up. 'But grandma's gonna send me some more, and we're gonna keep them in my bedroom now so those horrid mosquey people can't get them!'

'Good idea!' I said, in a strangled voice.

To make matters worse, they actually insisted on seeing the four pictures I'd done so far of the Seasons of the Doomed Trees, and absolutely fell about with praise and admiration. Brad even asked tentatively if, when I'd finished, he might be able to buy the lot. 'To remind us of our great time in London,' he added.

When they went I actually felt so guilty that if Father Emmanuel had pointed me to the entrance to hell, I would gladly have walked straight in.

24 July

Just had another meeting of the Residents' Association and Sharmie and Brad from next door came as well. Brad turns out to be a genius. He only has to scan the council's website, and he's picked up everything about local planning law.

177

He's drafted our letter brilliantly, citing sub-section 5 from the council's own planning recommendations, and pointing out that it is against their own policy according to item 19a in their Blueprint for the Borough . . . or something. I don't understand a word of it, but Penny says it's excellent, so I don't think we're going to have a problem.

I got a surprising letter this morning from the developer behind the hotel proposal asking if he could meet us, and when I told everyone he'd been in touch there was a general roar of delight, like Romans about to enjoy an excellent show of Christians being thrown to the lions.

'Yes! Let's 'ave 'im!' shouted Sheila the Dealer, through a haze of smoke. 'I'd like to give 'im a piece of my mind!'

Father Emmanuel sat quietly, absorbed, no doubt, in some spiritual thought.

We've got an enormous petition together, what with everyone going out and getting signatures and even Father Emmanuel came up with thirty signatures from his hell-bound congregation. Sheila the Dealer has got about a hundred—I don't know how she managed it but no doubt a lot of people 'owe her'. I can imagine her telling her hollow-eyed clients, queuing at her door and begging for further supplies of crack, 'Not until you've signed this petition, mate!' When you add them all up there are 560 signatures, so I don't think the council can possibly overlook our objections.

Penny's going to photocopy the petition and then we're taking it round to the council on Thursday.

25 July

Woke to find not only that the boiler had broken so there was no hot water, but also the news, in the *Rant*, that a 'TEEN HARLOT! *Loughborough sex-worker has ten children by eight different fathers, each one a dole scrounger . . .*' Thanks a lot. I really don't wish to know this. I think I might have to stop getting the *Rant*. How often have I said this? It has the extraordinary effect of geeing you up while lowering you, all at the same time.

The plumber came over this afternoon to stare at my boiler. We went through the usual 'Who installed this? Why are your settings like this? Surely you don't want it on all day? Why isn't the pilot light lit? What's your water pressure like?' and all kinds of questions that, like the computer questions, make me feel sick with fear, but he managed to get it working again, saying he thought the rads needed bleeding and there might be a leak in one of the valve sockets which would cause the boiler to lose pressure. He might as well have been speaking Japanese. He went round the house looking for leaks, and managed to fix one he discovered in Michelle's room, under piles of dirty underwear. It had been soaking into the carpet.

'That's your problem,' he said, in a monotone voice.

I wish someone could bleed *my* rads, I thought. Or fix *my* leaks. From the moment I wake up, I feel as if I'm losing pressure all day.

27 July

This morning the money came from the sale of the three pictures and the brooch at auction. Amazingly it's £9,000 altogether, so not only can I pay Mr P.'s fees, but I also have a bit over and with it I shall fly over to the States in style.

I was so enthused by the prospect that I started to look at flight times online. I have to say the idea of visiting the family in New York put a real spring in my step.

When I skyped Jack late this evening he was thrilled.

'Mum, that's great!' he said. He actually called out to Chrissie and Gene who were in another room, 'Mum's coming over!'

I was rather surprised to hear him being *quite* so enthusiastic. Could it be that he was actually missing me? Or, more likely, missing London?

'When?' he asked. 'Do come soon. Come as soon as you can—next month. Or early September. We've got a bit of time off then. It would be great to see you.'

Gene came running into the room in his aeroplane pyjamas and scrambled onto Jack's knee to join in the conversation.

'Granny, Granny!' he said. 'Are you coming over? I can show you my new school! And we're going camping next week! And it's so cool here . . .! We'll take you up the Empire State and we can go on a boat . . . Dad, we can go on a boat, can't we, you promised . . .? Just a minute . . .' And here he vanished from the screen and I was facing

180

an empty chair for ages. All I could hear was him chattering away in a far-away room. After about ten minutes, when I was just about to give up, Jack burst into view. 'Mum! You're still here! Sorry, I didn't realise Gene had left the Skype on.'

Of course all this sudden enthusiasm for New York from Gene changed my mood completely, as I realised he'd got completely hooked on the place, but I kept smiling. However, once we'd made arrangements for when I'd go, I suddenly felt like dancing. I put on an old Dr John record in the kitchen and cavorted about like a maniac.

28 July

I was having another dance in the morning when Penny rang the bell. I answered it gasping and sweating.

'What on earth have you been doing?'

'Dancing!' I said. 'I'm going to New York! Isn't it great?'

'When?'

'I hope maybe September.'

'Oh, but you'll miss my birthday!' she said, not joining in the spirit of the thing at all.

'But you hate your birthday,' I said, puzzled.

'Oh, I've had so many I've given up hating them these days.'

We sorted out the petition into piles on the kitchen table and put everything into respectable folders to look nice and professional.

On the way to the town hall the bus was rather crowded and a youngish woman with headphones offered Penny her seat, which Penny refused.

'It's not as if I'm decrepit!' she muttered angrily, as she clung on to the rail in the bus. 'How dare she offer me a seat!'

But when we got off I laid into her. 'You're so bad-mannered!' I said. 'If someone offers you a seat you should jolly well take it even if it does make you feel old. You've got to encourage young people to be polite and the more you turn down their offers of help the more you're discouraging them. I wish she'd offered *me* a seat! *I'd* have taken it like a shot!'

'Well she wouldn't have offered you a seat, would she?' said Penny, suddenly rather vicious. 'Because you look so *young* now, don't you!'

We walked on in frosty silence, but our row had blown over by the time we'd handed in the petition.

'Yes, all right, I *will* let people get up for me in future,' Penny muttered as we went back.

'Sorry I was so snappy,' I said.

AUGUST

2 August

I was standing in the street wondering what on earth I'd come out to do when one of the men from the mosque, a very nice-looking chap with a bushy beard and wearing a long white dress, came up to me. (How can they wear all that gear in this weather? It's boiling hot. Beyond me.)

'Can I help you?' he said. 'You look a bit lost.'

Golly, that made me think. I picture myself as the confident local, sauntering down the street on my way to the shops, but clearly he saw me as a barmy old lady, completely confused, only a step away from the Eventide experience.

4 August

Just back from the old school reunion organised by Marion. Crikey, what a bunch! The weird thing is that, despite the fact that we were all fifty years older than when we'd last met, we felt exactly as we did when we were ten or eleven. Wrinkles, grey hairs, middle-aged spread—they were merely incidental.

About eight of us met in Marion's house . . . and of course it's an ideal place to have a school reunion because it's like a time warp. She stopped paying any attention to stylish interior design or new wallpaper patterns in the early seventies. She still has old spider plants mouldering on the

183

window ledges, and jars of dried flowers now weighed down with dust. Each room is dominated by a faded—sometimes even split—round white (or once-white) paper lampshade, and she still has Dali and Che Guevara posters hanging on the walls in clip frames between the Indian wall-hangings. Her floor is covered in the most ghastly grass matting, which was tremendously cool and lovely when it was new but is now worn and frayed and held together with gaffer tape in the worn areas. Even the soap in the bathroom looks as if it's been there for the past twenty years, dried-up and ingrained with black lines of dirt.

But she's a sweetie, and even though her cuisine relies almost entirely on beans and lentils, and she's not a natural cook, she provided huge bowls of steaming soup and bread she'd made herself, and rather wodgy pasta salads, and I'd brought lots of wine, so we had a feast on the broken-down ramshackle stripped-pine kitchen table, another relic from the sixties. It's not that Marion and Tim, her husband, are skint, it's just that she's someone who believes that food is just fuel, and friends and feelings and books are all that matter.

Charming, of course, but it does mean that after lunch with Marion you feel a bit leaden round the old tum.

We all gathered round to stare, astonished, at the photographs of each other's grown-up children, children far older than the age we were when we last met. And as we all goggled at the old school photographs Marion had laid out on the table before lunch, grey heads bent earnestly, in that split second I was transported back to our classroom. The only thing that was missing was our battered old school desks.

Smothered as we all were in colognes and deodorants, I swear I could still smell the familiar odour of pencil shavings, stale milk and unwashed hair among us. We giggled as we reminded each other of how terrified we used to be of the old Austrian music teacher, we sighed about how sad it was that Mrs Leach had died ('But did you know? She *drank!*') and we gossiped about whether Mr Hitchin was actually gay.

There's a peculiar ease about being with people we've known in childhood, even if we haven't seen them since. Because although we've been changed and shaped by life's subsequent experiences, we remain essentially the same. Gilly, who was the netball captain, was dressed now in a designer suit rather than navy gym shorts, but she still bounded energetically into the house with the ease and poise of a natural athlete. And Emily, the class brainbox, might have settled down to make jam in her retirement, but she's still the only one of us who can remember everyone's names, the names of their parents or nannies, and even the dates of their birthdays.

A successful reunion is like a family get-together. They say that fate chooses our relatives, but we choose our friends. And fate, because we are powerless over who we end up in class with, also chooses our school friends. We were thrown together—the good, the bad and the ugly—and whether we liked it or not we had to get on with each other.

No one I know really liked their old school. Nor did the girls from ours, which was, according to most other people's accounts of their own schools, remarkably civilised. The food was inedible, there were only two loos for 140 young girls, but it was run on liberal Froebel lines, there were no punishments except being sent to the headmistress, and we called the teachers by their Christian names.

Yet, amiable as it was, we all bonded together in a loathing of school as a system and, as a result, we tolerated even the worst of each other's characteristics—something we rarely do as adults.

Crowning moment was down to Marion. She couldn't resist doing her old jug-of-water-passing trick on me, with the result that I was completely soaked. Luckily, knowing the state of Marion's chairs and having sat, frequently, in patches of honey and jam and found my elbows sliding on pools of drying yoghurt on her table, I hadn't put on my smartest clothes, so nothing was spoilt.

There were endless cries of 'But you look *just* the same!' and then the odd cry, to me, of 'But *you*, Marie, really *do* look just the same!' so I had to fess up about the facelift, whereupon they all got out their pens and notebooks begging for Mr P.'s details. Most pleasing.

We broke up at about four o'clock, and everyone was terribly affectionate, all clutching each other and hugging and saying 'I love you' as if we were never going to see each other again.

Which is, of course, probably true.

9 August

We had a very quick emergency evening Residents' Association meeting because the hotel developer man was so anxious to meet us. I don't think he yet knows that there's a 560-signature-strong petition waiting at the council.

He arrived—Ross Shatterton by name—with a whole retinue of designers, architects and personal assistants, and was extremely ingratiating and charming to everyone present. We all took an immediate dislike to him. Penny pursed her lips. James and Ned raised their eyebrows at one another. Father Emmanuel stared at him as if he were destined for the burning fiery furnace and Sheila the Dealer wore an expression that would have made the most penurious drug addict pay up. Tim looked cagey, Sharmie and Brad's expressions were totally blank, and only Marion gave her beaming smile. Ross ('Call me Ross, guys!') looked about twenty-five, with a shaven head and ring in one ear, and it was clear that he thought he was going to coast through the meeting charming the socks off a bunch of cantankerous complainers and then sail out, job done.

How wrong he was.

He gave us what he called a 'snapshot presentation' with slides and photographs, and drawings which made our triangle of green at the top of the road look like a naturalist's paradise, the blue skies teeming with birds, huge bushes surrounding the hotel, dogs jumping about—I wouldn't have been surprised to see he'd featured the odd rare rhino just to emphasise the thorough eco-ness of the plan—and he swore it would 'raise the tone of the neighbourhood', a phrase that made Sheila the Dealer's hackles rise at once.

'Bollocks!' she yelled, through a cloud of smoke at the end of the table. 'What's bleedin' wrong with the neighbourhood as it is now, might I ask, Mr Shitterton or wha'ever your name is?'

Ross gave what he thought was a charming laugh and looked around at all of us as if to say, 'I know this woman's mad, we all do, but we're just humouring her.' We all stared stony-faced at him. Even Marion's smile was fast fading. He was on his own.

'What I mean is,' he stammered, 'that it could raise the tone of the neighbourhood even *higher*. And if anyone of you are worried about parking . . .'

'We certainly are,' said Tim, in a loud voice. 'We can barely get a space in this, our own street, as it is.'

'Well, we have plans to build an underground car park to house fifty cars. And as members of the Residents' Association committee we would of course be very happy to allocate you free places if that would make your lives easier . . .'

'You tryin' to bribe us?' screamed Sheila the Dealer. 'Because it don't cut no ice with me. 'Arf the street don't even 'ave a car, so don't pull that one!'

'No, no . . . but I think you will like the design of the building. The interior will be entirely of marble, and it will only have forty rooms. It's more of a *boutique* hotel . . .'

'Forty double rooms,' corrected James. 'In other words eighty people. That's a hell of a lot. By the way, you will accept gay couples, won't you?'

'Well of course,' said Ross. 'That is the law . . .'

'Gay couples?' muttered Father Emmanuel to himself. 'Homosexuals?' He shook his head in a way that seemed to imply that all gays were

188

doomed and damned.

In the end Ross greasily told us what a pleasure it was meeting us and gave us his mobile number so that, 'if any of you have any concerns you can be in touch with me twenty-four seven!' and took his 'snapshot presentation' kit, his portfolios and his entourage of assistants off to 'another meeting.'

He left the committee even more determined to make a stand against the hotel than before.

'Twenty-four-seven! I like that!' said Sheila the Dealer, lighting a fag from the burning stub of another. 'What the 'ell does that mean? I'll try ringin' 'im at four in the mornin' to ask 'ow late the knees-ups will go on for and wevver they'll be servin' pie and mash in their fuckin' dinin' rooms! Hee-hee!' And she started coughing and wheezing.

Just starting the front of Gene's jersey. Hope the elephants look better on the front than they did on the back. They seemed to have trunks coming out of their bottoms.

10 August

Rather a sad Skype with Gene. He said his classmates are laughing at his accent.

'They keep asking me to say Harry Potter, Granny,' he said. 'I don't like it. And when I say I don't want to say Harry Potter they say, "Listen to the way he says I don't want—isn't it cute?" I don't want to be cute.'

'You're not at all cute, darling,' I said, indignantly. 'You're the least cute person I know.'

This of course was a great lie. Gene is the cutest, cleverest and kindest child in the universe. Really.

189

Gene smiled. 'It'll be great when you come over, won't it?'

It certainly will.

11 August

After Sylvie had reserved a place for Archie at Eventide, we had to wait for someone to die before he could move in. It does all seem utterly macabre, despite the fact that the decision is totally rational. Luckily, a place became vacant almost at once (in a darkly curious way I couldn't help wondering who it was), and we're moving him in next week. We've talked about it with him for a couple of weeks now, and he seems to understand, but of course you never know. One minute he's quite accepting and stoical about it, the next he says he's perfectly okay and doesn't need to move, but sometimes he's pitifully begging us to let him stay at home, and saying he'll try to be better. It's agony.

15 August

Just back from staying a couple of days with Penny at her bungalow in Suffolk. On Saturday, I said I was going to pop down to the shops—the high street is packed with all kinds of places you don't find in London, like a shop that only sells pet food, and the store which is stuffed with racks of practical jokes—packets of Itching Powder and Sneezing Powder and Floating Sugar Lumps. I always stock up for Gene. I'm keen, too, on the Cats' Rescue Centre which has offered up, in its time, a wonderful set of Victorian dinner plates and even a rock'n'roll skirt, complete with netted petticoats. Not to mention the famous Cats' Rescue jacket that I bought all those years ago, which still comes in useful on a nippy day.

Penny had said she had to do some cooking and then she'd pop out when I came back, leaving the door on the latch, but as I'd been so long browsing and shopping in the town I wasn't surprised to find her gone when I returned. I called and called, but no reply. After such a lengthy shopping spree, I staggered to my room, unpacked my enormous pile of loot, hopped into bed for a quick afternoon doze and fell asleep.

When I woke an hour later, I looked around the house and was very disturbed to find Penny still not back. Clearly, she had gone out and died. She'd had a heart attack in the vegetable shop and died. She'd fallen, foaming at the mouth, outside the grocers and died. What on earth was I to do? I had a vague memory that I'd kept her brother's phone number somewhere in case of emergency . . . at what point should I phone him? Or, even, the police? And how would I get my car out of the drive since hers was blocking mine in?

Shaking, I returned to my room to look for my address book and as I stumbled out into the hall again, I heard a noise. There was someone in the sitting room—obviously a concerned young policeman come to tell me the bad news. He'd been trained for such moments. It was the bit of his job he liked least. Bracing myself for this frightful confrontation, I opened the door and was astonished to see not a policeman standing with his helmet in his hand and a serious but compassionate expression on his face, but Penny, white-faced and trembling on the sofa.

She stared at me as if she'd seen a ghost. 'But I thought you'd died!' she said, as she rose, shakily, to her feet. 'You never came back from the shops and I was so worried! Where have you been?'

It turned out she'd had a brief kip in a hammock at the side of the house, and was out for the count when I returned. Finding no one in the house when she woke, she'd assumed exactly the same about me as I'd assumed about her.

'But I was just going to phone Jack! And then I remembered he's in New York and I don't have his number, and I didn't know what to do . . .' she said. 'And I'd already in my mind told him it was fine, that I'd pay for the transportation costs of your body back to London and he could pay me back later!'

We roared with laughter and opened a bottle of wine.

17 August

I've just got back from one of the most draining days of my entire life.

I drove down to Archie's in the morning, and then Sylvie, Harry and me went round Archie's bedroom while he was in the shower, collecting things we thought he'd like in his new home. We'd decided to take all his precious objects—his favourite chair (and get rid of the one in Eventide), and we gathered up a pile of dictionaries, the full set of Anthony Trollopes and the photograph albums. Harry had already gone

192

through his drawers on the sly, selecting bits and pieces. We can, of course, always return to get anything he particularly wants.

When Archie was dressed, Sylvie said, 'Come on, Daddy. We're going to take you for a nice stay at this special hotel.'

Archie looked pleased and was quite cooperative in packing. We'd decided that that was the best approach, to pretend it was only temporary and hope that by the time he'd settled in, he'd have forgotten about his old home. We dithered about the loden coat, but then Sylvie remarked that as he'd probably insist on wearing it just to go out of the house, there was no way we could leave it behind, tempting as it was.

Everything went swimmingly until the last minute, in the porch.

'I'm not going,' he said, firmly. 'I've changed my mind.'

He stood there in the sun, so brave and bold on the steps of his home, still, as Sylvie had predicted, in his strange loden coat—even though it's August he insists on wearing it, like a child with a security blanket. His hand was on one of the lions by the front door and he looked so noble and so like the old Archie, I thought my heart would break. To make it worse, Hardy was whimpering and cowering, looking at all of us accusingly and occasionally breaking into an anxious bark. He obviously sensed something disconcerting was about to happen.

'Nonsense,' said Harry, efficiently, taking his arm firmly. 'No going back now, old chap. It's all organised. All booked, and sorted. All done and dusted. Roger and out.'

Archie looked uncertain. It was a battle of wills. At first, it seemed as if he was going to hold on there and make a final stand when, before my eyes, you could see everything crumbling. Suddenly he turned from being a brave old home-owner to a frail old man, almost child-like. He almost seemed to lose height as I looked at him. His lower lip quivered and he allowed Harry to help him down the steps. 'I don't want to go,' he kept saying, muttering. 'But if you say I have to . . . I don't want to go . . . please don't make me go . . . Where's Philippa?'

This agonising talk went on until we got to Eventide, when Archie flatly refused to get out of the car.

'Where are we?' he said. 'I don't know this place! I want to go home!'

But again, Harry managed to cajole him out of the car and I took Archie for a cup of tea in the dining room, keeping up an endless patter of jokes and nonsense, while Sylvie and Harry did all the paperwork and sorted out his room to make it look as much like home as possible.

It was still light when they finally reappeared at supper time, and some sort of kindly carer figure, who had obviously seen all this hundreds of times before, led Archie to his room and settled him in. We looked in to say goodbye. Archie was sitting, already changed into pyjamas and dressing gown, even though it was only six o'clock, clutching a mug of tea.

He looked utterly confused.

'When am I having my operation?' he asked. 'Where is the doctor?'

'You're not having an operation,' said Harry.

194

'Don't worry.'

'We'll come to see you tomorrow,' said Sylvie. 'Have a lovely time.'

'Where are you going?' called Archie. 'Don't leave me! I want to come with you! Please don't leave me!'

But the kindly carer figure ushered us out, winking—which seemed horrifying in a way, though obviously it was only meant to reassure us. 'He'll be fine. You ring up in a couple of hours and you'll find he's settled in nicely. Lots of them are far worse. Don't worry about a thing.'

And we all drove off, feeling like murderers.

Oh God, I hope this never happens to me! I couldn't bear Jack to have to go through what I went through today. I think I shall have to check up that I still have my stash of sleeping pills to take the minute I feel as if I'm going off my head.

I feel such a mixture of relief and betrayal and satisfaction. It's so hard when you have all these conflicting feelings rushing around you at the same time, all competing for attention. First you feel relieved, and are just sinking into a chair with all the warmth of the emotion of feeling you've Done the Right Thing washing over you, and then Guilt comes stomping in like an uninvited guest, asking how you can possibly be sitting back and having a cup of tea when you should be scourging yourself with birch rods for being so cruel and deceitful to a poor old man. Then Sense bangs on the window and insists on joining the party saying, 'But you couldn't have done anything else, could you? He'd have done the same to you if it had been the other way round,' then a Warm Glow starts creeping in telling you what a wonderful person you are and

195

you start to feel relieved again and are about to sink back in the chair, but unfortunately Guilt's already sat itself down and is sitting there with a bed of sharp nails on its lap waiting for you to plonk yourself down on it.

Anyway, we did it.

I went to the kitchen, poured myself a huge glass of wine, gulped it down in one, standing up, and then poured myself a second one. Booze. What would we do without it?

18 August

Thank God Sylvie rang last night and said that Archie was fine. She'd even spoken to him on the phone and he'd sounded absolutely normal. He said the service was excellent and he'd just had a very good meal, and he didn't mention his old home once. Curiously, although this is very reassuring, it's acutely sad that he is able to forget in such a little time. A few hours of agony—and then his past is completely obliterated. Oh, I do hope it is. I couldn't bear him to go on suffering.

20 August

Spent the morning working on the August painting of the trees—a bit difficult this one because it's pretty much the same as July, so I've done them from a completely different angle. I must say the false acacia, with its yellowish leaves, is one of the prettiest trees in the world. Wish I had one in the garden.

196

Drove down to see Archie. Apparently he had a series of mini-strokes just after he moved in, and he's anyway worse than they thought, now they can monitor him properly, so he's been moved into Sunset. It's a long drive to Devon and it was pouring with rain and to make matters worse, just as I got on to the motorway, I discovered I'd got something stuck between my teeth. However much I sucked and hissed and even picked at it with my finger, it wouldn't budge. Funny thing about teeth. I really can't eat spinach any more, for instance. It's curious, actually, becoming the person one used to find so unappetising when one was young.

The sad thing is that far from being more tolerant now I'm older I find that I'm just as intolerant as my younger self. And now I have actually to *live* with this increasingly unappetising person, live *inside* her, *be* her, myself. So that's why I'm scrupulously clean, paranoid about getting stains on my skirt, pernickety about never going out without my make-up, and always making sure that my hair is not only well cut and well-coloured, but also always brushed into some kind of shape.

Anyway, back to the motorway. This bit of whatever it was stuck in my teeth was really maddening because, although I'm not the safest driver in the world, I do think that flossing your teeth on a motorway might not be very sensible, so eventually I pulled onto the hard shoulder and did it there. Luckily, no policeman came to ask me what I was doing because I'm not sure that flossing is a valid reason for stopping.

My satnav got a bit confused when I parked. The screen blinked a bit and I was all prepared for my lovely man to ask What The Hell I Thought I Was

Doing, but luckily he kept quiet. Frankly, I wouldn't mind marrying my satnav. He takes me to such lovely places. And he never gets cross when I get lost. He just says, 'Turn around when possible,' in a low, sexy, reassuring voice. Imagine going up the aisle with your satnav. 'Continue for 25 yards . . . ten yards, five yards,' he would say, until you reached the altar. And then: 'You have reached your destination.' And then, when you were married, he'd say, 'Turn around when possible,' and we'd go speeding back down the aisle and out of the church.

Satnavs are so safe, too. What a boon they are as you get older. Honestly, when I used to try to look at the map while driving on a motorway and had to change into my reading glasses when speeding along at seventy miles an hour to check the route, I'm amazed I didn't cause a pile-up of such newsworthiness that it would have made the *Daily Rant*. 'OAP CAUSES MOTORWAY CARNAGE HORROR!'

Penny was horrified when she discovered I'd chosen a man's voice for my satnav. I'd asked the man behind the counter at the Motor Accessories shop to put in all my details like my name and address. He then said, 'And you probably want a woman's voice, madam?' And I heard myself saying, 'Certainly not! Women have no sense of direction.' Whoops! Glad Penny wasn't there at the time. I wouldn't have heard the end of it.

Anyway, where was I? Oh yes, visiting Archie. Well, he'd managed to communicate to Sylvie that he wanted some papers from his desk at home.

'God knows why he wants them,' she told me on the phone. 'He can hardly read. But anyway, he's been banging on about them for days, so if you could get them that would be great. They're in a green folder, it seems. If you can't find them it doesn't matter.'

So before I went to visit, I popped into Archie's house. It looked so sad and lost all by itself, with its enormous Victorian-gothic windows and ancient porch, standing in its huge park, with no Archie inside it. It was a grey overblown sort of day, full of dark menace as if there were going to be a thunderstorm later. I noticed, sadly, that the grass on the front lawn was overgrown.

Mrs Evans came out looking twice her age, and, rather surprisingly and touchingly, flung her arms round me. 'Mrs Marie!' she said. 'Oh, we have missed you. And Mr Archie of course. I've tried to keep the place nice for when he comes home, but that's never going to happen, is it?'

'I'm afraid not,' I said. 'Not unless they discover a miracle cure in the next year or so.'

'Isn't it awful?' she said. 'I don't want to hang on like that, do you? I want to die in my sleep, that's how I want to die. Or drop down dead while I'm peeling the spuds. Or do it myself when the time comes. Or get a doctor to give me an injection. When it comes to euthan—you know, can't pronounce the name—I don't know what all those people are going on about, saying it's the thin end of the wedge. Why shouldn't we decide when to die? It's shocking. I don't want to be a burden to my children and have them spend all my money keeping me alive on a machine so they don't have no inheritance. No, I want them to have good memories of me . . . It's quality of life that's the thing isn't it, Mrs Marie? Not quantity. They say if you stop smoking you'll live a year longer—*but it'll feel like ten!*'

'I quite agree,' I said.

'Trouble is,' she went on, 'these laws are made by young people. They don't want to die. But you find when you get to my age, the idea isn't so bad after all. It's just something you do. By the time all these young people get to my age and decide we were right after all, it'll be too late. There'll be another bunch of young people deciding what's good for old people and what isn't. Interfering busybodies!'

I tried to find the folder Archie had been talking about and, while I was leafing through the papers on his desk, I found a pile of old poems he'd written. I sat down and read them. They were all about death. And one struck me with a dreadful poignancy. It was called 'Neither Here Nor There'. And it was in Archie's handwriting:

Once he was young and strong.
He'd lived and loved.
He was a man looked up to by his peers
Till, under the cover of advancing years

Others crept up and seized him unawares,
Right at Death's door.

Pulling him back without a by-your-leave
They hustled him on, ignoring his pale cry,
Into an ante-room to wait and lie
Hopeless, wishing God had let him die
The night before.

They were not enemies; they were not friends
Watching by night and tending him by day;

With one cold hand they took his life away
And with the other they kept death at bay
For evermore.

I felt so moved by it that I showed it to
Mrs Evans—who appeared to be polishing an
unwalked-on floor. I needed someone to talk to.
She read it slowly and then burst into tears.

'Oh, this is so true,' she said, in a wobbly voice.
'I hope they don't keep him hanging on like an old
vegetable, excuse me, you know what I mean . . .
how very sad. It's as if he predicted his own fate.'

'I know you understand, Mrs Evans,' I said. 'It's
so good you're here. You've been so wonderful. By
the way,' I added, as Hardy came up to me, eagerly
sniffling at my skirt and looking up at me, waiting
for a pat. 'What's happening to Hardy?'

'Oh, I've got him now. He'll go to Mrs Sylvie
soon. But at the moment she's so busy. My
husband takes him for walks. You can tell he
misses Mr Archie, but he'll be fine.'

She looked out of the window. 'You've probably
noticed the lawn. My husband's going to do it as
soon as he can, but his hip's not what it was.'

The close air had made everything become even
more claustrophobic when I arrived at Archie's
Eventide Home that afternoon. It emphasised the
slightly sinister atmosphere around the whole of
the place. It's so eerily calm: there are no screams
here, not even muffled ones. No conversation. No
machines whirring away. No life. Inside, there are
deep-pile carpets and sheets of paper pinned up on
notice boards listing future events—Old-Time
Singing with Roger and his Violin in the Green
Room on Thursday, Card-making with Gina on

Wednesday in the Sitting Room, and Take a Stroll Down Memory Lane with Bernard on Friday in the Dining Room. Gina, I noticed, also took Going for a Walk on Saturday, for those who could walk, I presume, and there was Have a Hair-Do on Sunday for those with enough Hair left to Do, with Roger.

In one way, Eventide couldn't have been a nicer place. The only thing was that to live in this particular bit of the nursing home, you had to be in a really parlous state. Despite the engraving on a brass plate by the reception area, reading 'The Age of Dignity', there's not a lot of dignity in being spoon-fed and having your bottom wiped.

I made my way down the overheated corridor to Archie's room. Full of his things, it looked really nice. There was a photograph of Sylvie in a frame on the chest of drawers, and one of Philippa. I noticed there wasn't one of me, but as we'd only been together for a few years, I couldn't complain. The walls are a pale yellow, and Sylvie has draped great Indian throws over the hospital chairs, which gives it more of a feeling of home.

There are some things that can't be disguised, however. The plastic locker by his bed. The cheaply varnished chest of drawers. The glimpse through to the over-lit and matless bathroom, with its toilet bolstered by a raised plastic seat, the sinister strings, hanging from the ceilings in both rooms, with a crimson alarm pull at the bottom.

Apparently, as the place is packed with women—we live longer—he's completely inundated by wobbly lady visitors, who imagine they're in love with him and endlessly totter in to engage in flirtatious banter. He's only been there a few days, but it's amazing how the roar of sexuality still drives people of the most unimaginable age. Archie's so very polite, it's touching. Even though he's now got very frail, he still always tries to get up when anyone comes into the room, bursting into a smile and saying, 'My dear! How lovely to see you! You're looking more beautiful than ever!' He does this to everyone: cleaners, consultants, me, and has even started to do it to the man who comes round every day with the newspapers. Of course he doesn't read the paper but he does manage to turn the pages and gaze vacantly at the pictures.

This afternoon Archie was sitting in his old chair with a blanket over his knees. He looked extremely gaunt and bony, and kept peering anxiously out of the window. I was amazed at how quickly he'd deteriorated after his strokes. I suppose institutions don't help. Put me in one of them and within half an hour I know I'd be sitting, craggy-faced, with a rug over my knees, sucking my gums, and unable to remember my own name let alone the name of the Prime Minister. When I came in he said the usual, 'My dear! How lovely to see you! You're looking more beautiful than ever!' But then it became clear he didn't have a clue who I was.

'Do you know who I am?' I asked, rather meanly. I sat down.

'Philippa?' he said, nervously. Then, 'No, Marie. Where is Marie?' he said.

'I'm Marie,' I said, taking his wizened hand and giving it a peck. The skin on it was so thin I felt I was kissing his very bones.

Then he pulled me towards him conspiratorially. 'Marie stole my . . . my . . .' He grappled around for

203

the word, plucking at his dressing-gown . . . 'my . . . pin . . . my . . .'

'Brooch?' I said, guessing.

'Yes, brooch. She said it was the cleaner, but she stole it, you know.'

We talked a bit. Or rather I talked. With one eye, I have to say, on my watch. It was just so hot in there. I got out my knitting, just to keep my mind busy, and did a bit more work on the front.

'Look at this!' I said to Archie, showing him the border. 'These are elephants, like the elephant game we used to play with Gene.'

'Jean?' he said. 'Who's she?'

A sour-looking nurse put her head round the door and Archie said, 'My dear, how lovely to see you! You're looking more beautiful than ever!' making a faint attempt to rise.

'A cup of tea, Mr Archie!' she shouted, suddenly, beaming at the compliment. 'You like a nice cup of tea, don't you! And a nice biscuit, too?'

Archie started to get upset. 'No biscuit,' he said. He shook his head, distressed.

'No, no . . .' She bustled around. 'No biscuit,' she said, winking at me. 'But perhaps your guest will want one?'

'No, no . . .'

'Whatever you want, darlin'.'

'Are you doing the crossword?' I said, noticing the puzzle in his paper. I thought perhaps we could do the crossword together, like we used to. I filled in a few clues and then said, 'Now, come on, darling, you can get this, I know. A vessel bearing right flag. Eight letters beginning with s.'

'Streamer,' he said, quick as a flash. 'Steamer with an "r" in it.'

204

That's what so sad about Archie. You talk for ages and it's all incomprehensible meandering nonsense, full of repetition and redundancy, and then suddenly the synapses click together and there's a flash of the old person you used to know. But is it really worth it? Being alive for the very odd moment—perhaps only once a week and only lasting a second—when you're back to your old self. My heart suddenly lurched as he smiled at me, his old smile. And then he went back to his own unknowable interior world again, a world in which I have no place at all.

Luckily Sylvie came at five o'clock and I was as delighted to be seen visiting her father as she seemed to be to see me.

As I left, she said, 'Thank you so much, Marie. But where are you staying?'

I told her I'd booked a B&B.

'No, come and stay with us . . . do. Oh, God, tonight's no good, Harry's sister's staying, but next time, will you promise?'

I was very touched at this offer, and kissed her and Archie goodbye. I could feel the skull beneath his skin. 'Goodbye, Philippa,' he managed to say. And that was it.

I headed off into the now-breaking thunderstorm, clutching the *Daily Rant* over my head to protect me from getting drenched.

21 August

Very grim time at the B&B so I'm delighted that next time I shall stay with Sylvie. It was one of those places so filled with knick-knacks you didn't

205

know where to move. Every chair in my room was occupied by a ceramic pierrot doll with painted tears running down its face, and the box of tissues was covered by a quilted chintz case—to match the cover for the lavatory paper in the bathroom. In a bowl lay some very dingy-looking shavings of wood impregnated with a sickly scent that pervaded the room, and all the drawer handles had plump red tassels hanging from them.

The pillows were those dreadful ones carved out of foam, utterly unyielding, like sponge boulders, and the sheets were made of some synthetic material so that within minutes of lying down one was drenched in sweat. On the bedside table was an electric clock with a blinking red light that I had to cover with a pair of knickers to stop it keeping me awake, and outside, early in the morning, the country road turned into a motorway for farm vehicles, with agricultural machinery grinding up and down.

The owner was, as they always are, an utterly delightful woman with a disabled husband who was proud as punch of her 'home from home' as she called it. All of which made me feel like an ungrateful old sourpuss when I thought of how much I'd loathed my night there.

To make up for my vicious thoughts I was effusive in my praise of the breakfast, which consisted of tinned mushrooms, bacon swimming in a white watery residue and scrambled eggs which must have been cooked the week before.

Before I left for London, I popped in on Archie again. He was staring at the paper, sightlessly. He suddenly pointed to a picture of a tree. 'Okay!' he said, excitedly. 'Okay!' I looked at the picture. It was of an oak tree.

'I think you mean "oak",' I said, gently putting my hand on his shoulder.

'Oak!' he cried. 'Oak!'

So you see it's pretty painful for all of us. Oh dear, I'm starting to cry as I write. It's difficult not to. Does one just get more emotional as one gets older? Sometimes I think I'm turning into a tough old boot and the next minute I'm bursting into tears at the slightest thing. Pull yourself together, Marie.

Of course it may sound very cold, put like this, but unless you've lived alongside someone who's getting Alzheimer's you can't conceive how gradual it is. For a couple of years you can see the same old person shining through, and the forgetfulness, rambling conversation, muddle and confusion are just rather annoying bits of nonsense that surround them. It's as if you had a really good friend who started to wear odder and odder clothes, until you could hardly recognise them, and yet you could still see little bits of them peeping out between the hats and veils occasionally, and still recognise them by their walk and the way they got up and sat down.

And then one day you realise the person has completely disappeared. Gone. Well, they've never quite gone, but the glimpses you get of them are so rare that they might as well not be there. Indeed, one never has a moment when one can actually mourn the time they disappeared because in a way they're still disappearing. So very sad.

It's a kind of death, but a very slow death. I mean, if Archie had changed from being the old Archie on a Tuesday, to the new Archie on a

Wednesday, I think I would probably have had a nervous breakdown. But as it all happened so gradually, over a period of years, I never had a single moment to actually feel the loss of him slowly disappearing. It's hard to grasp.

24 August

Finally got my act together and booked tickets to New York.

Later

A bulb went in the hall light. As it's a high ceiling I asked Michelle to hold the ladder while I clambered up.

'My fazair 'e fall off a larder,' she said.

'How could your father fall off a larder?' I said.

Eventually we understood each other. If anything, her English seems to get worse the longer she stays here. Perhaps she's not going to English classes at all and instead working as a call girl in the West End to fund her product habit. Last year I would have been worried sick. Now, frankly, I think she's old enough to look after herself.

But thinking about falling off a larder, and also with that ever-present faint but acute fear that the aeroplane might crash on the way over, and with the existence of Chrissie and Gene, I decided that, before I left, I should remake my will.

No good my disapproving of Archie's lawn, it's *my* lawn I ought to be concentrating on. It looks

208

like a forest. Pouncer can hardly be seen above the grass.

209

SEPTEMBER

1 September

Well, I've just got back from the solicitor's. He's going to make a rough draft of the will. I've got a great solicitor—a real old-fashioned one who wears a suit and a tie and sits in a dilapidated office surrounded by papers. He's called Mr Rankle, he's got a white moustache, and all I can hope is that he lasts long enough to do all the paperwork before he croaks. The man doesn't even have a computer on his desk. God knows how he copes in this day and age. He may not actually have a quill pen, but he looks as if he knows how to use one.

We chatted a bit about his family and mine, and then he drew a clean sheet of paper towards him and said: 'Well . . . let's get started . . .' and off we went.

He kept saying things like, 'But let's say the unthinkable happens and Jack dies before you . . .' or 'Let's say the unthinkable happens and Jack has a nervous breakdown and his character changes completely and he develops a wild gambling habit . . .' or 'Let's say the unthinkable happens and Chrissie develops multiple sclerosis and starts having an affair with someone . . .' He outlined so many unthinkable disastrous scenarios, all of which he assured me had happened to clients of his over the years, that I couldn't help laughing.

'Can we safeguard perhaps against my having a nervous breakdown, going bonkers and throwing all my money away in the street, or giving it to a young African gigolo I picked up in the Gambia?'

'Interesting point,' he said. 'Exactly the same thing happened to a client of mine some years ago. It's always useful, in such an eventuality, to have someone up one's sleeve to whom one is prepared to give power of attorney.'

I was laughing so much at this stage that he started giggling too, and try as he might he couldn't stop. I suppose it's the subject of death that is, at its heart, so frightening that one either blanks it from one's mind or finds it all, as I do, absolutely hilarious.

'Have you made any plans for your funeral?' he said eventually, after we'd made what's called an Advance Directive which gives Jack the power to tell the doctors to switch me off when I'm ready to go—I do seem to be obsessed by this.

I said I'd had quite enough of all this death, and I'd think about it over the weekend. Funerals. I'm torn between wanting burial in a recycled cardboard box in a quiet glade with no fuss, and a majestic show of pomp, circumstance and plumed horses at Westminster Abbey. So I'm leaving it all to Jack to do exactly what he wants.

That's probably the best.

After all, one can't control the world from beyond the grave. (And nor should one try to.)

3 September

Penny is very worried because we haven't heard anything from the council about the petition, and there's been no more news about the plans. We don't know whether they've been approved or not. They should have looked at them by now. James has asked Ned if he can find out anything, and according to his spies the developer now knows about the signatures and has submitted a slightly different plan. Not so different, however, that it needs further consultation with the residents. We are really worried about this. We feel that the council's in league with the developer and they've got him to make minor changes so our petition will be rendered worthless. I bet someone in the council is in his pay. Or perhaps he's promised to give the new parking spaces to the councillors. I wouldn't put it past him. Slimy old thing.

I've booked to go to New York next week, and today James came over to look at the house because he's going to take care of it and Pouncer while I'm away. Michelle has gone to Poland to see Maciej for a couple of weeks. I suppose partly to see him and partly to try to keep him in line. But I fear the worst.

I am of course terrified that in the three weeks I'm away gangs of drug-dealers will break in and steal my computer, Pouncer will perish after being attacked by a herd of oriental cockroaches, pipes will burst and the few remaining plants in the garden will die from drought. It took ages to explain everything to James, but he took notes and I made him go in and out of the house switching the burglar alarm on and off to make sure he understood it all.

'I've got a big surprise for you when you get back,' he said, mysteriously.

'Oh, is it the artwork?' I said, as enthusiastically as I could.

'I'm not telling,' he said. 'You'll just have to wait and see.'

'Are you and Ned getting married?' I suggested.

'That seems to be less and less likely,' he said, rather sadly. 'The problem is that the more I wean him off his vegan diet, the more he seems to change. He ate a bit of haddock the other day, and then I caught him eyeing up a woman in the Uxbridge Road.'

'A woman? I thought he was gay as a Christmas tree,' I said.

'Hmm . . . I'm not totally certain. Apparently he was married when he was young . . . I'm not sure he isn't bi-sexual, which does make things difficult. Now you're not to go stealing him off me,' he said, half-jokingly. 'Anyway, he doesn't look like a Christmas tree, does he?'

'No, he looks like a silver birch,' I said. 'At least that's what Penny and I think.'

James laughed. 'What tree would you call Penny?' he asked.

'She's a cherry tree,' I said. 'Not a very good shape but liable to burst into surprisingly lovely blossom now and again. You're definitely a pine of some kind.'

'Tall and boring, darling, don't rub it in,' said James, ruefully.

'Not at all. Constant, smelling lovely, always green . . .' Not much else you can say about pines.

'Well I think you're a plane tree,' he said. 'You're shady—in a good way—strong, reliable, and a real boon to the urban environment— particularly with all this work you're doing on the hotel.'

'Oh, thank you!' I said.

213

And funnily enough I *was* rather pleased. I love plane trees and always have. The other day I was walking down the road with my paints and easel, having just completed the September Season of the Doomed Trees, and there was some mad—and I mean mad—Indian woman in a bright red and yellow sari with very long, curved fingernails, standing by a plane tree systematically picking off its bark.

'Stop that!' I said. 'You'll kill it.'

'No, it is good . . .' she said, turning her obsessed plane-bark-picking eyes on me. 'It likes it.'

'It doesn't like it!' I said tersely. 'If you go on like that I'll report you to environmental health!'

She slunk away.

Most odd.

5 September

Spent the entire day packing. I know—it's ridiculous because I'm not going for a couple of weeks. But the older I get the earlier and earlier I start packing. I used to throw something into a suitcase the night before and that was that, but now I get my bag out from the elephant cupboard ages before I'm due to go. I've been to a toy shop and bought Gene the most enormous selection of dinosaur-making kits, books of origami, metal puzzles . . . all things we can do in the flat, or apartment as they call it. I also bought a kite, in the vain hope that it might be a windy day in Central Park. Then there's the virtual chemist's shop I have to take with me every time I leave home these days. There's practically no room for my clothes.

214

Looked at my passport photograph and I have to say I do look different after the facelift. I suppose I should have got a new one taken. Hope they don't refuse me entry because I look too young. Wouldn't that be awful? Awful and immensely satisfying at the same time.

7 September

David rang and asked if he could drop off some remote-control helicopter he's bought for Gene for me to take over. When I opened the door to him, he did a double-take as he entered, staring at me.

'Golly, you're looking well!' he said. 'What's happened? You look absolutely marvellous!'

I told him about the facelift and he kept sneaking little looks at me. 'You look just like you did when we first met!' he said, sentimentally. 'Takes me right back . . . we did have some fun, didn't we? Sometimes?'

'We certainly did!' I said. But then I asked him how he thought they were getting on in New York, and he said, 'Hmm. I thought they'd be back before now, I must say. But there's still time. Though I'm afraid to say whenever I've spoken to Jack he seems to be having a great time, and he's working really hard and Gene's loving his school now.'

It was the last thing I wanted to hear.

20 September

Feel really bad that I haven't been down to see Archie recently. Sylvie says I mustn't worry at all, and as he hardly knows who anyone is it won't make a lot of difference. I know it won't, but I still feel I ought to go and see him, for my own sake, really. Anyway, I'll go the minute I get back.

Been so busy packing and changing my mind about what to take, I haven't had a moment to write my diary. Off tomorrow. I've had to pay a fortune for my travel insurance. After a certain age no insurer wants to touch you with a barge pole. They imagine that the moment you're sixty-five you start getting ill and falling off ladders and costing them a fortune, and of course they're absolutely right.

On my way to the hairdresser to get a good cut for the trip, I went to the newsagent to tell them when I wanted the papers cancelled while I'm away. Afterwards, blow me, I couldn't find where I'd parked the car. I walked down the street I thought I'd parked it in, and then back down the other side, and it was getting later and later and I was sure the hairdresser would have given up on me, and I kept pressing the button on my keys hoping that one of the cars would start blinking encouragingly at me, as if it were saying hi to a friend, but *nothing*. All the cars turned their backs on me. It was like being sent to Coventry. I tried my mobile to let the hairdresser know I'd be late, but the battery had run out, and I was forced to walk home so I could ring her from there. As I got to my front gate I spotted my car on the other side of the road. I'd completely forgotten that I'd walked to the newsagent. Honestly! What's so weird about getting older is that you can remember the tiniest detail about the party dress you wore when you were three—or I can anyway—but can't remember where you parked your own car a quarter of an hour ago.

21 September

Last day of the *Rant* before I go. 'PAMPERED LIFE OF SERIAL KILLER!' read the headline. '*28-year-old Barry Bastard, serving life for torturing eight youngsters last year, lives Life of Riley. He has four widescreen televisions, one in each room of his spacious "penal quarters", which also feature a spa and internet access.* IS THIS JUSTICE??'
     I'll miss my daily dose of *Rant*.

Later

Now just sitting in the airport before I go through the departure gates. That's the good thing about a laptop. You can whip it out and write anywhere. I've got another horrible thriller from Penny to read on the journey, but with any luck I'll use the time knitting. I've nearly finished the front of Gene's jersey.
     Had a very jolly farewell drink with James and Penny last night. Penny says that I must watch out for evangelists. It's an urban myth that they spend a lot of time evangelising on long-haul flights,

217

imprinting on their neighbours the fact that if the plane were to crash, they wouldn't have made their peace with whichever particular god they're pushing. By the end of six hours you're so scared and bored, that before you land you find you've signed up to Mormonism, Scientology or some equally loony cult.

Half an hour later

Oh God, what a nightmare! Just got to the departure lounge, and security wouldn't let me keep my knitting needles! I begged and pleaded but they just removed them from the wool, with a look of contempt, and dropped them into some see-through box full of nail scissors, small tubes of hair conditioner, and all the other things that are so essential for hijacking. I could have killed them, but had to keep my temper or they wouldn't have let me on the plane. Surely they'll have knitting needles in New York! Or will they? I still think of New York as being so completely trendy that if you mentioned knitting needles they'd just laugh and send you to one of those weird towns they have in the South where all the inhabitants are forced to wear eighteenth-century dress.

Then, later, I thought I'd cheer myself up by checking my emails at one of those internet places and, to my horror, found an email from Penny with EMERGENCY!!! in the subject line.

Apparently the council has passed the plans! I feel utterly distraught. Here I am, just off to New York for three weeks, at the very moment we should be marshalling our forces. I rang Penny at once.

'What's all this?' I said. 'Can't we appeal? This is frightful! Have you been on to the local paper?'

Penny was almost in tears of rage. 'God, it's so maddening you're going!' she said. 'Shall I call another meeting? What can we do?'

'Yes, have another meeting and write to the MP,' I said. 'That would help. Invite all our local councillors along, and get hold of someone on the local rag. And organise a public rally. We ought to try a bit of direct action.'

'Oh God! I can't do it all on my own,' wailed Penny.

'Get James to help you,' I said. 'And Marion and Tim are brilliant and Sharmie and Brad will be great. It'll be fine. They can't build it before I get back and if the worst comes to the worst, I'll shin up the tree and stay there for a few days with a banner with YOUR COUNCIL WANTS TO KILL THIS TREE! written on it in bright red letters. That'd make them think.'

There was a slight pause. Then: 'Would you really?' said Penny. 'That would be a great idea.'

Of course I hadn't really meant it, but as I was sure it wouldn't come to that I said, 'Of course! If I can't do my bit now, I promise I'll do more than my bit when I get back! And, oh,' I added, remembering it must be some time soon, 'Happy birthday for when I'm gone!'

Later

I'd booked an aisle seat, but they'd made some muddle so luckily the very kind and rather dishy

219

young American man sitting next to me agreed to swap. (Well, I say young—I thought he was probably in his late forties). On those long flights I'm always up and down going to the loo and I don't want to disturb the poor person next to me, particularly if they're asleep.

He'd got a laptop, like me, which he was waiting to turn on when we got airborne, so I thought there wouldn't be much conversation during the flight, but as we were taking off he suddenly said, 'Oh, God!' as if he'd forgotten something. Then about ten minutes later, after rummaging around in a bag by his feet, he said, 'Oh Jesus Christ!' and for some reason I couldn't stop laughing, because it fitted in so well with what Penny had told me last night. I got terribly embarrassed, giggling on my own, but couldn't help it. Finally he looked up, turned to me with an amused expression on his face and said, 'Good joke? Care to share?'

He seemed so sympathetic that I explained as well as I could, and he laughed and said, 'So because of my cussing you thought I was going to inveigle you into my cult!' He gave me an admiring, even flirtatious glance. It was a look directly into my eyes, and with that I knew with absolute certainty that he fancied me. Ridiculous, I know, because there must be over ten years between us at least, if not twenty, but there was no mistaking it.

The reason I can type now, is because soon we'll be starting to land, and he's gone to a seat nearer the exit because he has to make a quick getaway for an urgent meeting, but oh, he was *terribly* attractive, with black hair and a really sweet smile and deep-blue eyes. He reminds me of a particular boyfriend I had in the sixties, and as soon as I remembered that he slotted into an entirely different groove. I felt I'd known him all my life. You could never do that when you were young, of course. But now I find that the people I meet for the first time often always remind me of someone I've known a long time before, so I just pop them into that category and behave towards them as I would towards the person I've known for years.

After we'd talked about evangelical Christians, he asked, 'What's bringing you over the pond?'

'I'm visiting my son and his wife,' I said. 'And my grandson.' I felt I had to get this fact in right away before he started asking for my phone number. (Fat chance.)

'You have a grandson? No way!' he exclaimed, apparently amazed, turning right round in his seat and assessing me. 'You must have started young! And so must your son, by the look of it. My name's Louis, Louis Bravon, by the way. I'm just returning to New York from visiting my mom. She still lives in England. My father was a Prof at Oxford—and my mom loved England so much, she stayed on after he died.'

And he held out his hand so I shook it.

'Marie,' I said.

'Marie . . . ?'

'Marie Sharp.'

'And do you work, Marie?'

'I'm ret . . . a teacher.'

Funny. I never used to know what to say when asked what I did when I was young. Sometimes I'd say 'I teach' but to actually be 'a teacher'—it didn't sound right. I think it was because when I was teaching and I looked at my life I was too much in

221

the middle of it all really to know *what* I was. It's only since I've retired that I can see the whole picture. And, yes, now I look back, it's true. I *was* a teacher.'

'And you?' I said.

'Guess,' he replied.

'Doctor?' I suggested, tentatively.

'Doctor!' said Louis, horrified. 'Jesus, no! Well, maybe not where you live, but in the States they're a whole bunch of crooks waiting to open you up, steal all your money, and then stitch you up again. No, I'm a freelance journalist. What you call a hack.'

'Hang on,' I said, 'I thought journalists were meant to be the evil ones, tapping people's phones, stealing photographs of victims from bereaved parents . . .'

'No, I'm a *good* journalist,' he said. His eyes were twinkling attractively as he spoke. 'I put the world to rights, uncover wicked financial and political scams, and am generally the scourge of conmen and criminals everywhere.'

'A bit like Batman,' I said.

'Exactly like Batman,' he said. 'With a touch of Superman thrown in. You are, at the moment, sitting next to a living fusion of the two mightiest superheroes in the world.'

I liked him. He was fun.

'And what do you read, in the way of newspapers?' he asked, noticing the copy of the *Rant* that I'd picked up free at the airport and stuffed into the pocket in front of me.

'*Daily Rant*,' I admitted. 'I'm ashamed to say.'

'The paper that wakes you up and brings you down all at the same time!' he exclaimed. 'Don't apologise. It's got a fantastic circulation and it's a fantastic newspaper. Not my politics, mind you, but still, you have to admire it.'

He started flicking through the movie list on the plane, and we talked about films we liked—*Sweet Smell of Success*, *All About Eve*—and didn't like—*The King's Speech*, anything by Almodovar or Mike Leigh—and, of course, agreeing on absolutely everything in that way you do when you meet a kindred spirit, and then he stopped and clicked a button. 'Here—what about this one—what's your opinion on this? *Bitter Quinces, Poisoned Souls.*' He put up a finger before he'd let me speak. 'This is the big test, Marie. Give it to me straight. Or haven't you seen it yet?'

Although I'd never met anyone except Penny who thought it was crap, I thought honesty was the only policy. 'Well, you probably won't like this,' I said, nervously, 'but I walked out after the first half-hour. I know everyone says it's a masterpiece, but I just didn't get it.'

'Let me buy you a glass of champagne!' said Louis, grinning broadly and clapping his hands. 'I have been searching the globe to find someone who thought it was balderdash, as you'd say in England, and you're the first person I've come across who's seen through the emperor's new clothes! Let's celebrate!' He caught the eye of a passing hostess and soon we were knocking back the bubbly.

'I still can't get that horrible opening sequence out of my mind,' I said. 'That dismal woman in the car park. Those fingers . . .'

'You didn't see the piano-playing bit? Oh God, excruciating! I was reviewing it. It was the only piece of mine they refused to print. They said, "You just can't say that about a foreign movie. We'll look like idiots!" And they sent someone else to review it who raved about it. Jesus!' He paused. 'You didn't get to the little boy, then?' he said, animatedly. 'Oh, my God, the little boy! He was the very pits!'

Before he moved to the front, and as he was getting his bags down from the overhead locker, he put his hand into his jacket pocket and fished out a card.

'Give me a call if you're at a loose end in New York,' he said. 'It's been great talking to you. I sure hope we'll meet again.'

'Unlikely, as I'm only going to be here for three weeks,' I said, regretfully.

'Oh, you never know,' he said, cheerfully. 'Remember I am a journalist. No door is ever closed to a good journalist!' And off he strode down the aisle, swinging his jacket on one finger over his shoulder, something I have never seen done except in films.

As I stared at his retreating back I had that awful kind of sinking feeling that I'd last had when Archie started making it clear he fancied me all those years ago. A kind of thrilling yet dreadful inevitability. In a way, I hoped nothing would come of it, because I'm about a hundred years older than him—or to be precise, because I did some quick mental arithmetic on the basis of a few dates he'd thrown into the conversation, a bit less than twenty years.

But then with a pang I was reminded of Archie, and I couldn't help being struck by guilt, and wondering how he was. Suddenly I felt really bad about having had such a good time with Louis that I'd hardly given him a thought.

But back to Louis . . . well! This facelift! I didn't have it done with the intention of picking up blokes, but as a side-effect it's not half bad!

27 September

Well, here at last! I am quite giddy with excitement and happiness, writing this in my lovely new bedroom in Jack and Chrissie's apartment.

After I'd got through customs I got my baggage trolley, or 'cart' as they call it here, and pushed it through to Arrivals, looking frantically for Jack and Gene. Nothing. I couldn't see anything familiar except dozens of people—Indians, Russians, Chinese—rushing about . . . and screaming children on piles of suitcases . . . and rows of cab drivers standing with handwritten notices, waiting for clients. There was no notice for me, and for an awful moment I thought they'd forgotten to come to meet me. All I could hear was the drone of flight announcements and the beeping of vehicles covered with luggage and the general hubbub.

And then suddenly I spotted Gene at the barrier, being held up by Jack and waving a big sign which read 'WelCOmE TO nEW YoRk GrANY!' It was covered with stars. Scrambling out of Jack's arms, he ran under the barrier and rushed to meet me. Then he stopped, and hung back slightly, obviously a bit shy of his emotional outburst. But as we walked out he took my hand and briefly pressed his cheek against it.

And when we'd gone a few yards, Jack joined us and gave me an enormous kiss and a hug, and said, 'Come on, Mum, we'll get a cab,' and before I knew it we were out of the airport doors, met by a huge wave of hot air—it was 24 degrees apparently as they're having a freak heatwave—into a cab and eventually we parked outside a huge old mansion block on, as Jack informed me with some pride, the Upper West Side. We then went up in a lift— 'elevator' said Gene, firmly, 'we call them elevators, Granny'—into their splendiferous flat. Or apartment.

I must say it looked a lot nicer than when I'd seen it on Skype, which gives a consistently unflattering view not only of people but of objects and apartments as well. It reminded me of those old mansion flats you get in London: it was all on one floor, corridors with vast rooms off each side, and a wonderful view of the Hudson out of the living-room window.

'Wow! Her company must think a lot of Chrissie,' I said.

Jack grimaced and nodded. 'They certainly do,' he said. 'They'll do anything to keep her. We only have to hint that we're thinking of going back home, and they up her salary or throw in an extra car or longer holidays. It's ridiculous.'

He showed me to my room, which looked extremely comfortable, and I was moved to see some of the bits and pieces were stuff I'd last seen in Brixton. The bedside lamp that had once belonged to my mother. The scarlet-and-green quilt that they used to have on their bed at home.

'Chrissie will be back for supper,' said Jack, after I'd unpacked. I joined him in the living room and sank into a comfortable armchair. 'We thought we'd all go out early tonight to a diner. Would you like that? We can have real American hamburgers.'

'And fries,' said Gene, as Jack left to make a cup of tea.

'Don't you call them chips any more?' I asked.

'No, only sometimes,' said Gene. 'Where's my jersey?'

'Next door, on a chair,' I said, as Jack handed me a large glass of wine. I was still a bit woozy from Louis' champagne, but never say no to a drink, I say. 'And you can get the presents as well. They're all on my bed, wrapped up. But be careful with the jersey, darling,' I shouted. 'Don't let it unravel! They pinched my needles at customs!'

He dashed to get everything and started unwrapping the presents. He was enchanted with the origami and the metal puzzles, and the various kits I'd bought, and disappointed only, I could see, with the kite. But there's always one present that doesn't go down as well as the rest. I'd brought Jack a vintage shirt from the seventies which I knew he'd like and then we tackled the jersey. This was the moment I was waiting for. I'd worked so hard to get it right.

But, unbelievably, I discovered, as I held the front part against Gene's chest, it was a terrible disappointment. It was far, *far* too small. My heart sank as I realised what I'd done.

'You can't have grown *that* much, darling!' I said, trying in vain to pull the jersey into shape.

Gene looked very disappointed. 'Wouldn't it stretch?' he said, tugging at it himself.

But there was absolutely nothing I could do.

'I'll start again,' I said, bravely. 'I haven't *quite*

227

finished it. I haven't done the arms. What a silly I am. I didn't realise how big you were, and how much you've grown in the last few months! We can unpick it together.'

And together we unravelled everything I'd already done, Gene holding it while I pulled at the thread and made it into a ball. All that work. Oh well, I'd enjoyed it. And this time I could get the ribbing right at the bottom—I'd made a mistake beforehand but couldn't be bothered to go back and correct it. And I knew there was something wrong with the elephants and had only got the hang of them with the last one. The ones which didn't look as if they had trunks growing out of their bottoms looked like grey wolves smoking cigars.

'You're looking very well, Mum,' said Jack, smiling as he topped up my glass. 'I was worried you'd look wan and haggard with missing us.'

'Well, I have a confession to make,' I said, nervously. And I told him about the facelift.

Jack leaned forward to examine me, looking absolutely astonished.

'A facelift!' He looked a bit put out. 'Honestly, Mum, you shouldn't have had a major operation before telling us. Why didn't you?'

'Because you'd have been worried,' I said, 'and I knew you'd have said don't decide to do it till you've come over to see us, and Chrissie would have given me all these products it would have taken me years to try, and I just thought, well, it was a treat to myself. I hope you don't think I'm a dreadful self-indulgent old thing.'

'Not at all,' said Jack. 'Good for you! You look marvellous! But you must promise me never to have anything like that again without letting us know. Of course we wouldn't disapprove. It's your life and your face. But you look great! You don't look young, exactly, but you just look—well, *well*! Doesn't she, Gene?'

'What?' said Gene, who was busy playing on the floor.

'Doesn't Granny look well.'

'Granny looks just like Granny. I don't know what you mean.' Gene was trying to build some kind of structure with Lego. 'Will you help me, Dad? Please, please, please help me.'

'In a minute. Well, I never! A facelift! My old mum! Chrissie will be amazed!'

Chrissie *was* amazed. But not quite so amazed as I was to see her, when she returned from work. She has always looked beautiful, but this time she looked like a film star. She kicked off her high heels before embracing me warmly.

'How can you work in those heels?' I asked.

'Oh, it's agony,' she said. 'The one thing I can't stand about this job is that I have to look like this all the time. It's so unnatural. But they say because I'm representing the company in my work, I've got to look absolutely marvellous all the time. I don't mind dressing up for special occasions, but every day . . .'

'She has to get up an hour earlier than us to tart herself up just to go to work!' said Jack, shaking his head. 'It's mad.'

'And I'm hardly ever here, it's so sad,' she said in a muffled voice. Gene was clambering all over her, kissing her. 'And how do you find Gene?'

'Fine,' I said.

'And I bet Gene hasn't said Gee whizz once,
229

have you?' she said to Gene, ruffling his hair affectionately.

'Gee whizz,' said Gene. 'Gee whizz, gee whizz, gee whizz.'

'Oh, God, what have I started?' said Chrissie. 'I'm so sorry.'

28 September

Today Chrissie was having to rush off to buy a cake for Gene to take into school on Monday because it was someone's birthday and everyone had to bring something in.

'Oh, don't do that,' I said. 'Gene and I can make some cakes here and ice them. That would be much more fun, wouldn't it, darling?'

Chrissie sighed. 'I know it would be nicer, but we did that once and everyone was horrified. It's because he's at a private school. Everyone's groaning with dosh, and making our own cakes— well, we were practically ostracised. No, here it's absolutely compulsory that we buy the cakes, and do you know how much we have to spend on a birthday present for someone in his class? About twenty quid! Back home we'd just buy something silly at the market. But here it's dreadfully frowned on. It's all about status.'

She rushed off and Jack asked if I'd mind if he went too because he had some work to catch up on and he was sure we'd have a good time, and so I was left with Gene.

I can't quite work out whether they're both enjoying it here or not. I noted the fact that Jack had said that whenever they talk of going home, the company responds with increased salaries and so on. So obviously they *have* thought of coming back. And it's pretty clear they haven't made many real friends, and the work is knackering. It's obviously very expensive living here, too, and I'm not sure that they're totally happy. But I can't bring the subject up or it looks as if I'm angling for them to come back which, of course, I am.

29 September

Spent yesterday afternoon sightseeing (still faint with jetlag), Gene mad keen to show me the Empire State and take the ferry to Staten Island. Both jaunts excellent fun. But today, Sunday, I was left with him while Jack and Chrissie went off to more work. Breakfast was a slice of flabby toast. ('Unless you go to delis, you just can't get nice bread here,' said Chrissie. 'There's no Waitrose!') And as for the tea—well, it was called tea but it was made with some strange sort of American bag which tasted of dust. However, a small price to pay for being in this fab—and here fab is the right word—city, with Gene.

I'm delighted they seem to be using me as a babysitter while I'm here, which is of course great for them, because they can catch up on all kinds of chores, and great for me. And, I hope, great for Gene, too. As it was raining we stayed in.

Gene started off by making me a necklace out of paperclips which I wore for a bit but found it soon got too painfully scratchy to bear. As I put them back a rather unnerving thing happened. I simply couldn't think of the word for paperclip. Crikey, I

231

really *am* going the way of Archie. I stared and stared at them, and finally had to ask Gene. 'Do you know what these are called?'

'Paperclips,' said Gene.

'Well done,' I replied, in order to conceal my ignorance.

'Had you forgotten?' asked Gene, with an amused smile on his face.

'No, no . . .' I brushed it aside, embarrassedly. We tried the origami and made a pelican and a butterfly—once we'd made one he wanted to make ten more and we stuck them up all over the flat. Then we tried the metal puzzles and managed to do all of them except one—two rings looped together which we had to unloop. Totally baffling.

He suddenly asked about Archie, and I said he wasn't very well, and had moved somewhere where people could look after him, and then, bless him, he suggested he make him a get-well card.

'Let's do one with elephants on it,' he said. 'That will make him laugh! Do you remember, Granny, that time . . . it was *so* funny!'

When the rain stopped I suggested we go out and get a lot of boxes from local shops and bring them home and make a mad robot of some kind, and paint it. Gene decided, rather unsettlingly, that he wanted to make a prison.

'Wouldn't you prefer to make a house?' I said. 'We could make your place in Brixton . . . or we could make a palace . . . a gym or, um, an art gallery. Or a hospital.'

'No, I want to make a prison,' said Gene, determinedly. So out we went into the now boiling streets of New York, and after posting Archie's card I started to feel rather like my old Polish

232

neighbour, going into shops and asking if they'd mind us taking their empty boxes away. However, they're used to this kind of behaviour. When we got back Gene spent hours drawing all the windows of the prisoner's cells on the sides of the boxes, glueing on toothpicks for the bars, and then we made a small garden for the prisoners to exercise in (my idea of course) and a large cardboard fence all around it so they couldn't get out. We made some prisoners out of Play-Doh, and I got quite into the whole project.

'Let's have a governor,' I said.

'No, there isn't a governor,' said Gene.

'But there has to be a governor,' I said, feeling quite upset. 'Otherwise the prisoners would all fight and everyone would get out of control.'

'There's no governor in *this* prison,' said Gene firmly. Whereupon he pushed all the prisoners together and, muttering, 'Punch! Punch! Take that! Ouch!', he managed to squidge all the prisoners into a single ball of multicoloured Play-Doh . . . 'Then there was this huge rocket which came down on the prison,' he said, 'It exploded . . . and bang! It was all squashed . . .'

And he jumped on it, crushing all the walls, and little flowers I'd made, reducing the whole thing to a flat piece of cardboard and Play-Doh.

'Oh, darling!' I said, rather disappointed. I'd been longing to show it off to Jack and Chrissie. But clearly he found the whole exercise—building it up and then destroying it—immensely satisfying.

After lunch it looked so enticingly sunny outside our rather chilly air-conditioned flat that we went out to Central Park and Gene took his bike. I was naturally expecting Central Park to be full of muggers and criminals, but actually it was peaceful and full of incredibly opulent-looking people with dogs on leads. I couldn't believe, when I asked the owners what their strange-looking dogs were, the astounding variety of deliberate cross-breeds like Yorkipoos, Maltipugs, Cockerpoodles, Labra-terriers, etc. It was teeming, too, with professional dog-walkers, all roaming the park holding up to six pooches on leads at a time.

Weird—and very nice—how talkative they all are, too. Not at all like in London parks.

I had a rather desultory game of football with Gene—not a game that grannies specialise in, I find—and when it started to rain again, we hailed a cab to get home. To my astonishment there was a television in the back of the cab playing loads of ads. And even more to my surprise, Gene seemed to know every word of them. 'Smith and Wollensky,' he recited in a pure New York accent. 'If steak were a religion, this would be its temple.'

After we'd got out and were going up in the lift, Gene said, 'You were right about arcon, Granny. It's not arcon. It's air conditioning. But,' he added decisively, 'I call it arcon.'

I made him an early supper and left him watching old Popeye cartoons while I emailed Sylvie for news of Archie.

Couldn't help thinking of Louis, though. Oh, dear. Hate to admit it but I haven't thrown his card away yet. Since I have absolutely *no intention* of getting in touch—it would be asking for trouble—why on earth am I keeping it? I suppose I've fallen for a younger man, like Penny did a while back. Always ends in tears.

OCTOBER

3 October

There is no bath in this splendiferous apartment. I don't know about other people of my age, but I can't bear showers. First of all, you have to stand in either freezing or scalding water while you adjust the temperature, then you get your hair sopping wet unless you wear some ridiculous shower cap, the floor is always slippery and I'm afraid I'll fall and, without taking the shower head off its perch and using it to spray inside all the cracks like under your arms and between your legs, you never get washed there at all. It is frightfully uncomfortable. But the worst thing of all is that not only do I have to read the *Daily Rant* to enrage me into life of a morning but also must have a bath to unseize my morning stiffness. A shower just won't do the trick.

Another disadvantage of showers is that it's impossible to play games with Gene in them. At home we had great bath times, with plastic duck and fish fights, and underwater diving adventures. Sometimes he'd crawl under my special non-slip bathmat, turn it upside down, and pretend to be a squid, with the suckers as part of its skin. Or, I'd be the hairdresser when we washed his hair, and say, 'And would you like a bit of mousse, sir?' at the end, with all kinds of pranks with the towels and sponges. The whole procedure took about an hour from beginning to end. Poor American kids. They know nothing of the hilarious, splashy and noisy pleasures of bath-time.

At least we still have laughs with the towel. After he's all clean, I love seeing his little glossy red face, beaming out of the fluffy towel, and him racing along the passage with me chasing after him (there being no stairs in this flat, the chase isn't quite as good, but still) and then doing him up as a Roman emperor in the towel or making him an enormous turban out of it so he's an Indian rajah . . .

Before he went to bed tonight, we measured the bit of the jersey on him, the bit I've restarted, and it seems to be fine. If anything, it's on the big side. Then, as he snuggled down, we had a chat.

'You should have watched Popeye,' he said. 'You see, Popeye wanted to go to this circus, and Bluto came with this big man, and there was this oven and Olive Oyl was in it and then it went bang, and this man, no not Bluto the other one, he got caught by this dragon, and Popeye rode on his bicycle . . .'

One thing *no one* is good at, not even children, is retelling the plots of films.

'Oh really?' I said. 'That sounds exciting.'

'It wasn't exciting, Granny,' said Gene crossly. 'It was *funny*. You weren't listening. Now listen properly. When Bluto came back there was this big explosion, and . . .'

I'm afraid to say that just at that moment and for no reason I could fathom, an image of Louis crossed my mind. I've finally thrown away the card. I couldn't possibly ring him up. But still, I couldn't help wondering whether, as he said, we *would* meet again. I did rather hope so, I had to admit.

4 October

Last night Jack asked an American couple over for dinner. He thought that the husband might be useful as he's a retired psychologist doing some research and Jack might be able to do some work for him. They arrived at 6.30—what strange times Americans eat—and refused anything to drink but sparkling water. Luckily Jack had got some white wine in for me and Chrissie.

The man, Lennie, was one of those lovely old-school American types—all grey hair, Brooks Brothers shirts and excellent manners, highly educated, interested in everything and absolutely unknowable. But although he was perfectly easy to talk to, and he appeared to be flattered by the interest I took in him, I just couldn't really imagine him as a human being. He was so wooden. As he is seventy-eight, we touched on the subject of illness and death, but suddenly he said, with a smile on his face, 'Oh, I don't think this is a very happy subject to discuss over cocktails!' and I said 'Why not? Isn't death one of the most interesting subjects there is now we're old?' But he continued with his bland smile and asked, 'Tell me, where do you live in London?' or some utterly banal question and I realised it would be rude to persist.

His wife, Martha, was what we used to call a blue-stocking. She was a graduate of Vassar and clearly a major feminist. She was tiny, feisty and spoke very loudly in a deep, Lauren Bacall voice. She wore wide silk trousers, had masses of frizzy grey hair and wore a minimum of make-up. Her face was covered with wrinkles and she was bubbling with energy.

During dinner she suddenly said, 'Well, as a feminist . . . and I'm sure I'm speaking for all us guys . . .' and I'm ashamed to say I butted in abruptly with, 'Oh, count me out, Martha. I'm not a feminist. I simply believe in equal rights.' That was a bit of a dampener, so when she turned to the subject of Jane Fonda, and how she'd let the side down by having a facelift, I kept absolutely mum.

'I would *never* have a facelift,' she said, 'and I guess you all feel the same. After all, my face is a palimpsest on which all my past is etched—my *journey*—the laughter, the pain. The joy! I'm a human being, for Chrissake. I don't want all my history air-brushed out of me! And you can always tell,' she added, looking slyly round the table. 'I always know when someone's had work done, don't *you*?' she added, patting me on the knee. 'They just look so stretched and expressionless.'

'Surely the only ones you can spot are the bad ones,' I said, cautiously. 'Isn't it like undiscovered murders?'

At this she looked a bit baffled. 'I don't know what you mean about murder,' she said, chuckling, 'but don't you agree these old people, they either have facelifts and try to be young, or they just give up. Some people my own age—they've lost all their sense of wonder. They can never be astonished by anything. It's so sad.'

'I've lost all sense of wonder,' I said, rather sharply. 'And very pleased to have lost it too. My sense of wonder has been replaced by wisdom and experience. Nothing surprises or astonishes me these days, and it's a very nice change, I can tell

238

you! Darling,' I added, sweetly, to make it sound less cruel.

Poor old Martha was a bit dumbfounded by this and seemed to lose some of her fizz, but I made up for it later on by telling her how wonderful she looked, and discussing various books we'd both read and feigning astonishment (if not wonder) at some of her rather clichéd revelations, so I think I repaired the damage. Oh dear, a terrible fault of being older is an inability to keep one's mouth shut. Americans are so keen to see the bright side of everything. 'What doesn't kill you makes you strong,' said Martha, several times in the conversation, while I was thinking, 'What doesn't kill you wounds you and leaves terrible scars.' When she said, 'When one door shuts another opens,' I felt like saying 'When one door closes another door slams in your face.' But I don't think my take on her sincerely held platitudes would have gone down too well.

'I'm so sorry, I shouldn't have said all that about wonder and undiscovered murders,' I said to Chrissie, as I helped her clear the table after they'd gone.

'Rubbish,' said Chrissie. 'Someone's got to tell them. That's the problem with Americans. You know, Marie, being here I sometimes feel so incredibly European. I can't describe it—I never felt European when I was in England—but here I feel like some old Italian olive-grower or an ancient Austrian philosopher. The mentality is completely different. It's all "Happy! Happy! Happy!" It does get a bit lonely sometimes, I can tell you. It does them good to have someone like you come along and tell them what's what. Good

239

for you. And wasn't it funny when she started talking about facelifts! I could hardly keep a straight face!'

I was grateful to her, because I thought I'd been rude. And also rather pleased, in a way, to learn that the family didn't fit into US society as well as perhaps they seemed to want me to imagine.

Went to bed and, as usual, put on the electric blanket they'd kindly provided. Although outside it's like a sauna, inside, the arcon, even though they've fixed it, makes it so cold you need an electric blanket to stop yourself from freezing to death.

5 October

Gene was at school today so I walked around the neighbourhood feeling rather at a loose end. Absolutely filleted, as Archie used to say, by the heat as well. I can't believe the contrasts between extreme heat outside and extreme cold inside are *good* for me.

I started off walking down Broadway all the way to Carnegie Hall. Continuing on, I passed the Russian Tea Room, still a wonderful emporium of mirrors, chandeliers and madness. I preferred it as it used to be, still glamorous though run-down and seedy. But life must go on, as Martha would probably have said. At least it's still there. Finally I walked to MOMA, the Museum of Modern Art—one of those buildings in which the architecture is so much more interesting than the art—and was so knackered after staggering around the place, I headed home, back up Broadway.

240

But on my way I couldn't resist nipping into a fabulous New York deli on Broadway, one that Martha had mentioned as being totally yummy and 'so New York', absolutely bursting with bagels and cheesecake, pickled cucumbers, smoked salmon and gefilte fish. I went in and ordered a cup of coffee, only to realise, after half an hour of people-watching, that I was rather bored. How was it possible, I wondered, to be bored in New York? Well, I've done all the usual touristy things. And I'm now at an age when another exhibition is just another exhibition.

Where I really want to be is with Gene or Jack or Chrissie, talking and doing things, or at home in Shepherds Bush and getting on with things there. As I sat staring out at the honking yellow cabs and the traffic I rather wished that I *did* still have a sense of wonder, like Martha. Perhaps I'd been rather hard on her, I thought. So when, from across the tables, a tiny grey-haired woman started waving at me, I was extremely pleased to see that it was the feisty old palimpsest in person.

'Sit down!' she shouted, beaming. 'The only woman in New York who isn't a feminist! You're looking great!' It's always rather maddening when the other person gets that remark in first. Replying, 'And so do you,' however enthusiastically, doesn't carry the same impact, I find. 'Have a sandwich. The pastrami here is to die for.'

'Well . . . I'm a bit squeamish about all that yellow fat,' I said, as I went over. 'But if you insist . . .' I discovered that even though it was only midday, I was suddenly rather hungry.

'Forget about it! Life's too short for yellow fat!'

she said with a raucous laugh, and she signalled over a waiter and ordered a couple of pastrami sandwiches.

'I'm waiting for my godson,' she said. 'He's doing an interview with one of those old beat poets who's still alive in the Village. We're going to go to MOMA together.'

I was just about to tell her about my morning's visit to MOMA, when I heard myself exclaiming, 'But I can't eat all that!' My meal—you couldn't call it a sandwich—had arrived amazingly quickly on an enormous platter. It consisted of two giant slices of bread full of enough seeds to fill a plantation, crammed with a hundredweight of salt beef, and surrounded by mountains of coleslaw and gherkins. The waiter plonked down a collection of small bathtubs brimming with sauces, relishes and salsas. And he'd provided enough napkins to paper a ballroom.

'Enjoy!' he trilled, and that was that.

It turned out that Martha has three grandchildren so it was quite easy to chat about how besotted we were. I recounted the fiasco at Heathrow security, and she howled with laughter and said she knew the perfect place for knitting needles. I was just wondering what was going to happen to the bill and whether it would be politer for me to insist on paying or politer to let her take me out, when a tall, nice-looking man threaded his way through the tables and I realised, to my amazement, it was Louis. Not only that, but he was coming our way.

'That's not your godson, is it?' I said to Martha, who was waving frantically at him. 'Louis?'

'Hello, darling,' she said, getting up and kissing

him warmly on both cheeks. 'Meet my new best friend from England . . . Marie Sharp.'

Suddenly I felt as if I were in some kind of fifties American film, full of coincidences. I started to wonder why I wasn't clutching a brown paper bag brimming with groceries, a stick of celery jutting out of the top, and why we didn't all push aside our tables and burst into song.

'Wee . . . ll!' said Louis, smiling broadly, as he pulled out a chair. 'You see . . . I'm always right . . . and I didn't even have to call in any favours from the DA's office!'

'You two met already?' asked Martha, catching the glance between us.

'We flew over together,' said Louis, sitting down. 'And I was certain we'd meet again. And *hoping*, too . . .' he gave me a knowing smile. 'And here we are. Hey, this is just wonderful! And how are you two lovely ladies connected?'

I found that because I'd been thinking about him so much, this time I could hardly think of anything to say. Speech wouldn't come at all. Indeed I'd become so dumb, I thought perhaps now I had had one of those mini-strokes and would never be able to speak again. However, perhaps by catching the waiter's eye and mouthing the word 'bill' I could re-enter the contest, as it were. Of course the American word is 'check' and the waiter looked at me blankly until I mimed the writing of a bill, or check, and he promptly came over. After that, the words started to flow. Martha suggested we all go to MOMA together.

'Great idea!' said Louis.

'But I . . .' I was going to say I'd been there already, but the words wouldn't come out. 'Come

243

on, we won't take no for an answer,' he said, reaching out to take my hand to haul me up. And as he touched me I felt that awful familiar spark that bodes so badly for any woman, whatever her age.

I could hardly bear to catch Martha's eye. Could she tell?

7 October

We had a wonderful time at MOMA—I just hoped that none of the museum attendants would recognise me and say, American style, 'Well, hi again—second time in one day, you must just love this place!' There was only one blip and that was when Martha insisted on dragging us off to a knitting-needle shop on the way, and I felt utterly humiliated. The last thing I wanted Louis to know was that I actually *knitted*. Were I some groovy young knitter who was knitting in a kind of retro way, fine, but the older knitting woman is not a very rejuvenating sight. But Louis took it all in his stride, and by the time I had to leave to pick up Gene from school, I'd taken back everything I'd said about poor Martha. Honestly, I can be such a crosspatch sometimes. When it comes to her ludicrously optimistic outlook on life, she may be 'full of shit' (as no doubt she'd charmingly put it herself) but there's no question she's a warm and life-enhancing woman.

That's the problem with Americans. They first of all make you feel like wise old olive-growers, like Chrissie said, but before you know it their good humour and kindness makes you feel like

244

some uptight, stony-faced repressed caricature of an English person. 'New best friend!' Well, I was quite bowled over.

Louis was funny, charming and flattering. Of course the age difference wouldn't be too bad if I were a twenty-year-old girl and he were forty, but then there's no getting away from it. It's different for men. If women are older than men in a relationship, then there's always something creepy about it. I know there is. I remember how I felt when Penny went out with Gavin, the man she met on the internet who was so much younger than her. It was quite pathetic to see her so besotted. But the awful thing is that I can feel it happening to me. I know Louis fancies me, too, because when one gets to my age (not a phrase I'd ever say in front of Louis, of course) one has had so much experience of relationships that one knows instantly. He catches my eye, puts his arm round my shoulder to steer me towards a picture he wants to show me, whenever a movie's mentioned (you see even I'm getting into the swing of New York lingo, now) he murmurs to me 'We must go see that'—it's clear as day. No doubt if we were ever together on a starlit night, he'd start showing me where the Great Bear was—always a sign of someone, in my experience, who fancies you rotten. He charmingly managed to get my mobile number by saying we both needed to swap them in case we lost each other among the Jackson Pollocks, and now I'm certain he'll be in touch.

So it was with a spring in my step that I left him to go to pick Gene up from school. I was standing there, surrounded by Puerto Rican nannies and New York mothers double-parked on the street in big jeeps, waiting for the kids, when my mobile beeped. I had two texts.

One was from Louis, whom I'd left only half an hour before, which read, *When can I c u again?*

The other was from Sylvie: *Daddy dying. Asking for you.*

For one awful disloyal moment I toyed with the idea of pretending to Sylvie that I'd left my mobile at home and had never got the message, but then I knew there was nothing for it.

I have to go back.

8 October

'But you've only just arrived!' said Jack, when I told him the news. 'You can't go back now! As you said, Archie barely recognises you . . . do you have to?'

'But you promised we'd make my Hallowe'en costume!' said Gene, pulling at me and making a sad face.

'There's nothing I can do,' I said. 'I'm furious, and I feel like screaming, but I just must. I would never forgive myself if he died when I was away. And particularly if he's asking for me.'

'Well, I think you're mad, Mum,' said Jack. 'You've spent all this money coming here, we've made all these plans, and now you just go back. You've barely got over the jet lag.'

But I knew I had to go. There was no getting out of it. After changing my flight back I went into my bedroom to start packing. I couldn't help but cry— tears of frustration, really. I'd just met a nice guy, I was having this lovely time with Gene and the

246

family, I'd got a new American best friend. And now this.

When I went to say goodnight to Gene he looked a bit sad. The sight of him in his aeroplane pyjamas, holding his teddy tightly made my heart break. 'When are you going away?' he asked, rather plaintively.

'As soon as I can get a flight,' I said. 'The thing is,' I explained, 'I have to. Archie's not at all well. There's nothing I can do. I'd give anything to stay.'

There was a pause while Gene sat staring down at the duvet. Then he looked up, a bit brighter. 'I know you have to go back, Granny,' he said. 'I just wish you weren't, that's all.'

There was something so grown-up about his simple, serious tone, that I felt like a child myself. But there was no changing my mind, I had to return. And I knew that, knowing he understood why I had to, I was actually setting him a good example for his later life. That sometimes there are just Things You Have To Do, whether you like them or not.

Jack and Chrissie and I had a rather silent, gloomy supper—I could tell they were disappointed too. But in the end, Jack put his arm round me and said, 'Sorry to be so snappy before, Mum. I was just upset you were going. We do know you've got to go. And look, in a couple of months, we'll see if we can come over or if we can scrape up some money for you to come back here. Perhaps for a much longer time.'

'I've got all these Air Miles, or whatever you call them these days, from flying with the company,' said Chrissie. 'I'm sure I could transfer them for a flight. We'll sort something out. Of course you've

247

got to go now. We'll miss you. But don't worry.'

I couldn't help thinking, while I was packing, that none of this would be happening if they were living in England. I could just pop down and see Archie and still be back to pick Gene up from school the next day. But there we are. Funny phrase that: there we are. One much used by oldies everywhere, I suspect. It's a phrase that signifies resigned acceptance of the status quo. Nothing you can do about it.

I was so choked up about it all, that I almost forgot to text Louis. But I did, and got a lovely text back: *c u in London then! over next month to see mom. Till then. xL*, which made me feel better. There we are.

10 October

Absolutely HORRENDOUS flight back from New York. First of all, they actually had the nerve to confiscate my knitting needles when I went through security AGAIN! I mean I know it was my fault, forgetting they'd been confiscated the first time round, but I'd already knitted half of the new back. I was so fed up, I was tempted to give them the wool and everything and simply abandon the whole project. But I didn't. I slid my New York needles out of the stitches very carefully—*again*— so that at least I could salvage something of the knitting when I got back to London and could buy *yet more* needles. I handed them over to the burly, blank-faced security man with an evil leer. I hope he fell on them and they poked him up the bottom. Or in the eye.

I mean *honestly*—how on earth could anybody possibly hijack a plane with a couple of size eight knitting needles? The whole thing is too preposterous. And when I turned to the queue behind me for support they all looked determinedly in front of them. I could see that none of them wanted to get involved in a wrangle at security in case they were carted off to Guantanamo Bay.

Then—when I got to Heathrow, cross-eyed with jet-lag, I hauled my suitcases off the luggage carousel, but just as I was turning a corner with one of the bags, it got kind of twisted—it's one of those suitcases on wheels—and I fell over. I felt so utterly ridiculous. Luckily, lots of people came rushing up, asking if I was okay. Though I'm sure most of them thought I was sozzled on in-flight hospitality.

Since the age of fourteen, when I remember flying off my bike on a country lane in Gloucestershire, I've never fallen over, and I was surprised how the first thing one wants to do is to jump up and pretend one's perfectly okay, even though one has probably broken one's spine and cracked one's skull and dislocated one's hips. Anyway, I managed to stagger upright, and because my tights were torn and my knees were bleeding I indulged in a taxi to get me home rather than hobbling onto the train to Victoria. Anyway, it was one of those grey, drizzling October days, and I didn't fancy going by train.

The taxi driver asked what had happened to me, and I explained. 'I think I might have done my back in,' I groaned, pitifully.

'These days my back goes out more often than I

do,' said the taxi driver. 'Geddit?' He was one of *those* taxi drivers. Later in the journey his mobile rang, and even though it's against the law he picked it up and started gabbling into it. 'So you done, it, eh? Did you just stand there or did you do a runner? Did you stamp on his 'ead when he was bleedin' and lyin' on the ground or did you call a hambulence? I know what you done. You done a runner, innit? Heh, heh!'

So I was extra pleased to get home. And thrilled to see dear old Pouncer, who was so delighted he seemed to shed all his hair over me as if he'd been saving it up specially for my return. But then my blood ran cold as I noticed a dreadful thing in the middle of my sitting room.

It gave me a real fright. The object—which looked some pagan ritual totem—featured a glaring white sheep's skull, festooned with barbed wire, on top of a broom handle, with piles of rusty cans at the bottom. It was mounted on an old dustbin lid, which had been squashed to turn it into a base. A sort of toga had been constructed around it, out of bubble wrap, luckily disguising the walking frame, held in place with metal clamps, and a garish plastic orange rose had been carefully placed in one of the eye-sockets of the skull, sticking up like an antenna. There were some pliers, a hammer and a pair of thick gloves on the carpet and I then realised that this was James's installation, based on me, and he was in the middle of perfecting it.

After the initial shock, I was so weary that I didn't know whether to laugh or cry, so, dazed, I rang Penny and explained everything to her.

'Oh, poor you!' she said. 'Well, come over and

250

have some supper this evening . . . you'll be exhausted! Or shall I bring something over and we can look at this dreadful thing together?'

'Come over tomorrow,' I said. 'I'm going to bed right now. I'm shattered.'

I left my suitcase at the bottom of the stairs. I simply couldn't manage to drag it up. I'll unpack everything at the bottom of the stairs and take my things up piece by piece to my room tomorrow.

An old person's trick.

11 October

Got up at noon, not sure what day it was or what, indeed, my name was, feeling dreadful. As I'd got back earlier than planned, my *Daily Rant* hadn't been delivered, but Penny had kindly pushed a copy through my door on her way past, which was very sweet of her.

'ANNIE NOONA FOUND DEAD BY ADDICT BOYFRIEND!' I was informed. Then, further down: *'Twenty killed in high-school massacre!'*

Poor old Annie. And poor old students. Still it makes a welcome change from the end of the world stuff.

The first thing I'd done before falling into bed last night was, of course, to ring Sylvie. Unfortunately her mobile just rang and rang, too. I tried Eventide, but they refused to tell me anything about Archie because I wasn't a relative, but at least I assume he's still alive.

So this morning, naturally, after glancing at the *Rant*, I rang Sylvie again. And I couldn't believe what she said. Though still very ill, Archie had pulled through! Emergency alert completely over! So I'd rushed all the way back home to see him and instead of catching him on his deathbed, he's still with us.

'Oh Marie,' she said, 'it was dreadful. You know how he's made a Living Will and everything, and I'd told them not to resuscitate him, but some new doctor was on one night and he refused to listen to any of that and pumped him full of antibiotics and he's still alive! Oh, I know it sounds so awful to say this about one's own father, but I can't bear to see him like this, so confused and unhappy! And instead of just letting him drift off, they drag him screaming back for God knows how many years! I've rung up the Matron and I've been absolutely furious and I've got a copy of the Living Will and I enlarged it and pinned it up above his bed, so everyone knows next time . . . it should never have happened! It was the one day I'd left my mobile at the office and I'd always said they should ring me on my landline, but they didn't so I didn't get the call . . . I can't forgive myself.'

I must say it was all very depressing.

'When can I come and see him?' I asked.

'They're not very keen on him having visitors at the moment,' she said. 'Except very close family. Basically only me, but I'll let you know the *minute* they say it's okay. They're scared stiff of the risk of infection.'

'Well, just say the word and I'll be there,' I said. 'I flew back from New York specially to . . .'

'Oh, you didn't!' she wailed. 'Oh, I'm so sorry!'

'Ah well,' I said. 'Nothing to be done about it. There we are.'

252

'Well, do at least come and stay, won't you?'

'Of course I will,' I said. 'Thanks so much.' At least I wouldn't have to endure the frightful B & B again.

And it's given me a chance to catch up on all the emails and bills that wait for you when you get back home. Not to mention, of course, the Seasons of the Doomed Trees. The leaves are turning yellowish-brown, and beginning to shed. Amazing how the things change over the months, particularly when you're really looking.

15 October

Penny came over today bringing a really delicious *salade niçoise* without any tuna in it. When she saw the installation, she screamed and nearly dropped the salad, but luckily I just prevented it. After she'd yelped with horror, we both got the giggles.

'If he thinks that's you, one of his best friends, God knows what he'd make of his enemies,' said Penny, sitting down, and wiping her eyes. 'Is that bubble wrap meant to be your dress? Is that rose your eye? Why is it sticking out on a stalk like an alien?'

Eventually we settled down with a drink, and because it was one of those peculiarly balmy, warm October evenings we had a very early supper in the garden, surrounded by late scented tobacco plants. The Calibans have completely disappeared, never to be seen again: £36.50 down the drain.

I always thought the whole point of *salade niçoise* was the tuna, but also its biggest drawback (and Penny said she quite agreed). Tuna is

253

disgusting, so she'd substituted a million anchovies and black olives and hard-boiled eggs and it was completely scrummy.

As we started to tuck in, Penny cocked her head, listening. 'Remarkably silent,' she said. 'What happened to the . . .'

'*Sshhh!*' I hissed, hoping Sharmie wasn't eavesdropping in her garden.

It was quite a relief to get the whole miserable story off my chest, and Penny shook her head, rocking with silent laughter. 'The granny chimes! My God! You must have felt awful!'

'Imagine if some dreadful neighbour had destroyed something in New York I'd given Gene to remind him of me and . . .'

'Don't even think about it,' said Penny. 'Much better in her bedroom, anyway. Now, what are you going to do about the installation?'

'Do you think I could suggest keeping it in the garden?' I said. 'Well out of sight? I was thinking I could put it round the side here—you could only see it if you were at the end of the garden looking back.'

'But would it be able to cope with the rain and wind?' said Penny.

'Hopefully not,' I said. 'But heaven knows what Sharmie will think when she looks out of her kitchen window and sees this ghastly thing from a Stephen King novel peering in at her.'

'Serves her right for putting up the—,' here Penny held up some imaginary chimes and flicked her finger against them and said, 'Ting!'

'If only Gene were around I could say I'd moved it because of health and safety and the risk he'd put his eye out on the barbed wire.'

254

'Bung it in the garden,' said Penny. 'James can't expect you to have it in the living room. Now,' she said, as I brought out the coffee. 'The Residents Association . . . and the plans . . .'

We decided to have a meeting next week and get the councillors and the local MP along too. We're going to ask Father Emmanuel whether we can hold the meeting in his church, and leaflet the entire area so that we get masses of people along. I said I'd chair it, and we'd get various people to speak for three minutes each. Like Ned, who'd say how important the tree was, and maybe one of the more respectable drug dealers to say how crucial it was to have somewhere to exercise their slavering dogs (we definitely want to make use of the drug dealers as they add diversity and authenticity). Then Brad from next door can talk about other legal aspects, and apparently Tim knows something about Open Spaces . . . then I'll do a kind of round-up of the whole thing, and there'll be questions and it'll all last about an hour. I'm sure there's a good enough story for the local paper.

'I'm absolutely shattered,' I said, as we wound the whole thing up, and Penny got up to go.

'Well, I'm not surprised!' said Penny. 'You've only just got back from New York, where you've had an exhausting time, you're knocked for six by the news about Archie, even though it turns out he's now okay, and you've had a long flight and jetlag and you've had a fall—what do you expect?'

The awful truth is that I expect to sail through things like this. I always used to sail through them. I was renowned for always coping and soldiering on, whatever happened to me. But sometimes now

I actually feel my age . . . isn't it dreadful? Indeed, this morning when I walked into the kitchen in my slippers I was aware of a funny rustling noise. Then I worked out that it was me—shuffling! *Shuffling!* Shuffler Sharp! I never thought I'd shuffle. Made a resolution in future to Lift My Feet.

10.30 p.m.

Just had a text from Louis, asking for my email address. Very flattering! Might wait a couple of days before I reply, just to pretend I'm not as desperate as I am. Next, a Skype from Jack, wanting to know if I got back safely. He sounded just as shattered as me. They'd been relying on me to look after Gene and had got an enormous amount of work organised to do while I was there, and now they're having to get temporary childcare and they've got some Dutch girl, recommended by a friend, who's over there doing a PhD and needs extra money. She'll only be there for a couple of weeks, but obviously my leaving has put them in a bit of a difficult situation.

How easy it would be if only they were here! I could just pop over and we'd all be happy as bees.

18 October

Michelle came back from Poland in a furious mood. Apparently Maciej has broken off their engagement and she found out that he *does* have a new girlfriend and she went round to her house and threw water all over her. Doesn't sound very edifying, but it obviously made her feel better. She didn't have a good word to say about him.

' 'E ees just seely leetle boy. I am better wizout 'eem. I 'av 'ad lucky escape. And 'e snore,' she added. 'And ees feet, zey are not good.'

'Perhaps you need to look for an older man,' I said. 'More mature.'

She rummaged in the fridge for a Yakult, took one out, and stomped upstairs.

23 October

No word from Louis despite my having sent my email address about three hours ago. Oh dear, I'm starting to feel like Michelle. I thought I'd never have to suffer all that 'Will he write? Won't he write?' ever again. And now look at me!

Sylvie rang to say that Archie is still out of bounds, but they're hoping he'll be up for visitors in a week or so. In the meantime, I've forgotten to mention James and his horrible installation.

'I love it!' I lied when I rang him. 'I just wish I could have it in the middle of the living room, but . . .'

'Oh, no, you can't do that,' said James. 'I thought it would be good just outside the French windows so everyone can see it.'

'That's a thought,' I said, non-commitally. 'Let's talk about it. You see, I was thinking, there's that kind of dead area in the passage alongside the house and I thought if I painted that bit of back wall white, it would really show up from the end of the garden. It would look as if it was in its *own private exhibition space* . . .'

I congratulated myself on this phrase. And I could see that the idea had made James think.

'But no one would see it,' he said, dubiously.

'Oh yes they would, because whenever anyone went into the garden, I'd show them,' I said firmly. 'It really deserves its own setting.'

I could hardly believe my ears. *Its own setting!* Sometimes I think I should have been a used-car salesman. By this time, I was starting to believe my own patter.

24 October

Sharmie rang this morning saying that there's been a muddle with childcare this afternoon, and she's got an urgent appointment, and if she were to drop Alice over, could I possibly look after her just for an hour or so?

Felt extremely touched and flattered by this request. And delighted of course, to have Alice over. No substitute for Gene, of course—little girls are so different from little boys—but any tiny person in a storm.

And today was made even more wonderful by the arrival, finally, of an email from Louis. He told me all what he'd been up to—investigating some Mafia story in the IT industry—and some party he'd been to—'but none of the women were up to your standard'—and ended with the news that next month he's got to come over to see his mother again in Oxford, because she has some grim hospital appointment, and he says he can't wait to meet up again. He ended, simply, 'xL', but that was good enough for me. I spent the rest of the day dancing on air.

Alice arrived on my doorstep with a rather white face, long fair hair held in place with a diamanté hairband, clutching not only an enormous stuffed rabbit but also a very pretty sparkly bag in which 'I keep my jewels,' she explained as she came in. She was wearing white tights, a very pretty green-and-yellow dress and pink ballet shoes, which she immediately took off in the hall. Naturally I said nothing about it being a shoes-on house. I'm not a monster.

She clung to her mother and didn't want her to leave, but I knelt down to her level, feeling the scabs on my knees cracking as I did so, and said, 'Now, you and I are going to do something very special for Mummy when she's gone . . . it'll be a surprise for her when she gets back . . . it's our little secret,' and then I whispered in her ear that we were going to dress her up as a princess and she started to smile.

Sharmie played along. 'What are you two plotting?' she said, pretending to try to overhear our conversation. Alice smiled and said, 'Go away, Mommy, it's a special secret!'

I hadn't prepared for this but soon we were up in my bedroom, going through the drawers, and finding an Indian shawl which turned into a long skirt, a sequined scarf that we tied into a top, another bright red stole to tie into a belt, and, having laden her with every brooch, bangle, bracelet, necklace, and earring we could scrape up from my jewellery box, and put her hair up with pins, we managed to transform her into the prettiest little princess I'd ever seen. Something I could never do with Gene.

259

Alice looked in the mirror, completely delighted by what she saw. Then she took my hand and said in a very serious voice. 'You have any make-up?'

'Of course!' I said, and let her loose on lipstick, blusher, eyeliner, and we even managed to pull off a winning stroke, a special Indian red dot between her eyebrows. With a spray of extremely expensive scent, she was finished.

After ten, when the bell rang, I'd just taken a couple of photographs of her (at her insistence) while she was admiring herself in my bedroom mirror upstairs, so I went down and let Sharmie in.

'Pretend not to recognise her,' I whispered. Then 'Alice!' I called. 'It's your mum!'

Alice came downstairs very slowly, and Sharmie played along.

'My, oh, my!' she said, putting her hands into the air. 'What a beautiful little princess! But where,' she said, turning to me, with a worried expression, 'is my Alice? You haven't lost her have you? I did tell you to be very careful of her.'

'It's *me*, Mom,' shouted the Alice Princess, shrieking with laughter and running down the stairs towards her. 'It's *me*!'

'No!' said Sharmie. 'It can't be! *You're* the little princess?'

'Can I show Daddy?' pleaded Alice. 'Can I show Dad? Huh? Huh?'

They all went off with promises to return everything once Daddy had seen the vision of loveliness and I was left with that wondrous, wonderful feeling that I remember so well with Gene . . . the feeling of fulfilment. Sometimes I think that being a granny allows you to be a child yourself, but without any of the unpleasant feelings

260

of powerlessness. Creating something with a child, letting your imagination roam, whether making a prison with a six-year-old boy, or turning a little girl into a princess—it's the most glorious, inventive and stimulating feeling in the world.

Well, I think so, anyway.

25 October

Finally got the all-clear to visit Archie and was, curiously, rather dreading seeing him again. It's odd, but I'd been so keyed up to expect his death that in a funny way—and I wouldn't admit this to anyone except my diary, not even to Penny—I rather resented the fact that he was still alive. I wonder if anyone else ever has that feeling? I mean I'd prepared myself for the grief, the funeral, the memories, and now here we were stuck in the same old pattern. I also felt, like Sylvie, very sad that he'd been so much forced to survive. I think it was that, selfishly, I was longing to grieve for what I'd lost. But, in the circumstances, I couldn't.

When I arrived at Eventide at lunchtime, I was told to sit in the corridor because the nurse was fussing about him in his room—taking his pulse, checking his blood pressure, draining away what little hope of a peaceful death was left inside him, leaving a hollow shell. I stared bleakly ahead of me. On Archie's door there was a small window set in, presumably so people can spy on him during the night to see he isn't doing anything naughty like dying peacefully on their watch. On the wall opposite me, there was a reproduction of Monet's Water Lilies, which I was trying to look at properly

261

despite being constantly interrupted by the passage of old ducks in wheelchairs being steered along the corridor, no doubt on their way to a collage class or some other distraction from the business of dying.

'Coming with us, dear?' said one nurse to me, as she sailed by. 'You'll have some fun. Armchair Aerobics. Everyone's welcome.'

The look of horror that crossed my face as I realised she'd mistaken me for a resident—or 'guest' as she was probably trained to call me—must have struck her because she immediately corrected herself. 'Oh, sorry, love,' she said. 'But do come, anyway, if you'd like.'

Armchair Aerobics? She must be joking. Did I really look like an Eventide resident? I got up to look at myself in a mirror, but couldn't find one. No doubt they keep mirrors away from the oldies in case they all drop dead the moment they see the ghastly shrivelled sights that stare back at them from the glass. However, as I got up, I did notice something odd. The hem of the skirt of my dress. I frowned. Surely it didn't have a border, this dress? I looked again. And then, to my horror and mortification, I realised I'd put the dress on inside-out. No wonder the nurse thought I lived there! Fumbling at the back of my neck, I could feel the label on the outside. Rushing into the nearest loo, I finally found a mirror. Briefly, I panicked that the facelift might suddenly have dropped and a kind of plastic surgeon's midnight bell might have been struck, like in *Cinderella*, and all my features had suddenly slumped back to how they used to be. But no. My new face was still intact. Applying a great deal more make-up and giving my hair a good comb, I made sure I looked emphatically like a visitor before I emerged into the corridor again. Whew! One moment later and they might have injected me with some kind of sedative and before I knew it I'd be slumped on a commode in a Sunset room, gawping at daytime television.

I took my place again opposite Archie's room and finally the nurse came out, bearing a chart.

'You can go in now, Mrs Ship,' she said. Thank God, everything was back to normal.

I tiptoed in. Archie was lying in bed, absolutely white-faced, haggard, just skin and bones, with eyes like dark hollow saucers. There were drips attached to his fragile arms. He was staring at the ceiling. Through the claustrophobic heat wafted the stifling smell of Dettol. I tried to open a window to let in some fresh air, but found it was completely sealed. In the end I opened the door to the garden, and for a moment the sharp air cut in, giving the room a breath of life. I left it slightly ajar and turned.

'Hello darling,' I said, gently.

He turned to me and gave a kind of throttled gasp. I could see him shifting himself, as if he wanted to get up.

'Hello,' he said, through a dry mouth. 'Lovely.'

I gave him some water and plumped the pillows up behind him. Then I sat beside him and stroked his hand, not knowing quite what to say. Occasionally he groaned and shifted or tried to form a word. In the end I just drivelled on. I told him about New York and about the family, the flight, the fall, James's dotty installation . . . with no idea how much of this he understood.

Then I thought: this is ridiculous. I'm being just

263

like those stupid nurses who pulled him through when he was ill, trying to pretend everything's all right. So I plucked up my courage. I remembered what had happened the last time I'd been with Hughie, and I knew this was no time to be polite or cheerful. Outside it was already starting to get darker.

'Darling,' I said, 'I want you to know everything's going to be fine this time. Sylvie and I are going to make sure you'll be able to go to sleep soon and there'll be oblivion. We know what you want, darling. It's too much for you, all this, I know. It's painful and hard work, and soon everything will be peace, endless peace. I promise . . .'

I put my hand on his dry, cold forehead and through my palm I could sense his whole body relaxing. The tension just drained out of it. His cheeks, so drawn, when I came in, softened, and he slowly drew my hand up to his lips and tried to give it a kiss. Then I said, 'You know, darling, I do love you. We had the happiest time ever. I don't think I was ever so happy with anyone as I was with you. In fact I know I wasn't. I do hope you know that.'

And for a moment our eyes locked, and I felt there was some strange connection. Even though he could hardly speak, he had got the drift of what I was saying, and he squeezed my hand for the first time.

'Marie,' he said. 'Are you Marie?'

'Yes, it's me, Marie,' I said. 'And I love you.'

He gave a faint smile, closed his eyes and then appeared to drift off to sleep. I waited a while and eventually tiptoed out of the room.

I sat down on the chair in the corridor. For some

264

reason I felt desperate for a cigarette. I'd stopped smoking years ago, but felt so drained and exhausted. I put my head in my hands. But my reverie was interrupted.

'Visiting Mr Archie?' said a nurse, bustling up. 'That's nice for him! And for you, too. You know he was very ill recently, don't you? But he pulled through. Oh yes, he pulled through! We're not going to let him go so easily! He's a fighter Mr Archie, make no mistake!'

I looked her straight in the eye, a cold fury stealing over my body. I could feel my heart starting to race with anger. 'To be quite frank,' I said, trying to control my voice, 'I think it would have been kinder if you'd allowed the poor man to die. What you did last month was little short of criminal. And I speak as one who loves him very much.'

She looked shocked and hurried on her way. For my part, I stood up and strode out of the overheated nursing home into the cool air outside. I walked around the grounds in the dusk, my mind in a whirl. I couldn't get my thoughts in order. I could feel the sharp air, hear the roar of cars in the distance, smell the supper cooking from Eventide's kitchens. But all I could see was Archie's hollow face, staring at me from the pillow. I couldn't cry. I felt too overcome with emotion for that. I so longed . . . longed for what? Longed for him to be reassured. Longed for him to be at peace. Longed, so longed, for him to die and be free from all this suffering. My heart felt full of longing and love.

As I blundered back to the car park, I bumped into Mrs Evans, who'd come all the way by two buses to visit.

'Oh, Mrs Marie . . . oh dear, oh dear, oh dear, isn't it sad?' she said. 'I keep thinking about that poem Mr Archie wrote.' She shook her head sorrowfully. 'You're staying with Mrs Sylvie tonight are you? You'll be very comfortable there. I go over now and help her out on Tuesdays. I like to stay in the family.'

And she bustled off down the path to the house.

What a trooper. Even though she'd been accused time and time again of being a thief, she's still loyal. (It says something not just for her, but for the great love that Archie inspired, and still inspires, in everyone.)

Briefly, an image of Louis came into my mind. But no. However I feel about him, nothing comes near to my feelings about dear old Archie.

30 October

Email from Louis saying 'Only another week and I'll be in London. It'll be great to see you again. xxL'

Hmm. I'd gone up an 'x'.

Skyped the family tonight. Gene looked rather cross. Apparently the Dutch girl thinks he's stupid to have a cuddly and calls him a baby.

'You're not a baby!' I said, angrily. 'You're a big boy! You're almost a man, like Dad. Dad,' I added, 'had a cuddly, a stuffed dog called Arno, until he was ten years old, and I used to suck my thumb till I was twelve and your granddad David *still* bites his nails sometimes, so don't let anyone tell you you're a baby because you've got a cuddly.'

'Did Dad *really* have a cuddly till he was

ten?' said Gene, barely supressing a slightly contemptuous smile. 'That's *very* old to have a cuddly!'

I didn't like to go into all the props that everyone leans on when they get older—cigarettes, alcohol, drugs, the ones that adults need to replace their innocent cuddlies—but I was outraged that this dreadful girl was jeering at Gene's old Ted.

'But she's going tomorrow,' said Gene, looking at me in rather a cheeky, victorious way. 'Mum's told her to go away.'

Well, that was something.

Oh, how I wished I were there or they were here!

NOVEMBER

1 November

Just back from Sylvie's. She lives in this very sumptuous converted farmhouse, not far from Archie's place. Every room looks as if she's had an interior decorator in to do it over, and there's not a cushion unplumped nor a curtain not held back by an embroidered tie. Even the National Trust tea towels in her kitchen have been ironed, and every cupboard is spotless, inside and out, crammed with sparkling arrays of glass and china. In the bathrooms she even has separate little hand-towels you dry your hands on and then throw into a bin in the corner, swank hotel-style.

That Saturday we spent a lot of time in her cosy kitchen as she prepared supper. Sylvie, thank goodness, does not take after her father. She believes in keeping warm, with a huge state-of-the-art Aga in one corner and central heating roaring away even in the corridors. We talked a lot, mainly wringing our hands about the Archie situation.

'Do feel free to have a bath before dinner,' she said, rather pointedly, I thought, as she wiped her hands on a piece of kitchen-roll. 'We're not changing, though.'

Changing? Baths before dinner? I realised that Sylvie lived in the same social circles as her father. I immediately went upstairs and had a bath, and, naturally changed, knowing that the translation of 'we're not changing' means 'we *are* changing, but not very much'.

Checking I hadn't got any clothes on back to front or inside out this time, and spraying myself extravagantly with Chanel No. 5 just in case any of the funny antiseptic smell of the nursing home still clung to me even after a bath, I made my way gingerly down the back stairs. (I'm still a bit shaky after the fall.) In the sitting room, I found Harry, Sylvie's husband, standing in front of the fire drinking sherry. Hardy lay on the hearthrug, having made himself completely at home in his new surroundings. I bet he appreciates being in the warm, after a lifetime of bracing temperatures.

Over supper I told them about the problems with the council over the common, and mentioned the appalling prospect of my going up the tree as a last resort, and at this point Harry suddenly became very enthusiastic. He's got quite a bit of land which involves forestry, so apparently he's got masses of tree-shinning-up equipment and he said if we needed something to help in this escapade he'd be happy to lend it to us. I said I hoped it wouldn't come to that, but it was very nice of him. Then, refusing coffee, I staggered up to bed. They were so kind and understanding. I think we are all quite exhausted by the situation.

5 November

Bonfire night! For the last few days fireworks have been going off everywhere, exploding into the cold, dark nights. I've been trying to keep Pouncer in because he's scared stiff of explosions. Who isn't? (Once, a few years ago, Pouncer actually rushed off when he heard a banger and didn't return for three weeks.)

Again, I couldn't help but reminisce over the old days. When Jack was small we'd let off a box of fireworks in the garden, little treats in coloured tubes with lovely names like Golden Fountain, Roman Candle or Erupting Vesuvius. There were bangers and rockets and squibs, and Catherine wheels that never managed to go round but remained motionless, shooting their sparks into the ground . . . and potatoes put in the fire to bake . . . and there was a wonderful smell of cordite afterwards and all the children had sparklers. The whole intense atmosphere of it came roaring back. And then, the morning after, there was that eerie moment when I had to go and clear the grass of all those damp, blackened shells and dirty, gritty, spent sparkler sticks.

Later

I haven't heard from Louis. Surely he'll be over any day now? I feel like emailing but have to resist. I don't want to make a fool of myself. However, I do keep checking my mobile for messages. He's never far from my mind. Oh dear.

Yesterday I had supper with James and Ned. It was James's birthday and Ned and I treated him. I'd told the restaurant—one of those jolly gastropubs—in advance that there was a birthday at our table, and one of the waiters brought in a tiny cake covered in candles, singing 'Happy Birthday' and the whole dining room joined in while James grinned, went bright scarlet, pointed his finger at me and mouthed, 'You naughty girl!'

270

Though most eyes were on the cake, I noticed James's look was directed at the waiter, a young chap who was so cool it was ridiculous. He was wearing daringly short trousers—the fashionable Oliver Twist look—a wonderful spiky haircut, a shirt that looked as if it was from Paul Smith, and great purple socks. He looked the last word in camp. (Though James was fixated on him, I noticed Ned was eyeing up one of the waitresses. I wonder if all's going well with that pair? There's certainly no slobbering over each other these days, that's for sure. Thank God.)

As we left, I said to the young waiter, 'I absolutely adore your get-up!'

He looked very pleased. 'I try to make an impression,' he said.

'You've certainly succeeded!' we said. And we left. But then I wondered. It must be rather awful if you're very young, as he was, to have ancient people telling you how stylish and wonderful you look. I mean it's hardly a compliment, is it? Sadly, young people are too shy to dish out random compliments to strangers, so if we, the oldies, didn't go round telling people how great they looked, no one would ever get any compliments at all.

When I got back I skyped the family. Gene had somehow solved the metal puzzle we'd been fiddling over for hours back in New York, and he insisted on showing me several times how he'd managed it. First, the two rings were together—and then, with a twist of his little hands, they were apart. It was baffling. I was so touched and proud.

The Dutch girl has gone, thank goodness, and Gene looked triumphant. 'She talked to her

271

friends on the phone all the time when Mum and Dad were out' (did he say 'mum' and dad or 'mom' and dad? I couldn't be quite sure, even though I was listening like a hawk), 'and Dad got cross . . .'

As I've been knitting with a vengeance since I got back—I managed to salvage most of the stitches, having bought yet *another* new pair of needles—I was delighted to be able to show Gene my progress and even tried to fit the new version on him via the computer screen. It didn't work very well, of course. But I'm really glad I've started again. I realise I made dozens of mistakes the first time, which I have now put right. The elephants look exactly like elephants.

Gene was absolutely disgusted to find that his school had sent out a note to parents asking them to discourage their children from wearing monster outfits at Hallowe'en. Having always been a big fan of Stephen King films, in which, as far as I remember, there is always a compulsory Hallowe'en scene just to build up the tension, I was most surprised. But no, things have changed, apparently.

'I wanted to wear my monster zombie outfit,' he said, sadly. 'It's got big hands with cuts on, and hair on the back, and I've got these special vampire teeth with blood on, not real blood, just paint . . . but mum said they wouldn't like it. And we wouldn't get any candy.'

'What did you go as?' I asked.

'I went as Snoopy,' he said, rather dejectedly. 'Snoopy's nice but not scary. But,' he added, cheering up, 'we got lots of candy.'

Later, Jack said Hallowe'en had been a fiasco and they'd ended up by handing out about fifty dollars'-worth of sweets to children who came calling. Not only that, he said, but the whole family was dismayed to find there were no Guy Fawkes celebrations at all.

'Of course, it's obvious when you think of it,' he said, 'and we were idiots to imagine they might celebrate it, but I do like a good bonfire night. Do you remember those fireworks we used to have, Mum, in the garden?'

'Of course I do, darling!' I said. 'I was only just thinking of them. And can't you hear the fireworks outside, now?' I added, as explosions burst into the air. The smell of bonfires had even crept through the cracks in the windows. But of course, like farts, you can't smell bonfires on Skype. 'Oh well,' I added consolingly, 'there's always Thanksgiving.'

Jack looked very grumpy. 'Haaappy Hullidays,' he said in a fake American accent. 'I can't think Christmas will be much fun here. You know, we can't get anything right. The other day Chrissie and I were invited to a party which had the words Fancy Dress on the invitation and we were just about to hire pirate costumes, when someone told us that 'Fancy Dress' means 'Black Tie'! It's like a foreign country.'

I said, rather pointedly, 'It *is*.'

We logged off, with much love and kisses.

Oh I do miss them! I worry so much—I feel certain they'll stay there and then eventually I'll just become some awful visiting stranger and Gene will turn into an American High School kid and join a fraternity and fall in love with one of those short-skirted cheerleader girls who march along with bands, twizzling sticks—tears are coming into my eyes just at the awful thought of it—and they'll

273

be complete foreigners. I just *wish* they weren't abroad.

Can't get out of my mind the way Gene called sweets 'candy'. I suppose it'll only be a matter of weeks before he calls biscuits 'cookies'. And calls maths 'math'. And rubbish 'garbage'. (Or is it 'trash'?)

6 November

Louis rang! From London! He's just arrived and he wants to take me out to dinner tomorrow, but it's the wretched Residents' Meeting—the huge one at Father Emmanuel's church—so there's no way I can get out of it. He says if I can make the next day, he'll hang on here one more day before going to Oxford to see his mother—he's staying with some editor friend of his in Notting Hill—so we're all set for the day after tomorrow. He says it makes things a bit easier for him, because he's got to interview the Foreign Secretary about something—foreign policy presumably.

'Have you seen the *Rant*'s headlines today?' he asked. "MAD MATHS GENIUS LEADS MOB IN MADRID RAMPAGE!" ' I expect that got you going.'

Did ask him if he wanted to attend the meeting, but he mumbled an excuse. 'But I know you'll be great. To the barricades!'

Longing to see him, but feel so nervous!

274

7 November

Penny and I have been beavering away to get this meeting off the ground, and thank God it's now over. I'd been up half the night making notes, we'd got an agenda, and Father Emmanuel had let us use the church as an evening venue.

But even though we'd leafleted the whole neighbourhood and put posters up in all the shops, we were terrified no one would come. I wouldn't have blamed them. The walls of the hall were plastered with pictures of Our Lord. Or, rather, in my case, Not My Lord.

By quarter to eight—the meeting beginning at eight—only a handful of residents had shown up and they weren't exactly the cream of the crop. Talk about the halt, the sick and the lame. I couldn't help thinking that some of them had only come because we'd promised them a cup of tea. But just as I was chatting to the people who were going to speak and apologising for the lack of attendance, there was a sudden commotion and blow me, people started to flock in from everywhere. The local policeman came, two extra councillors—apart from the ones who'd been hauled in to answer questions—a reporter from the local paper, and local residents starting to shove in from the back. Seats were filling up. Suddenly it was standing-room only. There was an enormous roar of noise, like an orchestra tuning up. Eventually there must have been at least three hundred people there, if not more—and then Penny nudged me and it was time to start.

275

I managed to kick off with an outline of what we objected to, which was met by a round of spirited applause, and I then introduced the speakers—first Ned, who really was brilliant talking about the trees and frankly made our piece of scrub sound as cherishable as the Galapagos Islands themselves.

Then Brad gave an eloquent delivery about planning. 'As you may realise from my accent, I'm from the States,' he began. 'And in the States they would allow this to happen. They build anywhere. But in this great country, this country of democracy, this country in which I am honoured and privileged to live as your guest—and what great hosts, might I add, you have been—in this great country, this Great Britain, and yes, I mean great, this is a place where you *care* about each other. And *you care for your environment, too* . . .'

He would have made Ross Shatterton himself sign up to the campaign.

Then Tim blathered on (giving a very good impression of the average bloke in the street, which, of course, he is), the rest of the committee gave their three-minute spiels and even Sheila the Dealer managed to stumble up onto the platform and rasp at the top of her voice about the 'bleedin' guvment' (not that the government has got anything to do with it), which of course got lots of the audience on her side.

Finally Father Emmanuel gave dark hints about what might happen to those who oppose the word of the Lord, implying that He was naturally on our side, and invited us all to offer up a prayer to God, asking him to intervene in our fight.

No one paid him any attention because by then the crowd was incandescent with fury. The poor councillors there to answer questions looked increasingly frightened, exchanging notes and whispering between themselves. And as they made their pitiful points about regeneration and jobs for the locals and investment for stakeholders (whatever they are), the crowd became more and more restless. People started getting up and shaking their fists. Slow hand-claps began. The chant of 'Save our Common! Save our Common!' grew into a such a crescendo I wished the *Robinia pseudoacacia* and the *Platanus acrifolia*, or whatever the trees' Latin names were, could actually have been there in person to hear all the voices raised on their behalf.

In the end the councillors agreed to have a second look at the plans (it was the only way they could prevent a full-scale riot), the fury slowly abated, and I felt so overwhelmed by the whole experience that I only just remembered to shout that I wanted everybody's phone numbers and email addresses and would those who hadn't signed the petition please add their names to the list so that we could send additional protests and would they please make a donation to Father Emmanuel's church as they went out.

Michelle came up to me afterwards. 'You vair' good,' she said. 'I am 'appy to leev in your 'ouse. It is like big rock concert! Next time, O2! Bravo! Yes, and you, too, actually!' she said, turning to Ned, who'd come up to join in the self-congratulatory throng. 'We all go for drink, *hein*?' and she made a coquettish drinking gesture and winked at him.

So off they went, while Penny and I, exhausted, had a congratulatory dinner *à deux* at the Indian restaurant next to the church. There is something

277

so calming about the spicy smells of a hot curry house.

'Thank *God* that means I won't have to shin up that wretched plane or Plantus whatever-it's-called,' I said, feeling mightily relieved as I scanned the menu. 'I was dreading it.'

'Don't blame you,' said Penny. And we ordered a delicious feast. Surprisingly, halfway through, the blue-and-red bead curtain at the door parted and it was James. He'd come to join us. He was looking a bit bleak.

'We thought you'd gone off with Ned,' we said. 'What's up?'

'He's decided he's not gay after all,' said James, rather sadly. 'He told me just before the meeting. He wants still to be friends, but he says he needs to find a woman and settle down. Usual story. I was just an experiment, it seems. Still. I don't think I could have stood a diet of nuts and soya milk for much longer. There we are.'

'I thought you'd got him on to haddock?' said Penny. 'What happened to that?'

'He only ate a tiny bit once, to please me. And it was then he realised it wasn't going to work. And that was that. Ah well, it was fun while it lasted.'

And he ordered a large tandoori chicken masala.

'Um . . .' said Penny, struggling to find the words. 'He *will* still help with the trees, won't he?'

'Of course. Don't worry,' said James. 'Nothing would prevent him from continuing in the tree fight. He's even more gung-ho about it than me. I was never sure about all that recycling stuff, and eco-environmental self-sustainability, plastic shoes and all that. He could never really let go and enjoy

278

himself. However, when I last saw him, half an hour ago, he seemed to be getting on rather too well with your lodger,' he said, turning to me. 'I left them to it. She's clearly got her eye on him,' he added, rather sourly. 'Though I would have thought he would have been a bit old for her.'

'Crikey,' said Penny and I, in unison.

We had just got down to having a really good post-mortem about the meeting, over the traditionally revolting coffee that Indian restaurants always serve, when I happened to mention my relief at no longer having to go up the tree. It was here that James put up his hand and stopped me.

'Oh, no, Marie, you've *got* to go up the tree! That's next on our campaign plan! Ned said it would be *mad* not to go ahead. We've got to push home our advantage. If the council is reconsidering, we really do need extra publicity against the scheme to tip the balance. No, I think it *all* hangs on your going up there. We need a bold gesture.'

As my face fell, Penny interrupted. 'Actually, James, that's a really good idea. I hadn't thought of that. Strike while the iron's hot and all that. You *did* say you would, Marie. And you said we could get all this stuff from Harry, so it'll be perfectly safe.'

Just then my mobile beeped. A text!

Hope meeting went well. c u tomorrow xxL, it said. Honestly, you would have thought I was a teenager: '*xxL*'—never have three letters meant so much. My heart started to race faster and I must have blushed because Penny said, 'What's the matter?'

'Oh, nothing,' I said, trying to force my smile away by helping myself to a large pinch of those funny coloured seeds they give you after an Indian meal, and spluttering.

'It's not a bloke is it?' said Penny, slyly.

'No, no,' I said. 'Just Jack. Yes, of course I'll go up the tree. It's fine.'

At that moment I would have agreed to anything.

8 November

Woke up this morning to find a letter from my doctor.

'Dear Mrs Harp,' it read. 'It is now the time of year that we ask all our vulnerable patients to make an appointment for an inoculation against flu . . .'

Well, firstly I'm not Mrs Harp and secondly, surely I'm not what you'd describe as 'vulnerable'? When I rang up the surgery they said everyone of sixty-five and over is described as vulnerable and I thought thank you very much. Anyway, why should I have a flu jab? When you get to a certain age, about seventy, say, shouldn't you allow yourself to be carried off by whatever fatal disease comes your way? Otherwise you risk going on for ever and being a Burden To Your Family, and costing them thousands of pounds in nursing home fees—like Archie. So I'm going to refuse.

Anyway, Louis. We're meeting tonight and I'm in an absolute panic. I have got my entire wardrobe out on my bed, and everything looks old and tatty. Even the Vivienne Westwood jacket that I bought

280

a few years ago in a sale, that I thought could never go out of date, somehow looks stupid. And it's frayed at the cuffs. In the end I decided on a very nice black skirt that shows off my slim tummy, and a top that's high enough to cover that slightly wrinkly bit that older women always get just above their boobs, but low enough to show I actually do have boobs.

This morning I slathered on a strange face pack I'd found at the bottom of the cupboard under the bathroom sink. I hadn't used the stuff since the sixties. It was a kind of green putty, and naturally enough the doorbell rang just as it was starting to dry.

When I opened the door I discovered Ned standing outside. I'd completely forgotten he'd texted last night to say he was coming over to talk about my going up this wretched tree. This morning, less dancing on air than I was last night, I'm increasingly wishing that I'd never agreed to this. Suddenly I'm starting to feel jolly vulnerable. Maybe my doctor has a point.

After he'd got over the shock of being welcomed by someone who looked like a Martian, Ned said he'd wait for me while I washed it all off. And as I was in the bathroom I heard Michelle coming downstairs and bumping into him in the kitchen. I came down, with my skin tightened and looking about forty-five years old and I noticed Ned was writing something down and Michelle was giggling.

So there *was* something going on, after all!

As she rushed off to her English class, Ned said kindly, 'If you don't want to go up this tree, I'm quite happy to do it instead. I really wouldn't blame you.'

'That's very kind of you,' I said, 'but somehow I don't think a fit chap like you going up the tree would have as much impact as a vulnerable old lady, i.e. me.'

'You're not vulnerable!' said Ned, taking the cue, and my heart warmed to him. 'You're tough as old boots.' My heart cooled a bit.

When I got to sixty I was always referring to myself as an old lady. I think it was to make myself seem a bit younger. In other words, I'd imagine whoever it was I was speaking to thinking I *was* an old lady, so I'd try to get the description in first. But these days I realise it's just a bit embarrassing. It's as if I'm trying to be one of the lads. So normally I keep quiet about it. It had certainly been a mistake to try it on with Ned.

I gave him Harry's number, so he could make arrangements to get the tree stuff, and he assured me that with the help of a couple of the drug dealers, he and James can make everything really secure.

'But we'll have to set it up at night, and get you up under the cover of darkness as well,' he said. 'James and I will get the banner up first—'YOUR COUNCIL WANTS TO KILL THIS TREE!'— and then you nip up. And we'll get the press round. It'll be a great story: "Pensioner makes brave stand to save tree . . . retired teacher Marie Sharp risks life to stop council desecrating centuries-old common."'

'What do you mean, risking my life?' I said, suddenly alarmed. 'I'm not risking my life, am I?'

'Well, I suppose technically, yes, if you were to drop out of it and there weren't enough drug dealers milling around underneath to cushion your fall,' said Ned. 'But no more than you risk your life crossing the road.'

'Hmm,' I said. 'Oh God.'

But I can't get out of it now.

Later

Waited in the most terrible state for Louis to arrive to take me to dinner. I'd put the Inkspots on to give me courage and was building up my confidence, usual Maori-style, in the kitchen, when he rang the bell. And on hearing the music he simply danced in, grinning, putting his paper down on a chair and then he seized me by the waist and insisted on finishing the dance till the next track.

'Nothing beats those old Inkspots!' he said. ' "I love coffee, I love tea, I love the Java-jive, and it loves me . . ." ' he sang. 'But Marie, what *is* the Java-jive? I guess if we knew that, we'd also know the meaning of life.'

'But I've *always* wondered about the Java-jive,' I said, laughing. 'In fact I've been relying on you, as an American, being able to supply the answer. If you can't do that, well, let's call the whole thing off . . .'

It all promised to be a terrific evening.

He'd booked a swanky Italian restaurant in Knightsbridge, with linen tablecloths and linen napkins and several glasses for each person as if they were going to have aperitifs, red wine, white wine, pudding wine and water one after the other, and it was full of glamorous young couples who looked Jack and Chrissie's age, holding hands across the table and murmuring things to each other. And it was here that I started to feel rather like an old granny. And yet I also felt, *at the same time,* which was what was so odd, just as I had done on my first ever date when I was seventeen. One gets pulled between two generational states. I knew how Schumann or whoever it was must have felt when he was trying to stretch his poor hands into playing two notes bigger than an octave at the same time. But over a delicious *escalope alla marsala* and a glass of champagne I started to relax even more.

Here I was with this young bloke (well, he seems young to me), eyes crinkled with friendliness rather than geriatric crinkliness, a lovely brown neck, hands with not a liver-spot in sight. Sexual desire flared up in me and I felt quite shy as I tried to fight it down.

We talked of his mother—suspected cancer, naturally. 'I'm so sorry, that is worrying,' I said. 'But quite honestly, is there anyone over sixty who *hasn't* got cancer these days?' And he burst out laughing and said, 'Marie, that is what I love about you. That remark is one that no American woman would *ever* say!' We then got on to painting, and were particularly scathing about the idea that art these days needed reams of explanations to accompany it, when he suddenly leaned over and took my hand.

'You know, we've gotten ourselves into a silly situation,' he said.

'I know,' I said. But I wasn't quite sure what the situation was.

'Part of me thinks I've completely fallen for you,' he said. 'And another part knows it's ridiculous. I mean, we hardly know each other . . .'

'I know,' I said again.

'But for some reason, the moment I met you in the plane . . .'

Before he went any further, I stopped him.

'Look, I'm ancient,' I said. 'Don't even go there. The whole thing would be ridiculous. I'm far older than you think. Let me tell you exactly how—'

'Whoa! Enough already!' said Louis firmly. 'Age has got absolutely nothing to do with it. Don't go there.'

'But I'm . . .'

'Shut up,' he said, firmly. 'I just know that I feel completely at home with you. You could be a hundred for all I care.'

'I feel at home with you, too,' I said. 'It's a funny feeling. Not one I've had for ages.'

'Since when?' he said.

And I suppose I meant since Archie was well.

And then I told him about Archie. And he suddenly leaned back and said, 'I hope you're not feeling this way about me because this old guy is dying, and you've got to find someone else . . .'

'I don't think so,' I said, rather startled by his analysis.

'When Dad died, I remember Mom falling in love with some other old prof almost the day after the funeral and it was all we could do to stop her running off with him there and then. This isn't like that, is it? You sure?' He was looking at me almost suspiciously.

I assured him that it wasn't, and if anything his kindness and perceptiveness about the situation had made me like him even more. Then I told him about going up the tree.

'Now you're not to tell anyone about the tree,

will you?' I said. 'It's a secret.'

He looked a bit annoyed.

'Look, Marie, just because I'm a journalist doesn't mean I'm a bastard. Of course I won't tell anyone. Anyway, who would I tell? It's not likely *The Times* is gonna run with it, is it? Unless maybe you fell out,' he added, grinning, 'and even then I'm afraid they wouldn't give a shit. But *I* would,' he added, taking my hand again. 'Are you sure you're doing the right thing, Marie? Are you sure you're going to be safe? I'm worried about you.'

His concern made me want to weep.

After supper we walked to the car and then I realised with a jolt he was so much younger than me that he actually walked faster. He took my hand and I scurried along like a dachshund, trying to keep up without panting.

He drove me back home and drew up outside the house—he'd borrowed the car from his host and it kept stalling at the lights. But before I could get out, he drew me close to him, put his arms round me and gave me a long kiss.

'I've been wanting to do that all evening,' he said, stroking my cheek. 'You're a beautiful woman, Marie. You're so lovely. But much as I'd like to come in, tear off all your clothes and take it from there, I don't think it would be a good idea. It's too soon. I don't want us to be like all the others . . .'

We cuddled up again, and when he finally pulled away, he said, 'Jeez, this takes me back to senior prom. She was called Marie, too, pretty little brunette . . . I took her home, kissed her in the car and looked up—her dad was waiting on the porch watching every move! I got out of there pretty damn quick, I can tell you!'

On hearing this, I looked nervously out of the window, hoping that no passing resident was staring in. But luckily, nothing.

'I so want to see you again, Marie. But I'm off to Oxford tomorrow to be with my mom while she has these tests. I'll try to get down in the next few days. I'll call you.'

I tottered to my front door, feeling absolutely sick with desire and confusion.

13 November

Four days and still no word from Louis, which isn't a good sign. He surely can't have gone back to the States without being in touch? I can't help feeling that there is something a little odd about him. He keeps blowing hot and cold. And anyway what was that about 'all the others'? Whatever, the result is that I'm left reeling. The awful thing is that I can't really tell anyone because I know it'll sound so stupid. I mean look at me when Penny fell in love with Gavin, so much younger? I couldn't have been less sympathetic. And now it's happening to me, and I'm just as goofy as she was.

Later

Had a very nasty moment this afternoon when I was looking through some old photograph albums (to see what I looked like when I was Louis' age, if the truth be known) and suddenly I spotted a picture of me and David, and Jack aged ten, sitting

287

by a very nice little table inlaid with mother-of-pearl that used to belong to my mother. With rather a sick feeling, I realised I hadn't seen it around for ages—presumably David had taken it with him when we got divorced. I felt really angry about this, and couldn't think of anything else except how to get it back. After all, we've been friends for years since then, and no doubt he's found a place for it, and I know it would look a bit churlish suddenly to want this table returned after all this time.

I shall just have to bide my time. Sometimes, if you wait around for a good moment to mention something it just comes up and you can slip it into the conversation naturally. But I still feel a tremendous resentment. Why, I don't know. It's only a table, for heaven's sake. But it really rankles.

James and Ned have suggested I start to brush up my climbing skills, not that I have any to brush up since, after making that promise to Jack, I haven't tackled a ladder for months. And after the chimes episode, I've been particularly wary of heights. So I'm starting to practise tomorrow afternoon in Ned's garden, where he has an old apple tree.

Spent the rest of the afternoon huddled in every jersey and coat I possessed, painting the November section of Seasons of the Doomed Trees. It was so cold I could have been in Archie's kitchen.

14 November

Ned has an extremely tidy, minimalist flat and a very tidy minimalist garden full of gravel. It's all a bit too Japanese for me, but still, he looks very good in it, with his bony figure and his silver hair. He gave us some tea, and, bless him, had specially gone out and bought some milk for James and me, which was decent of him because he obviously thinks of it as the Devil's Brew. He also gave us some strangely nice vegan biscuits which were made out of polenta and sugar and vegetable oil, but no eggs. God knows how it all stuck together. Probably with some vegetarian glue.

Being a tree man, Ned had got some kind of out-of-date contraption of his own for getting up the apple tree—the real sturdy stuff will come from Harry next week—and he'd slung it up over the branches of his apple tree and casually invited me to swing my way up like a monkey. It looked so easy when he did it, but when I tried I just found my arms weren't up to the job. And once I did get up to the top, with a lot of help from James and Ned shoving me up by my bottom, I felt absolutely terrified when I glanced back at the ground beneath me.

But they were really sweet, shouting and cheering, and Ned took a photograph and then they both said, 'Well, goodbye, see you tomorrow,' and pretended they were going off together and leaving me up there. Lots of jolly banter, and when I got back down to earth I found my knees were trembling.

'You did really well, darling,' said James. 'I'm proud of you!'

'Yes, well done,' said Ned. 'We'll make an eco-warrior of you yet.'

'Well, I hope I don't *look* like an eco-warrior,' I said, since most eco-warriors are renowned for their matted hair, generally grungy appearance and appalling smell.

'After a couple of days up a tree,' said James, 'you'll be unrecognisable. The birds will have made a nest in your hair, your clothes will be covered in leaves, squirrels will be hiding in your cleavage and ants and woodlice will be living under your nails. You'll come down with the ability to talk to the animals, like Doctor Dolittle. You will be Worshipped Like a God.'

15 November

When I was young I was always glaring at strangers in the street. I suppose I was terrified of them. I'd scowl and then stare at the pavement and stride past them furiously as if I were deeply offended by something they'd said the night before and I was never going to forgive them.

These days, however, I'm always smiling at strangers. Sometime I even speak to them. 'Hello!' I chirrup. 'Lovely weather we've having for the time of year, don't you think?'

Of course now strangers smile at *me* in the street and I've realised suddenly that it's not because I'm dancing on air and everyone is infected by my love of humanity—no, it's that they recognise me from chairing the Residents' Meeting. Most peculiar,

290

having all these welcoming faces around. And rather nice. It's fun being a celebrity for a while—which, of course, everyone wants to be in their weaker moments, even when it's not for the allotted fifteen minutes.

However, I was so busy smiling at someone in the street yesterday that I fell down *again*, this time grazing my poor old knees really badly on the pavement. I managed to hobble back home, but am rather worried. I thought I ought to visit the doctor because if there's something wrong with my balance perhaps there's something wrong with my ears, which is where balance is stored. Sometimes I think I could set up my own doctor's practice because I now know almost every ailment available to me.

I thought I'd go to bed for an hour to get over the shock, and as I reached for my glass of water, I suddenly noticed that it was actually sitting on the exact mother-of-pearl table I'd been so cross about David taking. It has been my bedside table now for years, but was so covered with books that I've never noticed it.

Thank goodness I never mentioned it to him! Particularly when it was under my nose all the time. I suddenly felt rather more sympathetic to poor old Archie and his delusions about the brooch.

16 November

Finally, an email from Louis! He says his mother's tests have come through, but now he's got to hang around because she's got to have some further scans. 'I did love our evening together. You're so often in my mind,' he wrote.

It all seems unreal. Perhaps it *is* unreal. I mean, I'm sure if someone else were to tell me the story of me and Louis, I'd say at once that he was just some serial charmer and not to believe a word he says. But I can't help it. I *do* believe what he says.

17 November

Still have that odd guilty feeling about going to the doctor. I know that I pay his wretched salary out of my taxes but (and I imagine it's some pre-welfare state habit, inherited from my parents), I feel I shouldn't really worry him (and mine *is* a 'him') unless I have a brain tumour or a lump on my nose the size of a marrow.

The doctor said there was nothing wrong with me, but suggested I practise my balance by standing on one leg every morning while I brush my teeth. I said I'd have a go, but the first time I tried it, I nearly fell over again. It's the action of cleaning one's teeth that makes it so difficult. If I remain absolutely still I can balance on one leg for about thirty seconds, but cleaning my teeth simultaneously—quite impossible. It's like that trick of rubbing one's tummy clockwise and one's head anti-clockwise at the same time. A trick I taught not only Jack but also Gene. And which was taught, in turn, by my own lovely granny to me.

This falling-over caper makes me glad I've organised a will. I mean if I hadn't, and I climbed up that tree and fell out, then though my money would go to Jack there might be a remote chance, if he were to drop dead at the same time, that all my money (I say 'all my money'—there's hardly any money, but I suppose the house is worth something) would go to the state.

18 November

Had a lovely email from Louis. He wrote, 'Thinking of you . . .' and ended it 'love, Louis'.

But I don't have a clue what's going on. I mean, what does he really feel about me? I feel a bit as if I'm living in some fantasy of his. He's wondering if I'm not keen on him because of Archie disappearing from my life. But *I* wonder whether he's not keen on me because I'm unattainable since I'm too old. I know that syndrome. I remember the number of blokes who used to fall for me when I was happily ensconced with a boyfriend and then, the moment I became available, they all scarpered.

Actually, I'm starting to wish he'd never started it. It's so irritating to manage to stifle all kinds of desires and feelings of longing for Archie and then have someone conjure them back up out of nowhere.

But however much I explain my feelings like this it doesn't make a blind bit of difference. I think about him far too much.

I am now of an age where I ought to be able to cope with it all. But of course I can't. I've spent the last few days feeling really weird and confused, and not sure whether it's about Louis or Archie, or the prospect of going up a tree, or because I miss Jack and Chrissie and Gene so much. I've shouted 'pull yourself together!' to myself so often that it doesn't have any effect any more.

20 November

Woken by the sounds of thunder in the night and now the rain is absolutely gushing down. *Daily Rant*'s charming headline today is 'NUCLEAR LEAK WILL BLIGHT GENERATIONS! *No more "normal" say scientists!*'

Since there's not much normal around here as it is, a nuclear leak isn't going to make a great deal of difference.

I braved the rain and went out to the newsagent to buy a new diary for next year. I waited in the queue and was so furiously impatient with the woman in front of me, fiddling about with her change, that I completely forgot to have my own purse ready when it was my turn to pay. Naturally I couldn't find it, and was patting my pockets, emptying my bag out on the counter and creating havoc in the queue behind me. Of course the people behind me got just as furious with me as I was with the previous customer. I apologised profusely but it didn't make any difference.

Feeling completely flustered I hurried out, and even though it was still pelting with rain—a real monsoon—I was so keen to get away quickly I left my head bare. Finally I got to a place under an awning where lots of other people were taking shelter, and tried to sort myself out. I put my bag down, did up the buttons on my jacket and pulled my hood over my head. Forgetting, of course, that because of the downpour it was full of water. I was completely soaked. It was all I could do not to scream obscenities into the beards of the men queuing up to go into the mosque, but I thought that would go down extremely badly, so I restrained myself by clenching my toes as hard as I could. Pretty painful, clenching ones toes at my age, I can tell you.

Being English, everyone stared straight ahead and pretended they hadn't noticed.

24 November

I am in a complete flap because Louis suddenly rang and said he was coming down from Oxford this afternoon, specially to see me, so I'm giving him a bite to eat here and then we're going for a walk in Burnham Beeches, the nearest bit of country. I tidied up the sitting room, leaving just enough books lying around to show that I'm not a neat-freak. I decided to put out a Christie's catalogue—the one my pictures featured in, because I thought that would give us something to talk about; a Beatrix Potter, to remind him I had a grandchild and wasn't ashamed to say so; and my current books on the go, the short stories of Chekhov and Bob Monkhouse's autobiography, *Crying with Laughter*. I know, I know . . . But it's amazingly well-written and he had an absolutely fascinating life. And I thought the juxtaposition of Chekhov and Monkhouse would confuse him.

To my consternation, Michelle, when cleaning the bathroom, had put my special rubber non-slip bathmat to dry on the radiator outside—it had got mouldy underneath, she said, and she'd had to bleach it to take the marks off—and I'd only managed to get rid of this evidence of infirmity, shoving it under my towel on the rail, just before Louis rang the bell.

Naturally enough, when he arrived he didn't give the books a second glance, but walked right through to the garden. Even though it was starting to look a bit like I feel these days—rather creaky and barren—he still raved.

'This is really neat!' he said. 'That's the problem with New York. No gardens, and not enough green. Jesus Christ, what the hell is that?' He'd spotted James's installation that I'd recently heaved into its 'special setting'.

'Er . . . um . . . it's by a friend,' I said apologetically. 'It's an installation . . . er, I put it as far out of the way as possible. It's meant to be me.'

'*You?*' said Louis, puckering his brow. 'All that barbed wire? It's not the you *I* know. With friends like these who needs anemones, as they say?'

'Oh, someone . . . he's very nice and kind, I've known him a long time . . . had to keep it . . . ghastly . . .' I mumbled disloyally.

But it had clearly made a great impact on Louis, and not in a good way.

'Marie, you can't keep that . . . that . . . that *thing* around, however much you like the guy,' he said. 'It looks like . . . like . . .'

296

'Something out of *Bitter Quinces, Poisoned Souls*?' I suggested. And he laughed.

As we came in to the kitchen, we passed an old walking stick I'd propped up in the corner to use after I'd had my second fall.

'Whose is that?' he said, slightly alarmed. 'Not yours, surely?'

'Oh, no, er . . . it's for visitors when they can't manage the er . . .'

Suddenly I saw the whole house as if he were appraising it in the way that I looked at Marion's house. Minimalist it is not.

Finally he said, 'You got a lovely home here. It reminds me of Mom's home. Very English.'

And at that my heart sank. For 'very English' read 'very old-fashioned'. Or, even worse, 'geriatric'.

I was glad when we drove out to Burnham Beeches. I've loved the area since I was a child. We parked the car and walked along a public footway through the woods, the beech leaves crunching under our feet. To start with, we didn't say much. But he put his arm round me occasionally as we walked, and squeezed me close.

It was one of those strange walks under the trees when you feel utterly in communion with your companion. Or at least I felt utterly in communion with him. I have no idea whether he felt in communion with me. He may have been thinking about the credit crunch or the foreign secretary for all I know. Sometimes I sneak little glimpses at him when he's not looking. And oh, his skin is so smooth and firm—and there's something about the back of his neck that just makes me melt. The truth is that the skin of older men just isn't quite so lovely. Even Archie's. Nothing one can do about that.

Halfway through our walk, we sat down on an old tree trunk and he looked at me.

'Look, I know I told you I didn't want to know, but now I do. I've been thinking. If this is going to go any further, we've got to be honest with each other. How old *are* you?'

'Well, I've tried to tell you but you wouldn't listen!' I said indignantly. Then I took a big breath. 'I'm sixty-five!'

And as I said it, I could see the surprise in his face. 'And I've had a facelift,' I added. I felt like someone owning up to cheating in maths at school.

'I hope you didn't tell Martha!' he said, laughing. 'She'd have had a fit!'

'I know,' I said. 'No, I tell most people, but I thought in Martha's case it might be best to keep quiet. But look, sweetie, you see the age difference is ridiculous . . . I have tried to tell you . . .'

'Oh Jesus!' he said, putting his head in his hands. 'What a mess! Oh why wasn't I born ten years earlier? Or you born ten years later?'

'Well, I wasn't,' I said, rather peremptorily. 'You've got to find a nice woman your own age, and start a family.'

'Couldn't you jet off to Italy . . . isn't there's some clinic where you can go and get pregnant, whatever age?'

The awful thing was I didn't really know whether he was joking or not. There was a sort of amused flirtatiousness about everything he said, but at the same time I could see there was genuine sadness and longing.

And for one absolutely awful moment I

298

suddenly wished I *were* younger and could have
another baby . . . the feeling of the loss of all that
flooded my entire body, and I could have wept. He
could see I was upset and, looking into my eyes, he
reached out and held my other hand.

'Gee, I'm sorry,' he said. 'It's not fair on you.
No, you're right.'

'But why aren't you married already?' I asked.
'You're pushing it yourself, if you don't mind my
saying so. You'd better get a move on.'

It was odd how easy it was to slide from the role
of lover, or potential lover at least, into the role of
mother. Sometimes with Louis I feel as if I'm with
Jack.

'There was an African girl I thought of
marrying, when I was doing my PhD,' he said,
looking into the distance. 'But then she was always
going to go back to Kampala and one day she
never came back. I think she got married. She was
the love of my life, to be honest. I was crazy about
her.'

Wasn't sure what to say, after that. So we just
walked on. He gave me another huge hug when he
dropped me off, and then he suddenly said,
'When's your tree thing?'

'Week after next,' I said. Surely he wasn't going
to offer to climb up with me.

'Well, the week after—you won't be up all week,
will you?—you said you were going to visit . . . who
was that old guy you told me about . . . Archie? I'll
still be at Mom's in Oxford, so why don't you come
down, meet her, on your way? I know you'd get on.
And it would relieve the tedium. I'm working most
days, but the evenings . . . there's a limit to how
many times you can play Canasta!' he added. 'And

299

you know, whatever age you are, my sweetheart, it hasn't changed my feelings . . . you do know that, don't you?'

'I do know, darling,' I said. Rather a risk, that 'darling'. But I didn't want to admit to myself that it was a blatant lie. So I tried to kid myself. 'And I'd love to come to Oxford,' I added. 'Assuming I haven't stayed up the tree and started talking to the birds and turned into Doctor Dolittle,' I added.

He laughed. 'And that's the other thing about you,' he said. 'You're so funny.'

Felt rather bad not telling him that the Dolittle gag wasn't mine, but what the hell.

Meet his mother! Funny, though, it didn't sound 'meet my mother' in a 'meet-my-mother-so-I-can-introduce-you-to-her-as-my-latest-girlfriend' kind of way. It sounded more as if he thought the pair of old dears would get along just fine.

That whole conversation has made me feel pretty bleak. But there's no getting around it. It's one we had to have. Though where it leaves us now, I don't know.

Later

Suddenly felt a bit creepy. I didn't like the way he referred to Archie as 'that old guy'. Oh well. Try to put it out of my mind.

29 November

Tomorrow evening is the time when we're planning to do this tree thingy. I am getting

300

extremely worried about it. I mean, could it be against the law? I'm sure it's not, but I would really *hate* to be arrested and put in prison. I mean *really* hate.

Harry's hauling equipment has arrived, and apparently Ned and James have got this kind of platform they're going to haul up and nail to a couple of branches, and they're going to put a sleeping bag and a bottle of water and some chocolate bars up there as well. But they say I mustn't drink too much water in case I want to have a pee. They estimate I can go for twenty-four hours without going to the loo, and if I'm desperate I'll just to have to come down, rush behind a bush, and then whizz up again. (Since these days I have to rush to the loo every ten minutes at night, I'm not too sure about this, but I'll just have to cross my fingers. Not to mention my legs.) I'm not to eat anything, either, for obvious reasons, but again, I'm sure I can last twenty-four hours without anything to eat.

We've now decided on a rota of people to go up, because no one can stay up longer than twenty-four hours, so Penny's going up the day after me, and then Marion and a couple of other doughty old girls from up the road. Sheila the Dealer said she wouldn't go up for love or money, and Father Emmanuel said he had a lot of church work to do. What a wimp.

I've got to sleep well tonight, but of course I'm writing this at three in the morning because I'm stricken with panic about it all. However, I can't wriggle out of it now. As long as the papers get a picture, that's all that matters.

Courage, old girl!

DECEMBER

1 December

Well! What a night! Although it was a triumph, I still feel a gibbering wreck!

We snuck out at 11 p.m. and there was only one drug dealer around (it being a bit early for drug dealers) and he was very much up for the whole thing. He thanked us for telling him what was going on because if there was going to be a media explosion he wanted to warn all the other drug dealers to steer clear until it was all over.

Somehow Ned and James had managed to get the whole thing rigged up. Ned had shinned up the tree as it got dark, without anyone seeing, and had fixed up a platform up there about the size of my front door. Then he'd let down a rope ladder for me to clamber up. James had to come up after me, pushing me from behind. They'd already got the banner into position, so I didn't actually have to do anything, except *be* there. Then they both went down, and I pulled the rope ladder up to the top. Frightfully heavy. It was an absolutely freezing night. I was glad I'd brought several extra jerseys, a pair of thick socks and an exceptionally warm, woolly hat with earflaps.

The odd thing was that I'd had no idea that up there the whole thing would move so much. You don't think of trees moving but when you get up as high as I was, there only has be a tiny breeze and the whole thing, even though it looks really sturdy, sways slightly. And the noise of those branches

302

rustling together! There must be a tremendous racket when the leaves are on. Of course it was incredibly scary but terribly exciting at the same time, and James and Ned had very sweetly pitched a tent at the bottom and they were going to sleep there so if I got panicky in the early hours I could yell down and they'd reassure me, but it was all okay. I was slightly nervous of rolling off in the night. But Ned had put planks around the structure so it would have been a bit difficult.

I'd been hoping to get on with some knitting up there—I've only got the arms left to finish—but of course I'd stupidly left it at home, so I had nothing to do but look out over the world below me.

It was so beautiful. As the night's blackness increased, the street lights glowed with their sodium brightness below me and soon I could make out the pattern of the roads. Cars roared by in the distance. Police sirens wailed. And far away I could see, incredibly, the outline of the London Eye and, even further away, the blinking light at the top of Canary Wharf. It was difficult not to be overwhelmed by this treetop panorama. I felt a wave of love for London, and a sense of belonging and, indeed, for the first time in ages (and Martha would be delighted to hear this) a real sense of wonder. I didn't think I'd be able to sleep at all, because every few minutes something new happened. New noises. New lights, on and off. New stars winking. The moon moving, ever so slightly, through the sky. The birds shifting around. An aeroplane passing. If it hadn't been for the loo arrangements I could happily have stayed up in what I gather is known as 'The Canopy', for a week.

It was also rather odd being inside a tree that I'd actually painted. I felt I was being intrusive in a way. Like asking a life model out for a date.

With a pang, I suddenly wished Archie could have been with me. He'd have been so up for it, bless him. And I knew he'd be just as touched as me, to see all this stretching out to infinity. And, in a funny way—though it sounds dreadfully sentimental—in a funny way I felt he *was* there with me. I started to cry. Not with misery, not with joy. Just because I was so utterly overcome by the . . . *everythingness* of everything. I can't put it into words.

I did finally get to sleep, however, and woke early, to see the dawn creeping up over the buildings. An hour or so later, James and Ned crawled out of their tent and started whistling to me.

'Are you okay?' they shouted.

'I'm fine,' I shouted back to the two tiny figures far below. 'It's brilliant up here.'

'We'll get you down by lunchtime! Just keep your legs crossed for another few hours!'

Luckily, though I'd taken a bottle of water up with me, I'd not had anything to drink for hours before I went up, *and* had also taken an anti-diuretic pill prescribed by my doctor five years ago that I had, very sensibly, kept in my medicine chest.

At eleven the local paper came round to take a picture, and, amazingly, even the *Daily Rant* turned up. That day must have been particularly disaster-free because normally something like this wouldn't make a story in a national paper. But apparently they're doing a big campaign about how local councils don't pay any attention to residents' wishes, so this is a brilliant illustration of it.

Local neighbours had arrived in support, too: mums with children in pushchairs, and their own banners, drug dealers, even the lovely Indian from the corner shop put in an appearance and gave me a wave, and Ned and James handed out cups of tea and home-made cakes to the journalists and cameramen. Even our local MP came along to lend his support—he's a different party to the council of course—and then I had to yell quite a few interviews from my treetop eyrie, and after a while they drifted off.

I remained up there, feeling like a weird tree nymph—a tree nymph who was desperate to go to the loo, I might add—and then at about one o'clock, Penny was ready to take over.

When I got down there was an enormous cheer and everyone wanted to congratulate me, but I was so bursting to go to the loo that I first had to rush to the nearest house and ask if I could use their toilet. After that, I came back out, and I felt like— well, I felt probably rather like Annie Noona must have felt at the height of her career, poor girl.

Several neighbours asked me over for a celebration supper, and I had no idea there were so many lovely people in the street. People I'd never met, people who lived across the road were all coming out of their houses and slapping me on the back, and even the drug dealers were giving me high fives and saying 'F'real, sister!' Sheila the Dealer gave me a thumbs-up, the height of praise from S the D, and Father Emmanuel insisting on getting on his knees and thanking the Lord that I'd come down safely. Almost felt like joining him in

305

prayer, I have to say.

Alice gave me a special card she'd made with glitter on it, and a drawing of me up the tree—so sweet!—and Brad and Sharmie insisted on asking as many people round as possible for champagne. Even though it was the middle of the day.

A couple of glasses and—because I'd had so little to eat up there—I felt pretty woozy.

'I must get some proper rest,' I said, as I left the party to go back to my own house. 'But thank you so so much! Let's hope the papers do something about it tomorrow!'

'Make sure you sleep like a log!' said James, unable to resist the joke—and everybody groaned.

And I did.

2 December

Louis sent me a text saying *I c u star! But knew that already! xL* (Notice there's only one x this time. Hmm.) And there, on one of the inside pages of the *Daily Rant*, was a photograph of me in the tree, with the headline 'TREE-MENDOUS! OAP IS ECO-WARRIOR! *Pensioner reaches dizzy heights in her bid to support* Rant's *campaign against councils' lack of concern for residents!*'

And underneath it reiterated the fact that the council was going to have a rethink about the whole scheme. And added that several environmental agencies we hadn't been in touch with were up in arms. The upshot seems to be that there's very little chance of the trees being cut down or a hotel being built after all.

As we'd got all that coverage, we decided there

306

was no point in prolonging the protest and hauled Tim, the latest in the tree rota to have been hauled up, back to earth. He, like me, had been enjoying his tree-top experience, and I think was rather put out to find his services were no longer required, but it was difficult for anyone to be grumpy when they saw the enormous amount of coverage we'd got.

'Weren't we just brilliant?' Penny and I said to each other as we prepared a celebration drinks party for the committee this evening.

'I love that Inkspots number,' said Penny as I put it on to encourage us in our work. 'But I never know—what *is* a Java jive?'

I put all the pictures I'd done of the trees around the room—it was like a mini-exhibition and I must say, though I say it myself, they didn't look at all bad. I must keep at it, though, to complete the cycle.

We'd also asked all the other people who'd helped, which meant there was a huge scrum and the party went on till about midnight. Unfortunately I'd said everyone could bring their children, and the result was that all the kids came, offered to hand round the food, and then disappeared down to the end of the garden, accompanied by Pouncer, with the plates of sausages, smoked salmon sandwiches and crisps, leaving the grown-ups with nothing but olives. Except Alice, of course. She very sweetly handed round the olives and the few remaining quails' eggs.

Still, it was a great evening, and James tapped a glass and said everyone should raise a toast to me and Penny, which was very nice, and Father

Emmanuel said we should all say a prayer of thanks, and that anyone who wanted to come to his church on Sundays was always welcome (somehow I doubt God had much to do with it all, but still, we all bowed our heads hypocritically while he droned on) and Ned said we should thank all our supporters who had written letters and gave a special vote of thanks to Harry and Sylvie for the loan of the equipment, and then the councillor (never one to miss an opportunity) banged on a glass even more loudly to get everyone's attention and implied it was all down to him and that he'd had a word with the leader of the council and in view of the publicity there was no way the plan would go ahead.

It was all a very pleasant orgy of self-congratulation.

Michelle sloped off with Ned and James, and while Brad took Alice home next door to put her to bed—he wants to give me £4,000 for the entire series of paintings when I've finished them! I can't believe it!—Sharmie gave me a hand with the clearing up. I've made a date to take Alice to the circus next week. Tragic—I'm just so desperate for children to do things with! And still harbour such terrible feelings about destroying her dear old granny's chimes.

Penny braved the bottom of the garden to retrieve the plates the children had taken down there, and came back saying that not only had they broken one of my favourites, but they'd obviously had a sausage fight and there were bangers scattered all over the beds.

Felt like such a heroine, I couldn't have cared less. And if the cockroaches have a feast on the sausages, then good luck to them. May their little black tummies burst.

3 December

Very odd Skype with Gene who assures me that Christmas is a non-existent festival in New York. They don't hang up stockings, he tells me, and they have, in any case, just celebrated Thanksgiving. I think he was wondering why I hadn't sent him a present.

'There's no Father Christmas here,' he said, 'we have Santa Claus. And Mom says we mustn't say Happy Christmas we've got to say Happy Holidays instead. And we had a horrid turkey at Thanksgiving, all slimy.'

Turned out, as Jack told me during the same Skype, that their friends at Thanksgiving insisted on going out into their yard and deep-frying the bird in peanut oil, and serving it with some vile concoction of Campbell's mushroom soup with green beans stewed in it, and crispy fried onions sprinkled on top. Then they had sweet potato puree as a complement, with marshmallows as a nightmarish garnish.

'Completely inedible,' said Jack. 'And what are you doing for Christmas, Mum?'

I wanted to say I was hoping to come and stay with them, or that they'd say they were coming back here for a holiday, but because of Jack's question I didn't like to.

'Oh, I'll probably spend it with Penny—or Marion and Tim, who asked me over for the day, or Sylvie, who said, really sweetly, that I'd be very welcome. So it's not as if I don't have any perches,' I said, casually. Then I screwed up my courage. 'But I suppose there's no chance . . .'

'Oh, we've got no idea about our plans,' said Jack, rather impatiently. 'Everything's up in the air at the moment. There are lots of options.'

After we'd logged off, I felt very blue. Christmas without the family. It doesn't bear thinking about. Suddenly I wondered what on the earth the point of me actually was. No doubt everyone has these moods, but when you're my age you can't say, 'Well, who knows what the future will bring, tra la?' quite so confidently as you used to, because we all know what the future will bring. Oblivion.

Marie! Stop it! You sound like a *Daily Rant* headline! Who was it—Don Marquis?—who wrote 'there's a dance in the old dame yet toujours gai toujours gai?'

I'm jolly well going to try to get rid of all thoughts of Louis and Archie and Christmas just for tonight and . . . and . . . I'll ring Penny and we'll go out and have a yummy supper and a couple of lovely drinks and I'll be right as rain.

4 December

And, do you know, I was! Right as rain, that is. There's nothing like wallowing in the Slough of Despond and then getting really irritated and then having supper with a good girlfriend to put a jollier slant on everything. I realise I've got terribly behind with the knitting, too, so I've decided to knit at least three inches a day and that way I'll have finished Gene's jersey by Christmas. And

310

maybe I'll be able to go out to New York in the New Year anyway. Something to look forward to.

In an article in the *Rant* about How to be Happy, someone was quoted as saying that the key to happiness was having three things on the horizon. One in the next few weeks, another in the next few months, and another next year. Well, I've got visiting Louis and his mum, then Christmas, and as for the next few months, well, who knows. But I know something will turn up.

5 December

Woke this morning with a start, a funny feeling coming over me at 5.30 a.m. It was a Feeling of Dread. It's not all that uncommon of course, but I wondered if it Meant Anything. Sometimes I make a note of these strange moments, thinking that if I see a headline in the *Rant* the morning after, saying that there was a fatal air crash at exactly the time I woke with the Feeling of Dread it would mean I had psychic powers. But unfortunately these Feelings of Dread never seem to relate to anything.

But the phone rang at 7.30 this morning, just as I'd finally got back to sleep, and it was Sylvie.

'Daddy died in the night,' she said simply.

'Oh dear,' I said. I felt a wellspring of emotion, and for a moment everything seemed completely unreal. It didn't feel as if I were in the room at all but floating, somehow, at ceiling height.

'But thank God he didn't suffer for long in that awful state, Marie,' said Sylvie, with a catch in her voice. 'Oh dear, poor old Daddy. I know we were all expecting him to die, but it's different when it happens isn't it? I still can't believe it. I still think he's alive . . . it hasn't come home to me yet.'

'Come home to me.' I wonder if such deaths ever really 'come home'. I know that were my father or mother to walk into the room right now, I wouldn't be at all surprised. They still live on daily in my mind. I don't think I've ever really understood they're dead. They've just gone away somewhere.

I tried to feel sad, but I couldn't. It was as if I've used up all my sadness over the past few months. I just felt like crying with relief.

'Oh Marie,' said Sylvie, down the telephone. 'Don't be too upset. You know Daddy would have wanted it like this.'

'I know,' I sobbed. 'It's just that it's been such a long time coming . . . oh poor old Archie, thank God he's at peace at last.' Finally, trying to pull myself together, I added, 'Can I do anything? How are you feeling? I know we knew it was coming and I know it was what we'd all hoped for in a way, but . . .'

'No, don't worry,' she said. 'Mrs Evans is the one who's taking it most badly, of course. Losing Dad means she loses more than just him, but her job, her role in the house, everything. She was with him for forty years, you know! But I'm getting her to come and work for us, and I know Daddy provided for her in his will . . .'

'What about the funeral?' I was trying to get out of bed and pull on my dressing gown without her hearing. Very softly and quietly and switching the phone from ear to ear while I put each arm in a different sleeve while she was talking so she

312

wouldn't know I was doing something else. I hate it when I can hear people feeding the cat or peeling potatoes—or even writing emails—while I'm talking to them on the phone. I like full concentration.

'We'll probably have it next week,' she said. 'We want to get it over as soon as possible, so it doesn't get in the way of Christmas.'

Later that morning, I rang up as many people as I could to tell them about Archie. It made it feel more real, the more people I told. Everyone was very sad and kind, and Penny and James even offered to come round, but most of my older friends just said, 'Ah well. There we are.' They're used to death. It was the young ones who seemed so appalled.

Even Jack was upset, surprisingly, when I skyped him.

'Oh, Mum, how sad!' he said, and I could see he was upset. Tears came into his eyes as he looked slightly up and to the left of my shoulder. 'Oh, I wish I'd been able to say goodbye. He was such a good bloke. You must be devastated.'

'Well, devastated*ish*,' I said. 'I just feel weird to be honest.'

'Oh well, it will make you a bit freer,' he said. 'Looking on the bright side.'

'Yes. And talking of being freer . . . you're definitely not coming over at Christmas, are you?' I asked daringly. 'I just need to be certain so if you're not I can make other plans.'

Again, at the mention of Christmas Jack seemed irritated. 'I've already told you, it's all a bit difficult at the moment, Mum. I don't quite know what we'll be doing at Christmas . . . assume that no,

313

we're not coming over . . . but we'll talk later.'

And then I wondered: oh dear Lord, maybe they're planning to go to California for Christmas?

Gene came on next and started gabbling on about some go-kart track he'd been on. 'It was *awesome*, Granny,' he said. 'I came second! And I wore a special hat and all these things, it was cool. And you know?' he said, leaning forward so all I could see of him was his nose, 'at Christmas, we . . .' but here Jack stepped in and said: 'Not now Gene, another time . . . sorry, Mum, but all our plans are up in the air. But we'll see you very soon, whatever happens, I'm sure . . . lots of love.'

Oh God! At Christmas what? They were becoming US citizens? Having a beach holiday in Miami? Spending the entire holiday in Disneyworld? Joining the Scientologists? I tried to put it all out of my mind. Get Archie's funeral over, that was what was important now. Golly, another funeral. They come thick and fast these days.

Then I was struck by a mind-blowingly vile and greedy thought. *I wondered if Archie had left me anything in his will?*

Isn't it awful when some mind-blowingly vile and greedy thought like that pops into your head without so much as a by-your-leave? I mean, one can't help one's thoughts, but thoughts of this sort that pop into my head make me feel so mercenary and ashamed of myself.

Still, I couldn't help wondering . . .

7 December

Spent all morning making Christmas cards. Looking at my list I see there are about seventy people I've got to send them to, and this year I've had rather a nice idea. I've cut out lots of Christmas tree shapes in green paper, stuck them down the centrefold of a red card, so their branches stick out when the card's opened, then I've drawn in the pots and added on some festive silver sparkle. At the top I've glued on a small gold star—I've still got loads left over from when I used to correct homework at school.

They look utterly charming, though I say it myself. And, finally, I've realised who Angie, Jim, Bella, Perry and Squeaks are. They're Marion's daughter and her family. Resolve to send them an extra affectionate message, and determined to pop down next year to make the acquaintance of Squeaks, whoever or whatever he or she or it might be.

Phone rang and it was Jack and Chrissie's agents saying the tenants have done a runner, without paying last month's rent. Bang goes their hefty deposit, then. Charming. Just before Christmas. Still, that's Jack and Chrissie's problem. Maddening, though.

This afternoon, I took Alice to the Moscow State Circus. She had dressed up in a pink skirt, a glittery top and a pair of bright yellow tights. She looked delightful. She was very shy about coming out with me on her own, but after I'd promised we'd get her some candyfloss and reassured her

315

that I wouldn't let any scary clowns drag her into the ring, she agreed to get into the car, and after finding somewhere to park we made our way to the circus and got settled into our ringside seats.

'My grandma takes me to shows,' she said, through an enormous pink cloud of floss. 'And I told her about you on Skype, and she says you sound real nice and she says to send you lotsa love. Grandma to grandma, she said to say.'

In the interval I looked at the programme—ten quid!—and said that it was a pity it was all printed in Russian. Alice quickly pointed out that I was holding the programme upside down. Hope she doesn't tell Sharmie and Brad about this. If so, I'll never be allowed out alone with her again. Will have to claim I didn't have my specs on.

8 December

Of course now Archie has died, I've cancelled any plans to travel, but told Louis I'd pop up to Oxford anyway, to see him and his old mum. I was curious to have a good peer at her. And desperate, in any case, to see him again. So I decided to go.

As I drove down, I found myself wondering what she would be like. God knows, I thought, what she thinks my relationship with her son is, if indeed she knows anything about it at all. No doubt I'm seen as some kind of aunt-like figure who has befriended him. I'm sure she doesn't see me as a romantic liaison, even though no doubt she's been introduced to quite a few of those, I was certain. Just as I was starting to dread the meeting, my satnav announced, 'You have reached your destination!' and I drew up outside a large, detached red-bricked house in north Oxford. And getting out of the car, I pulled myself together and plastered on the old smile. It was half past two.

I knocked and waited. After a while the door was opened by a woman who can't have been a great deal older than me. And yet those few years make such a difference. It seemed to me as if she'd been born into a different generation. Her hair, unlike mine, was undyed, white and all over the place. She wore a stained old denim skirt. It was so strange—although the age difference between me and Louis was about nearly twenty years and the age difference between me and this dear old fossil was less than ten years, the gap between Louis' mother and myself seemed like a vast and unbridgeable chasm. It was the sixties that did it. Anyone born before 1940 never experienced all that sex, drugs and rock-and-roll that we post-forties generation did. Well, I'm sure some did, but not on the same scale.

'Oh delight!' she said, clapping her hands. She only had a faint American accent, no doubt worn away by living so long in the city of dreaming spires. 'You must be Marie! I've been expecting you! I'm so sorry, Louis' not arrived yet . . . he's out interviewing some friend of his father's about Iran or something. But come in and have a nice cup of tea. I've heard so much about you, as the saying goes!'

But what *had* she heard about me? I only wished I could have asked. I felt immediately out of place. I just couldn't work out how I fitted in. For the first time I felt my facelift put me at a disadvantage. She obviously thought I was younger than I was—

and she seemed to be treating me, confusingly, as something between a child, a friend of Louis' and a contemporary. I felt like some awful fraud, looking all young and stylish on the outside and all run-down and dilapidated on the inside. I consoled myself by promising myself I could leave the following day. It was all too uncomfortable.

The time crawled by. Three o'clock came and went, and still, at four, there was no sign of Louis. Joan—that was her name—and I sat in her living room, making polite conversation. The walls were lined with old books, and new books were piled on tables and chairs and on a baby grand and everything was covered in a fine layer of dust, a sure sign of someone who Lives in the Mind. I noticed the absence of a television set. Joan had put on a small electric fire with only one bar, and it wasn't really doing the job. We drank tea out of chipped mugs and ate home-made biscuits, chatting, oddly enough, about grandchildren— Joan has three grandsons by her daughter. I was surprised Louis hadn't mentioned his nephews to me. It made me feel slightly uneasy.

She tried, poor woman, to start a conversation about an article in the *Times Literary Supplement*, then questioned me about Stephen Pinker's latest book, and when that failed even started questioning me about the upcoming US elections and what I thought would happen in the banking crisis. But when it became completely clear that, unlike her (and, presumably, all her brainy Oxford buddies), I knew considerably less than her about books or politics (especially as I receive most of my political information from that notoriously unreliable source, the *Rant*), we moved on to the subject of Martha, Louis' godmother. She'd known her since high school apparently, and filled me in on their friendship, and then we ground to a halt.

Rather hopelessly I dragged in my latest views on Tolstoy and luckily scored a hit. She agreed completely. Totally over-rated. So that was good.

Finally, I courageously asked her about her current ailments, and much to my relief that took up at least an hour. Quite interesting, actually. Halfway through she asked me about the tree escapade—Louis had obviously filled her in quite a bit about me. Then, at about quarter past five, she paused slightly, looked at her watch, and leaned back in her chair.

'Oh dear, he's so very late, isn't he? You must think he's so bad-mannered. But you know he's just always so busy, poor boy. Deadlines. You've got a son, too, haven't you?' And then we nattered on about the odd relationship between sons and mothers. 'Of course I worry so much about Louis not being married,' she said, confidingly. 'The trouble is that he's always falling in love, poor boy. He just has to meet a girl, any girl, it seems, and he's promising to marry her and then before I know where I am it's all over and I'm being introduced to the next one. I feel sorry for those poor girls, as well.

'There was this Ugandan girl who we liked very much, Masani—my husband and I met her and she was just perfect. But she went back to Kampala. Louis has probably told you about her? He still thinks of her, he says. But quite honestly, he ought to get married soon or no one will want him, I mean he's nearly fifty . . . I don't think any young girl would want to marry a man of fifty, do you?

319

Too much responsibility.'

She sighed again. And then she leaned forward to me, and smiled confidingly. 'And that's why it's so lovely to see *you*, Marie!' she said. 'At last Louis seems to have made a proper friend, someone he respects. Oh, he *does* respect you, believe me. And I'm so hoping you can persuade him to settle down with some nice girl and have children, and stop all this falling head-over-heels stuff.'

I just sat, speechless, absorbing this appalling piece of information. He *respects* me? But I thought he felt quite differently about me!

Then the bell rang and I felt a great wave of relief. But although Louis gave me a perfunctory kiss, and his mother a hug, saying, 'Sorry I'm late! Got held up! But great to see you've had time to get to know each other!' he barely stayed more than ten minutes chatting before he got a text and said he was sorry but he had to do some more work and would we excuse him. I felt like saying, 'No, actually, we won't! Come back here and have a proper conversation! We've waited long enough! Where are your manners?' and then I remembered that only last week we were clasped in a long embrace after our walk. And I'd called him darling.

After half an hour he came downstairs, head bent over his mobile. He stood for a moment at the door, and then immediately went into the corridor to reply. When he finally came back into the sitting room he complained that the tea was stewed. He threw me an affectionate smile, but that was about it.

'By the way, you haven't put me in Dad's study, have you, Mom?' he said to his mother, rather

320

sulkily. 'You *know* I can't sleep there . . .'

'Oh, I'm so sorry, have I taken . . .?' I stammered.

'Sweetheart, just for a couple of nights,' said his mother, soothingly, tousling his hair as she rose to make yet another pot of tea (and I noticed he didn't flinch, as Jack would have done, which seemed a bit odd). Then, from the kitchen she called back 'You can't expect Marie . . .'

'Oh, I'm only staying the one night,' I said hastily. 'Please don't worry. I have to get off to see my friend's daughter . . . the funeral . . .' And while Joan and I chatted on about death and funerals and losing a loved one, Louis picked up a paper and starting reading it. The lazy and adored son. It wasn't a pretty sight.

After supper ('I've made your favourite, darling,' said his mother, as she helped him to a giant portion of frankfurters, beans and coleslaw, which he wolfed down without a word of thanks) he left us both to do the washing up—which took ages because Joan was one of those loopy people who rinse the dishes before they put them in the machine. (What's the point?) And she was also one of those people who washes the saucepans by hand instead of bunging them in too. Then we reassembled briefly in the sitting room, where Louis was working on his laptop, and I left them so I could nip to the loo. By the time I'd got back, Louis was just gathering his things together to go upstairs to bed, turned, gave me a warm hug, and left. As we heard him walking upstairs, his mother suddenly put a finger to her lips. 'He's just told me that Masani's back on the scene!' she confided in a happy whisper at the bottom of the stairs. 'Fingers

321

crossed it's The One! Sleep well, my dear!'

I passed the night in an orgy of rage and misery. I should never have come. Louis was totally useless, totally selfish and totally horrible. I'd been a fool to think there might be anything in it. I felt utterly humiliated and completely idiotic to have believed a single word he'd said. Having left my temazepam at home, I spent the entire night punishing myself for my naïvety and raging at Louis in my mind for what seemed like wanton cruelty. And when I finally got to sleep, I dreamed that I was on holiday with the family and a huge tsunami came and washed everyone away. I could see Jack and Chrissie carried off by the waves, and then I spotted Gene. I reached out to get him and I held his hand, but he, too was swept away, and there was nothing I could do. I woke up, shaking and tearful.

I got up before dawn and left a note with a feeble excuse on it, explaining I'd had an urgent call from London and thanking Joan profusely and, before either Louis or his mother got up, I leapt into the car and sped back home as quickly as I could.

I didn't want to see Louis ever again. It was all too complicated and I felt I'd been used. I missed Archie more than I can say. Maybe, I wondered, for all his faults Louis had been right about my feelings for him. Maybe I *was* trying to cling on, in some wretched way, to the loving feelings I felt for Archie by transferring them, randomly it now seemed, to another person. Any person. Someone I sat next to on a plane. But now Archie had died, and I'd just had that horrible experience in Oxford, my feelings had changed dramatically.

322

The moment I got back, put my key into the lock of my own front door and entered my own house I felt better.

After a long bath to wash every vestige of that loathsome slimeball and his beastly brainy mother completely off me (I know she was actually very friendly, but at that particular moment I loathed the whole family), I made myself a cup of tea and sat in the garden, wrapped up warm in a coat. It was one of those wonderful crisp, bright December days, and Pouncer was leaping about the grass in the cold blue sunshine. My life wasn't really so bad. And in a way it felt all the better for having made a decision about Louis. I could get on with things now, and not have that yearning all the time, wondering when or whether Louis was going to ring.

Last night's dream crept back into my mind, and I realised how much I longed to see the family again. Perhaps I could move to the States? Perhaps . . .? But get Christmas over and then make a new plan, I thought.

12 December

Daily Rant: 'GAY SHAME OF CELEBRITY COCAINE CHEF'. Honestly, if you believed everything the *Rant* said you wouldn't think there was a single pleasant, hard-working or reasonably intelligent person in the whole of the country. And yet the place, as far as I can see, is thronging with them.

Got up and had my bath in a pleasant rage.

Tomorrow is Archie's funeral. I'm driving down

323

early so I can help Sylvie—there're having a do back at Archie's old place after it. She asked if I could bring down maps of how to get from the church to the house to distribute in the church because their printer has gone wrong, so I've printed off two hundred. Nice to know I'm needed, even in such a small way. I'm also taking down all the tree tackle to give back to Harry.

Sylvie's asked me to read that poem of Archie's I found. I'm not sure how well it'll go down, but I think she's brave and decent and kind to ask me. It shows how much he wanted to die, when he was old and ill, and not linger on, half alive. That will be a comfort to some people, I know.

I got out all my clothes from my wardrobe—again—and put them on the bed. What a sorry sight! This New Year my resolution will definitely be to get some new outfits! There were piles of washed-out jerseys covered with those little bobbles ('pills' I think they're called), skirts stretched out at the bottom, and dresses with all the colour bleached out. I thought I'd wear black—no one wears black to a funeral now, so I thought: why not? And it made life easier because there's a really lovely designer black cocktail dress which I got for a song at a charity shop, and the most brilliant felt hat from a craft fair which collapses into a flat shape so you can put it into your suitcase. Once I'd got myself togged up, I was surprised to find I looked really much more than pass-muster presentable. A spot of make-up and bingo—quite fancied myself! That facelift? I must say, it was the best thing I've ever done!

I was just trying on a necklace when it fell on the ground. As I groped around to pick it up, I

324

remembered an old joke of Archie's: 'Now we're old, whenever we reach down to pick something up, we wait a bit before straightening up in case there's anything else we can do while we're down there.'

I found myself laughing by myself in my bedroom. Lovely when you make yourself laugh, I think. All by yourself.

Text from Louis: *Sorry not to have a chance to see you properly! What happened? Miss you! Big hit with Mom! Meet soon? xxxL*.

But it didn't matter how many 'x's there were on his texts any more. I felt nothing.

13 December

It was a really charming country funeral. And the church was absolutely packed with people I'd never seen before. That's the thing about the country—people from all over Devon who'd known Archie since he was four all crammed in. It was a much more social occasion than it would have been in London. Sylvie had done the flowers, a great mass of white lilies, and the slow movement from Mozart's concerto in C was playing softly as we all filed solemnly in. Oh dear, another coffin. It all reminded me so much of Hughie's funeral. And of course that reminded me of my mother's funeral and that reminded me of my father's—when you get older every funeral rings old bells of past losses until in your head there's an endless peal of bereavement going on.

Sylvie read a passage from the Bible and some elderly cousin played something on the cello, and when I read the poem (with difficulty: I nearly broke down)—there wasn't a dry eye in the house. Even Hardy played his part, sitting mournfully by the coffin and whimpering occasionally.

The only blot on the landscape was the female priest. Am I the only woman on earth who finds women vicars a bit creepy? They always look like some ghastly old aunt one used to know when one was a child and was forced to kiss. They never have their hair done or wear lipstick because they think the scrubbed, unadorned look will make them look more pious. Somehow male vicars always have an air of mystery about them. Particularly when they're wearing a long wafty dress, which on a woman just looks normal. Men look more mysterious anyway, not just because of the dresses but because they're so peculiar and unlike oneself. But women—I can't really see a woman as *holy*, in a mysterious way, because she's too familiar—a woman who has periods, and has had children, and cooks scones. At the least the old saints or saintesses or whatever they're called never had kids or drove cars, and were virgins. They were a pretty peculiar bunch of women to start with. But of course I take rather a dim view of holiness anyway. I remember Archie, who didn't like women priests either, said the reason we feel uneasy around them is because they remind us of pagan times, and we associate them with witches.

Something in that, I think.

Afterwards there was that usual shuffling around outside the church in the cold with no one knowing what to do and everyone keeping their heads down and saying how sorry they were. And then we sped off to Sylvie's and had a drink and everything cheered up.

Well! At breakfast Sylvie came down looking pretty exhausted, I must say. But she said how strange it was to be a fully-fledged orphan now, and be in the front line as far as death went. And she said she could smell Archie and hear his voice, still, and wasn't it all odd? And of course what was so strange to *me* was hearing her say all this as if she'd stumbled across something that no one else had discovered—when of course I remember feeling exactly the same when my parents died. Sometimes I read these confessional pieces in the *Rant* by celebs who write really movingly about a parent's death, and it touches me to think they imagine they're the very first people to have experienced all these feelings, when in fact other people have had exactly the same feelings, all over the world, for generations.

However, just after the scrambled eggs, she suddenly reached across the table and squeezed my hand.

'Marie!' she said. 'I've just remembered. The will. Daddy left everything to me, but he did leave a list of wishes. He's left something to Mrs Evans, obviously, and he wanted you to have something, too. He thought that you should have £10,000 and perhaps something to remember him by? I know this is very embarrassing. How does that sound to you? It's what he would have wanted. I know it's not a lot when you look at the whole estate, but most of that will go on death duties ... and ... and

327

if there's anything you want from the house, you know something, just a little something . . .'

I was completely taken aback. Despite my earlier vile and unworthy speculations, I really had no idea that he wanted to leave me anything at all! I stammered out my gratitude and said it was absolutely wonderful, and thanked her very much. And I said I'd look in on Mrs Evans at the house on the way back—she was just clearing up there before the estate agents come round to value it.

How lovely of him to remember me! I drove off feeling a huge surge of warmth and love towards Archie, which made his death even more poignant.

I hated going back to the house. But there was dear, loyal Mrs Evans—and I could see that though she was sad it was a great relief to her, knowing that everything was settled and she had a new job at Sylvie's.

'She's been ever so kind to me,' she said. 'They're a lovely family. And the funeral. Weren't it beautiful? And that poem—weren't it sad? Oh, of course you know about it, you read it, Mrs Marie, so silly of me. I shall miss this house, though. Now—Mrs Sylvie told me you was going to choose something so I'll let you look around and decide on your own and then I'll have a cup of nice hot coffee waiting for you.'

Going from room to room wondering what piece of furniture, picture or ornament would best remind me of dear Archie, I felt like a vulture. I could almost feel the great claws on my feet and practically had to check my nose to see it wasn't an enormous beak. It was so odd, but each room, though when I entered it seemed full of promise, turned out to be surprisingly empty of anything I actually wanted.

What I wanted was the light coming through the curtains. I wanted the smell of the apple logs burning in the grate. I wanted the birdsong in the garden. The feel of the worn-out towels on my back when I got out of the bath. The sound of a distant lawnmower. I wanted the smell of Archie's cigarettes in the library. I wanted to hear his voice calling to me from the vegetable garden. I wanted the sound of his laughter, and the touch of his hand. I wanted the smell of damp in the hall and the creak of the boards in the dining room . . . even the cold in the kitchen. *Especially* the cold in the kitchen. And just to take a *thing* didn't seem at all satisfactory. The important things in life aren't things.

I eventually settled, oddly, for some linen sheets.

'I know, it's odd—rather than taking a picture or something,' I said to Mrs Evans when I eventually came downstairs. 'But these sheets really remind me of staying here. I never have linen at home. And to be honest I've got enough 'things' at home, pictures, ornaments, etc. But these sheets will be lovely.'

'And they'll see you out,' said Mrs Evans, repeating that weirdly comforting phrase that never gets said to you when you're under sixty.

'Yes,' I agreed. 'They'll see me out.'

Then I thought of something else. 'And do you think I might be able to have his old fishing hat as well?' I asked. 'Or would that be too greedy, do you think?'

'Take it!' said Mrs Evans, going out into the hall to find it. 'I know Mrs Sylvie won't mind. She's already taken his gardening hat to remember him by. But we've taken that horrid old Alpine coat of his down to the charity shop with the other stuff. Bad memories.' She paused. Then, 'And take the pillow cases with you, as well. They go with the sheets. There are so many here . . . they're all due for the auction. They won't be missed.'

Later

When I got home I immediately put the sheets on my bed and they're absolutely lovely. The cool, slippery feel of them just takes me back instantly to Archie's house, and our lovely cuddly nights together. I've hung his hat in the hall, too—just like nervous spinsters used to do in the old days to give burglars the impression that there was a Man in the House.

15 December

I wasn't really expecting to hear from Louis ever again, and certainly didn't want to, *at all*, but I got a call from him, asking if I'd see him. He was just on his way to Heathrow to go back to the States and he needed to talk to me, he said. Urgently.

This time I didn't prepare the house to make it appear as if I were an interesting person. I slapped on a bit of make-up, pulled a comb through my hair and that was that. I was on the phone to Penny when the doorbell rang and instead of telling her I must go, and rushing down the stairs like a breathless teenager, I kept the phone to my ear and opened the front door with the other hand, signalling Louis to come in. When I'd stopped talking to Penny, I put on the kettle rather sourly, preparing to make him a cup of coffee as he stood uncomfortably by the kitchen table. I was determined not to rage or cry or show my emotions at all. I would remain cold and dignified. In the event, it wasn't difficult.

'I have to explain,' said Louis, putting his arms on my shoulders and turning me round to face him. 'I'm sorry. You must have thought I was so rude the other day, when you'd come down specially.' He shook his head. 'I had this assignment, and then I guess I've been so worried about Mom, and there's you. It's been wonderful, but to tell you the truth, it's broken my heart, all this . . .'

'This age difference?' I said rather icily. 'And, no doubt, the return of Masani.'

'How did you know about that?' Louis sat down, looking a bit taken aback. 'You should get a job on the *Rant*, Marie. You'd make a good journalist!'

'Your mother told me,' I said, coldly, as I sat down opposite him. 'And she also told me you did this all the time—fall for women, and then unfall for them. And it was clear I was just another one.'

'Marie, with you it's *different*, I swear it,' said Louis, seizing my hands. And for a moment I felt the old flicker of sexual longing. But I battened it down. 'You *know* it's different! If you and I were more the same age and I'd met you years ago, we'd be married with kids by now. I love you! There! I've said it! And I want us to know each other for ever and ever! And I want you to meet Masani and love her, too, and . . .'

He blathered on to such an extent that in the end I felt positively sorry for him. The awful truth

331

was that he meant every word he was saying. Right at that moment. He was one of those men who have been cursed with this ability to charm women, and he uses it not because he's a slimy creep, but because when he meets women he really *does* love them at that moment. And he can't help telling them.

'You've got a lot of charm, Louis,' I said, looking intently into his eyes and hoping I appeared like some mad old witch. 'But you should remember to use it carefully. If you don't watch out, you could hurt someone. As I'm sure you already have. Frequently. You nearly hurt me. Very much. Now don't get up hopes about this Masani. I hope you'll be happy with her, but try to think ahead before you blurt out your feelings this time—for her sake,' I added, feeling suddenly very sorry for this poor little African girl who was all ready to fall into Louis' web of charm.

But I don't think he'll change. He left, swearing undying love and friendship, and yet I have a funny feeling I won't hear from him again.

But who knows?

And who, I'm afraid, cares?

16 December

'Well,' said Penny, when I rang her, 'You could always spend it with us . . .' She was going to spend Christmas with her daughter and son-in-law. But I knew that really she wanted to have it with her relatives on her own, and why not? I do. It's funny how much you can tell just by the faintest pause in someone's voice what their real feelings are. 'I mean, we'd love to have you . . . couldn't bear to think of you sitting at home all on your own.'

'That's really kind of you,' I said, 'But I'm sure I can find somewhere . . .'

I thought of Sylvie or James or even Marion—they'd all offered. But otherwise, would Christmas on my own really be all that grim? Mightn't it actually be rather a relief? There'd be no one in London, I could do exactly what I wanted, and I know quite a few friends who say how much they hate Christmas and just spend it curled up watching old films on the telly by themselves, and having a great time.

I was just sitting down and wondering what I could do, and feeling a bit empty now all the excitement of the trees is over, Archie gone and Louis out of the picture, when the phone rang. It was Jack, asking if I would go on Skype.

I logged on, and there he was. Gene was by his side, hopping up and down.

'Stop hopping, darling!' I said. 'I can't see your face! By the way I've nearly finished your jersey!'

'We've got some news for you, Mum,' said Jack. He had a big grin on his face.

Gene pushed in the way. 'Yes, Granny! We're coming back!'

'For Christmas? How lovely!' I said. That was *wonderful* news!

'No,' said Gene, 'We're coming back, coming back properly. To stay!'

'Stay for how long?' I asked, nervously. I still couldn't quite believe it.

'No, no, stay . . . live!' said Jack, beaming. 'I'll tell you all about it when we get back properly, but we've been thinking about it for a few months.

That's why we've been so hopeless about Christmas. I'm *so* sorry. I know how much you've been wanting us to come back and I couldn't bear you to get your hopes up and then disappoint you. The fact is, we just can't adjust here. Chrissie's working too hard. And although everyone's so friendly, we haven't made any real friends. And you know we don't want Gene being brought up American. All the usual reasons. You were right, Mum. It's the gee-whizzness of it all. And Chrissie's been offered her old job back and she's taking it part time and I'll have a much better chance of working . . . and anyway London's our home . . .'

Well, I didn't know what to do or say. I just felt wave after wave of happiness flooding over me. Tears came to my eyes. I felt as if a huge boulder had been rolled away from my shoulders and suddenly I felt, well . . . would it be too much to say *born again*? I couldn't speak.

'Mum? Mum? Are you all right?' said Jack, leaning forward.

'I'm so so happy,' I sobbed, reaching out to touch his face on the screen. 'Oh darling . . . how wonderful . . . and when are you coming? I'll be at the airport to meet you . . . oh darling . . . what wonderful, *wonderful* news!'

'We'll book a flight as soon as possible. It'll be a nightmare and terribly expensive, but we'll be home for Christmas if it kills us,' said Jack.

20 December

Haven't written the diary for far too long, because I've been doing nothing but rushing about making mince pies, ordering the turkey, putting up the decorations (I was *very* careful with the ladder and got Penny to come and hold it) and finishing Gene's jersey, as well as trying to sort out Jack and Chrissie's house for them. The tenants have left it in a dreadful state and I've had to repaint bits, and had a huge rush to get the carpets cleaned so it's now looking absolutely spotless and just as Jack and Chrissie left it.

They're coming back tomorrow and I can't speak for joy. I can hardly type this. Forget facelifts, I feel about ten years younger just with happiness and have been dancing in my kitchen like a whirling dervish. Suddenly realised, however, that Brad and Sharmie next door would be able to stare out of their upstairs windows through my glass roof, and get an extraordinary view of the old neighbour capering about. Then I thought, 'Well, let them! Who cares!' And continued cavorting about the kitchen to Gladys Knight and her marvellous Pips.

I've bought Chrissie an art nouveau lampshade which I know she'll like, and Jack a book on surrealism and Gene's getting a *huge* set of Lego. It's all just so wonderful. As if all the stress of this past year has been wiped out at a single stroke.

And to cap it all, I've finally cancelled the *Daily Rant*! I'm giving it up for good!

21 December

They're all back!

I drove down to Heathrow and parked the car and went on legs that were quite shaky with excitement to the barrier. There were the usual Indians and Arabs and Chinese, all no doubt with their stories to tell, and none of them knowing what I was feeling, all staring desperately at the gate and scanning the faces of people emerging with their trolleys. There were loud flight announcements, the sounds of some computer game bleeping and whizzing in the background, and the general buzz of the terminal. I was so excited I could hardly contain myself, hanging on the rail and willing them to come through. I was even trying to read the flight numbers on the labels on people's suitcases . . . impossible, of course. Why is it that when you're waiting at the barrier the people you're waiting for are always the very last to come through?

And at long last, there they were! Gene was pushing the trolley—far too big for him—and looking around everywhere. The moment he saw me, he left the trolley, dodged under the barrier and raced up to me. I held on to him for dear life, as if I'd just rescued him from that raging dream tsunami. Then Jack and Chrissie came up and we all got a bit tearful. I could hardly speak.

'Oh, it's wonderful to see you!' I said, in a breaking voice. 'I can't tell you . . . !'

'Where's my jersey, Granny?' said Gene. 'I want to see my jersey!'

I produced it from my bag with a flourish and he immediately threw off his coat and pulled it on. 'It's brilliant!' he said, twirling round in it. 'And I like the elephants. How did you do them, Granny?' and he started making elephant noises, followed, after a moment, by elephant pooing noises.

'That's enough,' said Jack, as we tried not to giggle at these head-turning sounds. 'Come on, Gene, we've got to get back now. I can't wait to be home.'

'Nor can I,' said Chrissie. 'Oh, it's *so* good to be back!'

'You go ahead to the car, Mum,' said Jack, as he took the trolley from Gene. 'We'll follow you.'

Gene and I forged ahead to the car park. He took my hand and started jumping up and down as we walked. 'I want to come over and see your house, Granny,' he said. 'And then can we play the elephant game? And can I tell you what I want for Christmas?'

'Of course, darling,' I said. 'What *do* you want?'

'Well, I want some Lego,' he said. 'And a guinea pig. But what I want as well,' he said, looking down, rather shyly, 'well, you see, Granny, there are these people in Africa, and they're so poor, they've got nothing to eat. And Dad says you can buy a goat and give it to them for Christmas, and they can get lovely milk from it and that will give them vitamins and they'll be happy and well. And it'll say 'love from Gene' on it. Could we do that Granny? Could we? Would it be too expensive?'

And as he looked up at me, his big eyes full of trust and warmth, I felt my heart break.

'Of course, darling,' I said, squeezing his warm little hand in mine. 'We'll send just as many goats

337

as you like.'
And we did.